THE LASKO INTERVIEW

A NOVEL BY CLAY JACOBSEN

BROADMAN
& HOLMAN
PUBLISHERS

Nashville, Tennessee

0-8054-1660-9

Published by Broadman & Holman Publishers, Nashville, Tennessee
Acquisitions & Development Editor: William D. Watkins
Page Design: Anderson Thomas Design
Typesetting: SL Editorial Services

Dewey Decimal Classification: 813
Subject Heading: FICTION
Library of Congress Card Catalog Number: 98-24177

Unless otherwise stated all Scripture citation is from the Holy Bible, New International Version, copyright © 1973, 1978, 1984 by International Bible Society. One verse is from *The Message*, the New Testament in Contemporary English, © 1993 by Eugene H. Peterson, published by NavPress, Colorado Springs, Colo.

Library of Congress Cataloging-in-Publication Data
Jacobsen, Clay, 1956–
    The Lasko interview / Clay Jacobsen.
        p. cm.
    ISBN 0-8054-1660-9 (pbk. : alk. paper)
    I. Title.
PS3560.A2584L37   1998
813'.54—dc21

                              98-24177
                                  CIP

1 2 3 4 5 02 01 00 99 98

To my wife Cindy. You planted this seed, and through your encouragement, God has brought it to fruitfulness. Thank you for your loving support. Also to Sharayah and Shelby, our daughters, who put up with the many hours Daddy was busy writing. I love you all more than words can say.

ACKNOWLEDGMENTS

I wish to express my heartfelt thanks to the following people that helped in bringing *The Lasko Interview* to print.

To my parents, Gene and Jo Jacobsen. Since my earliest memories, you've been a shining example of what it means to walk with Jesus daily.

To Torey Johnson, criminologist for Las Vegas Metro Police Department, and Tony Miano, a deputy in the Los Angeles County Sheriff's Department.

To Jack Wallen for his knowledge of computers and the Internet.

To my friends and family who critiqued early manuscripts: Wayne Jacobsen, Rod and Kathy Jacobsen, Dan Lovil, Val Gray, Lee Coate, and Eve Adair.

To my editor Angie Kiesling, and the great staff at Broadman and Holman, especially Bucky Rosenbaum, Bill Watkins, Lisa Parnell, and Mark Lusk.

And special thanks to Chaz Corzine, Matt Jacobson, and Sara Fortenberry.

PROLOGUE

TUESDAY, MARCH 16
6:27 P.M., MALIBU, CALIFORNIA

The killer crept along the hallway leading to the only lighted room in the house. He listened for any strange sound that could interrupt his plans, but all he heard was the soft tapping of fingers on a computer keyboard coming from the small office just a few feet before him. Although the intruder had broken into countless places as he worked his way up through the criminal ranks, tonight those talents had not been called upon. It was a lovely spring evening, so all the windows and the patio doors at the back of the house had been open. Tonight's only challenge would be in keeping with his orders: "It must look like a suicide. We can't afford anyone asking questions!" The words still echoed in his mind. That demand would make the next few minutes even more challenging.

Each time the typing stopped the killer froze, not making a sound. Only when he heard the soft patter of fingers again did he resume his approach. Reaching the end of the hallway, he peered around the doorframe. He knew the desk faced the window, and, as he expected, the target had his back toward the doorway. The killer pulled out the unmarked .357 handgun he always had tucked behind his back, then entered the room quietly. Looking over the victim's shoulder, he stopped short as he saw what was on the computer screen. He smiled. Once again, his timing was perfect. If he'd waited any longer . . . well, he didn't want to think about that.

The man at the desk kept his focus on the task before him. He'd just completed writing the last sentence of his E-mail and moved his cursor to the address window at the top of the screen. He began typing in the familiar characters—Dbernstein@idt.co—

The killer stepped into the pool of light cast by the lamp on the desk, and the target saw him for the first time. The man pulled his desk drawer open and lunged for the Taurus semiautomatic pistol he had stashed there. Just as he got a grip on it, the killer's large gloved hand engulfed his own—and the gun. Breaking into a smile, the killer slipped his own weapon behind his back.

"Wait . . . nobody has to know . . . I can explain . . . ," the man pleaded. As he babbled, the killer tightened his grip and forced the gun around so that it pointed at the man's face.

"Please . . . just listen for a minute—"

"You don't have a minute," the killer whispered into his ear, enjoying his victim's terror. He brought more pressure against the arm and raised the gun toward the man's head. The victim's face reddened as he struggled to point the gun away, but he couldn't match the strength of the figure before him. As the gun was forced the final few inches toward the victim's mouth, the two men's eyes met. The man in the chair froze in horror as he looked into the killer's eyes.

He recognized the face.

He kept his gaze on the killer as he reached for the computer with his free hand. If he could just enter the last character before . . .

The killer pushed the gun inside. The victim's last thought was how bitter the metal tasted. It seemed odd that he would think of a thing like that when—

The blast echoed through the house. The slide jammed into the back of the killer's hand when it recoiled, tearing a deep gash into his glove and flesh. Cursing, he released the man's hand and the gun as the body jerked and then went limp. The room was deathly quiet. The killer savored the moment, smiling—until a beep from the computer caught his attention.

He looked at the screen—paralyzed. "Your mail has been sent."

How could his mail . . . then the killer noticed the dead man's hand resting on the keyboard. He couldn't panic. He had to finish quickly. He had watched the wife leave a few minutes before he made his way around back and jumped over the wall. Still, someone next door might report the gunshot, and he could have a visitor within the next couple of minutes.

The killer pulled out his handkerchief and wrapped it around his left hand before any of his blood could drip to the floor. Then he reached for the computer. It was difficult working the track pad with his gloved hand, but he wasn't about to take the glove off. He quit the America Online application, disconnecting the computer from the service. Then he reached into his back pocket and extracted a three-and-a-half-inch computer disk. The victim's computer was a Macintosh Powerbook. The killer was more comfortable with an IBM or one of its clones, but he had spent the previous night on a friend's Macintosh preparing the disk.

He looked at the screen, surprised that a letter was now visible, addressed to David Bernstein. He was in luck—that was the name he'd seen on the E-mail. Now he had the full name and location: a law office in Beverly Hills. He memorized the information, then quit the document.

The computer beeped, asking if he wanted to save the changes before closing. He clicked "no" as he shoved his disk in the floppy drive.

The phone on the desk rang. He ignored it, allowing the answering machine to pick up the call instead. It was one of those models where the outgoing message couldn't be heard in the room, so the killer continued in silence. He copied a document titled "Good-bye" from his disk onto the computer's hard drive. As he waited, the answering machine beeped, and a woman's voice projected through the speaker.

"Wade, it's Cassie. Josh wanted me to let you know he got out of here a little late, but he's on his way. With traffic, I'm guessing he probably won't get there until after seven. He thought you'd be there ... I'll try your cell, so if I reach you on it, ignore this message."

The phone call disconnected and a male computer voice droned, "Tuesday, 6:35 P.M." The killer removed his disk, then erased the document the man had been working on. In one fluid movement he moved the cursor to the document he'd placed on the hard drive and opened it, then selected "print." He'd noticed a laser printer sitting beside the desk in the corner, a green light steadily glowing from its top. *That should add a nice touch.*

Before leaving, he grabbed a box of computer disks and the victim's appointment book from the top of the desk. There had been a note made on today's calendar to call a Mr. Mortenson at 555-3764. He thought it best to take that with him.

The killer left the way he had come, through the back door and over the wall, grimacing from his injured hand as he scaled the stone wall. He heard someone knocking on the front door as he landed on the other side. Another job finished just in time. He quietly made his way down the hillside and found his car near the road, tucked behind a tree.

Back in the house, the knocking went unanswered as the lifeless head of the victim lay illuminated by the computer screen:

Becky,
    I've had it. Life just isn't worth it anymore. For whatever pain this adds to your life, I'm sorry. You'll find someone better for you. You deserve it.
                 Wade

CHAPTER 1

Cassie hung up the phone and glanced at the digital clock display in the upper right corner of her computer screen. If she was going to get over to Kathy's house in time for their weekly home fellowship meeting, she'd have to hurry. But something felt wrong. Wade should have been at home. He had called the office and talked to Josh less than two hours ago. Now, with Josh on his way to meet him, Wade should be there. She had tried his cell phone but only got the recording: "The cellular customer you have dialed is unavailable or has traveled out of the service area."

Cassandra Petterson wasn't what people would call a classic beauty. She was more like the girl-next-door type—the very cute girl-next-door type. She had wavy brunette hair that fell down over her shoulders, and an attractive figure that she usually concealed beneath conservative clothing. Her large hazel eyes and infectious smile complemented a personality that was the very opposite of the intensity-and-intimidation combo so often found in Hollywood.

She was the assistant to Josh Abrams, producer of "The John Harold Show," a late-night talk/variety show that was gaining popularity across the country. Recently Harold's ratings had surpassed Letterman's, and the show was now a close second to Leno in the late-night ratings race.

John Harold and Josh had become good friends after coproducing a comedy special for Showtime three years ago. They kept in touch, brainstorming ideas until they came up with their successful late-night format. "The John Harold Show" had the normal instudio interviews and musical guests that allowed celebrities to push their latest project. But what set the show apart was one unique segment—a hard-hitting feature about an issue facing the nation. All the guests joined in a lively discussion centered around the topic. It was an unlikely combination, but the show had found a niche by adding substance to late-night entertainment—a balance between "The Tonight Show," "Nightline," and "Politically Incorrect."

Cassie had only worked in the entertainment industry a few years. She had intended to become a lawyer, but when her bank account continually slid to double-digit balances, she was forced to leave law school. A roommate who worked in television helped her land a couple of production assistant jobs.

During the pilot for "The John Harold Show" last spring, Josh had been so impressed with her work that when National Studios bought the show, he asked her to be his personal assistant. Now the excitement of the show's success had dulled the ache of not completing her law degree. Cassie found herself enjoying the controlled chaos that surrounded the production office and thinking less and less about becoming a lawyer.

Wade Bennett, the show's director, and the rest of the team were on hiatus for the week, airing reruns while taking a much needed break after a great showing in the February sweeps. It was quiet around the office. Normally they would have just finished up their nightly taping.

Cassie couldn't get the unanswered phone calls off her mind. *Oh well, maybe it'll all make sense tomorrow.* She picked up her purse and began to hum "Give Thanks," one of her favorite worship songs, as she began locking up the office.

She hoped they'd sing the chorus at the fellowship tonight. The thought lightened her mood as she let the unanswered phone calls drift from her mind.

6:45 P.M., BURBANK

Rick Treadway looked up from his script to the array of video monitors stacked in front of him.

"Ready two with Sam; we're coming to the close," he said.

Allan, the technical director sitting to his right, tensed the finger that was resting atop camera two's button on the switcher. The cameraman zoomed in and checked his focus on Samantha Steel before framing the shot from the waist up, careful to include the stunning shape that kept Samantha's career on the upswing.

"Cue Sam. Two," Rick said, accented with a snap of his finger, Allan's cue to take the camera on-line.

The harried look on Samantha's face transformed into a brilliant smile the instant before the tally light on her camera flashed red. "So remember," Sam said as the stage manager pointed to the lens giving her the cue, "all you have to do is call our toll-free number . . ."

"Dissolve to still store. Stand by tape and Chyron with credits," Rick continued directions as she spoke.

". . . 1-800-555-7887, that's 1-800-555-7887. Our operators are standing by to assist you in getting the home protection that your family deserves."

"Sell it, Sam. We're almost through," Rick interjected with a laugh over the communication system.

"Thirty seconds to black," yelled Miguel, the associate director beside Rick.

"Dissolve back to two. Roll closing music. Cue Ted in," Rick instructed.

Samantha's cohost entered the shot and stood beside her as she continued, "So join the rest of the families you've seen tonight, who have chosen to be safe and secure within their homes. You'll sleep more peacefully. Call now."

Sam stopped speaking as Ted's name came up on the TelePrompTer in front of her. She smiled and turned her head toward Ted as he picked up the dialogue. "Please make that call today. I'm Ted Wells. For Samantha Steel and the rest of us here at Alert One, good-bye and be safe."

"Roll tape, key Chyron, and roll credits." As Rick directed, the large color monitor in the center of the wall changed to images of an upscale house with lights coming on and alarms sounding as a would-be burglar ran down the street. The names of the production team scrolled over the footage on screen.

Miguel began counting backward from ten as they neared the end of the show.

"Stand by black," Rick said, then matching Miguel's count, "in three . . . two . . . one, and fade it out. Whew!"

Rick let the tension drain from his body as he released a deep breath. "That should do it. Nice job, everyone. I think this one is in the can."

He looked up at the digital display above the monitors that registered the time—6:52. *Thank God,* he thought, *no overtime. Right on schedule.*

"Great! That's a wrap, everyone," Rick said to his crew listening on headsets, then he pressed the red button that sent his voice over the speakers in the studio. "Sam, Ted, and everyone on the staff and crew, great job. Thanks for all your hard work. Let's hope we sell a lot of these so we'll all be back together making the Alert Two infomercial." Secretly he hoped it would happen quickly. He had been out of work for more than four months, and the money from this job would only put a small dent in his accumulating debt.

Rick Treadway ran a hand through his thick dark hair, which always looked half combed. Even when dressed for work, he kept as comfortable as possible with faded blue jeans and tennis shoes complementing his dress shirt and navy blue sport coat. A graduate of UCLA Film and Television School back in the mid-eighties, he had forged a moderately successful career in television while climbing through the ranks of different productions. In the last five years he had been able to make the difficult transition from stage manager to director. Then last October, the daytime talk show he was directing got canceled abruptly. Now it was early spring, that time in Hollywood when the current shows were all fully staffed and it would be several months before the fall shows started production. Rick wasn't thrilled about taking the infomercial job when it came up, but his empty calendar helped make the decision for him.

"Nice job, Rick. We'll be able to get this on the air late tomorrow night as scheduled." Rick looked up as Norm Valentine came around the back bench to shake his hand. Norm was producing the show for Alert One and would be taking the project from here. Rick's work was done.

"It's been great working with you, Norm," Rick responded. "I'll make sure Miguel gathers up the tapes and brings them to the production office. If I can be of any more help, just give me a call."

"Well, we don't have anything on the boards at the moment, but hopefully soon. We'll have your check mailed to you within a week. Thanks again," Norm said, then turned and stepped out of the room.

Rick turned to Miguel, Allan, and his production assistant, Sharon. "Thanks so much, gang. You make a great team. Hope we'll get the chance to do this again real soon."

"Always a pleasure, Rick," Miguel said as he closed his script binder. "Do you have anything else coming up?"

"You know me, always something in the works. But the next few weeks are probably going to be pretty quiet," Rick said, grinning. The appearance of not working wasn't good for a freelance director's career.

"Well, the time off should do you some good," Miguel said, reading between the lines. "I'm off to Atlantic City for a few days for that boxing match on HBO. I'll give you a call when I get back."

"Sounds good. Let's get together for some golf. Well, I better head back to the office and get my stuff packed up," Rick said as he walked out the control room door.

He made one last sweep through the studio, thanking the crew, then decided to go by the dressing rooms to say good-bye to Samantha and Ted as well.

One of the most trying aspects of his job was dealing with the egos of the celebrities he had to work with. Ted Wells wasn't so bad, having worked in a variety of game shows and commercials. Samantha Steel was another story. Everything had been a problem to her: she wanted rewrites on the script, her wardrobe wasn't right, the lighting was too harsh—and several other minor headaches.

Still, in spite of it all, Rick found himself attracted to her. Coming from a modeling background, she was now a field reporter covering entertainment stories for a news magazine show on the ABC affiliate in Los Angeles. Like most on-air talents in LA, she was young and beautiful. She always portrayed just the right amount of perkiness when the lights and camera were on her. But the tension she had brought to the set had kept Rick enough off balance that he wasn't sure how to respond to her.

"You guys were terrific!" Rick put on his best smile as he entered the green room, the holding area for the principles of a show.

"Thanks, Rick. It was a lot of fun," responded Ted from the floral sofa.

"I'm just glad it's over. I can't believe my agent got me into this lousy piece of . . . ," Samantha graciously decided not to finish the sentence. "It's just that some of the copy was so amateurish."

"Well, at least everything worked out," Rick said. "The producer seemed to like your suggestions," Rick tried to answer diplomatically.

"I'm thrilled," Samantha responded sarcastically. "Anyway, I know you had a big part in keeping this show on track."

Rick smiled. He couldn't tell if this was the sincere Samantha after the pressure was off or just a flirting comment to catch him off guard. He made a mental note to give her a call in the next few days to follow up on which way she intended her compliment. "I don't know about that. I was just trying to do my job," he finally responded.

Samantha grabbed a glass of champagne and held it out for Rick. "Care for a celebration toast?"

He accepted the glass with a smile and raised it in the air. "To a wonderful job by both of you."

The three touched glasses and drank to the toast.

After a few minutes of small talk, Rick turned to go.

"I hope I'll see you soon," Samantha purred, smiling coyly.

"Take care, Rick," added Ted.

Samantha's eyes lingered on him, enjoying the view as he walked away.

7:05 P.M., BEVERLY HILLS

The man sat with his feet propped on top of a huge cherry desk and looked out his penthouse office window. The twinkling lights of the Los Angeles basin made a breathtaking view, yet he hardly noticed.

If he leaned back one more inch in his black leather chair, both the chair and his short massive body would be sent sprawling to the floor. He puffed on the Cuban cigar he had pulled from the humidor just moments before, smiling as he imagined how his biggest problem was in the process of expiring. The private extension on his phone lit up as the silence was broken by a ring. He slowly reached over and hit the speakerphone.

"Yeah."

"It's done."

"Just like I said?"

"Yeah, and there's more." The killer, talking from his cell phone, sat on the hood of his car near a Union 76 station about ten minutes from Bennett's ranch house in the Malibu hills. The handkerchief was still wrapped around his left hand, holding back the flow of blood. He winced as he spoke.

"Well, what?" The boss didn't like surprises.

"He'd put it all together and was in the process of spilling the whole can of worms."

"The Lasko interview?" he sat up, grabbing the receiver off the hook and bringing it to his ear.

"Yeah, he was working on a letter about it when I kind of 'interrupted' him." The killer knew he had the man's full attention and didn't intend to offer up any information about the E-mail problem. "Now what's it worth to you?"

"Why don't we add another five grand, as long as you're sure that the file is destroyed."

"Make it ten, and no one will ever know anything more about Lasko."

"Fine." The man in the office scowled, suddenly irritated. It wasn't the money; that was walking change to him. He just hated being manipulated by anyone. "But there's one more loose end you have to tie up for me. Come by tomorrow afternoon, and I'll explain it to you."

The killer watched as a red mustang pulled up and parked next to his BMW.

"OK, I'll see you then."

"Rudy, one more thing—did you leave the place clean?"

"You know my work!" he shouted and cut the line. An attractive blonde stepped out of the Mustang and walked toward him. Rudy whistled as he stood to his feet and brushed by her. She didn't even bother to look up at him. On any other night that would have made his blood boil, but tonight it was just as well nobody noticed him. He still had one last job to perform in Beverly Hills, then he'd get a good stiff drink and find somebody to celebrate with. A sheriff's car sped down Las Virgenes Road toward Malibu as he calmly got into his car and drove away in the opposite direction.

CHAPTER 2

Becky Bennett pulled off the Pacific Coast Highway, spinning her tires in the gravel as she made the corner onto Malibu Canyon Road and headed toward the hills that would take her home. She gripped the wheel, resenting the "shopping spree" Wade had urged her to take. This was supposed to be their week together. The schedule from the new show he was directing had hardly given them any time together over the last seven months. With the show on hiatus, she had looked forward to having him to herself.

Wade had come home from an edit session last night so pre-occupied with something that their romantic plans for the evening were totally destroyed. Now he sent her off shopping while he planned for some important meeting with the producer. If he expected her to sit quietly through this kind of treatment, he was in for a rude awakening. She should have forced the issue about the Hawaii trip she wanted to take. She made the last turn onto her street, flooring the gas pedal as her anger grew.

To her amazement, she couldn't get close to her own driveway. The path was blocked by a tangle of vehicles with flashing lights. Becky's stomach dropped like a boulder as her anger quickly melted into fear. She left her car double-parked and darted for the front door. A deputy standing next to a yellow tape barricade took a step forward to stop her.

"This is my house. What's going on here?" she demanded.

"Come with me, ma'am," the officer said, changing his posture. He pulled back the tape to let her through. "I'll get Detective Phillips. She's the one in charge here."

Just then a woman stepped out of the house, as if in answer to the squeal of tires from Becky's car. "Are you Mrs. Bennett?" she asked, hardly waiting for Becky to nod. "I'm Detective Stephanie Phillips."

"Is Wade all right?" Becky asked, her voice trembling.

"No, Mrs. Bennett," she said as gently as she could, "he's dead."

Becky's knees went limp. She reached out to steady herself against the side of the house. The detective watched her reaction, evaluating its sincerity. She waited a few seconds to let her deal with the initial blow. Oh, how she hated this part of her job.

"One of your neighbors, Mr. . . . ," Stephanie looked down at her notepad, "Jenkins, has already identified the body for us, Mrs. Bennett."

Becky felt herself go numb inside even though, remarkably, her legs were still standing. Wanting to see for herself, she tried to push past the detective to get into the house, but an arm blocked her.

"I'm sorry, Mrs. Bennett," Stephanie said, reaching out to steady her. "You don't want to see him."

Becky stared at her, shock and anger reflecting in her face.

"Besides, I can't let you. It's a crime scene and we have to protect the evidence," Stephanie continued. She didn't tell Becky the more serious reason for barring her from the office. If she became the prime suspect, as is often the case with widows, she wouldn't have an excuse as to why her fingerprints or some other piece of evidence that implicated her might be found at the scene.

Instead, Stephanie led Becky inside the house and into the living room.

"Is there anyone you'd like us to call?" the detective asked.

"No, I mean yes . . . I don't know, maybe my sister . . . How did this happen?"

"Well, according to the note on the computer, it appears he took his own life."

"What? That's not possible! Not Wade," Becky said through her tears. Stephanie handed her the computer printout, already neatly protected in a plastic evidence bag.

> Becky,
>   I've had it. Life just isn't worth it
> anymore. For whatever pain this adds to
> your life, I'm sorry. You'll find someone
> better for you. You deserve it.
>   Wade

Becky stared at the paper, her face going blank. What she was reading didn't make the least bit of sense.

Detective Stephanie Phillips and her partner, Bill Brier, were quite a pair. She was a blonde, big-boned woman in her mid-forties, but she carried herself in such a way that men were easily attracted to her. Bill, an African American, was shorter than

Stephanie and built like a linebacker. Their five-year partnership had resulted in one of the best arrest records in their department.

They had been driving through the southern part of the San Fernando Valley, following up leads on one of their other homicide cases, when the call came in about the death in Malibu. The first officers on the scene were dispatched from the Lost Hills sheriff's station. Once they found a body, it was standard procedure to alert a homicide team to investigate. Unfortunately for Stephanie and Bill, no one else was available, so they got the call.

They had arrived on the scene only thirty minutes before Becky, so they were still putting the pieces together themselves. All they knew so far was that the victim, Wade Bennett, apparently shot himself with the pistol lying on the floor in front of his body. An hour earlier, the neighbor had heard the gunshot, called 911, then waited a few minutes before getting up the nerve to come across the street and knock on the door. When no one answered, he walked back out to the street and waited for the first patrol car to arrive. The patrol deputies entered through the back door, which they found open, and discovered the body in the office. So far, none of the witnesses interviewed had noticed anything out of the ordinary, except the sound of the gunshot.

Stephanie and Bill were pleased with the way the deputies had protected the scene, and the neighbor had filled them in on Mr. Bennett's background. The only other point of interest was the message on the answering machine. Evidently, someone named Josh was on his way to meet with Wade in the next few minutes. It looked like a fairly open-and-shut case. Stephanie left the crime scene analysts (CSAs) gathering evidence and asked Bill to call Mrs. Bennett's sister. She turned back to Becky.

"Did your husband own a gun, Mrs. Bennett?"

Becky paused, still stunned. "Yes . . . I know he kept one somewhere in the office."

"Do you know when he bought it?"

"No," she said. She pulled a tissue from a box on the coffee table and blew her nose. "You can talk to our business manager. He might know."

Stephanie wrote down his name and number as Becky recited it. She'd need to trace the serial number of the gun and make sure it was indeed Mr. Bennett's.

"Did you notice your husband being depressed or overly stressed during the past few days?" Stephanie asked.

Becky didn't respond, staring blankly past the detective.

"Mrs. Bennett?" Stephanie repeated.

Becky's eyes focused again on the detective. "Oh, I'm sorry. What did you ask?"

Stephanie repeated the question.

"No, not at all, Detective. That's why this doesn't make any sense."

"Any trouble in the marriage? Family problems?" Stephanie continued as gently as she could.

Becky dropped her head, the tears returning. "Nothing more than any couple goes through." She paused. "The show took a lot of Wade's time."

"That would be 'The John Harold Show'?"

"Yeah, any new show has long hours and a certain amount of pressure. But Wade is used to that. The show was down this week. We were supposed to have some time together."

"Why were you out?"

The question stung Becky with its implications. *Maybe if I'd been home he'd still be alive?*

Stephanie hated to continue the painful interrogation, but it was her job. Every spouse was a suspect in the initial stage of a case like this.

"I'm sorry, Mrs. Bennett. I know this is hard on you. Just a few more questions," she said as she placed her hand comfortingly over Becky's. "What were you doing out?"

Becky looked back up, wiping tears from her eyes. "Wade asked me to go do some shopping. He wanted to be ... alone ... some work he wanted to get done before Josh came over."

Stephanie remembered the name from the answering machine. "Josh?"

"He's the show's producer. I thought it was strange for them to be meeting here during the hiatus. As a matter of fact, I was pretty upset about it as I was driving home—" Becky abruptly stopped, covering her face with her hands. Through the tears Stephanie could hear, "... and now he's ... gone."

She sat awkwardly while the widow cried, searching for words of comfort, but none came. She was relieved when a woman came through the front door and Mrs. Bennett ran into her arms sobbing uncontrollably. Through the introductions, Stephanie found out it was Mrs. Bennett's sister, Melissa. She allowed the two women to go back to the master bedroom for some private moments, away from the chaos.

8:00 P.m., BURBANK

Rick sat at what had been his temporary desk for the three days that he'd been hired for the production of the Alert One infomercial. With the exception of a picture of his two children, everything was packed. He could have been on his way twenty minutes ago, but something kept him in his chair, staring mindlessly at the photograph.

It wasn't that he'd loved the job. Putting up with the lack of professionalism on the staff had bothered Rick as much as it had Samantha. It was the fact that walking out of this office once again left him unemployed. The last five months had taken their toll on him—from his bank account to his self-confidence. He had hit rock bottom.

He brought his eyes back in focus and reached out and grabbed the picture frame. He gave Jennifer and Justin one last thought as he placed their picture back into his briefcase. How he missed them!

He'd parked near the studio door, so the quickest way to his car was by walking back through the stage. The darkened studio felt strange. Only a short time ago it had been swarming with energy. Now most of the crew were gone, and only a few technicians were left putting equipment away.

"Another great job, Rick."

He was in such a daze he'd walked right past Gary Hall.

"Oh, Gary, hi. Sorry, I guess I was lost in thought."

"No need to apologize. I'm surprised you're still here. Everything go OK from your end?" Gary asked as he placed some headsets into a case. He was one of the top experts in communications, and Rick tried to always have him be a part of his crew when he was directing.

"Yeah, I guess it did. Appreciate all your help," Rick said, putting out his hand to shake Gary's.

Gary closed the headset case and reached out to take Rick's hand.

"You're welcome, Rick. I always enjoy being around your productions." Then, before Rick could turn to walk away, "And, Rick, you've been on my mind lately. When you get some time, let's get together. It's been too long."

"I'd like that, Gary," Rick answered truthfully.

Gary watched Rick walk away, sensing that something wasn't quite right. Even when exhausted, Rick was usually upbeat. Gary breathed a prayer for his friend. *Lord, whatever is going on in Rick's life, use it to bring him closer to you.*

8:15 P.M., MALIBU

Inside the Bennett house, Stephanie and her partner examined the crime scene as the CSAs combed the office collecting evidence. Ray Kokka, one of Stephanie's favorite lab technicians, was going over the details of what they'd found.

"I checked the gun; it's a Taurus PT-101, fairly new model. It handles Smith and Wesson .40-caliber rounds. He had hollow points loaded."

Stephanie sighed. Now she knew why there had been so much damage to the victim.

Ray continued: "The magazine holds a total of ten rounds; there are nine left. We found the bullet lodged in the wall. We'll test fire a round and compare it with the recovered slug. The casing caught in the chamber."

Stephanie had noticed that earlier. In some suicides, because the hand holding the gun goes immediately limp as the gun is fired, the chamber doesn't recoil cleanly, catching the hand as it snaps back and causing the spent cartridge to get stuck. But that alone could not definitively determine if Bennett had killed himself or not.

Bill was pointing to the victim's right hand. "Did you guys notice these marks here?" There were some abrasions on the outside of the hand.

"Yes, we did. I'm not sure what to make of it, but I can tell you it wasn't caused by the recoil. The coroner will have to take a closer look. But there's something else I want to show you." Ray turned to the desk.

"I found a pattern on the desk where the blow-back isn't consistent."

Stephanie gave him a questioning look.

"You can see the spray of blood and tissue covers the whole desk and his computer except for two areas, here and here." Ray pointed to the spots beside the keyboard.

"What could cause that?" Stephanie asked.

"Could be just a weird spray, or something was removed after the gunshot."

Bill and Stephanie looked at each other. She flipped open her pad and scribbled some notes in it.

Bill looked over at the phone sitting beside the computer, having an idea.

"Look, it has a redial button," he said as he punched the speaker button and hit redial.

CHAPTER 3

The three listened as the dial tone, then a series of beeps, filled the room. The instrument displayed the number it was dialing; Stephanie jotted it down. After two rings, a voice-mail system answered the call.

"Hi, this is Josh Abrams. You know the drill; leave your message at the beep."

Stephanie raised her eyebrows at Bill as she wrote down the name.

Josh frowned and sped up Rye Canyon Road and the last few hundred feet to Wade's house. An accident on Pacific Coast

Highway had kept him on the road for nearly two hours. His irritation turned to alarm when he saw a group of patrol cars with flashing lights and a remote van from a local TV station parked outside the house. As he pulled up to park, the coroner's car stopped next to his. His stomach churned, nearly emptying its contents on his car's upholstery. He got out and walked over to where a sheriff's deputy was standing by the yellow tape.

"I'm Josh Abrams, Officer. I have an appointment with Wade Bennett. What's happened here?"

"Just a minute, sir." The officer communicated Josh's name and information into his radio mike clipped near his shoulder. A moment later he gestured for Josh to follow.

"Detective Phillips would like to speak with you."

Ray, Stephanie, and Bill all stared at the laptop computer on the desk.

"I haven't seen too many electronic suicide notes, Steph." Bill brought up what she had already been thinking.

"It kind of makes it hard to do a handwriting analysis, doesn't it?" Ray added.

Stephanie kept silent, glancing up as the deputy led Josh down the hallway toward the office. She went to head them off.

"Mr. Abrams? Detective Phillips," Stephanie said, stepping down the hall to lead Josh to the living room. "I'm sorry about your friend."

"What happened?" Josh cast a quick glance into part of the office. What he saw there shook him to his bones.

"Mr. Bennett is dead," she said, watching his reaction. "It appears he took his own life."

Josh suddenly wished he was sitting down. "I can't believe it . . . are you sure?" When the detective didn't quickly respond, he turned his eyes away.

"We found a suicide note on his computer," Stephanie said.

"How about Becky? Is she here?"

"Yes, she's back in her bedroom with her sister."

"May I see her?" Josh asked.

"Yes, Mr. Abrams, but the deputy will have to stay with you. When you're finished, there are some questions I'd like to ask you."

Josh made his way back to the master bedroom. Becky was sitting up against the headboard cradled by a woman Josh had never met before.

She looked up as he entered.

"Becky," Josh said, walking up to the bed. The deputy stayed by the door. "I'm so sorry! Is there anything I can do?"

Becky released her sister as Josh sat down next to her and gave her a hug.

"Josh, how could this happen? It just doesn't make any sense . . ." Her voice trailed off as she started crying again.

Josh's mind went blank. He couldn't think of a thing to say, so he just held her.

Suddenly Becky looked up. "Just this afternoon he wanted me to get out of the house, do some shopping. That wasn't like him, but he said he wanted to get some things done. So I went." Her sobs intensified. "If I had stayed with him, this wouldn't have happened."

"No Becky, you can't blame yourself," Josh reassured her uncomfortably. "There's nothing you could have done differently."

He turned to Becky's sister to distract from the awkwardness of the moment. "I'm Josh Abrams."

"I'm Melissa, Becky's sister. The police called me after Becky came home."

"I'm glad they got hold of you. What have they told you so far?"

"Not a whole lot," Melissa said, recounting the events as she knew them.

Josh shook his head, the nausea returning, "Well, let me go talk to the detectives, see if they've found out anything new." He turned back to Becky, "I'm sorry, Becky, so sorry. We'll be with you through this. If you need anything, anything at all, you let me know."

He got up and turned to leave, then looked back at Becky. "By the way, do you know why Wade wanted to meet tonight?"

"No, I thought you called the meeting," Becky replied, thinking his question odd. "He told me you were coming and he needed to get organized, but that's all he said. If he did kill himself, he just wanted to get me out of here." With that, another flood of tears released. Melissa wrapped her arms around Becky as Josh left the bedroom.

The deputy sat Josh down in the living room, then went into the office to get the detective.

"It's rare that a suicide note is left on a computer, not hand-written," Stephanie said as she walked up. She had seen Josh reading the note on the coffee table. "But this is the nineties, I guess. Tell me, Mr. Abrams—"

"Please, call me Josh."

"Mr. Abrams, when was the last time you saw or spoke to Mr. Bennett?"

Josh noticed the formality. "Friday, after we finished taping."

"Have you noticed any depression or strange behavior?"

"Nothing unusual. I know with the success of the show there's been a lot of pressure on all of us. But Wade seemed to be handling it. I can't imagine him taking his own life. How did he do it?"

"Gunshot through the mouth."

Bill came in from the office and stood beside Stephanie as she continued.

"There was only one shot fired, from a gun we believe belonged to Mr. Bennett. It was loaded with hollow point bullets, so there was massive damage." Josh winced at the words. Stephanie noted his reaction.

Josh dropped his head. "I don't understand. What could bring Wade to want to kill himself in the first place?"

"That's why I wanted to talk with you. No one we've inter-viewed saw anything strange, like someone entering or leaving the house, and we've got the note on the computer. At this point we're calling it a suicide. There's just one odd thing."

Josh looked up, "What's that?"

"Well, his right hand, the one that apparently shot the gun. There are some abrasions on it. Probably nothing, but we're going to take a look at it. Let me ask you something; do you know anyone who would benefit from Mr. Bennett's death?"

"No, not offhand ... certainly none of us at the show. We just lost an Emmy-winning director. You know there's always the rivalry, cutthroat reputation of Hollywood, but I can't think of any enemies he might have had that would seriously want to hurt him."

"Well, give it some thought and we'll be in touch with you in a day or two."

"Is there anything else?"

"I'd like a staff list from your show. We might want to talk to some of them."

"I'll have my assistant get that to you tomorrow."

"Great. Here's my card. Fax it to the number on the bottom."

"Fine. Oh, and Detective, there's one more thing. This computer will have a lot of files on it relating to our show. How long until you'll be done with it?"

"Well, if everything checks out, it shouldn't be too long. Maybe we'll be able to get it to you by the end of the week."

"I'd appreciate it. I'm sure it will be helpful to our new director ... whoever that's going to be."

"Well, thank you for your time, Mr. Abrams," Stephanie said as Josh stood up. She paused, a question framed on her countenance.

"Yes?" Josh replied.

"We noticed that the last phone number Mr. Bennett called was your office. You don't remember that call?"

Josh glanced down to give himself a moment to think. "He must have called while I was on my way out here."

Stephanie nodded, "I guess that would explain it. Thanks again, Mr. Abrams. You're free to go."

Josh turned and walked toward the door, the words *free to go* reverberating in his mind. Once he was out of sight, Bill spoke, "Well, Steph, I'm surprised at you."

"What did I do now?"

"You mentioned the marks on the hand. Usually you don't give out any piece of evidence."

Stephanie nodded, her eyes trailing back to the door Josh Abrams had just walked through. "I don't want everyone involved with Bennett to think we're going to close this case too quickly, although I, for one, would like to get it off our books."

What made me lie about talking to Wade. What an idiot! Josh thought, nearly spinning out on a curve as he maneuvered his Porsche down Malibu Canyon Road. He picked up the cell phone and punched in the number for the executive producer of "The John Harold Show," Gabriel Flint. He answered after the second ring.

"Yeah."

"Gabe, it's Josh. Wade's dead."

"What do you mean dead? I thought you were meeting with him," Gabriel answered, his voice void of emotion.

Josh shivered and noticed his hands were shaking on the steering wheel. "I mean dead. He shot himself before I got here—"

"You're at the house now?"

"I just left. His body was in his office, still in the chair. The cops are all over the place."

"What did you tell them?" Flint asked.

"Nothing, just that I was shocked that Wade would take his own life. We were supposed to talk tonight. Whatever was bothering him would have been dealt with; everything was going to work out." Josh was starting to speak faster.

"Josh, calm down," Gabriel stated flatly. "He must have been dealing with some problems we didn't know about. Now, tell me what you saw."

Josh took a deep breath, then told Gabriel all he could recall.

"I'm sorry to hear this, Josh. We'll have to make sure we take care of his wife. Becky, isn't it?"

"Yeah, it's Becky, and she's really upset."

"I can imagine, but we'll all get through this. You just hang in there and don't freak out, OK?"

Josh agreed lamely before he disconnected the call. His body shook with a deep fear he'd never experienced before.

CHAPTER 4

Face to face, Jesus, I'm drawing near,
The warmth of your presence melts away my fear.
Mold my heart, put everything in place,
Transformed by your glory, face to face.

Cassie sat on the floor of her friend's living room singing softly with the group clustered around her. Some had their heads bowed, others were looking toward the ceiling, several had their hands extended upward. The song ended and everyone sat still, enveloped by the peace that settled over the room.

After a few moments, the silence ended when the middle-aged man sitting next to her spoke out, "Cassie, do you mind if I pray for you?"

Cassie looked up. This was a little out of the ordinary for Jack. He smiled and waited for a response.

"No, I don't mind at all," she said, swallowing her shyness.

"Is there anything specific you need prayer for?" Jack asked as the group gathered around her.

"Nothing out of the ordinary. There's the constant struggle at work of knowing when to speak up and when to keep silent about my faith. I know God has a purpose in my being there; I just don't want to miss it."

A few moments passed while Jack led the group in prayer. Then, thumbing through his Bible, Jack looked up. "Cassie, as we were praying, this verse came to mind, Psalm 32:8. I think it's for you: *I will instruct you and teach you in the way you should go; I will counsel you and watch over you.*

"I believe God has a specific plan for you, and he wants you to rely on him. He will lead you step by step."

Kathy, who was sitting next to Cassie, agreed. "I felt the Lord impressing on me that there's something coming up he's preparing you for as well. I'm not sure what that means except to encourage you to keep your eyes on him. He'll guide you."

Cassie smiled and took in a deep breath.

"I wish I could give you more details of what God is going to do," Jack said, "but he doesn't seem to work that way."

"If he did, we wouldn't call it walking by faith, would we?" Cassie laughed.

10:55 P.M., STUDIO CITY

Rick stepped through the garage door into his kitchen, relieved to be home. He had bought this condo last summer when it looked like the show he was directing would be on the air for awhile.

It had taken nearly all of his savings for the down payment, and now making the mortgage without a steady income had depleted the rest.

His mood sank even lower when he looked at his message machine and saw the number zero displayed. He had hoped for at least one call about some upcoming work.

He grabbed a soft drink and flopped down in front of the TV with his mail. Flicking the set on, he let whatever station he had last watched fill the screen.

The mail consisted of several bills, a couple of advertisements, and a *Hollywood Reporter*. He'd take the time to search through the *Reporter* classifieds later. He did a quick mental calculation of how much money would be left in his account after paying the new bills. Even with the paycheck coming in from the infomercial, he'd still be several hundred dollars short.

"Wade Bennett, Emmy-winning director, currently working on 'The John Harold Show,' was found dead tonight at his Malibu home." The lead story on the eleven o'clock news grabbed Rick's attention. "Details are still sketchy, but our own Samantha Steel is in Malibu with this live report. Samantha?"

Rick nearly dropped his soda in his lap. Wade Bennett dead? And what was Sam doing in Malibu? She wasn't a news reporter.

The station switched to Samantha standing in front of Bennett's home. "Thanks, Rob. You can see the Bennett's house behind me, fairly quiet now. The police and coroner have completed their work. It appears that Wade Bennett committed suicide earlier this evening. A neighbor heard a gunshot at approximately 6:30 and called 911. Sheriff's deputies arrived on the scene, went into the house, and found Bennett dead, sitting at his desk with a single gunshot wound to the head. . . ."

Rick had worked with Wade on two different occasions as a stage manager. The man should have been on top of the world with the success of "The John Harold Show." Why would the guy want to kill himself?

". . . Although the police were cautious in saying the investigation is still open," Samantha continued, "there was a suicide note left for his wife on his computer. No other details have been released. Back to you, Rob."

"Samantha," the anchorman interjected as a split screen between the studio and Malibu appeared, "any reaction from the family?"

Sam again filled the screen. "Mrs. Bennett has been deeply affected by this tragedy," she said with just the right touch of somberness. "We understand her family is with her in the house, but there has been no comment."

"Thanks, Samantha. We'll have a retrospective on Wade Bennett's influence in Hollywood later in the broadcast. In other news . . . ." Rick tuned out.

Unbelievable, Wade Bennett committing suicide. He had been a difficult director to work with, abusive to his on-air talent, and often termed "a screamer" by the crew. But he was very well connected to the right people, and in Hollywood that was the bottom line.

Rick made a mental decision to follow up on that call to Sam he had planned to make. Maybe he could learn some of the inside scoop on Wade's death, plus it would give him a good reason to reconnect with her. Amazing! He would kill to have Wade's job, and, apparently, Wade had just thrown it all away. *Perhaps* kill *wasn't the best choice of words,* Rick thought to himself, chuckling.

As he surfed through the channels, a single thought lodged in his mind: sad as the man's death was, it left one very prominent show without a director.

11:10 P.m., BEVERLY HILLS

David Bernstein was exhausted as he made his way to his Mercedes-Benz parked around the back of his Beverly Hills office. The preparation for his court appearance in the morning had taken a lot longer than he'd intended. He hoped the confrontation with his wife over the extended day wouldn't keep him out of bed too much longer. He needed some sleep.

His car chirped as he hit the unlock button on his key ring. He tossed his briefcase in back and got behind the wheel. He started the car, the lights coming on automatically, illuminating the sign in front of it proudly claiming his parking space.

He was too tired to notice anything around him as he pulled out of the parking lot and headed home toward the Hollywood Hills. That prevented him from seeing the silver BMW pull out from across the street and settle in behind him.

Ten minutes later, Bernstein's car turned right on Mulholland Drive, one of the most dangerous, winding roads in Los Angeles County.

The killer in the car behind him smiled. He couldn't have planned this better if he'd wanted to. He knew a corner coming up with at least a hundred-foot drop off the edge of the road. He stepped on the accelerator and narrowed the gap between the two cars. Bernstein was irritated by the blinding headlights that suddenly appeared in the rearview mirror. He reached up to flip the mirror to night reflection when the BMW slammed into the back of his car, just as he should have been turning left. With only one hand on the wheel, he couldn't get control of the vehicle as it skidded off the road and over the bank.

The Mercedes rolled several times as it made its way crashing through the underbrush along the hillside, ending in a bent heap at the bottom of the ravine. Seconds later, as Rudy watched from above, the Mercedes burst into flames.

11:45 p.m., STUDIO CITY

Rick got up from his recliner, grabbed a glass of water and the latest Tom Clancy novel he'd been reading, and headed for the bedroom. After undressing and brushing his teeth, he crawled into bed. He couldn't get his mind off of Bennett's successful career. *Why would he have ended it with suicide?* Rick was sure if he were directing a show like "The John Harold Show," he'd be the happiest man in Hollywood.

But he wasn't, and the reality of it all gave Rick the beginnings of a first-class headache. He leaned over and opened up the dresser drawer next to his bed, reaching for a jar of aspirin. As he pulled it out, he noticed his Bible toward the back of the drawer, covered by a thin layer of dust.

How long has it been since I spent time reading that? he wondered. He unscrewed the aspirin bottle and dropped out three caplets into the palm of his hand, hoping they would deaden the pain around his temples. He gulped them down with the water, then stared at the open drawer.

His eyes went from the Bible to the novel before closing the drawer and picking up the novel. He felt a twinge of guilt for his decision, but he just wasn't in the mood for any spiritual reading. *I'll find some time in the next few days to get back into the Word,* he tried to convince himself as he settled in under the covers and opened the paperback.

CHAPTER 5

Jacob Weinberg bounced the ball several times with his left hand, then paused and looked up at his opponent. The morning sun still sent shadows over half the court facing him. It was set point. He was up five games to four, leading this game 40–15. It had been a long time since he had taken Ralph in a set of tennis. Jacob tossed the ball into the air, waited until it began its descent, then brought his racquet around with all the force he could muster, slamming the ball straight into the net with a slap. *That's what I get for going for the ace,* Jacob thought. He pulled the second ball out of his pocket and repeated the ritual of the bounce.

Concentrate, Jacob thought to himself. He tossed the ball up and sliced across it with his racquet, sending a spinner toward

Ralph's forehand. It wasn't hit hard, so Ralph ran up and sent the ball back down the line to Jacob's left. Jacob anticipated the strategy and was already moving left, preparing his backhand. He had two choices as he saw Ralph charging toward the net: go for a passing shot, hard down the left sideline, or play more defensively and lob it over his head. He was feeling a good ten years younger than his fifty-eight years and decided to go for the winner. He added his left hand to the racquet, planted his feet, and sent the ball racing back over the net. It was the best backhand return he'd hit in a decade.

Ralph was caught with his weight leaning toward center court and couldn't make the adjustment to get his racquet on the ball. It shot past him, landing just inside the line before bouncing to the back fence.

"Yes!" Jacob yelled, punching the air. "Finally, the great Ralph Grambling is mortal."

"Great game, Jacob." Ralph chuckled as he walked around the net. "You played like a man possessed today. I demand a drug test."

"Wouldn't do you any good, pal. It's just determination. When you're number two, you try harder."

"Well, if we didn't have to get back to the office, I'd make you play until I won or you had a heart attack, whichever came first."

Jacob laughed heartily as he reached for a towel to wipe the sweat off his face. The two had played tennis together a couple of times a month over the past several years. They were partners, co-owners of The Coast to Coast Talent Agency, which handled actors, directors, writers, and a few other Hollywood specialists. Jacob, the senior of the two, was silver-haired, with a little paunch to his mid-section. He'd been around the industry for many years and could wield great influence in certain areas of film and television. His partner, Ralph, was a distinguished looking man with dark hair that was frosted with gray. Although he hadn't been around quite as long as Jacob, he had a reputation of being more ruthless in negotiations than his partner.

"So what do you think about Wade Bennett?" Ralph asked as they gathered their things and headed for the showers of the Bel-Air Golf and Tennis Club.

Jacob pulled a cigar out of his bag and stuffed it in his mouth. "Quite a shock, quite a shock. I heard it on the news this morning coming over here. It's not too often one of the more successful people around here commits suicide, is it?"

"No, usually it's the long-forgotten ones, and by that time they aren't worth too much news coverage. This one surprised me. We need to get one of our directors in there."

Jacob stopped walking, having noticed an old friend on the court next to theirs, then looked back at Ralph. "Everyone in our stable is working except Treadway. I still can't believe they pulled his show off the air last fall. Have you talked to him lately?"

"It's been a couple of weeks, when I finalized his deal with that infomercial. He seemed a little down about his lack of work."

Jacob started walking again. "I wish he had more credits under his belt to pitch him for the Harold show. Do you think he can handle it?"

"I think he can. From what I've seen, he's talented. It's just a matter of getting him the right opportunities, then he could make us a lot of money."

"You get in touch with him, make sure he's comfortable with us pursuing this." Jacob motioned to the two men playing tennis on the next court. "I'm going to catch Walter over there between sets and see who we have to sell Treadway to."

Walter Reed, one of several lawyers at National Studios, the syndication arm behind "The John Harold Show," just might be the one they'd have to negotiate with if Rick was offered the job. He'd know who held the power to decide Bennett's replacement.

Ralph walked on to the locker room while Jacob waited for a change of courts in Walter's game. As Walter made his way around the net, he noticed Jacob. "Good morning, Jacob. How'd your match go?"

"A victory for a change. How about you?"

"I'm down 5–2, but I've got him just where I want him," Walter laughed. "Jacob, this is Kent Turlock; he's vice president in charge of distribution for National."

Kent and Jacob shook hands and exchanged pleasantries. Then Jacob got down to business. "I'm sorry to hear about Wade. It must have the studio in quite an uproar."

"It's really sad, Jacob, although I haven't been in yet to see everyone's reaction. It sure shocked me."

"How well are you tuned in to the show's production people?"

"A lot. I worked out the contract with Wade. Josh Abrams is the producer, but he really doesn't make a major decision without involving Harold as well."

"So those two will be deciding on Wade's replacement?" Jacob casually interjected.

"Oh, I see where this is going," Walter said. "Actually they'll have to clear it with the executive producer, Gabriel Flint, over at Starfield Enterprises. He keeps a fairly heavy hand on the show. You must have somebody in mind for the job."

"As a matter of fact, I do. Thanks for the names. I'll see if I can get my client in the door on this one. I owe you one, Walter."

Walter shook his head, smiling. "That and a quarter won't even get me a cup of coffee in this town. But good luck, Jacob."

"Nice to meet you, Kent." Jacob waved as he started off the court. "Attack his backhand; it's his Achilles heel."

"Hey! He's already winning. He doesn't need your help," Walter called out, as he stepped over to his service line.

Jacob walked back to the clubhouse, pleased with himself. It always helped to know who he had to deal with before attempting a meeting for one of his clients. He knew getting Rick the job was a long shot, but if he could pull it off, he'd be the talk of the town, something his inflated ego had sorely missed.

8:37 A.m., WEST LOS ANGELES

Vanessa felt the sunshine on her face as it streamed through her bedroom window, pulling her toward consciousness. She moved her head to get a look at the alarm clock by the bed. The slight movement sent a shock wave of pain through her whole body. She lay still, trying to shake the cobwebs out of her head while taking stock of her physical condition. She had a pounding headache, her lips were swollen, and when she tried to moisten them with her tongue, she tasted caked blood. Her chest burned with searing pain around her rib cage.

The man beside her moaned and rolled from his side, lying flat on his back and filling the room with a loud snore. His presence at first startled her, then the events of the previous night began to resurface in her memory.

It had started as a quiet evening for a change since she had not been forced to "entertain" any of the associates of her keeper. Vanessa remembered she had watched some TV, then smoked a little marijuana while taking a long, hot bubble bath before going to bed. Her apartment faced the ocean, and on clear days she had a beautiful view. She could no more afford the rent on the place than she could the payments of the Corvette she drove, but these little extras were all part of her "job."

Vanessa had run away from home just after she turned sixteen to escape an alcoholic mother and a stepfather who often spent the night in her bedroom instead of her mother's. She was a beautiful girl with long, sandy blond hair and bright green eyes. Everyone at school said she should be a model or a movie star, but there weren't too many opportunities in Bismarck, North Dakota. So one night she sneaked out of her house, hitched a ride west, and never looked back.

Now, after four years, her clear, bright eyes were dulled and lifeless. She had spent many nights on the street, quickly prostituting herself just to be able to get something to eat. She'd been surprised how easy that was for her; she gave her stepfather credit for that.

Nothing had broken for her in modeling or film work until two years ago, when she ran into someone who got her an interview with a director doing an adult film. Once she made it through the audition on his couch, she was launched on a short film career doing movies for a company called Sextasy.

On the set of one of her films, the top executive of Sextasy took a liking to her. Before long she was out of the movies and living in this beautiful apartment with a nice weekly allowance. All she had to do was entertain him, or one or two of his friends, from time to time.

She pulled herself up, trying to get out of bed. The man next to her was Rudy Vanozzi, one of her keeper's hired hands, who often took her as a bonus when he knew the boss wasn't around. He had come in sometime early in the morning, using a key he had made for himself, and reeking of alcohol.

Vanessa at first refused to have sex with him, and she had paid for it. She could have saved herself the pain; he was so drunk he didn't have the ability to complete the act anyway. That in itself would have brought more abuse to Vanessa had he not mercifully passed out before any more damage could be done.

She made it to the bathroom and splashed some cold water over her face, feeling the sting from the split in her lip. The water helped clear her head. She took a rag and wiped carefully at her mouth.

What was it Rudy had said last night before he passed out? None of it made any sense. Something about a guy named Bennett who was now out of the picture, and another comment about Laslo, or something like that, being buried forever. Vanessa didn't understand any of it, and it would probably be better for her if it stayed that way.

She walked back into her bedroom and eyed the pile of clothes Rudy had left by the bed. The sight of his huge bulk lying face up on her bed made her stomach turn. There was some blood on the sheets, but she couldn't tell if it was hers or blood from his bandaged hand. She went through his stuff, hoping to find compensation for the punishment she suffered last night. He had quite a wad of bills in his pants pocket, so she grabbed a clump of them, hoping he wouldn't remember how much money he'd had. Lying next to the clothes were an appointment book and a small white box. She opened the box first and saw a bunch of computer disks. Then she opened the notebook; it belonged to a guy named Wade Bennett. As she thumbed through it, a rate card for the Directors Guild of America fell out. She wasn't so dumb as to think his being "out of the picture" referred to his being dropped from a film.

Getting nervous, Vanessa put the rate card back into the appointment book. On impulse she grabbed a couple of the computer disks before closing the box and putting everything back the way she had found it. She padded back into the bathroom and hid the money and the disks behind some cleaning products under the sink.

She needed to get dressed and get out of the apartment before Rudy awoke. As she stood to walk back into the bedroom, a wave of nausea hit her. She barely made it to the toilet in time. The horrible retching sent waves of pain from her rib cage that nearly left her unconscious.

8:52 A.M., NATIONAL STUDIOS

Cassie pulled into the parking lot, a few minutes early as usual. She was surprised to see that Josh was already in his office and on the phone. Usually he didn't arrive until ten.

As she was setting her purse down, she heard Josh end his phone call.

"Cassie, get in here," he yelled gruffly. She grabbed her notepad and rushed into his office.

"This is going to be one hell of a day," he said.

"What's going on, Josh?" Cassie inquired innocently.

"You mean you haven't heard? Wade killed himself last night."

Cassie's heart seemed to stop. She had just talked with him yesterday when he'd called in to talk to Josh. Then she remembered how she had been unable to reach him by phone to tell him Josh would be late to their meeting. "When? How did this happen?"

"Last night, around six. Evidently he shot himself. Now listen, I know this is quite a shock for you. It is for me as well. But there're several things I'm going to need you to take care of this morning." Josh looked up at Cassie and saw tears welling up in her eyes. She hadn't heard a thing he'd just said.

"I'm sorry, Cassie. I've had a whole night to deal with this." The phone rang in the outer office on Cassie's desk, and she stood to go answer it.

"Let it ring. The voice mail will get it. I want to make sure you're OK, and that we have a plan to deal with everything."

"I'm OK, Josh. It's just so startling," Cassie said, wiping the tears away before her mascara ran. "I can't believe he could do that. How is Becky handling it?"

"Not too well as of last night. I'd like you to call her later today and check on her for me, but first we've got some business to take care of. Are you ready?"

Cassie nodded silently.

"First, here's the card of the detective who is handling the investigation." Josh slipped it across his desk.

"I thought you said it was a suicide. Why is there an investigation?"

"I think it's just routine stuff, but she wants a fax of our staff list. They might want to contact some of them. See to that first. Then I want you to arrange a staff meeting tomorrow morning at ten, everyone attending. We may have to adjust our schedule next week. I don't know if we'll be able to find a director by Monday. Get any of the production assistants that are in today to make those calls. You're going to be too busy with other things, believe me."

Cassie jotted everything down as Josh spoke, trying to overcome her shock. She wondered what the other things would be, but he quickly answered her question.

"You haven't been around this business long, Cassie, but you're about to find out what the piranha are like when there's blood in the water." She shuddered at his graphic visual image. "We're going to be inundated with two types of calls. First, the press. There's a story here, at least until the police officially call it a suicide. Sad to say, but any kind of press brings ratings. So I've made a list of networks, newspapers, and possible magazines that I'll receive calls from—anyone else just give them this comment from the show." Josh handed over two pages he'd prepared early that morning.

"The second group will be from those most anxious to get at Wade's job. I'm not taking any of those calls today. Any agents who want to talk to me about their clients, just put on a list. Have them fax the résumés and we'll worry about those tomorrow. Later today, I'll come up with a list of directors who might be suitable, then you can call their agents and see how many are available. You got that?"

"No problem."

Josh smiled reassuringly. "It'll be harder than it sounds. Your best bet with any agent is to tell them I'm not in the office. They can be pretty persistent, and they don't like to take no for an answer." Cassie didn't like the sound of that. He was asking her to lie.

"The last thing is getting back to Becky. You've had a chance to get to know her, haven't you?" Cassie nodded. "Good. Give her a call and offer any assistance she needs from us in arranging the funeral, memorial service, anything at all. Oh, and find out a charity that Wade supported. We can set up a fund for people to donate to in Wade's memory. Any questions?"

"No, Josh, I think I've got it." She paused, blinking back tears. "You and Wade were pretty close, weren't you?"

"Yeah, we were. I can't believe this happened." The phone rang again. "You'd better get that. Like I said, it's going to be hell today."

No, Josh, not as bad as hell, Cassie thought. She made her way back to her desk and picked up the phone. As predicted, it was a reporter. His name wasn't on Josh's list, so Cassie read him the official statement.

After she got off the phone, she rounded up the two production assistants who worked on the show. She had one take the staff list and head off to fax a copy to the detective as well as notify the staff for tomorrow's production meeting. She kept the other one on a phone extension by her desk to screen calls while she collected her thoughts. *Lord, I'm beginning to see why you led the group to pray for me last night.*

CHAPTER 6

The phone rang, bringing Rick out of a restless sleep. He looked at the clock on his nightstand. He couldn't believe he'd slept past ten. He cleared his throat several times as the phone rang a second time, then he lifted the receiver and forced out a hello.

"Rick! It's Ralph Grambling. I didn't wake you, did I?" said the exuberant voice on the line.

"Hi, Ralph. No, of course not," Rick lied. "I've just had this little cold. It's good to hear from you. I was thinking about calling you today." Rick tried to pull his mind into full gear.

"Really, what was on your mind?"

"Have you heard about Wade Bennett's death?"

"Yes, I have. What a tragedy," Ralph said, giving a low whistle.

"I was thinking, even though it's sad and all," Rick struggled, "I think I'd be perfect for 'The John Harold Show.'"

"Well, we must be on the same wavelength today, buddy." Ralph grinned as he propped his feet up on the desk. "Just this morning, Jacob and I were talking about that very same thing. He's going to pursue an interview for you; we just wanted to make sure you felt comfortable and didn't have any reservations about being able to handle it."

"Not at all." Rick sat up, wide awake now. "I'm made for this type of show. Get me in the door, and we're home free."

"Glad to hear you say that, Rick. We'll work on it from our end. Everything we have, résumé and directing reel, up to date?"

"They sure are. I haven't been doing much else for the last couple of months, remember?"

"Except for that infomercial, which we don't need to add. We'll be in touch."

Rick stared into space, not wanting his hopes to get away from him. He knew that his chances of landing this job were as slim as winning the lottery.

Rick looked up toward the ceiling and said, "God, this job would be perfect. I know it's a long shot, but please, open the doors for me. Let my agent get me that interview."

He decided to get up and take a shower. He hadn't intended to let the day get away from him by sleeping so late. But as each day went by without finding any work, he had fallen into a pattern of getting up later and later. If only this show would come through, it would be the answer to all of his problems. Or so he thought.

11:00 A.M., SHERIFF'S HEADQUARTERS

Stephanie sat at her desk, lost in the pile of papers—reports and lab results from the cases she had been working on with Bill before the Bennett death. Their desks sat facing each other in the corner of a large office space that housed a dozen other desks and an equal number of detectives.

Bill sat down in his chair and tapped a pencil on the desktop. "I talked to Ray about the computer. He's really backed up, but he promised he'd sneak a peak at it this afternoon. Any luck with the phone records?"

"We should have them in a couple of hours." Stephanie's intercom buzzed. She picked up her phone. "Phillips."

She listened for a few seconds, then responded, "Right away."

Bill's eyebrows rose.

"That's the captain. He wants an update on Bennett. Let's go give him what we've got."

The two walked down the hall to the captain's office. Stephanie tapped on the door before opening it.

"So, how are my two finest overworked detectives today?" Captain Vance Lipton looked up from his desk as Stephanie and Bill entered.

"We could be doing a lot better if you'd send us on some investigation to Hawaii," Bill joked. The captain didn't laugh.

"The press is all over us this morning on the Bennett thing. Is it clear-cut suicide so we can put it behind us, or have you come up with something fishy?"

Stephanie took the lead. "So far we don't have much to go on. I'd like to get the autopsy report and take a look at the lab work before we make any official conclusions."

"What have you got that's keeping you from concluding suicide?"

"Just some marks on Bennett's hand and a unique blowback pattern around his desk. Not to mention no one can substantiate a suicidal frame of mind."

"So you don't have squat. Go ahead and get your lab and autopsy findings, but if nothing more concrete turns up, I want this case closed. We've got too many pressing investigations to clear up to waste time on a stupid Hollywood suicide. And I don't need the aggravation of the press breathing down my neck. What about that councilman?"

"Perkins," Bill filled in.

"Yeah, the one who was found in a dumpster. Any leads?"

"Not since we talked yesterday. We were working on that case when the call came in about Bennett."

"Another reason to get it wrapped up quickly. Then see what you can do about wrapping up the councilman's case. If he was mugged, then let's call it that and move on," the captain continued. "It's been more than a week, and I don't like the pressure I'm getting. Between Hollywood and downtown politics, I'm about ready to become a department store security guard. Now, get outta here and get to work."

The Perkins murder was a difficult case to crack. His body, beaten and shot, had been found a week ago behind a bar near Los Angeles International Airport. It had taken two days to identify him as Jerry Perkins, the city councilman. It was another high-profile case that the two detectives didn't have any good leads on. This was not going to be a fun week.

11:24 a.m., STUDIO CITY

Rick opened the morning paper and saw a small picture of Wade Bennett in the lower right-hand corner of the front page with the caption, "Emmy-Winning Director Found Dead" written above it. He read through the story, not learning anything new except the wording of the suicide note. What a tragedy. Even during Rick's darkest time, when his wife Connie divorced him three years ago and they were fighting over custody of the children, he never seriously contemplated committing suicide. But the thought had crossed his mind.

Rick finished his cornflakes, breezed through the rest of the paper, then went upstairs to his loft, where he kept his office. Since he'd already heard from his agent, that left Samantha on his list of calls to make.

He grabbed his script binder from the Alert One infomercial and looked up Samantha's phone number from the staff list. She'd probably be at the studio this morning if she was still covering the Bennett story, so he tried her there. Unfortunately, she was out, so he left his name and number for her to return the call.

That left him with the stack of bills piled on his desk. He knew he needed to figure how much he owed and compare that to how much he had left in his checking, but he didn't have the heart to do it now.

He tossed the bills back onto the desk, deciding he'd deal with it all later. Without thinking, he grabbed his wallet and keys and headed out the back door into the garage. He jumped on his ten-speed bike and headed into the street, peddling furiously.

Something needed to break soon or he'd lose everything he'd worked so hard for over the past several years. For the first time since he had started directing, he was seriously considering going back to stage managing. It was a decision he'd been avoiding for a few weeks, but now it seemed inescapable.

The wind in his face refreshed him. He was a block away from his condo before he realized he'd forgotten his helmet. Several miles later, he pulled up at one of his favorite delis off Ventura Boulevard to get a drink. He parked his bike outside, then walked up to the counter to order an iced tea.

"Rick, nice to see you again."

Rick turned, surprised. It was Gary Hall.

"What brings you around this neck of the woods?" Rick responded.

"My shop is just a few blocks from here. I just came in to grab a quick sandwich. Would you care to join me?"

Rick looked at his watch. "I guess it's nearly lunchtime. I'd love to."

Rick ordered a sub to go with his iced tea, then Gary led him over to his table.

"You look like you're feeling a little better today than you were last night," Gary said as they sat down.

Rick grinned apologetically. "Sorry about that. I had a lot on my mind after the show. I probably came off a little cold."

"I figured it was something like that, but I've been praying for you today anyway. Figured you might need it."

If you only knew, Rick thought.

"Now that your project is over, what do you have coming up next?" Gary tried to lighten the mood.

Rick sighed, unable to keep up the busy freelance front anymore. "To be honest, I don't have a thing. Every lead I check out is a dead end. Everyone's trying to sell shows right now, not produce them."

"Don't worry, Rick, I'm sure something will come along soon," Gary said, twirling the straw in his drink.

"I hope so. I'm not sure how much longer I can stay afloat."

"Didn't you make quite a bit last year when you were doing that talk show?"

"Yeah, but I thought the show was going to run a lot longer than it did. The down payment on the condo took up the bulk of it. It's getting tough with the expenses still coming in, but no income."

"Well, we'll just have to pray that God brings you something quickly."

"I'd appreciate that. How about you? Work still keeping you busy?"

"Oh, yeah," Gary replied. "We're at the tail end of the awards show season. It's always a hectic time of year."

"I miss doing those shows. I had a lot of fun back then."

"And we miss you, too, but now you've moved up, and sometimes that's a rough transition. Actually, I'd say you've done very well so far. I've seen a lot of others try and make the move to directing. It took years before they established any kind of reputation. Some didn't make it at all. You've had a pretty good couple of years. Maybe God is just stretching your faith a little," he grinned.

Gary's words rang true. Maybe he was right. Rick remembered why he liked Gary so much—he always seemed to have a positive outlook on life.

"That group I attend, Christians in Film and Television, has a meeting coming up Thursday night." Rick's attention snapped back as Gary spoke. "Why don't you come with me? I know you can't say you'll be working," he smiled.

"I don't know if I need to add another church service to my life right now," Rick said. Already he tried to squeeze in two or three services a week, somehow expecting to curry favor from God by steady attendance. But it didn't seem to help, and Rick was left with a growing restlessness he couldn't quite pinpoint.

"This isn't a church service," Gary countered. "It's people like you and me, getting together to study God's Word and pray for whatever needs arise within the group. Just being supportive of one another."

Gary paused, a thought coming to his mind. "Let me ask you a question. How many people do you know at your church?"

This took Rick by surprise. "Know? Well, lots, there's . . ."

"I mean really know, as an intimate friend. Someone you'd run across town to help change a tire, or help move out of an apartment on a Sunday afternoon, spend time with in the hospital, or counsel through a difficult marriage. That kind of friend."

Rick thought for a moment. Off the top of his head he drew a blank.

"I guess not very many the way you describe it," Rick said.

"If you're ever in the market for that kind of friendship, drop by," Gary said, jotting down the address of the group and sliding it across the table to Rick.

When the sandwiches arrived, Gary bowed his head to give thanks.

Rick looked up and glanced around to see if anyone in the deli was looking at them. He was relieved to find they weren't.

Later, as he mounted his bicycle for the long ride home, Rick reached into his pocket and pulled out the slip of paper from Gary. Below the address was a note: "1 Peter 4:8–11. Read it when you get the chance. Then let's talk some more."

CHAPTER 7

Cassie checked the time display on her computer screen as her phone rang once again. She had never looked forward to a lunch break as much as she did today. If she had to talk to one more agent or reporter, she would scream. Josh had made an understatement when he called them piranha. She breathed a prayer for more patience and picked up the phone.

"Josh Abrams's office. This is Cassie; may I help you?"

"Yeah, this is Jacob Weinberg. Is he in?"

"I'm sorry, Mr. Weinberg, but Mr. Abrams is not available at the moment. If you'd care to—"

"Tell him this is important. I've got the perfect director for his show."

"I'll be happy to do so, sir, when he is available," Cassie said, her teeth clenching.

"If you'll tell him it's me on the phone, I'm sure he'd want to make himself available," Jacob said, trying to intimidate Cassie.

"Mr. Weinberg, if you have a director that you'd like Mr. Abrams to consider, you'll have to follow the same procedure that everyone else is following. Our fax number is 555-1400. You may fax your client's résumé to us at your convenience. I'll be compiling them all later today for Mr. Abrams to go over."

Jacob changed tacks. "Look, sweetheart, I didn't mean to come on too strong. It's just that Josh and I go way back." He tried to recall if they had, in fact, even met before. "I want to let him know how sorry I am for what happened to Wade. Besides, I really think I could save him a lot of time looking around for another director."

"Well, I'll give him the message," Cassie said, standing her ground.

"Fine, you win. I'll fax his résumé over directly. But let Josh know his name is Rick Treadway. I'll be in touch with him later about this."

Cassie hung up, relieved. She had gotten through another one. Already, more than a dozen résumés had been compiled for Josh. She hadn't even had a chance to call Becky yet. That would be her first priority after lunch.

Chad Overton, the associate director for the show, walked up to her desk muttering, "I can't believe what's happening around here. You must be having quite a day."

"Well, it hasn't been a picnic," Cassie said blandly. "You must be pretty shocked by the news."

"I am. I don't know how we're going to replace him. Is Josh in, Cassie? I've got something I need to go over with him."

"He's real busy, Chad, but let me check." Cassie grabbed her phone and buzzed Josh.

"Josh, Chad's here. He's got a quick question he needs to ask you."

"Send him in," Josh said through his speakerphone, "and Cassie . . . I've got that meeting at Gabriel's office in a couple of hours. I need to have that list of directors by then."

"They'll be ready." Cassie could see her lunch break flying out the window. She hung up the phone and looked up at Chad. "You're on."

Josh put some papers aside and stretched back in his chair as Chad came in. "Cassie said you had a question," he said, getting right to the point.

"It has to do with some of the remote segments we were going to try to catch up on this week." Chad placed a videocassette on Josh's desk. "We finished the off-line on the immigration piece yesterday; you just need to sign off on it."

Josh took the cassette. "It'll be a day or two before I can even get to this. There's so much in the air right now."

"I kind of figured that. I just had one other question. Did you want me to finish up the Lasko interview Wade started?"

Josh's head snapped up. "Is that what Wade was working on? Were you with him Monday?"

"No," Chad said, suddenly defensive. "I'd finished my session and left. Sid told me Wade was coming in that afternoon to do Lasko, and I didn't know if you needed that finished or not."

"No, we don't. We've decided not to air that piece. What I need you to do is to get some more reruns ready for us in case we don't go back into production on Monday. I'm going to be swamped, so just look back into the October and November shows. Pull five good ones for me."

"I'll take care of it. Any leads on who's going to be taking over?"

"Not yet. I've got a couple of directors I'm thinking of, but I don't know if they're even available. Anybody come to your mind?"

"Not really. Everybody I've thought of is already working on something else."

"That's what I'm worried about. That's why I may need those extra reruns. Get together with Schu and book some editing time."

"I'll do that. And good luck, Josh. I know you've got your hands full."

"That's an understatement," Josh answered under his breath as Chad left the office.

As soon as Chad was out of listening range, Josh picked up the phone and dialed the off-line bay's extension. After three rings he heard Sid's voice.

"Hi, Sid. Josh here."

"Josh, I'm really sorry to hear about Wade. What a shock! I couldn't believe it when I heard the news."

"I'm finding it hard to believe myself. Listen, Sid, I just wanted to ask you a quick question. Did you stay and work with Wade on Monday?"

Sid paused before answering. "Not really. Wade came in while Chad and I were working on the immigration piece. He was anxious to get started, so we held over the immigration stuff and finished it this morning. After I got him set up with his tapes, he wanted to do it on his own. So I left just as he was getting into it. Why do you want to know?"

"Just curious. How far did he get with Lasko?"

"It looked like he gave up. The tapes were put away and he erased the footage off of the hard drive."

"OK, Sid, thanks," Josh said relieved. "We're killing that story anyway so don't worry about it. Chad's on his way back. We need to prepare another week of reruns."

"We'll get 'em ready, boss," Sid replied, blowing out a soft whistle as his sweaty hand placed the receiver back down.

John Harold sat in his living room still in his underwear, half covered by his robe. A bowl of cereal was on his lap and the morning paper lay next to him. On the tube, some poor woman was sobbing about how her twin sister had sex with her husband on their wedding day. John chuckled. Maybe he should get the twins on his show—could be worth some ratings. He noticed the picture of Wade in the corner of the paper's front page.

"I really won't miss you," John said to the picture. Although he hated to admit Wade had directed his show well, he was tired of the ego clash the two had become famous for around the set. John had tried to keep reminding Wade of whose name was on the show, but that didn't seem to work. Well, that problem was behind him. Now he had to make sure the next director was someone who understood who was in charge.

John looked at the wall clock across the room from his large-screen TV. A little after one. That gave him nearly two hours to get presentable and make it over to Beverly Hills for the meeting with Josh and Gabriel. If he'd learned anything in show business the last couple of years, it was to take all the control you can get before someone else does and you're left holding the short end of the stick. John had no intentions of letting that happen with his show.

1:27 P.M., MALIBU

Becky had spent most of the day in her bedroom. Decisions were still to be made, yet whenever she tried to focus on one, her emotions overtook her and she broke down and cried. Life must go on, she decided. With what determination she could muster, she got up and left the bedroom.

She passed by the entranceway to the house, noticing several arrangements of flowers delivered from friends and business associates of Wade's. She didn't have the heart to stop and read the notes. Maybe sometime later.

"Becky," her mom broke into the silence, "would you like something to eat?"

"I don't think so, Mom. I think it's time to get things in order."

Her mother nodded in agreement. She and Becky's sister had managed to clean up the office before Becky had come out of the bedroom. Now they weren't sure what to do.

Becky continued, "Today is Wednesday, right? Let's have a memorial service on Saturday. That way a lot of the people Wade would have known in the industry will be able to attend. Just a simple ceremony at the funeral parlor. I don't want everyone at the graveside."

"Have you given any thought to the eulogy and who will give it?" Becky's sister asked.

"No, I haven't. You know Wade never went to church. Don't they have someone at the funeral home?"

"They might have someone on call. I'll ask them for you," Melissa offered.

"If they don't, I'll ask Pastor Riley. I'm sure he'd do it for you. Just the other day he said he really missed seeing you at church," her mother said, searching her daughter's face for a reaction.

Becky cringed. Her family hadn't been excited about her relationship with Wade because he wasn't a Christian. Soon after they started dating, Becky's church attendance, sparse enough since she'd been a teenager, dropped off altogether. Her mom continued to apply subtle points of pressure to try to get her back to church. With Wade gone, there'd be no stopping her now.

"Melissa," Becky turned to her sister, deciding to change the topic, "come into the office with me. I'm going to need to get things in order. Let's call David and see what legal steps I need to take with Wade gone. His number will be in Wade's book."

"Are you sure, Becky?" Melissa asked.

Becky just turned and headed down the hallway. She came around the corner and stepped into the office. She felt as if she'd stepped back in time. Everything was clean, and she almost expected to find Wade sitting at his favorite chair, working. Except the chair wasn't there. Melissa knew what was on her mind.

"We left the chair out back. We couldn't get it clean."

Becky nodded and then made her way over to the desk. Wade's computer was gone; she'd expected that. The detectives had said they'd need it for a few days because of the suicide note. She slowly took stock of the whole room. It felt as empty as her life did. Friends who had been through divorces told her it would have been better if their husbands had died rather than go through the pain of rejection. Before, she'd agreed with them. Now, she changed her mind—especially if the death was self-inflicted. A suicide was worse than a divorce. It was the ultimate rejection. It said that life with you was so bad, death was preferable.

That's what kept tugging at Becky. They had had a happy life together. Sure, Wade could be arrogant, a bit self-indulgent, and the show kept him busy; but that's when he was the happiest. Their life together had its share of adjustments, but judging from her friends' marriages, theirs was a good one. Suicide just didn't add up.

Becky scanned the room looking for Wade's appointment book. When he was home, it was always between the phone and the computer. Now that spot was empty. Becky reached beside the desk and picked up her husband's briefcase. She laid it on the desk and flipped it open. Inside were his cell phone, some paperwork relating to the show, a stopwatch, and his collection of pens, but no appointment book.

"Melissa, did the police give you a list of the things they took into evidence?"

"No, they didn't. I think the only thing they took was the computer," her sister responded.

"His appointment book is gone. It has his calendar, phone numbers, and stuff in it. He always kept it with him."

Becky turned and yelled out the office door, "Mom, look up David Bernstein's number in the phone book and call his office for me."

"Maybe it's in his car, or he might have left it at the studio," Melissa said.

"I don't think so; he always had it with him." Becky suddenly looked into her sister's eyes with steely determination, "Melissa, Wade didn't kill himself. I can't accept that. Maybe I'm grasping at straws, but I want to find that appointment book and look through his computer myself. There's got to be something that will tell me what is really going on here."

Melissa didn't know what to say. What was it psychologists say is the first step in dealing with death? Denial? Maybe this was Becky's way of handling the shock of it all.

"Why don't you go out and check his car? You'd know what you're looking for. I'll call the detectives and see if that was something they took, OK?"

Becky nodded. "Thanks, sis. And see when they'll let me have that computer back, would ya?"

Becky's mother stepped into the office, her face drained of any color. "I just spoke to Mr. Bernstein's secretary. His car ran off Mulholland Drive late last night. He's dead."

2:03 P.M., COUNTY SHERIFF'S LAB, NORTH HOLLYWOOD

Ray Kokka turned on the Powerbook computer and glanced at his watch while the laptop was booting up. If he was lucky, maybe he'd get out of the office by seven tonight and have dinner with his wife for a change. The computer was ready, displaying Wade's desktop before him.

Most of the computers in his crime lab, and the ones he'd worked with in the past, were IBMs or IBM clones. He wasn't comfortable with the Macintosh models. Nor was he excited about wasting his time on this case when things were so busy in the lab. In spite of some of the questions he'd had at Bennett's house, he couldn't see any evidence that it wasn't a suicide. But to complete the formalities of the investigation, he copied all of the data from Bennett's computer onto a portable disk drive. He wanted to make sure that if there was something on the computer that could lead to a suspect, it wouldn't get damaged.

With that process finally done, Ray set aside Wade's Powerbook, hooked the portable drive into one of the departmental Macintosh computers, then spent the next hour perusing Bennett's various files. His address book, résumé, folders from past shows, computer games, and several documents associated with "The John Harold Show" flashed on the screen. Still, nothing suspicious emerged.

Ray decided he'd better analyze the suicide note itself. He moved the cursor to the proper icon and double-clicked the mouse to open it up. He reread the note. Nothing.

He wondered when Bennett had typed up the document, but wasn't sure how to access the time and date of creation on a Macintosh. Suddenly his desk started shaking and the light fixture above him started to sway.

"Earthquake!" someone screamed behind him. He was about to crawl under his desk when the shaking abruptly stopped.

Someday I've got to move out of this city, Ray thought. Ever since the Northridge quake in 1994, Ray and his wife had talked about relocating out of Southern California. Even after several years, any tremor still rattled him.

"That was fun; probably a 4.0 or higher," Ray's assistant, Daryl, shouted from across the room. Ray shook his head. It was just like Daryl to enjoy being shaken by the earth. "Hey, Ray, could you come over here a minute?" Daryl called out.

Ray turned and headed over. "Yeah, what is it?" Daryl was holding up the Bennett gun, analyzing the chamber.

"Did the victim get his hand caught in the slide?" he asked, looking up at his boss.

"We didn't see any evidence of that at the scene. Why?"

Daryl pointed to the area he was inspecting as he slid the chamber back. "I think I found some skin tissue and something else in here that looks like latex. Take a look."

Ray inspected the gun, intrigued about locating something out of the ordinary. *Maybe this case has some merit after all.*

CHAPTER 8

Rick was getting nervous. His checkbook was down to only $467, and that included the $3,000 he had borrowed on his home equity line of credit two months ago. He was still a couple of months overdue on his child support, and the condo payment had to be paid in a couple of days.

He mentally added in the money he'd receive for doing the Alert One infomercial, but that only covered the condo payment. He'd have to talk to Connie to see if she could get by without the child support for a few months. She'd remarried into a well-to-do family, and her new husband was a lawyer. They didn't really need the child support, and what a lousy occupation for her to marry into when he was behind on his payments. He drummed his fingers on the desktop and glanced at the phone.

He'd hoped to hear something from his agent about the show. He was tempted to call, but that wouldn't do any good. If they knew something, they'd call him. But being patient was next to impossible while sitting here staring at his bills.

He paid what he could, working through the bills in order of their due dates until his account hovered just above zero, then shut his computer off with a sigh. He walked back downstairs, not really sure what to do with the rest of his afternoon. Then he remembered his conversation with Gary. He grabbed the scrap of paper Gary had given him and headed to his bedroom.

Opening the nightstand drawer, he pulled the Bible from under the Clancy paperback. He thumbed through the New Testament, passing through the Gospels and heading toward the back until he found 1 Peter. He looked up chapter 4 and read verses 8–11: *Above all, love each other deeply, because love covers over a multitude of sins. Offer hospitality to one another without grumbling. Each one should use whatever gift he has received to serve others, faithfully administering God's grace in its various forms. If anyone speaks, he should do it as one speaking the very words of God. If anyone serves, he should do it with the strength God provides, so that in all things God may be praised through Jesus Christ. To him be the glory and power for ever and ever. Amen.*

Rick studied the words for a minute and thought back to what Gary had said. Would he run across town to help someone with car trouble or help move a friend on a weekend? Rick considered himself a giving person. Sure he'd do that. But when it came to hospital visits and counseling people, he paused. That was the pastor's job, wasn't it?

Then he flipped the question around. Who would come to him if he was in one of those situations? Dan Black came to mind, the sound engineer for the church. He and Rick had forged a friendship when Rick helped with the Christmas pageant. But Dan had a wife and a couple of young kids. Rick wouldn't bother him even if he did have car trouble. As far as moving, he had been doing fairly well financially when he moved into the condo, so he had a moving company do it for him. And if he was in the hospital or needed marriage counseling, he'd expect the pastor at his church to be there for him.

Rick thought back to three years before, when his marriage was failing. As a last resort, he'd gone to his pastor, hoping for a miracle. It didn't happen.

Sweethearts from college, Rick and Connie had had a couple of happy years together. Connie's nursing salary helped stabilize the finances as Rick entered the up-and-down world of television production. Eventually he found a niche as a stage manager and built a solid career, allowing them to start a family. Jennifer came along, and then Justin. Unfortunately, with Rick's rising career came a lot of travel, long hours, and a growing separation between him and Connie. Rick didn't seem to notice, but the loneliness eventually got to Connie, and she went searching. She found what she was looking for in the love of another man. The attempt at counseling with the pastor hadn't helped at all. Connie divorced him and remarried right away, while Rick plunged into the darkest period of his life.

His eye caught the middle verse, snapping his attention back to the present. *Each one should use whatever gift he has received to serve others.* Did that include counseling or hospital visits? How did a person know what gift he had received? Rick thought of different people who served around his church—the pastoral staff, the church secretary, the custodian, the choir director, the organist. But those people were all paid to be there.

His mind worked a little harder to identify the ones who weren't paid: the ushers, the sound people, the Sunday school teachers, the nursery helpers. *Is that what the verse means?*

Rick remembered those couple of weeks before Christmas during the pageant rehearsals. Some of the people he had to work with didn't exactly inspire a heart of love—especially the mother of a couple of kids who were part of the play. She was on Rick constantly to keep them in front, fussing about their costumes and demanding speaking parts. She could put to shame some of the worst Hollywood mothers he had come across.

Rick read through the passage one last time. It seemed to be giving him more questions than answers. He dialed Gary's office number.

The receptionist answered, then Gary came on the line.

"Hi, Rick," Gary said. "Long time no see."

"Funny. Hey, you left me with a couple of questions. Do you have a minute?"

"I've got just a second. I'm headed over to a meeting about the People's Choice Awards. Give me one of your questions and maybe we can meet later."

"OK, how about this one: What does the passage mean when it refers to each one having a gift? Does that mean like the ushers or the choir director, or like when I helped with the Christmas play? Or is it referring to something else?"

"Wow, that's not easily answered in thirty seconds or less. Did you look up any of the cross-references?"

"Well, no."

"Tell you what, why don't you take some time to see what other Scriptures say about those gifts, and then Jill and I can come by your place after dinner tonight and we'll discuss it."

"That sounds great. How about 7:30?"

The evening planned, Rick hung up. He reached back into his drawer and grabbed his Bible again. In the margin, next to chapter 4 was a cross reference for Romans 12:6–8. He turned to Romans and read: *We have different gifts, according to the grace given us. If a man's gift is prophesying, let him use it in proportion to his faith. If it is serving, let him serve; if it is teaching, let him teach; if it is encouraging, let him encourage; if it is contributing to the needs of others, let him give generously; if it is leadership, let him govern diligently; if it is showing mercy, let him do it cheerfully.*

Rick compared this list with the one he'd been thinking earlier. Things still weren't adding up.

The phone rang. It was Samantha.

"Rick. Hi. I just got back into the studio and found a message that said you called."

Her voice brought Rick to attention. He shut his Bible with a snap and laid it on his nightstand. "Yeah, I was trying to reach you earlier. I caught your report on Bennett last night. Since when did you start reporting the news?"

"Well, actually, that was the first time. I dropped by the studio last night after we wrapped the show. The news about Wade was just coming in, so I went to the news director and said I wanted to cover it. I twisted his arm until he finally agreed, and the exposure's already been fantastic."

"I'll bet it has. Have you learned anything new? Was it really suicide?"

"You'll just have to watch the news tonight like everyone else," Samantha teased. Rick's pulse quickened.

"How about I meet you after you're off the air and take you to dinner. I want the exclusive firsthand."

There was a slight pause as Samantha thought it over.

"I don't know if I'm doing a live cut-in tonight or not, but the news is over at seven. Why don't you meet me at the Columbia Bar and Grille at 7:30?"

Rick was thrilled. "I'll see you then." As he hung up he remembered his plans to meet with Gary and Jill, but he could meet them anytime. He redialed Gary's number, but he was already gone. Rick left word that they'd have to reschedule their meeting. Something important had come up.

3:30 P.M., CRISIS PREGNANCY CENTER, SANTA MONICA

The Crisis Pregnancy Center of Santa Monica was housed in the corner of a small shopping center. Jill volunteered her time as a counselor three days a week, but this afternoon her mind was pre-occupied with her husband's friend Rick. Gary had told her last night about his concern for Rick, who had seemed so depressed after the show. Then Gary had called to ask her if it was all right to spend some time at Rick's house that night.

Jill's thoughts were suddenly interrupted when a red Corvette pulled up outside and a young woman wearing sunglasses approached the door. This wasn't the typical client for the center; usually they dealt with troubled teenagers or low-income wives who couldn't afford a physician's care.

"Hi, my name's Jill. Can I help you?" Jill said with a smile as the woman came through the door.

"I sure hope so," the woman said through swollen lips.

"Here, take a seat." Jill motioned to the chair in front of her. "Do you think you might be pregnant?"

"I hope not, but I'm late, and I've felt nauseous the last couple of mornings. I thought maybe you could let me take one of those tests."

"We'd be happy to." Jill pulled out a patient information form. "Can I get your name."

Vanessa paused for a moment, sizing up the young woman across the desk from her. It had been a long time since she'd trusted anyone.

"Rachel," she finally got out.

"Rachel . . ."

"Let's just keep it at that for now."

"Sure, I understand. Do you remember when your last period was?"

"I'm two weeks late."

Jill made a mental calculation and wrote down the date. "Have you been using any kind of birth control?"

"I've been on the pill, but I haven't been real consistent lately."

"Have you given any thought to what you might do in the event you are pregnant?"

Vanessa shook her head.

"I'll tell you what—come with me into the back room. We'll get the test started, and you'll be able to get the results in just a couple of minutes."

Jill led Vanessa through the doorway leading to the counseling room and the bathroom. After the test was complete, she sat Vanessa down in the conference room.

"Well, Rachel, you're pregnant all right. Are you excited or scared to death?" Jill held the test kit up, showing the positive blue result.

Vanessa's face was expressionless. "I don't know what I am."

"Look, Rachel," Jill began, "you seem to be someone who is in need of a friend right now. The bruise on your lips tells me you've been through some pretty rough times lately. Was it your husband, or a boyfriend?"

"I just fell, that's all. Look, I appreciate your help today." Vanessa got up to go, clutching her purse.

"I don't want to scare you off, Rachel. I just want to help you. If you're going back into a dangerous situation, maybe there's something we can do."

Vanessa hadn't thought about that. She'd be all right for awhile. But when it came out that she was pregnant, she'd be forced to get rid of the baby, and she wasn't sure she wanted to do that. This child might be the first person in her entire life who would love her unconditionally. Something inside her screamed out for love. There was a spark of hope still left within her. She couldn't let that die with her child.

"I'll be OK—really." Vanessa tried to sound confident.

"Well, listen. Here's our phone number at the clinic." Jill held out a card. "If you need anything, anything at all, just call here. I work Mondays, Wednesdays, and Fridays." Without thinking, Jill did something she had been instructed not to do. She wrote her home number on the back of the card. "And that's my home phone number. You don't have to go through this alone. I'll help you if you'll let me."

Vanessa took the card and placed it in her purse, touched by this stranger offering her personal assistance. "Thank you. You've been so helpful already. But I have to leave now."

Vanessa drove away, heading out of the shopping center toward her apartment in West Los Angeles, tears forming in her eyes. *A little baby is growing inside of me,* she thought. For a brief moment while inside the center, she had contemplated ending the pregnancy. That would be the easiest solution. But as the reality of what was inside her settled in her mind, she knew she couldn't do it.

4:00 p.m., BEVERLY HILLS

It was exactly at four in the afternoon when Josh stepped off the elevator on the twelfth floor where Starfield Enterprises had their executive offices. He walked over to Mr. Gabriel Flint's executive secretary to let her know he was here. She ushered him right in. John Harold was already there.

Josh walked over to the sitting area where Gabriel and John were talking together on a couch, a panoramic view of Santa Monica behind them. Gabriel's office stretched across nearly half of the building's top floor, the other side facing the huge metropolis of Los Angeles.

"Come in, Josh. Take a seat." Gabriel motioned to the chair adjacent to his end of the couch.

"You guys wouldn't believe what it's been like around the office today," Josh said as he flopped into the chair.

"I can imagine," Gabriel said, quickly taking charge of the meeting. "I know we're all sorry about what happened to Wade. He was an excellent director whose talents helped get this show running. Josh, make sure the show is well represented with flowers and stuff at the memorial service. Maybe you could have the staff donate to some charity Wade was into. We might be able to get some positive press with that in the trades."

"Already taken care of," Josh answered him.

"Fine. Now let's get down to business," Gabriel said. "First, we need to decide if we're going to continue with the production schedule as is, or delay things until Wade's replacement can be found. What's your feeling, John?"

John shifted his position on the couch as he spoke, "I think we should get another director in there—fast. I don't want to continue with reruns after our success in last month's sweeps. We've got to keep the momentum going."

Josh thought for a moment. "Offhand, I'm inclined to agree with you, John. My only fear would be moving too fast and putting the wrong person in that position. We've got a great-looking show; ratings are on the upswing. The wrong director could kill us. On the other hand, it could cost us a lot to stay on hiatus. We'd still be charged for the studio, and I'm not sure how much of our staff and crew we could extend the hiatus for without paying them."

"I'm not worried about the money," Gabriel snapped. "I just want what is best for the show. Wade's suicide could affect a lot of people, including the writers. I want to make sure when we go back into production, we have as good a product as we did for the February book."

"The writers will be fine; you know how jaded they are. I'll bet they're all home writing suicide jokes as we speak," John interjected. He wanted to be back in the studio Monday. "Josh, do you have any leads on a new director yet?"

"Well, our office has been hearing from a lot of agencies. I've got a list of twenty directors whose agents have called in with résumés already." Josh pulled out a large batch of papers from his briefcase as he spoke. "I gave Cassie the names of a couple I would love to bring in. She's checking today to see if any are available. The ones I'm checking on have all been in the business a long time, have great credentials, and could step in immediately."

John thought of the egos that would accompany those credentials. "Who are we talking about here, Josh?"

"Well, Bob Michaels is one. He's done the last couple of American Music Awards, and he used to do late night. Also Carl Drake is a wonderful director. He won an Emmy for the special he did with Whitney."

John didn't like where this was headed, so he responded carefully. "Josh, Wade set a wonderful framework for our show, and we've still got our booth personnel intact. I think we'd be OK with someone who doesn't have an impressive track record or an Emmy, as long as they are willing to fit into our mold."

Gabriel, primed for this argument by John, joined in, "I think John may have a point. If we bring in a big-time director, there's going to be a longer adjustment period for them to try and make their mark on the show. We don't need that. We need someone who can step in and leave things as they are. I don't want some high-priced egomaniac coming in and demanding their own staff, changing the set on us, or trying to change the way John works."

"I assure you, I wouldn't hire a director who didn't fit our mold. I've got to work with him, too," Josh said.

Gabriel nodded. "Go ahead and check your names out for availability. Let's meet Friday morning at ten, at National. Have three or four of your top choices who are available and can start Monday there for us to meet. As a back up, bring us names of those who can start full-time a week from Monday, but no later. Fax us their résumés so we can come in with some idea of what they've done. If we find a satisfactory director who can jump in with us, we'll stay on schedule. If we can't, we'll continue searching and possibly air another week of reruns. Agreed?"

When Gabriel said "agreed" like that, there wasn't anything left to do but agree. Josh was more than a little frustrated. Waiting until Friday morning to decide if they would continue production next week didn't give him much time at all.

Josh and John made their way out the main entrance to the office. As soon as the door closed behind them, another door across the room from Flint opened.

"It sounds like they bought the suicide," Rudy Vanozzi said smugly.

"Don't get overconfident. There are still a few loose ends to tie up." Flint reached for another one of his Cuban cigars.

"How long have you been in that room listening?"

"Long enough."

"Well, fill me in on last night," Flint said, as he lit the cigar. "I want to hear all the details."

After recounting the events of the murder, Rudy pulled a couple of objects out of his coat pocket. "I took a box of computer disks in case he had made a copy of what I saw him working on, and I kept his little calendar book. Here—" Rudy handed it to Flint, "he had this written over today's date."

Flint looked down and saw the name Mortenson and a phone number. "I checked. I'm still not sure who Mortenson is, but the number is the DA's office," Rudy said, wiping the back of his hand across his nose.

"I know who he is. It's a good thing you grabbed this. Keep it in a safe place where no one can trace it back to you, but don't get rid of it. You can trash the disks."

"Whatever you say. Now, what other loose ends were you talking about?"

"I'm talking about the tapes. If we don't want this happening again, you've got to destroy the tapes as well."

"How do you propose I do that?"

Flint reached across his desk, grabbed his lighter, and flicked it on. "Torch them!"

"Are you sure? As old as those studios are, the whole lot could go up."

"Well, make sure that doesn't happen. Make it look like a cleaning person left some chemicals or something. They'll have fire crews there in time to save everything else."

"Why don't we just have our man inside get rid of the tapes?"

Flint shook his head. "I don't want there to be any questions about just one set of tapes missing. Just take care of the whole vault."

Rudy hesitated a second. "When?"

"Better wait a few days. I don't want anyone to connect this with the suicide. Besides, our man on the staff assures me no one will be looking at those tapes for awhile." Flint rubbed his chin as he thought. "Let's make it early next week, and make sure nobody gets hurt. If there's a death in the fire, they'll be an investigation. If it looks like a cleaning mistake, everyone will carry on, business as usual."

A knock on the door interrupted them.

"Yeah," Gabriel called out. The door opened and a beautiful, scantily clad woman walked in with a couple of drinks in her hands. Rudy took this as his cue to exit. He sauntered out of the office, but not before seeing her hand Flint his drink as she nestled onto his enormous lap. Rudy shook his head, smiling. *Money sure does make for strange bedfellows.*

4:15 p.m., NATIONAL STUDIOS

With Josh out of the office, Cassie was finally able to get a bit of a breather. She munched on a chicken salad sandwich from the deli across the street as she reached for the phone. *Lord, give me your words,* she prayed as she dialed Becky's number. After the third ring, a voice she didn't recognize answered.

"Hi, this is Cassie Petterson. Is Becky able to talk?"

"May I ask what this is concerning?" It was Becky's mother.

"I'm a friend of Becky's from the production office, and I wanted to see how she was doing—see if there was anything I could do for her."

"Hold on, Cassie, let me see how she feels." Cassie waited on the line, then heard Becky's voice.

"Hi, Cassie. Thanks for calling."

"Becky, I want you to know how sorry I am. If there's anything I can do for you, I will. I'm sorry I haven't called you earlier. The phones at the office have been ringing off the hook."

"It's been the same out here. That's why my mom is answering the phone."

"Have you decided on a memorial service?"

"We were just in the middle of discussing that. I think we'll have something on Saturday. I'll make sure one of us calls the production office so the staff will know about it."

"Saturday sounds good. That way a lot of them can come. But what about you personally? How are you doing? Do you need someone to talk to about anything?"

Becky was silent for a minute. "I honestly don't know how I'm doing. I still don't know what to make of everything."

"I understand. Well, if you think of something, anything at all, just give me a call, OK?"

"As a matter of fact, there is one thing."

"Just name it, Becky."

"I haven't been able to find Wade's appointment book, and he always kept it with him. Could you check in his office to see if he left it there?"

"I'll go check right now. If I find it, I'll call you right back."

"Thanks, Cassie."

"You're welcome . . . and Becky, I'll be praying for you."

Cassie hung up, wishing there was something more she could do, but theirs was only a casual acquaintance, not enough of a friendship that Cassie could just run over there. Frustrated, she got up from her desk and headed over to Wade's old office. Fortunately the door was open. She stepped inside and turned the overhead light on. It felt a little eerie. She wondered who would fill this space next week.

Cassie scanned the desk and went through the drawers. All she found were scripts, interoffice memos, ratings sheets, and other papers associated with the show. No appointment book.

Back at her desk, the phone rang once again.

"Josh Abrams' office."

"Cassie? It's me—Jack."

"Jack, what a relief. It's nice to hear a friendly voice on the other end of the phone."

"How's it going? I haven't been able to get you off my mind since last night at the group. I've really been praying like crazy. Is everything all right?"

"You haven't heard? Our director committed suicide last night. We've been swamped with press calls and agents trying to get their clients a job. It's been unbelievable."

"I hadn't heard. Wow! I guess God knew what he was doing when he had us pray for you. How are you holding up?"

"Pretty well really. I just got off the phone with Becky, the widow, and I felt so helpless. I didn't know what to say to her."

"Just be yourself and let the Holy Spirit flow through you. Have you got a second? I'll pray for you now."

Cassie looked around the office. All was quiet for the moment. "That would be great, Jack."

As he prayed, the Scripture from last night came back to Cassie: *I will counsel you and watch over you.* The words breathed new life back into her spirit.

"Thanks, Jack. I know God is with me."

"Excellent. Well, I'll let you go. Keep me posted if anything more comes up. I'll make sure a few others in the group know what's going on as well."

"You're a dear. Take care."

Cassie leaned back in her chair and exhaled slowly. Already the burden felt lighter.

4:34 P.M., BEVERLY HILLS

Ralph walked into Jacob's office and sat down heavily in a chair across from Jacob's desk.

"Did you get through to Harold's producer?" he asked.

"Don't ask. I got the runaround from his assistant, and I couldn't get through. She said he's not taking any calls today, just to fax a résumé over. What about you with Treadway? Does he feel confident he can do the show?"

"He's chomping at the bit, and he's hungry. We'll have a hard time holding him back for any contract extras. It sounds like he'll grab their first offer."

"Let's just hope we get far enough to get a first offer. I've got to find a way to make sure Treadway gets serious consideration—" Jacob's intercom buzzed.

"Jacob, 'The John Harold Show' is calling on two," came the voice over the speaker.

He punched the blinking line on his phone.

"Jacob Weinberg here."

"Hello, Mr. Weinberg. This is Cassie Petterson from 'The John Harold Show.' I'd like to talk to you about one of your clients to see if he is available to take over our show."

"I know, we talked this morning, remember?" Cassie did not remember. "His name is Rick Treadway."

"No, I was referring to Carl Drake. You represent him, don't you?"

Jacob stopped cold. This had nothing to do with his attempt to get Rick onto the show.

"Yes, we do represent Mr. Drake. He's currently in production on an NBC special that will wrap up late next week. When would you need him?"

"That's still in the discussion stage. Right now we're just compiling a list of possible replacements and when they could be available to us."

"Well, I'll check with my client. He has another project that's supposed to start in three weeks. I'm not sure if he'll consider changing his schedule or not." Jacob tried to change topics and bring out his best sales pitch. "I did call earlier today about a very good director that we think would be perfect for your show. His name is Rick Treadway."

Now Cassie recalled the conversation—and how pushy Jacob had been on the phone. "I've just been asked to call and check on Mr. Drake's availability. You say he won't be available until at least a week from Monday, which would be . . . ," Cassie glanced at a calendar in front of her, "March 29. Is that correct?"

Jacob looked at his calendar. "Yes, and that's only if he is willing to pass this other show onto someone else in order to do your series." He didn't know how far he should push his next comment. "I can't say that he'd be willing to do that. I really wish I could talk to Josh about the other director. He would be much better for your show, and he could begin immediately."

"I'll let Josh know that." Cassie decided it was time to get off the line. "He'll call back if he has any more questions for you."

"If he's there, I could—"

"He's out of the office right now." It felt good to finally use that line. "I'll let him know how you feel."

"Thank you. I know he won't be disappointed." Jacob hung up the phone and looked over to Ralph.

"They want Carl. They're reaching. I don't think Carl would even consider a series at this point."

"Well, at least we know the direction they're trying to go. If they're looking for a director like Carl, they're going to have a hard time finding one available." Ralph rubbed his chin. "We still might be in the ball game."

"I hope so. For some reason I really want to make this work. Right now, though, I wouldn't bet the farm on it."

"I don't know, Jacob. You used to be known for your miracles. Maybe it's time for one."

"Right. Just call me Moses," Jacob shot back. He wasn't at all happy with how things were progressing.

5:10 P.M., SHERIFF'S HEADQUARTERS

Stephanie and Bill sat in the office and digested what they had just heard on the phone with Ray Kokka. He had found nothing in the computer that would lead them to suspect anything other than suicide. The autopsy report would state the obvious, that death was caused by a single gunshot wound to the head. The bullet was found and compared to a test-fired round from the gun found on the floor of the office. They matched. Bennett's business manager had been contacted, and the gun did indeed belong to him. But he'd bought it only six months before, not a few years ago like the widow had thought.

There was nothing conclusive about the abrasions on the hand, although the gunpowder residue had the same inconsistency they'd noticed about the blowback on the desk. His right hand seemed to have the residue, but instead of an equal covering of powder, there was a large section where no residue was evident. But one new piece of information Ray had been excited about caught the detectives' attention. Daryl, Ray's assistant, had found some blood, skin tissue, and possible latex under the slide chamber of the gun. Nothing on the victim indicated that it would have belonged to him.

Bill also had the phone records from Wade's office. The day of the murder he had placed three calls from his main line. One placed earlier in the morning, at 10:16, to an extension at the production office called "off-line bay" that cross-matched to a Sid Ratcliff, the "off-line editor." The second call was placed about an hour later at 11:08 A.M. to Los Angeles information. The third call, made at 5:15 P.M., was matched to the extension of Josh Abrams. That call lasted six minutes. On the second line, the one Bennett used for his fax and modem, there had been a couple of calls to a local access number for America Online. The last one came at 6:20 P.M. That call lasted ten minutes.

"So, Steph, I think what we have here is an open-and-shut case of suicide," Bill said with a smile, summarizing everything they knew so far, "with a lot of questions still unanswered."

"You're not kidding. Those abrasions on the hand, the inconsistent blowback, and especially the blood and skin on the gun sure make me think something is rotten in Malibu. If latex is confirmed to be there, I'd say we've got something. Not to mention the fact that it looks like Bennett did indeed talk with Abrams that afternoon. Abrams was lying about the call being made while he was on his way to Malibu. I think we need to reconstruct exactly what Wade was doing the last day before his death." Stephanie sat across from Bill, looking over her own notes from the death scene. "From what Mrs. Bennett told us, he went to edit something for the show on Monday afternoon. When he returned, she said he seemed preoccupied, but he wouldn't say with what. Then their romantic evening was ruined, which is when she started to get a little miffed. The next day he spends in his home office making three phone calls, spending some time on the Internet, before he sends her off to do some shopping so he can evidently meet with the show's producer."

"Doesn't sound like the schedule of a man ready to end it all, does it?"

"No, it doesn't. I know the captain wants to close this case quickly, but there's something wrong here."

"What are we going to tell the press?" Bill asked.

"What else? Until we have a suspect, it's a suicide. Plus it'll keep the captain off our backs. But—unofficially—you and I are going to keep digging. I smell something, and I want to get to the bottom of it."

CHAPTER 9

The sun was setting into the Pacific, casting a brilliant orange glow over Flint's apartment as Vanessa opened the door and stepped in. She was too tired to notice the sunset's beauty, and her stomach was so queasy. It looked like Rudy had made his exit. Great. She had spent most of the afternoon driving around, trying to sort out her feelings. She didn't even know who the father of the baby was, or did she really care? One thing she was sure of: if she told Gabriel she was pregnant, he'd immediately want her to get an abortion, or she was history. He didn't like complications. But she was resolved to bring this baby to term. Unfortunately, she had no idea how she was going to pull it off.

She walked into the bathroom and checked under the sink to see if Rudy had discovered the disks and cash she had hidden there. Everything was just as she had left it. She grabbed the cash and reached for her purse.

Her hands were shaking as she pulled out a little vile she always kept with her. She poured some of the white powder inside it onto the countertop, formed it into a thin line with a razor blade, then rolled up one of the crisp hundred-dollar bills. She was about to bend over and sniff the coke through her nostrils when her mind suddenly pictured a tiny baby, tucked warmly away inside of her. Disgusted with herself, she swept the powder into the sink. She threw the vial into the trash, ran back to the bedroom, and sprawled onto the mattress, sobbing.

The phone beside the bed rang; Vanessa ignored it. After several rings, the answering machine took the call for her. It was the voice she least wanted to hear—Gabriel Flint.

"Vanessa, where have you been all day? You better be back by nine. I've got someone I'm bringing over. We're going to have dinner and then come by for a little party time. Put on that frilly red number I bought you."

Vanessa's shoulders shook as tears still moistened her cheeks. She couldn't let those men defile her again. She had to get out.

Quickly grabbing a suitcase, she began stuffing as many of her things into it as she could. She made a pass through the apartment, making sure nothing of value was getting left behind. Satisfied, she stepped out the door and was about to lock it when she remembered the computer disks. She ran back in and stuffed them into her purse. As she was locking up the apartment, a great relief washed over her. She knew her life here was over, but she had no idea what life lay ahead. She hadn't been this afraid for a long time—but neither had she felt so alive.

7:19 P.m., THE COLUMBIA BAR AND GRILLE, HOLLYWOOD

As usual for this time of night, there were four cars ahead of Rick lining up and blocking traffic, trying to get a valet to take their cars from them. There was never a parking place in front of this restaurant, and during rush hour, it could be a mess. It took Rick another fifteen minutes to actually make it inside and be seated at a table. Samantha still hadn't arrived, so he had a few minutes to relax, but all that did was make him more nervous.

It had taken more than a year to get over the devastation of the divorce enough to even desire another relationship. But in Rick's line of work, he didn't often run into what he felt was his type of girl. He wasn't sure Samantha fit that bill either, but he did like the outside packaging.

He rose from the table as he saw her making her way toward him. He gave her a brief hug and a kiss on the cheek, then pulled out her chair and helped her sit down.

"I hope you didn't have to wait long, Rick. The producer of the newscast stopped me to tell me he loves what I've added to the show. He's talking about using me more. Pretty interesting, huh?"

"Intriguing is more like it," Rick countered. "I didn't know you had any interest in being a journalist."

"Well, you never know. I kind of enjoyed covering the story on Bennett last night, but I'm going to talk it over with my manager. I don't want to get off track with my acting career, but the exposure has already started opening up some doors."

"I'm sure you've got what it takes to scoop the best of them if that's what you want."

Samantha's eyes locked onto Rick's. "Why, Rick, you're so sweet." She cast her eyes down and scanned the menu as she talked. "I just want to make some headway. I don't think I can stand doing that news-magazine show much longer, and I certainly don't want to be doing any more infomercials either. No offense."

Rick laughed. "None taken. As a matter of fact, I feel the same way. I'd hate to picture myself in twenty years doing Alert Forty-three: Keeping Your Doghouse Safe."

Sam laughed and flung her hair back over her shoulder. Rick eyed her. It felt good to be seated with a gorgeous woman in a restaurant. He hoped everyone noticed them. His ego could use a little perking up.

"What's the latest on Bennett? Still suicide?" Rick asked, moving the discussion along.

"We haven't heard anything different from the police, but they haven't been talking too much. From what I can tell, there isn't any evidence to change their mind."

"That's amazing to me," Rick confided. "I'd give anything to have 'The John Harold Show,' and here he's so depressed he kills himself? It sounds bizarre."

"Did you know him?"

"Yeah, we worked together several times before I started directing."

"I didn't have the pleasure, but from what I hear from those who did, he was a real jerk."

"Well, I can vouch for that. He did have a way of treating people . . . well, let's just say a lot like Napoleon Bonaparte might have."

Samantha snickered, then leaned closer to Rick and lowered her voice, "My theory is, he just snapped."

"Maybe you're right. Have you talked to his wife?" Rick asked.

"No, she's not doing any interviews. I'd love to figure out a way to get her to talk with me though. If anybody could see a suicide coming, you'd think it would be her. I hope it wasn't a suicide though. I could get some great exposure out of this if it turned out to be a murder."

"Now you're beginning to sound like you belong on 'Hard Copy,'" Rick chuckled.

"Maybe there's a journalist in me after all," she laughed, then steered the conversation toward other new developments of her career.

Toward the end of dinner, as the dessert cart headed toward their table, Sam suddenly noticed the time. She finished her glass of wine in a big gulp.

"Oh, Rick, I didn't realize how late it was getting. If you don't mind, can you take care of this while I run back to the station?"

Samantha rose, gave him a quick hug and kiss, then headed out the door. Rick sat back, dazed at her sudden exit. The waiter came by and offered Rick a dessert. He politely declined. He sat and thought about the evening as he waited for the check. She was stunningly beautiful, intelligent, and totally self-centered. What more could he ask for in a woman? He had his credit card out when the check arrived, thankful he'd have thirty days to try to come up with some way to pay for their lovely dinner.

9:35 P.m., WEST HOLLYWOOD

Gabriel Flint walked his guest out of the elevator and headed down the hall toward his "fantasy apartment."

"You're going to love this one, Steve. I found her on one of my movie sets and quickly decided she was too good for the public. So I put her away, for just me and certain guests." He winked at his friend.

Steve smiled, anticipating the night. He'd had a couple of evenings like this with Gabriel before, and he'd never been disappointed. Steve's father, Jeff Parillo, was the money and muscle behind Gabriel's less-than-legal ventures. Whenever Steve paid a visit to check on things, Gabriel rolled out the red carpet.

They made it to the door of Vanessa's apartment; Steve imagining the beauty that lay ahead, Gabriel thrilled to once again be able to enjoy his little game. Once he set up somebody to have an evening with Vanessa, Flint would retreat to the second bedroom, ostensibly to give the two some privacy. What his guests didn't know was that he had Vanessa's bedroom designed with two-way mirrors, hidden cameras, and audio embellishments that made the second bedroom the perfect viewing spot for Gabriel.

Gabriel opened up the door, expecting to see Vanessa in her red negligee, welcoming them in with a couple of drinks. Instead he found the apartment dark and empty. Gabriel felt a wave of panic, although Steve didn't notice—he thought this might all be part of the fun.

"Wait here, Steve. Let me go bring her out."

Gabriel went directly to Vanessa's bedroom. She wasn't there either, and on quick inspection he noticed that most of her things were missing. She'd left him. No one left Gabriel Flint. He grabbed the lamp off the nightstand and hurled it into the bathroom with a crash, swearing up a storm as he looked for something else to break.

Steve came rushing in, gun drawn, ready to shoot anything in sight. When Gabriel saw the pistol, he stopped dead in his tracks. He called Vanessa a few choice names, muttered something about her paying for this, and then addressed Steve.

"The evening isn't lost, Steve. Look, I'll take you down to Club Royale, and you can take your pick of the strippers. How's that?" Gabriel didn't want Steve heading back to Las Vegas with anything but kind words to say to his father about the trip.

"Sure," Steve responded, then with a laugh, "but let me have one of those movies this Vanessa was in. I want to see what I missed."

Gabriel laughed, attempting to cover up the intense anger he was feeling. He'd call Rudy later tonight and tell him to find her. Then he'd enjoy one of his other perverse pleasures—watching someone who crossed Gabriel Flint suffer.

CHAPTER 10

Rick stepped into his kitchen and stared at the familiar surroundings. The brief dinner with Sam had managed to take his mind off his problems for a few hours, but coming back home brought it all back. The number two lit up the display on his phone machine. His heart quickened as he pressed play. *Please let one of these be from my agent.*

"Rick, it's Connie. I just wanted to make sure you were taking the kids this weekend like you promised. Don't forget, I've got that partner's dinner for Phil with the law firm, and we're counting on you. By the way, we haven't received the support check for this month yet. What's going on? Give me a call so we know that Saturday's covered."

That certainly helped lighten the mood. Maybe the second message would be the one he wanted.

"Hi, Rick. It's Gary. Sorry something came up for you tonight. Jill and I were really looking forward to meeting with you. Listen, you asked a question about gifts, so I wanted to give you something to chew on until we get together. Read Romans 12. The whole chapter has some great stuff, but especially verses 6–8. Then read 1 Corinthians 12 and take special notice of verses 4–7. Hope that'll keep you up tonight. I have a pretty free day tomorrow, so if you want to get together for lunch again, give me a call."

Rick sighed. Why hadn't his agent left some word? In this case, no news was definitely not good news. If something didn't break for him soon, his career would slide into oblivion.

He left the kitchen and plopped down in his recliner. Maybe he should cry defeat and go back to being a stage manager. The thought was humbling. How would he begin the process of calling up the other directors he had been in competition with and beg them for a job as a stage manager? He decided to give it a few more days, at least through the weekend, before he made any rash decisions.

"God, why?" he wanted to know. "Why is it taking so long for me to get a job. Just when I'm finally getting back on my feet after the divorce, everything falls apart. The show gets canceled and I'm left with a stack of bills. I've been doing my best. Going to church more. Helped out with that stupid Christmas play. What do you want from me?"

Rick sat quietly in his chair, his emotions spent. He felt as if his words just bounced off the ceiling and lay right at his feet. *There has to be more to being a Christian than this,* he thought.

11:55 P.M., WESTWOOD

Jill lay awake in bed, her husband breathing deeply beside her. Gary had fallen fast asleep after the two of them had finished their nightly prayer time, including remembering that strange woman Jill had met earlier at the center. Jill was half awake, on the verge of sleep herself, when she felt a stirring that brought her fully alert. She wondered why she was troubled, then just as quickly thought of Rick. With the thought came a strong urging to pray for him.

THURSDAY, 12:14 a.m., STUDIO CITY

Rick was still up, stretched out in his chair with the TV blaring before him. He'd caught the news, seeing Samantha get another small part updating the Bennett suicide. Evidently the police hadn't issued any new statements, so there wasn't much else to tell. He had watched the first half hour of "The John Harold Show," listening to the comedian's monologue and watching how Wade had cut the show. Rick knew he could direct it. It was a simple five-camera setup, a lot of talk on the couch with a musical number now and then. But watching the show only depressed him. Getting the chance to direct it was a dream he'd never see to reality.

He clicked the set off and was headed for the bedroom when he heard a knock at the door. It was past midnight—who would be coming over at this hour? He walked to the front door and looked through his peephole, pleasantly surprised at who he found there. It was Samantha.

He opened the door. "What are you doing here? How did you even know where I live?"

"If I'm going to be a reporter, I've got to be able to research these things," she said with a coy smile. "Can I come in?"

"Of course," Rick said, stepping aside. "Come on in."

CHAPTER 11

"Gary, wake up. I need you." Jill nudged her husband.

Gary turned over and looked up at her groggily. He reached up and turned on the light on their headboard. "What's the matter, honey? You hear something? Do you feel all right?"

"I'm feeling fine. It's just that . . . I haven't been able to sleep. I feel like something's going on with your friend Rick, and we should pray for him. I've been trying alone, but the feeling persists. I think we should pray together if you can wake up."

"My spirit's willing, although my flesh is weak."

Jill elbowed Gary in the ribs as he snickered.

"Sorry. Do you have any sense of what we're praying for?" Gary asked, sitting up and trying to shake the cobwebs out of his head.

"Not a whole lot more than what we talked about earlier. You said you thought the Holy Spirit is trying to draw him closer. Maybe there's something going on, something trying to get between him and the Lord."

"That could be. I've been feeling that Rick is in a place of decision. He's going to have to choose between God's leading and his own."

Gary wrapped his arms around his wife, then took her hands in his. They spent the next several minutes praying quietly, opening their hearts to the Holy Spirit's direction. They prayed fervently for Rick, that Jesus would be victorious in his life and bring him into a deeper relationship with him.

SAME TIME, STUDIO CITY

Samantha walked past Rick into the family room. He smelled alcohol as she made her way by, taking a seat on the couch. "Actually, I looked up your address on the staff list from the amazing Alert One. Turns out I live just a couple of miles up Ventura Boulevard." Then with an alluring smile, she added, "I thought I'd surprise you on the way home."

Rick followed her. Sam certainly was an intriguing woman. He sat down next to her on the couch, their knees nearly touching. "I am definitely surprised. Can I get you something to drink? I don't have much here, maybe a soft drink or a beer?" He usually kept some beer on hand for his friends.

"No thank you, I'm not thirsty. I just enjoyed our dinner so much, and I hated to run off so quickly. I was hoping we could pick up where we left off." She reached out her hand, lightly touching her fingers over Rick's arm.

Rick's body responded while his mind raced. A mental alarm went off, telling him that this wasn't right, but it was quickly overshadowed by his physical reaction to Sam's touch.

Samantha giggled as she rubbed her fingers over the goose bumps that had appeared on his arm.

"Wow, you must be cold," she teased. Samantha took her other arm, reached around Rick's neck, and drew him toward her. Rick kept his eyes locked on hers until their lips met. He knew he should do something to stop himself, pull away, slow things down. Then he breathed in the fragrance of her perfume, felt her moist lips on his. He reached his arms around her and felt her body stirring. He suppressed the inner warning, closing his eyes and running his hand through her silky blonde hair. It had been a long time since he had been this close to a woman. He melted into her.

Rick's depression quickly vanished—no more thoughts about not having a job, how he'd pay his bills, giving up his directing career. He was living in the moment, and that moment was Samantha.

She brought Rick's desire up to match her own. He didn't resist. He was under her full control, his inner alarm silenced. The passion consumed him as their bodies embraced, clinging to each other.

Her mouth nibbled his ear as she whispered, "Do you have anything?"

That caught Rick off guard. "What?"

"You know, something for protection."

Protection!

The mood broke. Rick straightened up on the couch, disentangling himself from the embrace.

"It's all right; I've got a condom in my purse," Samantha said, reaching for it.

She was exactly what he wanted—beautiful, sitting there next to him with her hair tossed about, her tempting low-cut blouse, willing and ready for him.

But in that one word—*protection*—Rick's spirit had been awakened. What was he doing with this woman? He was about to do something totally against the will of God, looking for a minuscule amount of latex to protect him. As much as he wanted to complete what they had started, Rick found the strength to stop.

"No, Sam. I think we kind of got ahead of ourselves."

She reached for him, trying to recapture the intensity they had both felt. "Come on, Rick, don't back down now," she pleaded.

Rick held his ground, standing up to keep his distance. "You're a beautiful woman, Sam, and right now you're very inviting—more than you know. But it just isn't right."

"Isn't right? This is the nineties! What kind of antiquated morality is that?" She straightened her blouse, her passion replaced by a seething anger.

"It's just that I have a great deal of respect for you, and I want to take things slower," Rick said.

Samantha swore viciously at him. She grabbed her purse and headed for the door. "I should have known you weren't man enough for me!"

"Sam, please don't leave like this. Let's talk it over for a bit; maybe you'll understand—" Rick was talking to an empty doorway. She was down the sidewalk and into her car in a flash, squealing her tires as she sped away.

Rick walked back into his kitchen and banged his fist on the counter. He felt wretched. Why had he allowed it to go as far as it had? He could have stopped her after the first kiss, knowing she'd had a little too much to drink. But he had felt so down about himself, he'd used her attention to uplift his deflated ego. Now he'd probably blown any chance at a real relationship with Samantha. What a mess his life was turning into.

He opened the refrigerator, grabbed a soft drink, then started off to bed when his eye was caught by the light on his answering machine. What was it Gary had said? He reached over and manipulated the controls until Gary's voice filled the room.

"Hi. Rick. It's Gary. Sorry something came up for you tonight. Jill and I were really looking forward to meeting with you. Listen, you asked a question about gifts, so I wanted to give you something to chew on until we get together. Read Romans 12. The whole chapter has some great stuff, but especially verses 6–8. Then read 1 Corinthians 12 and take special notice of verses 4–7. Hope that'll keep you up tonight. I have a pretty free day tomorrow, so if you want to get together for lunch again, give me a call."

Rick made a quick note of the verses on a pad he kept by the phone. Romans 12 sounded familiar. Then it hit him. *That's where I was reading when Samantha called back this afternoon.* He took his drink and headed for the shower, a cold one. Maybe he'd check out the Scriptures Gary had given him before falling asleep. He didn't have anything to lose—once again, there was no reason to get up early in the morning anyway.

12:26 A.M., HOLLYWOOD HILLS

John Harold sat back in his easy chair, once again clad in only his robe and underwear. It was late and he had just finished watching his favorite TV show—his. He was pleased with the way things had gone this afternoon with Gabriel. Although he'd agreed with everything Josh had said, John just wanted to have a director he could manipulate when they went back into production.

He started flipping through the TV channels. Somewhere in the upper channels John stopped as Samantha Steel's face filled the screen telling him about a home security system he couldn't live without. John had seen her covering Wade's suicide story. She caught his attention long enough for him to listen to her sales pitch for the Alert One.

For an infomercial, the production seemed amazingly smooth. John decided to stay with the show through its close to see who directed it. The credits went by fast, as they usually do, but John caught the name: Rick Treadway. Now there's a name he'd never heard before.

Perfect, just what I need. An unknown who would die for a break into major late-night television. Someone who would fall in line with whatever I say, John thought to himself with a smile.

12:45 A.m., STUDIO CITY

There are different kinds of gifts, but the same Spirit. There are different kinds of service, but the same Lord. There are different kinds of working, but the same God works all of them in all men. Now to each one the manifestation of the Spirit is given for the common good.

Rick read through to the end of 1 Corinthians 12. He'd settled into bed after taking a long shower, letting the water wash over him as he asked the Lord to forgive him for his escapade with Samantha. For the first time in a very long while, Rick felt like his prayers were reaching somewhere. Standing there naked in the shower, he felt he also stood naked before God. He knew it was time to let the Lord take over—he just wasn't sure what that really meant.

He'd already tried to call Samantha and apologize for letting things get so far—then reacting the way he had. She wasn't home, or not answering the phone, so he left a brief apology on her machine, hoping they could talk tomorrow.

Now his full concentration was on the words before him. He'd already read over the twelfth chapter of Romans where he'd been reading earlier in the day before Sam's call interrupted him.

The rest of 1 Corinthians 12 contained a listing of what Rick remembered was called "the gifts of the Spirit": the word of wisdom, the word of knowledge, faith, gifts of healings, the working of miracles, prophecy, discerning of spirits, different kinds of tongues, and the interpretation of tongues. Rick thought back through his life in the church. He couldn't remember a time when any of the things mentioned in this list had happened in his presence. *Maybe a really good sermon could be called a word of knowledge,* Rick thought. But he'd never seen a miracle, or a healing.

Verse 12 through the end of the chapter centered on the same theme he had been into earlier that morning—the teaching about everyone being part of the body of Christ, all having a function. *But what does all of this have to do with our discussion at the deli?*

Rick knew he wasn't living his life up to the standards of Scripture, that his church experience didn't seem to model the body of Christ as he had just read. Was that Gary's point to all this? Still, there was one thing Rick knew; he was beginning to enjoy the journey he was on more than he had enjoyed anything in a long time. Maybe if he kept at it, the pieces would start to fall into place.

Rick decided to plunge in and see where things would take him. Tomorrow night he'd give Gary's group a chance. *God, help me to understand where you're leading. It's hard, but I want to be able to trust in you.*

Despite all of the confusing events of the day, Rick fell asleep quicker than he thought possible. A peace settled over him—something he hadn't felt in quite some time.

CHAPTER 12

8:30 a.m., SHERIFF'S HEADQUARTERS

"Well, which case shall we break this morning?" Bill tried to start the day off on a high note as he walked up to his desk, doughnut and coffee in hand. "We can wrap up the councilman's murder, jump into that gang slaying from the other night, or trip through Hollywood until we figure out what happened to Bennett." He fell into his chair and smiled at Stephanie.

"What side of the bed did you get up on this morning?" she shot back wryly. "Did your wife leave town and make you the happiest man in the precinct?" Stephanie had already been at her desk for nearly an hour, trying to make some headway on the cases.

Bill laughed, "No, I just feel that with all the dead ends we've hit lately, today might be our lucky day. Besides, the taxpayers of this great metropolis need to get their money's worth from us."

Stephanie didn't look up at him. "I'm underwhelmed by your enthusiasm."

"I'll tell you what; I've got a deal for you. Today's Thursday, and I'll bet you by the end of the weekend, we'll have nabbed ourselves a killer."

"Really?" she asked.

Bill nodded, as he took a bite of the doughnut, leaving powdered sugar all over his mouth. "You're on," Stephanie said, "and wipe your face. You look like a cokehead. So, what are we bettin'?"

"Lunches for a week. If I'm right, you buy; if I'm wrong, they're on me."

"Oh great. We'll be having Taco Bell for seven days if I lose."

The two laughed, knowing Bill's favorite feeding trough.

"So, which murder is it you think we'll solve?" Stephanie asked.

"I've got a hunch it'll be either the councilman or the director," Bill responded.

"You've concluded the director was murdered then?"

"Something in my gut says so, yeah."

"I have to say I agree with you, but what's the motive? Let's start there."

"Sounds good to me." Bill took a sip of his coffee, washing away some of the powdered sugar. "First we need to find out exactly what Wade was doing on Monday and Tuesday."

"Good, I agree." Stephanie got up, grabbing her purse. "Let's go by the lab. We'll pick up the computer and take it out to the widow's house. That'll give us a good excuse to ask her a couple more questions. On the way, let's drop by the production office and talk to the producer and editor about the phone calls on Tuesday."

Bill gulped down what was left of his coffee, then had to step quickly to catch up with Stephanie. Once she picked a course of action, she was full speed ahead.

Although Rick had read and prayed until after one in the morning, he found it easy to crawl out of bed and start his day at a respectable time. He couldn't put his finger on it, but he knew he'd had a breakthrough in his life last night. For the first time in quite a while, he was actually excited about facing a new day.

After breakfast, Rick pulled out the *Hollywood Reporter* he'd received in the mail the day before. He glanced through it, hoping to see an article on some production starting up that was in need of his services. Unfortunately, as had been the case for the last couple of months, there didn't seem to be anything.

He went back into the bedroom and was changing into his cycling pants when the phone rang.

"Hi Rick. It's Gary."

"Gary, thanks for the message last night. I spent some time looking through those Scriptures. I've got to say you have my interest piqued."

"That's great to hear. Did you want to try and grab another lunch to discuss some of the questions you said you had?"

"I'd love to. Do you have a place in mind?"

Gary thought for a second. "I'll be working at the office today. Why don't we just hit that deli again?"

"Sounds good here."

"Oh, and Rick, before you go, was everything all right with you last night?"

Rick was taken aback. "Why, what do you mean?"

"Well, sometime around midnight, Jill couldn't sleep; she kept thinking of you. She prayed for you awhile, then eventually woke me up and we prayed together. It wasn't until after 12:30 that we both felt at peace and went back to sleep. I just wondered if there was something going on last night?"

"Are you for real, Gary? There wasn't—" quickly thinking back to last night, Rick realized that this matched the exact time of his interlude with Samantha. "Actually there was something going on last night. And if you two were praying for me about midnight, thank you. I was in a . . . ah . . . situation that really needed some prayer."

Gary didn't want to pry any further. It was exciting to hear that Jill's leading had been genuine.

"That's interesting, Rick. I guess the Lord's keeping his eye out for you. Listen, I'm looking forward to lunch. Let's meet about 12:30?"

"I'll be there." Rick hung up the phone, amazed. While he was fooling around with Sam, a couple he really didn't know that well were praying for him. Rick shuddered at what could have happened if the mood hadn't been broken with Samantha's question. He thought back to the Scriptures he'd read last night, about each part of the body having a different function. Suddenly, deep within Rick, a spark ignited. The things he'd been studying were beginning to come into focus.

The discussion with Gary brought the events of last night back to Rick's mind. He wanted to get through to Sam and try to apologize personally. He looked at his watch, deciding it was worth giving her another try.

Rick's heart raced as her line rang. After three rings he heard a very groggy hello. *Oh no,* Rick thought, *I woke her up.*

"Hi, Sam. It's Rick. Did I wake you?"

"Oh, it's you," Sam said in a deeply irritated voice, not answering Rick's question.

After a short pause, Rick continued, "Look, I just wanted to apologize for last night—"

"Rick, I'm not feeling too well right now," Sam said, cutting him off. "I don't want to hear your apology. I don't even want to hear from you. We could have had something special last night, and for whatever sick reason, you freaked out on me. It's your loss." *Click.*

Rick held the phone away from his ear, looking at the receiver as if trying to wish Sam back to the phone. He had hoped to heal over the damage from the night before, but it seemed like that was not to be.

9:45 A.M., NATIONAL STUDIOS

"Bob Michaels is somewhere in England shooting a video for some rock band. He won't be back until mid-April. That leaves you with Carl Drake. He's wrapping up a special, and there's a slight possibility he could be available a week from Monday, but that's only if he passes up some other project he's supposed to be starting the week after."

Cassie could tell by Josh's expression that he wasn't at all happy with the news. "Did you find anybody you liked from the faxes that came in yesterday?"

Josh looked over the list he'd been studying the night before. "There's a couple of possibilities, but no one with the credits that either of those two come with. I like Frank Straton; he was around NBC when I was with the 'Tonight Show.' He seems to have a few good shows under his belt. And Tina Livingston might be a possibility, but I don't know if Harold or Flint would go for a woman director. One other name sounded familiar, but I couldn't place it— Rick Treadway."

"Treadway," Cassie remembered the name. "He's the one that this Weinberg guy was trying to sell me when I called about Carl Drake. He handles both directors and thinks Treadway would be perfect for us."

"Wow, what a surprise," Josh smirked. "Still, there's something about Treadway that rings a bell. Let me see his bio."

Cassie shuffled through the papers in her hands, handing over Rick's résumé and biography. Josh scanned it, first looking at his list of credits to see what show they might have met on, but nothing that Rick had directed coincided with any shows that Josh had worked on. Then he looked at the background information on the biography sheet. Something caught his eye toward the bottom of the page.

There it was: UCLA graduate, 1982. They'd been in college together. Now Josh could picture him. He tried to remember what Rick had been like. They'd run around in different circles, but crossed paths a few times. Josh recalled he was talented in a lot of different aspects of production. They had teamed up with a couple of other students on a news show in their senior year. Josh had favorable memories of that project.

Cassie could see by the look on Josh's face that he'd remembered the connection to Treadway. "Are you going to share your revelation with me, or do I have to figure it out for myself?"

That brought Josh back from the past. He glanced up. "He was at UCLA when I was in school there. We worked on a project together our senior year. I didn't even know he was directing—last I heard, he was a stage manager, I think. Cassie, contact Treadway, Livingston, and Straton. I want to talk to each one, and if they are available, we'll bring them in for interviews tomorrow. Also, get back in touch with Drake's agent. See if he's been able to pin him down on our show." Cassie got up, ready to leave. "And Cassie, don't mention anything about my interest in Treadway, OK?"

"You got it." Cassie glanced at her watch. "I'll have to wait on those calls; it's almost ten. You called a staff meeting in the conference room, remember?"

Josh swore. "I forgot. I thought I'd have something to tell them by now, and we really don't. Did you find out about the memorial service and a charity Wade liked?"

"Yes, I wrote a memo concerning both. I'll pass it out at the meeting. Schu said he'd collect all the money for the donations, then write one check from the show."

"Thanks, Cassie. You're a lifesaver." Josh got up and headed out of the office, with Cassie right behind. "Let's go tell the staff what we don't know."

Fifteen minutes later, thirty-seven people on the production staff attempted to squeeze into a room designed to seat ten around a conference table. Trying to speak loud enough for the employees standing in the doorway and hall to hear, Josh said, "So as of this moment, we still don't know if we're doing a show on Monday."

"This is going to be a last-minute decision. Hopefully tomorrow by noon we'll know one way or the other." Josh looked over to the talent department headed by Sylvia O'Reilly. She'd been around the business a long time and knew all the tricks of the trade. But get her Irish dander up by messing around with the schedule, and she was a real fighter. "I know this is putting an extra hard burden on you and your staff, Sylvia. But I'm confident that any inconvenience we place on our guests will be understood because of the nature of Wade's tragedy."

For once Sylvia didn't jump up and attack. She just nodded her head in understanding as he spoke.

"Any hints on who our next director might be?" one of the segment producers called out from the back of the room.

"At this point we're still in the process of narrowing the possibilities. I'll be interviewing a few tomorrow with John. If we can find someone we like, we'll stay on schedule. If not, we'll do another week of reruns to give us some more time. By the way, if any of you know of a great director who is available to jump in with us, give Cassie or me the name. But we need it quick."

Josh's eyes glanced through the doorway. Behind the employees crowded there he noticed the two detectives he had met at Wade's house walking toward the room.

Josh turned toward Cassie beside him. "Cassie's going to go over the details of Wade's memorial service and the charity donations we're setting up."

As Cassie stood to speak, Josh squeezed himself out the door to meet the detectives.

"Mr. Abrams, I hope we're not interrupting something important," Stephanie said as he approached them.

Josh extended his arm to shake both their hands. "We just called a staff meeting to update everyone on what's going on. What can we do for you?"

Bill took the lead. "We just wanted to speak to you, and one or two other staff members."

"Is there some question in your mind that it wasn't suicide?" Josh seemed surprised. He hadn't expected a serious investigation. "I thought this was a pretty open-and-shut case."

"We're just completing our initial investigation," Bill tried to reassure Josh. "There are some holes we'd like to fill in concerning the events prior to Wade's death."

"Well, we're happy to cooperate. Would you like to address the staff while they are assembled?" Josh could hear Cassie in the background winding down, and he knew he should get back in there.

Bill looked over to Stephanie, then she responded to Josh, "That won't be necessary. We want to keep a pretty low profile with this visit. If you need to get back to your meeting, we can spend a few minutes with you afterward."

Josh agreed and showed them to his office where they could wait while he wrapped up the meeting.

"Thanks for waiting," Josh said minutes later as he returned to his office and closed the door. "Now, what do you want to know?"

"We're mainly trying to reconstruct what Wade was doing during the days before his death," Stephanie began.

Josh nodded and waited for her to continue.

"We know that he left his home around noon on Monday, headed here to do some kind of editing—"

"Actually," Josh broke in to clarify, "Wade didn't come here. Our off-line editing bay is in a bungalow near stage seventeen, about a five-minute walk from our stage. As far as I know, Wade didn't even stop in here."

"Do you know what he was working on?" Stephanie inquired.

"Not specifically. There are several remote shoots that haven't been edited yet. Between Chad, our associate director, and Wade, they were trying to use this week to catch up on some of it. I don't know exactly which segment Wade would have chosen to work on."

"We'd like to talk to the editor. Is he in today?" Bill asked.

"Yes, his name is Sid Ratcliff. He's over in Bungalow C. I'll have Cassie walk you over there when we're finished."

"That would be fine," Stephanie said, remembering the name from the earlier call Bennett had made the day of his death. "You told us Tuesday night that the last phone call made from Bennett's house to your office didn't reach you." She paused to watch his reaction closely. "His phone records indicate a six-minute call to your office at 5:15 P.M. on Tuesday."

Josh mentally kicked himself. He knew it was stupid to have lied. "That's right, I'm sorry. We did talk, but I was so distraught at Wade's house I didn't know what I was saying."

Stephanie's expression told Josh she wasn't buying it.

He continued, "Wade called to talk about something that was bothering him. But he didn't want to go over it on the phone; he wanted to see me in person. I assumed it was about the Las Vegas trip. We're taking our show there in November and there were some logistics Wade and I needed to work out, so we decided I'd stop by his house later that night. That's how I ended up being there."

"Did you notice any sign that he was a man who was about to commit suicide?" she asked.

"That's the weird part. He seemed fine to me. I was shocked to find out what happened."

"Wanting to talk to you in person didn't alarm you?" Stephanie persisted.

Josh shook his head. "Not with Wade. You have to understand his ... ego. It would be just like him to want me to come all the way to his place to talk about something trivial like the Las Vegas trip."

Stephanie looked over at Bill, and, as if some mental communication had occurred between them, they stood up in unison.

Bill presented his hand, "Thank you, Mr. Abrams. You've been very helpful."

"If there's anymore I can do, please let me know."

"We certainly will. And if anything else comes to mind, give us a call," Stephanie said as she shook Josh's hand. "We'd like to speak with the editor now."

"Yes, of course." Josh opened his office door and introduced the detectives to Cassie, asking her to show them to the bungalow. As the three of them were heading out of the office, Josh called out.

"I was wondering when you think we'll be able to have Wade's computer back."

Stephanie stopped and turned back to look at Josh.

"Was the computer the property of the show or was it Wade's personal computer?"

"It was his own computer. We just need to get back the files pertaining to the show."

"Then I'm afraid you'll have to take that up with Mrs. Bennett. Actually, we're giving it back to her today."

Cassie saw a look of frustration cross Josh's face. She figured that when she returned after helping the detectives, she'd probably be placing another call to Becky at Josh's request.

The early spring sunshine made for a beautiful day as the three walked across the studio lot. For Cassie it was a welcome relief from the pressure in the office.

"You were the one who left the message on Wade's answering machine the day he died, weren't you, Cassie?" Stephanie asked.

"Yes, I was. I was really surprised he didn't answer. I knew he'd just talked to Josh and was expecting him that night. I tried to call his cell phone right after, but didn't get through."

"Do you know why he called Josh that afternoon?"

"No, I don't. I do know that he didn't sound normal though. He was . . . ," Cassie tried to find the right words, "agitated, kind of frazzled. If you knew Wade, you'd know how different that would sound. He always appeared in complete control."

"Did you hear any of their conversation?"

"A little bit of Josh's side of it. His door was open, and the office was pretty quiet with most everyone gone. It sounded to me like it was a personal call, not something related to the show. I wish I could be more helpful."

"You have been, Cassie," Stephanie reassured her. "If you remember anything else, please give us a call."

"You don't think he committed suicide, do you?"

"To be honest with you, Cassie, we're not sure," Stephanie said. "There are a few unanswered questions we'd like to get to the bottom of before we make any official conclusion."

Cassie couldn't believe it. *God, if there's something fishy about this, let your truth come out,* she prayed silently. They were coming up to the bungalow as she pointed across the street. "That's stage seventeen where we shoot. Our off-line bay is over here in Bungalow C."

The three entered the building, and Cassie led them through the narrow hallway to a back room. It was dark with only a few track lights illuminating a work counter that held a computer and two large color monitors. They could see a man seated at the computer, working the mouse as different video images appeared on one of the monitors. He turned as the three entered.

"Sid, I want you to meet Detectives Phillips and Brier. They're handling the investigation of Wade's death and want to ask you a few questions."

Sid stood up, his face showing lines of concern. He greeted the detectives and offered them a seat on the couch against the wall by the door.

Bill opened up his notepad. "We understand that Mr. Bennett was editing here on Monday afternoon. We're hoping you can fill us in on what went on around here that day."

Sid cleared his throat. "I don't think I can be of much help. You see, Chad and I were in here Monday morning, but when Wade came in, we both packed up and left. Wade knows how to operate this system, and sometimes he preferred to do it himself."

"How long were you here after Wade came in?" Stephanie asked.

"Just a few minutes. I made sure he had the beta machine hooked up for digitizing." Sid noticed the puzzled look on the detectives' faces. "That's what we call the process of transferring the footage from the original tapes to the computer's hard drive. Then we can edit right on this thing." Sid tapped the top of the computer screen as he continued explaining. "We call the process 'off-lining.' It saves the production company a lot of money by making all the creative decisions before going to the 'on-line' edit with the original tapes. Once I had Wade set up, he said he would be OK and told me to go home to my wife."

Chad stepped into the room as Sid finished. Cassie introduced the detectives, then Bill continued with Sid. "What specific project was he working on?"

"I'm not sure. I just got him started, then took off."

"I thought you said he was working on the Lasko interview," Chad interrupted.

Sid's eyebrows edged together, looking at Chad. "You're right, I nearly forgot. I believe he did say he was going to edit Lasko."

Stephanie took the lead again. "Was he acting strange in any way that day?"

"Not that I noticed. I gotta tell you, though, it sure surprised me when I heard that he killed himself."

"How was he acting when he called you on Tuesday morning?"

Sid stopped short and looked up at Stephanie, a quick flash of fear crossing his face. "He seemed normal. He called to tell me that after working a couple of hours he didn't like how it was turning out, so he erased what he'd done and put the original tapes back into the vault."

"Did that seem strange to you?" Bill interjected.

"A little. It takes some time to transfer those tapes onto the computer, and to erase them means we'd have to start over. But Josh said they've killed that story now, so I guess it won't matter."

Bill looked over at Stephanie. A flash in her eyes told him: *We've got enough. Let's get outta here.* They thanked Sid and gave him their cards, requesting he call if anything else came to mind.

As Cassie showed them the way back to their car, Stephanie stopped and looked her in the eye.

"Cassie, I'm going to trust you and ask you to do us a favor, without letting anyone at the office know about it. Can you do that for us?"

Cassie looked very serious. "I'll try. What do you want me to do?"

"I'd like you to get me all the details you can on this Lasko interview. Do you think that will be possible?"

"That shouldn't be any problem. All the notes should be in the filing cabinet."

"Good. When you get them together, fax them over to us at the station." Cassie agreed, then said good-bye as the officers drove away.

"Good morning, Cassie," a voice startled her from behind as she watched the car drive away.

Cassie turned and saw Reggie, a security guard on the lot who had befriended her when she first began working there. He was a large African-American man, a former linebacker for the Los Angeles Rams. Underneath the rough exterior, Reggie had a heart of gold, and Cassie had come to appreciate their friendship. He was also the only one on the lot Cassie had been able to identify as a Christian, so they often stopped and spent a moment together whenever they could manage the time.

"Reggie, good to see you. How's the family?"

"They're all doing just fine, thank you. How's the office? It must be hectic with Mr. Bennett's suicide and all."

Cassie looked up at Reggie and smiled. "It's been pretty rough actually, but I've felt God's presence through it all."

Reggie motioned to the car that just drove away. "Were those the detectives handling the case?"

She nodded. There wasn't much around this lot that got past Reggie. "I guess they're not too sure it was a suicide."

"Now, that is interesting. Who in the world would want to kill Mr. Bennett?"

Cassie thought about how abusive Wade had been to some of the staff and crew and almost responded: "Who wouldn't?" Instead she answered: "I wish I knew the answer to your question. They want me to get some information out of the office without any- one else knowing about it. So keep me in your prayers, would you?"

"You bet I will, Cassie. You just be careful now, OK? I'll try and keep my eyes out for you if you get into any trouble, but I know God will be with you."

Cassie thanked Reggie and gave him a quick hug as she headed back toward the production office.

On her way back she remembered her little prayer about finding the truth. What had really happened to Wade? And who was involved? She knew she had to get ahold of the three directors for Josh, but she decided to call her friend Jack first and update him on the situation. She could definitely use some more prayer support if she was going to try to play amateur detective.

CHAPTER 13

Rick walked his bike out of the garage, placed his left foot on the pedal, and let the bike roll down the incline toward the street. He swung his right leg up and over the seat like a cowboy mounting his favorite horse. He headed toward a park nearby, looking forward to a good workout. The sunny day made for a beautiful ride as the wind whipped past his face. The smell of flowers blooming and freshly mown grass filled his nostrils.

His mind kept going over the events of the night before. It was just too weird that Gary and Jill had been praying for him at the exact moment he needed it. It challenged his whole concept of God.

The fact that Jill couldn't sleep because of the urge to pray for him blew him away. He wanted to know more about what kind of relationship Gary and Jill had with God that enabled them to hear from him like that.

If Samantha hadn't come up with that question about protection, nothing would have stopped him from fulfilling his lustful desires. It had to have been God's hand that kept him from getting into any further trouble.

Now he was actually looking forward to the lunch with Gary. He wanted to know more about how this all worked.

He turned the corner into the park, joining the bike path that circled the grass area. Glancing at his watch, he decided he had enough time for a couple of laps before meeting Gary at the deli. With each pump of his legs, Rick felt revived as he sped around the track.

11:40 A.M., WEST HOLLYWOOD

The unmarked police car cruised down Sunset Boulevard, heading west, toward Malibu and Becky Bennett's house. Bill concentrated on the traffic around him as Stephanie looked over her notepad.

"Did you get the sense that Josh was a little evasive about why he was going to Wade's house?" Bill asked, turning onto the Pacific Coast Highway.

"He was lying through his teeth," Stephanie said bluntly. "According to what Cassie overheard, it sounded more personal than business."

"That still doesn't mean Bennett was murdered. It could have been something innocent to do with the show that Josh doesn't want us to know about."

"Well, it would have to be something pretty big to risk being suspected of murder, don't you think?"

"That's a valid point, I'll give you that. What do you think of the editor?"

"His story sounded OK, but he sure was nervous. And for some reason he didn't want us to know about this Lasko interview. Did you see his face when I mentioned the phone call? I don't think he would have volunteered the information if I hadn't brought it up. Everybody seems to be hiding something, and not one person has put Bennett in the frame of mind to blow his brains out. The more we find out, the more I lean toward this being a homicide."

"I hate to say I told you so, but—," Bill smirked to his partner.

"If memory serves me right, I was the first one at the scene to bring up that possibility," Stephanie chided back.

"You can't ever be wrong, can you!"

"I was once."

"Oh really? I can't recall. When was that?"

Stephanie looked over at him, enjoying the moment. "When I accepted you as my partner."

Bill laughed, enjoying their banter. It kept the stress of their work at a greater distance. "Well, that was a day we've both lived to regret, haven't we," he said with a big smile. "Seriously, do you think we should let the widow know we suspect something?"

"I don't know yet. I'd like to have a suspect before we send her on some mind trip trying to figure it out. Let's just play it by ear, see if she suspects anything. OK?"

"I'll let you lead. She seemed to relate better to you the other night."

11:47 a.m., HOLLYWOOD HILLS

John kept a current Director's Guild membership directory in his office at the house. After his daily routine of a light breakfast, reading the newspaper, and checking the overnight ratings of his show, he made his way into the office and pulled the directory off the bookshelf.

He'd been fortunate to land a director like Wade Bennett when they started up the show last August. John's rise to television stardom had come through nightclubs and small comedy rooms across the country before he landed the Showtime special where he first met Josh Abrams. He had not had a lot of television experience, and therefore didn't know a lot of television directors. Wade, although a great pain to John's ego, got the show off on the right track and had set a good foundation. But now John felt it was time to make his presence felt behind the camera as well as in front. He was looking for someone he could have some control over to sit in that middle chair in the booth.

He flipped through the directory, slowing down as he reached the *Ts*. He hoped he had the name right from the credits of that infomercial he'd seen the night before. Travis, Trayno, Trbovich . . . there it was, Treadway, Rick C., Director, Stage Manager. John glanced through the credits listed under his name. There were no Emmy awards noted. The only show John recognized besides a game show four years earlier was a daily talk show called "Cathy & Friends" that was canceled last fall. It wasn't impressive compared to Wade's credits, but to John it was perfect.

He needed to talk to someone who knew Treadway and how he worked to make sure he was the right choice. After a moment, John decided who better to talk to than the star of Treadway's last show. He picked up his phone, deciding his agent would be able to get him a phone number on Cathy, whatever her last name was.

A half hour later, with a glowing report of Rick's character and competency from Cathy Westland, he began designing a plan that would allow him to get Rick's name into the running for the director of "The John Harold Show."

CHAPTER 14

"I just have a sense that all is not as it seems," Cassie said in a lowered voice, not wanting anyone to overhear her phone conversation with her roommate, Amy.

"Funny you should put it that way," Amy said, grabbing some lunch at their apartment. "In my devotions this morning, I came upon this verse in 1 Corinthians and thought you might want to hear it. It's verse 5 of chapter 4."

Amy continued reading from the Bible she held before her: *Therefore judge nothing before the appointed time; wait till the Lord comes. He will bring to light what is hidden in darkness and will expose the motives of men's hearts. At that time each will receive his praise from God.* I believe God's placed you in the middle of what's going on there for a reason, Cassie. Keep trusting in him to guide you, and whatever is hidden, God will bring to light."

Cassie scribbled the reference verse on a notepad she kept by her phone. She fought back some tears, not wanting anyone to see her cry at the office. She hadn't realized what a strain she was under until that moment. Having Amy lift her up in prayer and hearing the Scripture touched her greatly. "Thanks, Amy, you've really helped me. But listen, I'd better get back to work. I'll see you tonight."

She looked at the list of directors she needed to contact. Since Josh was here and wanted to talk to each of them, she'd better try and get them on the phone now. At this point in the process, Josh wanted her to avoid their agents, so she called their home phone numbers listed on the résumés. She easily got to Frank Straton and Tina Livingston, putting them through to Josh, but all she got at Rick Treadway's was his answering machine. She left a brief message.

Now for the phone call she'd been dreading. How was she going to get through to this agent about one client, when he would be pushing so hard for Treadway? She picked up her phone and dialed.

"Mr. Weinberg, please. Cassie Petterson from 'The John Harold Show' calling." As she waited, she whispered: "Help me, Lord."

"Ms. Petterson, nice to hear from you again," Jacob's resounding voice came on the line. "Are you calling to set up an appointment for Rick Treadway?"

"No, Mr. Weinberg. Mr. Abrams wanted me to find out if you'd spoken to Carl Drake about our show."

Jacob hated talking to the middleman—or woman in this case. "Why don't you connect me with Mr. Abrams so we can talk directly."

Cassie could feel the tension rising in his voice. "I'm sorry, Mr. Weinberg, he's in conference right now." She was relieved to have seen Jim Schu walk into Josh's office as she spoke, so it wasn't a lie.

Jacob was running out of patience. "I probably won't be able to get that answer until later today, or even tomorrow. I spoke with Carl late last night about it, and he . . . ," Jacob paused, searching for the right words, "wanted a day to think about it before responding."

"Then I'll be waiting for your call when he gets back to you."

"I'll let you know as soon as I do, but what about—"

"I'm sorry, Mr. Weinberg. Mr. Abrams has the information on your other client. He'll be getting back to you if he's interested." Cassie set the phone down, hating it that she had to be so abrupt, but relieved to have the call completed. She wasn't looking forward to speaking with him again.

12:22 p.m., MALIBU

Stephanie and Bill walked up the sidewalk to the Bennetts' front door. What a change from the other night, when emergency vehicle lights had flashed, obscuring the peacefulness of the canyon and the beauty of the ranch house before them.

Becky answered the door and let the two detectives in.

"How are you doing, Mrs. Bennett?" Stephanie asked as they walked through the entryway and into the living room.

"I'm getting by, Detective," Becky said as she sat down in a living room chair.

"We don't want to add to your grief, but your sister called and requested the computer back, and there are a couple of questions we want to follow up on." Stephanie took a seat as Bill placed the computer on the coffee table.

"Did you find anything on the computer?"

"No. We made a copy of what was on it to check later if something comes up. The disk will be kept confidential and then erased when the case is closed."

"And you didn't take my husband's appointment book that night?"

"No, Mrs. Bennett, we didn't," Bill said, glancing at his partner. "Have you asked the office to look for it?"

"Yes, and I haven't heard anything back, so I assume they haven't located it either."

Stephanie added that to her notes, then phrased her next words carefully. "Mrs. Bennett, I hate to distress you any further, but I need to ask you about your relationship with your husband."

Becky stared wide-eyed at Stephanie as she continued. "Were there any marital problems between the two of you? Any extramarital . . . relationships that you were aware of?"

Becky shook her head.

"Was there a time recently when you were contemplating any relationships?"

"No. Nothing at all like that. Look, detectives," she leaned forward in her chair, trying to decide how to proceed. She'd spent two days vacillating between feeling like she was going crazy because she hadn't noticed her husband's despair, to being convinced that he'd been murdered—but not knowing how to go about proving it. "I've thought a lot about this since Tuesday night, and I'm positive that my husband did not kill himself." She looked straight into Stephanie's eyes, hoping for some outward sign of agreement.

Stephanie wrestled with her next step. Should she tell Becky about the gut feeling she and Bill had, possibly risking a leak to the news media, or keep their suspicions quiet? She decided to play it safe. Most families had a very hard time accepting that their loved ones could kill themselves.

"Do you have any proof, or do you have any idea who would want your husband dead?"

Becky dropped her eyes. She'd hoped for a different response. "No, I don't. Look, maybe you hear this from other wives in this situation, but I know he didn't do it. He was happy; he had a successful career, a good marriage, no deep dark secrets. There was no reason for him to take his life." She couldn't keep her emotions from slipping through as her voice quivered. "But I don't have any proof; that's your job." She folded her hands nervously in her lap.

"Mrs. Bennett, we don't have the answers yet either, but the way this case is shaping up, we don't believe your husband killed himself."

Becky grabbed a tissue from the coffee table and wiped at her eyes. Relief flooded her. If they were doubting the suicide, maybe she wasn't crazy after all.

The three spent the next hour going over anything Becky could remember about the last few days, piecing together the string of events that had led up to Wade's death.

12:28 P.M., WEST HOLLYWOOD

Rudy Vanozzi was fuming. He'd spent the better part of last night, and several more hours today, looking for Vanessa. Flint had called him late last night to let him know she'd missed an appointment at the apartment. He had made it clear, in no uncertain terms, that he wanted her found and brought to him immediately.

Combing the areas of Hollywood where Vanessa used to "work," he had asked her former associates if they had seen her. No one had, nor did Rudy ever spot her red Corvette. After checking the apartment one last time, he decided a different course was needed.

He picked up the phone in the apartment and started calling all the pimps, drug runners, even cops, that were on Flint's payroll. Once contacted, he would tell them, "It's Rudy. Listen, I need a favor. If you come through for me, it'll be worth a quick grand. Keep your eyes peeled for a red Corvette, license number 2RYE477. A real looker drives it—tall, built, long sandy blond hair. If you see her, get ahold of me right away, and try to follow her until I can get there."

He hoped Vanessa was dumb enough to still be driving the car. He was looking forward to witnessing Flint's revenge, as well as enacting a little of his own. He remembered just enough about the other night to know she had refused him. No one did that to Rudy Vanozzi. He wasn't sure how much he had punished her that night, but he'd pick up where he left off when he found her, that was for sure.

CHAPTER 15

Rick wove through the traffic, waiting for the light on Ventura Boulevard to turn green. He peddled his bike into the parking lot of the little shopping center and rode over to the deli.

As he locked his bicycle outside the restaurant, he could see Gary sitting at a table by the window.

"Are you always early?" Rick asked as he approached the table, looking at his watch.

"Only when I'm looking forward to the appointment," Gary smiled. "How was the ride?"

"Invigorating. I enjoyed it even more today than yesterday." Rick reached out and grabbed a glass of ice water set before him. He didn't realize how thirsty he was until the refreshing water washed down his throat. He emptied the glass before placing it back on the table with a gusty sigh.

"I guess it piqued your thirst too?"

"It sure did. You know what else is piqued? My curiosity. What trip have you sent me on?"

Gary looked puzzled.

"First you start asking questions about relationships at my church, then you send me on some scavenger hunt through the Scriptures, and this thing last night about Jill having an urge to pray for me. You've really got my head spinning. Are you planning to answer some questions today, or just keep me in limbo awhile longer?"

Gary laughed. He had had no idea how much the Holy Spirit had been working on Rick since their discussion. "What questions do you have?"

"That's part of the problem. I'm not even sure what questions to ask to get the answers I'm searching for."

Gary started to respond, but decided this could take awhile, suggesting they order first.

"Let's start with this," he continued as they returned to their table. "What are some of the thoughts that have come into your mind since we last talked?"

Rick scratched his chin. "Boy, let's see, there's been a lot of them. After our lunch together I read the verses in 1 Peter. It really got me thinking about love, relationships, and serving others. Those questions you asked me about helping someone, especially praying for them or counseling with them, really had me going. Isn't it the pastor's job to do the praying and counseling? I mean, that's what they're paid for, isn't it?"

Gary smiled. He, too, had once believed that to be true. "I would say that is the belief of a lot of Christians in America, yes. But I wouldn't say that makes it necessarily true."

"What do you mean? If that's not their role, then what is?"

"Let's shelve that question for a second. What's more important right now is what is your role?"

Rick smiled at Gary's tactics. "OK, if that's the way you want to play it, fine. I know from what I've read lately that we're all part of one body and each has his part. That much is evident. But I don't have the foggiest notion what my part is. The first time I read 1 Peter, I would have said it was helping out by directing that little Christmas play we put on, or doing some job within the church, like being an usher or being in the choir, something like that. Now I'm not so sure."

"Good, you're thinking. That's the first step." Gary leaned forward on the table that separated them. "Look, Rick, I didn't plan to send you on this path. Yesterday, over lunch, that question just popped out. Part of it was because you compared the group I'm in to just another church service, and I wanted to point out the difference. The other part, I believe, is the Holy Spirit working. You see, I've been where you are now. I've done the church thing—where you attend every week, hear good sermons, even help out on certain projects if your talent fits in. But even after all that, I still felt empty. I felt like I was just going through the motions."

Rick nodded, signaling that he wanted Gary to continue.

"God sent me on a search just like the one you're on, and you know what I found? I found out there's more, so much more, to the Christian walk. Jesus is alive and real, and our relationship with him can be much greater than attending services twice a week. That first Scripture you read in 1 Peter said, above all, to love each other deeply. Jesus said it in John 13—that the world will know we're his disciples by the love we have for one another. Generally, I haven't seen the church live up to his words. Don't get me wrong; there have been some rare instances where I've seen that kind of love conveyed in some people through the years, but in most of my church history I've seen more bickering, gossiping, and struggling for position than in many of the production companies you and I have worked for."

They both laughed, knowing that wasn't a favorable comparison.

Gary kept going, "When people look at the church and see us treating each other just like they do, why would they want anything to do with Christianity? However, if the world saw a church where love was expressed the way Jesus talked about, there'd be no question that we'd stand out as his disciples. Unfortunately, most of the time we give back to the world a mirror image of itself rather than the image of Jesus."

Rick couldn't argue; he just kept listening.

"The Bible says we, as Christians, are supposed to relate to each other in love. At our fellowship meetings we have a little card that compiles what we call 'one anothering' Scriptures. I'll get you one tonight. Things like love one another, serve one another, pray for one another, uplift one another, and bear one another's burdens are all part of that list."

Gary paused, nudging Rick's mind back to his earlier question. "Aren't those the things that pastors are supposed to do?"

"Traditionally, yes, and there are some wonderful men and women of God working themselves to the bone trying to do them. Unfortunately, those are not their jobs alone. Those are the roles of everyone in the body of Christ. I don't see how we can fulfill the 'one anothering' thing unless we're in a dynamic relationship with a small group of Christians. Seeing people sit in a pew near you once a week doesn't build this kind of relationship. Since I've been going to the fellowship group, my relationship with Jesus has become more real. It now feels natural for me to pray with somebody about a problem in his life, or confess an area of weakness that I struggle with, or even be led by the Spirit with a word for somebody else around me."

The waiter brought over their sandwiches. Gary gave thanks for their meal, and they both plowed into their food. After a couple of bites, Rick finally spoke up.

"What you're saying makes a lot of sense. To be honest, I've had some of those same thoughts about going through the motions of church stuff, not feeling like it's making a big difference in my life. But you've given me a lot to chew on. I need to digest some of it."

"No sweat. I'm not pushing you into anything, believe me."

Rick's mind went back to his earlier question. "You still didn't totally answer my question about the pastor thing. If what I thought the pastor was supposed to do is being done by the whole body, or church, then what is the pastor's role?"

"There is a section in Ephesians that's pretty clear on what the role of leadership is in the church, but I think there's somebody else who can answer that better for you. I don't know if I've mentioned him to you before or not, but Rob Stevenson was the founder of Christians in Film and Television. He used to be a pastor, and he'd have a lot more to say about your question than I ever could."

"Will he be at your meeting tonight?"

"As a matter of fact, he will be. Do you think you can make it?"

Rick nodded, "Yeah, I do. It's time I see firsthand what you're talking about."

1:15 P.m., MALIBU

Becky stared at the computer in front of her, cursing herself for not having spent the time with Wade to learn how to run the stupid thing. Maybe there was something in here the police had overlooked that would give her a clue. She knew Wade had been working on it that fateful afternoon he'd sent her out shopping. There must be some clue in there.

She needed some help. But who?

Her mind recalled a conversation she'd had the day before with Cassie, from the production office. She'd offered to help with anything, hadn't she? Becky's determination returned as she picked up the phone.

Most of the press had stopped calling Josh Abrams's office, evidently content to let suicide be the conclusion of the story. Josh had set meetings with the two directors he had talked with on the phone earlier, Frank Straton and Tina Livingston. If Treadway returned their call, he'd get the eleven o'clock slot. Mr. Flint and John Harold had already been told about the meetings as well. Hopefully, by this time tomorrow, they'd have a new director and be able to get back into production.

The phone rang beside Cassie.

"Josh Abrams's office," she said automatically.

"Cassie?" the voice on the other end asked.

"Yes, can I help you?"

"It's Becky."

Cassie felt a quick flash of panic. *What am I going to say to her?*

"Becky, it's good to hear from you. Are you hanging in there all right?" she managed to ask as she mentally prayed for the right words.

"I'm doing OK, Cassie."

"By the way," Cassie said, "I didn't have any luck finding Wade's appointment book. I know I should have called, but it's been frantic around here."

"That's all right. I understand. That's strange, though, because it hasn't turned up here either, and the police didn't take it. Say, Cassie, remember the other day when you offered to help in any way with anything that might come up?"

"Of course I do, and the offer still stands. Is there something you need from the show?"

"No, not from the show. But there is something I think you can help me with if you're willing."

"Just name it."

"Well, I don't want to go into it over the phone, but I'm convinced that Wade didn't . . . ," she paused.

"I understand what you mean. I've been having my doubts as well."

"Well, the police brought his computer back, and they say nothing suspicious turned up on it, but I'm hoping there might be something they missed. Unfortunately, I don't know the first thing about computers. Would you feel comfortable coming over and going through it with me?"

"I'd be happy to, Becky. When do you want to get together?"

"Would after work tonight be OK?"

"That'll be fine; I don't have any plans. Why don't I call you when I'm ready to head out of here, and we'll meet sometime this evening."

"That'd be perfect. Thanks so much." She hung up.

Lord, whatever you've got planned here, open up her heart to your presence, Cassie prayed.

The office seemed deserted. Cassie decided this would be a good time to try and locate the file on the Lasko interview. She opened the spiral notebook she kept by her desk and turned to the schedule for March, looking back toward the first of the month. None of the schedules showed the name Lasko. She thought about calling Mark Richards, one of the show's field producers, and asking him about the name, but she remembered the detectives warned her not to let anyone know what she was doing.

Cassie walked over to the filing cabinets where they kept the field scripts on different topics. She glanced around the room, then opened the cabinet drawer, her pulse racing. She rifled through the section of upcoming segments. There was a file on immigration that contained shooting scripts for March 7, but no mention of Lasko. There was a file on welfare, but nothing had been shot on it yet. Under censorship, she saw a schedule relating to the shoot on the ninth, but nothing there about Lasko either. Then she saw a folder labeled Adult Entertainment. Maybe this was it, she thought. But when she pulled the folder out, its lack of weight told her it was empty before she opened it. Another dead end.

She heard Josh's line ringing. She quickly put the empty folder in the file cabinet and rushed back to her desk.

"Josh Abrams's office."

"Hi, Cassie. Jacob Weinberg here."

Great, Cassie thought. *All I need is for him to call again.*

"Hi, Mr. Weinberg. What can I do for you?"

"Well, you wanted to know as soon as I heard from Carl Drake if he was interested in your show or not, remember?"

"Of course I remember. What have you found out?"

"Well, is Josh there? I'd really like to talk to him directly." Jacob never gave up.

"I'm sorry—"

"I know, I know. He's not available," he finished for her. "Tell him that Carl is interested in doing the show but won't be available until after his next project, which should take him four weeks to complete. So if Josh wouldn't mind an interim director for the next month, we might be able to strike a deal."

"I'll let Mr. Abrams know that, Mr. Weinberg. If he has any more questions, he'll call you himself."

"Good. By the way, Rick Treadway would make an excellent choice in the meantime."

"I'm sure he would. We'll take that under advisement," Cassie said as she disconnected the call.

"Who was that?" Josh yelled to her from inside his office. Cassie rose from her desk and walked to his doorway.

"It was Jacob Weinberg, Carl Drake's agent."

"Is Carl interested in the show?"

"Yes he is, but he can't get out of the other commitment. So he's offering to take over the show in a month and suggesting we hire an interim director to cover us until then."

"That may work to our advantage. If we offer one of these three directors the job, but they don't perform that great, we can always bring Carl in. That way we're covered either way." Josh's mouth spread in a big grin. "By the way, has Treadway called back yet?"

"Not yet. I'll put him through as soon as he does. That agent was pushing for him again, you know."

"You didn't tell him we'd called Treadway, did you?"

"No, I figure it'll be a great surprise for him when Treadway tells him. By the way, Josh, I had a question," Cassie said.

"What is it?" Josh asked, his eyes focused on his computer screen.

Cassie hesitated. "I was organizing the remote files, trying to stay ahead so that all the information would be available for the new director. I know we had a remote crew out under the heading of Adult Entertainment, but I can't find a script or any information on it. The file's empty."

Josh looked up at Cassie. She didn't know if it was her imagination, but she thought she saw a scowl cross his face.

"That's odd, but don't worry about it. We've decided to kill that segment. Anything else?"

Cassie knew the meeting was over. "No sir," she said, and headed back out to her desk.

She sat down, amazed that she was having such difficulty finding out anything about the Lasko interview. She wanted to be able to help the detectives, but it was as if every bit of information on the piece had simply disappeared.

CHAPTER 16

Rick rushed through the door, breathing heavily from racing home on the bike. In spite of the physical drain, he felt invigorated from the time spent with Gary. He was looking forward to the meeting that night with the home group. He tried to remember the last time he had been excited about going to a church meeting. He couldn't think of one.

He noticed the flashing light on his answering machine as he placed his keys on the kitchen countertop. There were two messages. Rick hit the play button.

"Mr. Treadway, this is Cassie Petterson from 'The John Harold Show.' Our producer, Josh Abrams, would like to speak with you. If you could return the call at 213-555-9583 when you get this message, we'd appreciate it."

Rick's heart leaped. The second message was even better.

"Rick, this is John Harold. I'm sure you've heard about the tragedy with Wade Bennett. Well, we're in need of a new director, and you sound like someone who might be right for my show. I'd like to speak with you. Give me a call at 310-555-4421 when you can. Thanks."

Rick laughed. His first thought was how lucky he was to be represented by such a wonderful agency. Then he paused for a minute and thought again. This had to be God's work. To get a call from the producer and the star had to be God's doing.

Now, who to call first, the producer or the host? Rick chose the host. He'd learned early in his career: never keep the star waiting. After the second ring, John picked up the phone.

"Mr. Harold, this is Rick Treadway returning your call," he said, trying to keep his voice steady to hide his nervousness.

"Rick, thanks for calling back. I've heard some great things about you, so I wanted to touch base with you."

"I appreciate that. Who's been telling stories about me?"

"Well, among other people, I talked to Cathy Westland. She spoke very highly of you and your working relationship."

Rick hadn't spoken to Cathy in several months. He'd have to give her a call of thanks later.

John continued. "I'm sure you've heard about Wade."

"Yes, I have. That must have been quite a shock for you."

"Oh, a shock it was. He was fabulous, and I want to find someone who can fill the job as well as fit into our growing family here. What's your situation, Rick? Are you currently involved in a project?"

"Actually, my last show just wrapped up Tuesday night. I'm available for whatever you need."

"Well, I haven't talked to the producer about you yet; I wanted to talk to you first."

"Mr. Harold—"

"John, please."

"OK. John, as a matter of fact, I also received a call from Josh Abrams this afternoon. I haven't returned that one yet; I wanted to speak to you directly first."

John smiled. That was a very good sign. It looked like Rick could be just the person he was looking for.

"Well, that's great. I think they're having a couple of directors come into the production office tomorrow for interviews. It looks like they're planning to include you already." *That'll make my job that much easier,* he thought. "Tell you what, Rick. Don't mention this phone call; I'll bring up my feelings on you at the right time, OK?"

"Whatever you say. Hopefully, I'll see you tomorrow."

"I'll look forward to it."

Rick hung up the phone, amazed at how things were falling into place. He dialed the office number with a bit more confidence.

"Josh Abrams's office."

"Hi, this is Rick Treadway returning Mr. Abrams's call." As Rick spoke the name, something sounded familiar, but he couldn't place it.

"Hi, Mr. Treadway. This is Cassie Petterson. I've been waiting for your call."

The warmth of Cassie's voice had a soothing effect on Rick. "Is Mr. Abrams in?"

"Yes, he is. I'll get him for you right away."

There was a moment's pause. "Rick, it's been a long time. How are you?"

That caught Rick by surprise. He must have worked with this man before, but where? He tried to recall what show it could have been but couldn't place it. "I'm doing just great, and how about you? It has been a long time." He played along, frantically racking his brain for the memory.

"I'd say so. College seems like a lifetime ago, doesn't it?"

That was it! They had been at UCLA together. What a relief. "I didn't realize you were producing the show. Congratulations, Josh. You've done pretty well for yourself."

"Thanks, Rick. Things have been going great the last few months, until this suicide thing hit. We'll really miss Wade over here."

"You have my deepest sympathy. I worked with Wade a few times; he was quite a director."

"That he was. Speaking of directors, I didn't know you were in that line of work, and from what I can see, doing pretty well at it too. Last I remember hearing about you, weren't you stage managing?"

"Yes, I was, but about five years ago I got a shot at directing a game show. One job led to another, and eventually I gave up stage managing altogether. It's been an interesting transition, but I feel like I was able to take the best from a lot of the directors I had worked with and make a career for myself."

"Well, that's why I'm calling. Are you interested in coming over here and working for me?"

"I'd love to. Since I heard about Wade, I have to admit your show has been on my mind. My agent said he was going to try to get an interview for me, and I'm thrilled at the chance."

"Well, we've kind of been running around your agent. He never really got through to me. But when your name crossed my desk, I remembered working on that news project together our senior year, and I wanted to give you a shot at the job."

"Just let me know what you need me to do."

"Well, tomorrow morning we're having a couple of other directors come over. I'd like you to join us as well, say around eleven o'clock. You'll be interviewed by me, John Harold, and Gabriel Flint, our executive producer. I'll be honest with you, Rick, the decision won't be mine alone; it'll be a consensus."

"I understand. I'll be there at eleven. Do you want me to bring any tapes or résumés?"

"We've got your résumé already, but do bring a demo tape if you've got one handy. We might want to take a look at some stuff."

"You've got it, Josh. And thanks for including me. It'll be great to see you again."

"I'm looking forward to it as well. I'll put Cassie back on, and she'll give you the information you need to get on the lot."

After the call ended, Rick dialed his agents' office to let them know the good news. Neither one was in so he left a message.

He had to share the news with someone. Here it was, his one-in-a-million shot, and he had an inside track with the producer.

Rick decided to call Gary. He told him the good news, then asked if he and Jill would pray that this job would happen—if it was God's will.

After he hung up, Rick leaned against the counter, staggered by all that had happened. Less than fourteen hours ago, he had been at the lowest point in his life since the divorce. Yet his new outlook now was due to more than just this job possibility. He'd felt a rejuvenation in his spirit since last night when he poured out his heart to God in the shower, and it had continued on through the lunch with Gary. He knew that his relationship with God was deepening because of all the struggles he'd been through, and that was more encouraging to him than any job-possibility.

2:20 P.m., SHERIFF'S HEADQUARTERS

"Wow! Do you know what we've missed?" Bill motioned with some papers at Stephanie.

"No, what?" Stephanie tried to keep the frustration out of her voice. She'd gone over and over the information they'd received through the day, from the show's staff, and from Mrs. Bennett. She wanted something to break open this case, or Captain Lipton was going to force them to close it as a suicide, and soon.

"Well, we know Abrams is hiding something, not only about why he was going to see Wade that night, but probably what Wade was doing in the edit room the day before."

"Yeah, so what? What we need to know is exactly what the Lasko interview was about," Stephanie said irritably. They'd covered this already.

"That's true, but until we find that out, there's one other avenue we need to investigate." Bill waited for his partner to give him her full attention. When she looked up at him, he continued, "Remember, the fish rots from the head down."

"Is this something you learned from your fortune cookie at lunch?"

"No, just an old saying. If there's something bad going on around that show, bad enough to get Bennett killed, we need to get to the top, and I don't think Josh Abrams is it. When they faxed over the show's staff list, it only included people at the production office. While we were there, I grabbed a more complete list, including the National Studios executives, the distributors, the executive producer . . ."

Bill handed Stephanie the page he was holding, pointing to the credit for executive producer.

Stephanie's eyebrows went up, "Gabriel Flint?"

"Does the name ring a bell?"

She thought for a minute. "Something about it sounds familiar, but I can't place it."

Bill smirked; he loved being one up on his partner. "I can. It wasn't that long ago that I moved up here from Vice. Flint is not your typical Hollywood producer. He's involved in prostitution, big into pornography, owns some strip joints around town, probably a few other activities we don't even know about. But we were never able to nail him on any of it. He covers his backside pretty well, and if I remember correctly, that takes a lot of coverage."

Bill had Stephanie's full attention now. "And this slime ball is the executive producer?"

"Unless there're two guys in this town named Gabriel Flint, yeah. Tell you what." Bill got up out of his chair and slipped his coat on. "Let's take a trip down to Vice and see what Mr. Flint has been up to lately. You game?"

Stephanie nodded. "You bet. We don't have any other leads, and until Cassie can get us the info on this Lasko thing, we're kind of at a standstill anyway."

2:45 P.M., BEVERLY HILLS

Gabriel Flint scowled.

"How could she disappear? You can't find a lousy whore in this God-forsaken town?"

Rudy stood tall before the verbal abuse. "I've got people looking for the car and checking out her old hangouts. She'll turn up; just give it some time."

"I was lucky Steve found something he liked at the club. I can't imagine the grief I'd get when he got back to Vegas and told his father I didn't show him a good time down here. What's gotten into Vanessa anyway? Where is she?" Flint swore and threw his pen across the room.

"I'll find her, boss."

"You'd better, and fast. But that's not the only reason I called you down here. We've got another problem."

"Which is?"

"Some people are asking questions about Lasko in the production office."

"So what? By now the police have closed the Bennett case. Suicide. Fineto," Rudy answered with a cocky grin.

"If you'd done your job right, that'd be true," Flint said, coldly. "But would you believe the police were over at the production office today trying to retrace Wade's movements on Monday? Evidently their case isn't as shut as we'd like it to be. We're going to have to step up our schedule. I think you should plan to go in tomorrow night and make sure those tapes are never seen again."

"Why not tonight?"

"I've got to go over there tomorrow for some meetings. I don't want to be around when the police might be asking questions."

"You're the boss."

"Don't get cute with it either. I don't care if it looks like arson anymore; just make sure those tapes are history."

"You got it."

"Now get outta here and find Vanessa. I want to know why she's running out on us. That no good . . ."

Rudy made his exit as Flint kept on raving about Vanessa. He'd have to make sure she didn't talk to Flint about being with him the night before. If Flint blamed him for her disappearance . . . well, he didn't want to think of the consequences.

CHAPTER 17

Rick drove his car along Mulholland Drive, enjoying the breathtaking view of the city lights as he rounded each turn. He'd taken Laurel Canyon from his side of the San Fernando Valley to where Mulholland begins winding its way through the Hollywood Hills. The meeting was being held at the home of a screenwriter.

Spotting Skyline Drive, he turned left, driving down the hill a bit until he saw the house. He pulled up behind a gray Jeep as a couple got out and headed up the walkway. Rick felt a little nervous going up to the house by himself; he hoped Gary was already inside. As he made his way around his car, he spotted Gary's car pulling up on the other side of the street.

"Hi, Rick," Gary called as he opened the car door. "See, miracles do still happen—you finally made it to one of our meetings."

"Lately I feel like my whole life is a miracle. I'm excited about tonight. Maybe it'll put some of the questions I've been having into perspective."

"I hope so."

"Where's Jill?"

"She had to go over to her mother's house tonight. I forgot that her sister's having a baby shower," Gary replied as the two headed up the sidewalk. "Any news on the show?"

"Nothing since I called you. I've just got to get through that meeting tomorrow morning."

They walked into the house and were greeted warmly by the owners, Warren Tuttle and his wife Penny. Gary introduced Rick to several people until one of the men in the group grabbed a guitar and started singing. Everyone settled into a seat and joined right in.

Most of the songs were new to Rick, but he was given a small song sheet with the words on it and found that the melodies were easy to pick up. He glanced around at the faces of the people in the group as they sang. Many lifted their hands up in worship. It was obvious they were not just singing songs together, but singing to the Lord. It didn't take long for Rick to realize that no one was looking at him, which helped him feel more comfortable. After a while he found he was singing along with them, allowing the words to be a prayer from his own heart.

After several songs, the group stopped singing as the guitarist continued playing quietly. Rick could hear different people around him verbalizing their adoration and love for the Lord. He heard comments on God's greatness, his holiness, his awesome love. He heard prayers for the Holy Spirit to come and move among them as they waited. It was all very new to him. He wasn't sure what to call it, but he felt a warmth and a peacefulness surround him. In all his days, through many different church services, he'd never felt anything like this. It was wonderful.

"I've got to confess something," a voice spoke out. It was Warren, the owner of the house. "I've had a rough day; the details aren't important. What is though, is that as we were worshiping, I found my thoughts centering on myself: 'God, cheer me up. Make that frustrating situation in my life go away'—those kinds of things.

"Then God started showing me how I judge worship to be successful depending on how it makes me feel. But that's backward. What's important is how God feels during our worship. When we sang 'I wonder how he could love me, a sinner condemned and unclean,' it really hit home. God loves me. Even during my weakest moment, he still loves me. How can I not respond with an expression of love that is pleasing to him?"

A chorus of amens spread throughout the room. Rick silently agreed, realizing that he also had been concentrating on his own feelings.

Then another man spoke up. "Let's sing that song again, and I encourage anyone who can relate to what Warren just said to turn the focus on the one who is truly worthy, Jesus. Warren, before we sing, why don't you lead us in a prayer that God would do that in our hearts tonight?"

Warren began praying, and Rick silently prayed along with him that God would work in his heart, that he'd learn what it means to bless God rather than to look for a blessing from God.

As they sang through the song again, tears came to his eyes. In the quietness after the song, Rick knew he was sensing God's presence in the room.

As the night progressed, several people around the room read Scriptures and shared thoughts they felt the Holy Spirit had impressed upon them for the group. Rick had never heard the Holy Spirit mentioned so much in one evening. These people spoke of him as if he were right there with them, orchestrating everything. Other than the guitar player, Rick couldn't spot a specific leader who was in charge of the meeting. But somehow it all flowed together. Rick thought of a Scripture he'd read the other night, and turned to

1 Corinthians 14:26: *What then shall we say, brothers? When you come together, everyone has a hymn, or a word of instruction, a revelation, a tongue or an interpretation. All of these must be done for the strengthening of the church.*

He was watching this Scripture being lived out right before him, and it thrilled him. This was the church in action.

8:05 P.M., MALIBU

"Thanks so much for coming over this late, Cassie," Becky said as she opened her front door.

"I'm sorry I couldn't get here sooner. The office has been so hectic from all that's happened." Cassie stepped into the house and followed Becky into the family room.

"Oh, the time's no problem for me, but I know you have to work tomorrow. I feel bad for you."

"Well, to tell you the truth, I'm anxious to be of help. There are things going on around the office that are just too strange. I hope we find something on the computer that will clear things up."

The laptop sat on the coffee table. Cassie recognized it; she'd seen Wade use it in his office numerous times.

"I brought the computer in here. It's hard to be in that office after what happened . . . ," Becky's voice trailed off, and Cassie could see grief written on her face.

"Do you have the computer case he used to keep it in? The batteries are probably worn down by now, so I'll probably need to plug it in."

"Sure, I'll be right back."

With Becky out of the room, Cassie quickly prayed for God's guidance. She not only wanted to be God's instrument to find the truth about Wade's death, she also wanted to be God's lifeline to Becky.

Becky came back in carrying the black travel case Wade had used to transport his computer to and from the office.

"You still haven't found his appointment book?" Cassie asked.

"No, I haven't, and since it wasn't at the office, I believe someone was in here that night and took it when he killed my husband."

Cassie pulled the AC adapter from the case and plugged the computer into a wall outlet. "This must be so hard on you, Becky. How are you holding up?"

"Sometimes, OK; sometimes, not so good. Keeping my mind on trying to solve the murder has helped, and my family has been supportive, but there's a huge hole in my life and I'm not sure how to fill it."

I know how you can fill it, Cassie thought, but she sensed that this wasn't the right approach. She got everything connected and turned the computer on. It would take a few moments to boot up and be ready to use.

"I lost my father a few years back when he died of cancer. It was a really tough time," Cassie said as she watched the computer screen flicker to life.

"Does the pain ever go away?"

Cassie turned and looked at Becky, "It depends on how you view it. I still miss him terribly. Everyone says time heals all wounds, but I think time only deadens the pain. I've found, personally, that only Jesus can heal the wounds."

Cassie paused to see what kind of effect her words had. Becky was still looking at her, listening intently, so she continued, "I wasn't walking that closely with the Lord at the time, and I think it was Dad's death that brought my priorities into focus. He had a strong relationship with God, and the way he faced death spoke to me louder than a thousand sermons I'd heard. He was so at peace with it, ready to go and be with his Lord. I, on the other hand, was living out the rebellious kid thing, having nothing to do with the church, although I had kept a close relationship with my dad."

Cassie paused, "I don't want to bore you with my life, Becky. I know you're probably going through even more pain, losing your husband."

"Oh, no," Becky pleaded, "it's all right. I grew up in a Christian home, too, and . . . well, I haven't been around the church much myself."

"Well, my father's death made me realize how short life can be. Even though I was out pursuing my own desires, I still knew deep down that what I'd been brought up with was the truth. I wish it hadn't taken his death to wake me up to that fact."

Cassie took Becky's hand as she saw tears forming in her eyes. "When you go through a tragedy as you have, Becky, there are two responses people can have. One is to blame God, get real mad at him, and run the other way. That's a very normal response, and if you're feeling that way now, God understands."

Becky was crying steadily now.

"Or, you can turn to him. He understands, he loves you, and he wants to walk you through this, letting you know how real he can be in your life." Cassie paused again to let Becky contemplate what she was saying.

"Well, I'm at the mad-at-God stage. How could he let this happen to Wade? To us? My parents have been trying to get me back into church, especially since Wade's death. Right now that's the last place I want to be."

"Church isn't the answer, Becky, Jesus is. He's the healer, the peace giver, the one who can bring life out of death."

Becky's head shook slowly and her tears continued as Cassie spoke. Cassie felt this was as far as she should go for now. Becky needed some more time to deal with her feelings.

The two had forgotten about the computer sitting next to them until a beep broke the moment. Becky laughed through her tears, "I think something's trying to get our attention."

"Well, let's see what secrets are going to open up to us," Cassie said, focusing her attention back onto the computer.

Cassie noticed a document labeled "Good-bye." "This must be the suicide note," she said to Becky as she pointed to the screen. "In this mode—what Macintosh calls the icon view—all you can see is that it's a Microsoft Word document, but if I go up here—" she placed her finger on the track pad, moving the cursor to go under the view heading and selecting "by Name." The whole computer image changed, and instead of small folders, they now saw a vertical row of items listed by their names on the left.

Cassie stretched out the display area so they could read all the information on the page. "That's interesting," she whispered as she noticed something on the far right of the screen, her eyebrows furrowing.

"What?" Becky said anxiously as she looked for anything on the page that would give her a clue as to what had happened to her husband.

"What time did the police say Wade killed himself?"

"I think the police said it was around 6:30. That's when the neighbor heard the gunshot."

"And that was on the 16th?"

"Yeah, why? What have you found?"

Cassie pointed to the titled document and ran her hand across the line as she spoke. "See, here's the suicide note. It was titled 'Good-bye.' Notice the information that follows it. It's size, 4K. It was created with Microsoft Word, and here's the interesting part. It was last modified, which probably means it was created, on Monday, March 15 at 10:35 P.M. According to this, Wade wrote the suicide note on his computer the night before he shot himself."

For Becky, it took a second for the information to sink in.

"That's impossible!" she exclaimed. "I can tell you exactly what Wade was doing at that time on Monday, and he wasn't anywhere near this computer. We had been looking forward to the week off for such a long time. He had a couple of things he wanted to get caught up on at work, but we were going to try and make the best of the time that we had.

"He'd spent the afternoon over at the studio editing some field piece they'd shot, then we'd planned to have a romantic dinner at home. He was late; I remember how mad I was because the dinner was ruined. I tried to get over it, but he was in such a weird mood. Something at work was bothering him, but he wouldn't tell me about it. He can be that way sometimes, but after a while, he usually comes around. That night was different; he kept dodging the issue, and stayed in a terrible mood. He was worried about something.

"Anyway, at 10 o'clock we went out to our Jacuzzi to try and recapture the romance of the evening, but that didn't work either. We finally gave up and came upstairs. I remember because I looked at the clock and couldn't believe we were in bed watching the sports scores on the early news at 10:30. I know he didn't sleep much that night, but I didn't fall asleep until about midnight, and he hadn't left the bedroom. So at 10:35 on Monday night, Wade and I were upstairs together, nowhere near this computer."

Cassie was excited. Finally, something concrete. "You said the police didn't find anything suspicious, didn't you?"

Becky nodded.

"Then they're going to want this thing back, but I hesitate to return it if they missed this." Cassie thought for a moment, then looked back up at Becky. "We've got two options. Stop right now, which is probably what we should do. Or we could jump in and look for more, but that could jeopardize whatever evidence the police might be able to find."

Becky sighed, realizing her excitement was going to be short-lived. As much as she wanted to find out whatever else the computer held, she didn't want to jeopardize any evidence that could bring the killer to justice.

"You're probably right. We better not take the chance of messing up any evidence."

Cassie agreed, although somewhat reluctantly.

"But you keep the computer with you," Becky added. "You'll need to show the detectives what you found out. I couldn't begin to explain it."

"I'd be happy to. I'm sure they'll be by the office tomorrow anyway. I'll call them first thing in the morning and let them know what we found," Cassie said as she shut the computer off and carefully placed it in Wade's carrying case.

8:15 P.M., HOLLYWOOD HILLS

"One Anothering"

Love One Another—*John 13:34*

In honor prefer One Another—*Romans 12:10*

Edify One Another—*Romans 14:19*

Serve One Another—*Galatians 5:13*

Be kind to One Another—*Ephesians 4:32*

Encourage One Another Daily—*Hebrews 3:13*

Bear with One Another—*Ephesians 4:2*

Confess sins and pray for One Another—*James 5:16*

Stimulate One Another **to love and good**
        deeds—*Hebrews 10:24*

Admonish One Another—*Romans 15:14*

Bear One Another's **burdens**—*Galatians 6:2*

Forgive One Another—*Ephesians 4:32*

Comfort One Another—*1 Thessalonians 4:18*

Submit to One Another—*Ephesians 5:21*

Be Hospitable to One Another—*1 Peter 4:9*

Share with One Another—*Acts 4:34–35*

Teach One Another—*Colossians 3:16*

Rick was looking at the white card Gary had given him. There sure were a lot of Scriptures encouraging the "one anothering" concept. The list was a bit overwhelming to him. *Trying to follow this would put me in full-time ministry,* he thought.

"I have to confess, instead of this being exciting to me, it became a heavy burden."

Rick's attention was pulled back to the group. Terry Stanfield, a talent coordinator Rick had worked with before, was speaking.

"The reason? Because I thought I had to do it all. If it was in Scripture, then I had to be out there, looking everywhere for ways that I could be doing all these things.

"Well, last week I had to fly to New York for the American Comedy Awards. For some reason I was booked on a flight that had a two-hour layover in Dallas. I obviously had some time to kill, so I found an empty gate a little distance away from my connecting flight to try and get some work done. It was very peaceful, for awhile. Then people started congregating around, waiting for a flight to arrive at my quiet little spot. The noise level began to increase, and it became harder and harder to concentrate. There was a kid, probably about five or six years old, a little boy, that was getting rowdy. He was climbing over the chairs and stuff, being a nuisance, and his parents were oblivious to it all. Then he ran by and knocked over a folder I had sitting next to me, sending booking sheets flying all over the place. All in all, I was getting pretty irritated. How dare these people come around where I was working and mess up my life!

"Then something in me began to take notice of my surroundings. I now know it was the Holy Spirit at work. I noticed the little boy was with his family, a younger sister and his mom and dad. They were Japanese, and I could hear the father talking excitedly about the kids seeing their grandparents coming in from Japan.

"I looked over in the corner of the gateway and noticed a young woman standing nervously with a single rose in her hand. I began to imagine who she could be waiting for, a boyfriend coming home from college, or maybe her young husband returning home from a long business trip.

"Then I saw a single man, fairly young, sitting nervously in a seat across the gate holding a huge white teddy bear. I imagined he probably was divorced recently, and about to be reunited with his young child."

That one struck Rick's heart. He identified with the awful feeling of being separated from his kids.

"I became involved with the lives of the people around me. I was still just a bystander, but I began to have compassion for what was happening in their lives.

"As the plane came in and people started to come through the gate, I watched the ones I had taken a personal interest in. One of the first ones off the plane was an older Japanese couple. The Japanese father ran to hug his parents, and then he proudly introduced them to that little boy I had been so irritated with.

"Then I noticed the young girl with the rose. She was nervously looking among the crowds of people coming through, standing on her tiptoes at times to get a better look, but the man she was looking for hadn't come out. I felt for her; maybe he missed the flight, or something else might have happened. The stream of people trickled down to just a few, and I found myself praying for her, that she wouldn't be disappointed. Then a tall young marine came walking out of the jetway carrying a bouquet of flowers. The girl's face brightened into the biggest smile as she ran and threw herself into his arms."

Terry had to pause, his voice cracking with emotion. "Then the single father with the huge white teddy bear was standing there alone. It took a few more moments for the flight attendant to come up through the walkway, holding the hand of a beautiful blonde-haired girl, about six years old. She ran into the waiting arms of her father, crying, "Daddy, Daddy," as he dropped the teddy bear aside, spinning her around in his own bear hug."

Rick's hand reached up and wiped a tear from his eye.

"That day changed my whole way of thinking about all this 'one anothering.' I felt the Lord speaking to me right there in the airport. This was how Jesus loved, caring about individuals and their lives. When I thought of John 3:16, that God so loved the world, I had this misconception that God loves the whole world; therefore, he loves me. But I had it backward. You see, God loves me. He loves all of us as individuals; and then, when you add it all up, he loves the whole world. He loves you and me, one at a time. He loves Gary, Warren, Penny, Janet, Bill, Rick."

Terry looked right at Rick when he said his name. As he did, the Holy Spirit penetrated right into his heart.

Terry continued, "I'm not called to 'one another' everybody. I'm called to love the person God has placed before me. I'm called to love—one at a time. I'm called to serve—one at a time. I'm called to bear someone's burden—one at a time. You get the picture? When this finally sank in, I felt so free. The burden that I had been under lifted. I'm still learning what this all means in my daily walk, but I now look ahead with great expectation to see who God places in front of me to 'one another.' Let's pray."

Rick bowed his head as Terry ended his teaching time in prayer. The words touched Rick. He marveled at how God could be leading him in his search through the Scriptures, and then tonight respond to so many of his questions through this man. He felt so thankful that God was showing him a path he hadn't seen before. This journey was definitely an exciting one.

In the quiet moment, Rick opened up his heart toward the Lord. *Jesus,* he prayed silently, *I'm realizing that a walk with you is so much more than doing the church stuff. Forgive me for being content with just going through the motions. I want to have a living, intimate relationship with you. Tonight, Lord, I want to rededicate my life to you. Lord, please help me to understand the work of your Holy Spirit that I've been hearing so much about tonight. I want to hear your voice, follow your will.*

The meeting ended a little before nine, but then refreshments appeared and there were many who stayed and talked, breaking into smaller groups. A silver-haired man approached Gary and

Rick. "Gary, is this the friend you've been telling me about?" he asked.

Rick shook the man's outstretched hand as Gary spoke up, "You bet. Rick, I want you to meet Rob Stevenson. He started Christians in Film and Television or C.I.F.T. as we sometimes call it."

Rick was surprised. He had assumed that the head man wasn't at the meeting because he was sure if he had been, his leadership would have been evident. "It's nice to meet you, Rob. This is quite a group you've got going here."

"Thank you, but as you can see, I don't make it happen. I've found through the years that if you get Christians together and just let them love Jesus, he'll get the work done."

"How many fellowship groups do you have like this?" Rick asked.

Rob thought for a moment. "We have fifteen groups that meet on different nights. We also have some smaller groups that meet in the mornings for devotional time before work. Then we have our combined meeting once a month. That's coming up Sunday night; I hope you can make it."

"I'd love to."

Gary turned to Rob. "I've been sharing with Rick some of the 'one anothering' principles, and what gifts really mean in the church. It's amazing how God orchestrated tonight's meeting to fit into that. But there are some questions Rick has that would be right up your alley. I thought it would be good to get you two together sometime and have a little chat."

Rob turned to Rick, "Do you have any time this weekend?"

"Saturday morning would be good for me, if you're available. Maybe we could meet for breakfast before I pick up my kids for the weekend."

"I'd like that. Gary, you want to join us?"

"If I'm free. Let me check with Jill; I'm not sure what we have planned this weekend."

Rick spent the rest of the night getting to know others in his industry who shared his faith. He realized he hadn't met very many Christians at the workplace, but then again, that wasn't something the old Rick would have been on the lookout for. The new Rick would be a different story.

11:39 P.M., SANTA BARBARA

Vanessa looked at the clock beside her bed in the hotel room. She hadn't realized how late it was. After leaving her apartment, she'd driven north on the Pacific Coast Highway, not having a clue where she was running to. She just knew she had to get out of there.

At Santa Barbara she decided to stop and find a place to stay for the night. She had pulled off and found a Motel 6 with a vacancy. She used some of the money she had taken from Rudy to pay for a couple of night's rent in advance.

Her body, still sore from the abusive hands of Rudy, cried out for some chemical that would make her feel better. Her mind wanted relief from the depressing reality she was now living. Even her stomach, so nauseated since that morning Rudy lay beside her in her apartment, cried out for nourishment. Life couldn't get any worse than this.

She finally summoned the resolve to get up and walk into the bathroom. When she looked in the mirror, she didn't recognize the reflection staring back at her. Her eyes were bloodshot, lost in dark circles. Her hair was knotted and looked like it hadn't been brushed in days. Out of frustration, instead of calmly looking through her purse for a brush and makeup, she dumped the contents onto the countertop.

She reached for the brush but noticed the card she'd received from the Crisis Pregnancy Center lying on top of it. The image of the woman who had been so nice to her flashed through her mind. *What was her name?* Vanessa turned the card over and saw the home phone number with the name Jill written over the top. She had seemed to really care about Vanessa. But how could she? If the past few years had taught Vanessa anything, it was that you don't trust anyone. Look out for number one, and that's it.

She dropped the card back into the pile and grabbed the brush instead, working at the tangles in her hair. Still, she couldn't stay on the run forever. Her choices came down to running until the money ran out, going back to Flint, or trusting somebody—this woman Jill—one last time. If she could get some food in her and make it through one more night, maybe she'd go back to that center in Van Nuys tomorrow and see what kind of help Jill could offer her.

CHAPTER 18

Stephanie arrived at the office a few minutes before nine in the morning. Bill hadn't arrived yet, so it would give her a few minutes to review the cases they were working on. Talking with Vice the night before had been rather enlightening. They had an extensive file on Gabriel Flint but had not been able to put enough evidence together that would lead to a conviction. His latest adventure, Starfield Enterprises, was his first legitimate business attempt, and it had paid off well with the success of "The John Harold Show."

Stephanie was sure Bill was on to something. The key to Wade's death would probably be found somewhere near Flint.

Bill walked up behind Stephanie, the usual morning doughnut in hand.

"Anything new?" he asked.

"Not yet," she said, spinning her chair toward him. "I was just trying to come up with a way to get a look at those Lasko tapes."

"I don't think our producer is going to exactly hand over those tapes, do you?" Bill asked.

"No, I don't. If there's something on those tapes and they haven't already been destroyed, calling up and asking for copies will certainly get that result. We'd better get a search warrant and get over there ourselves."

"I agree with you, Steph, but this is still pretty flimsy stuff for a search warrant. I'm not sure a judge is going to give us one. Besides, I doubt those tapes are still around."

"You may be right, but we've got to pursue it."

"Agreed," Bill said, as he noticed their captain approaching from behind Stephanie.

"Good morning you two. How's the Perkins investigation coming?" the captain asked as he stopped by their desks.

Stephanie realized they'd been so engrossed with Bennett's case, they hadn't even thought about the councilman's murder. "We still haven't found any leads. By all appearances, it could be just a simple street mugging. He was in a bad part of town at the wrong time."

"Then why isn't it closed?" he asked, an edge rising in his voice.

"We've just got a few leads to finish up on, Captain," Bill stepped in to save his partner.

"All right, but we need to nail this one soon. The Mayor is hounding me. At least the press hasn't been all over us about the Bennett suicide. You have closed that one, haven't you?"

Stephanie swallowed hard, "Not yet."

"What am I paying you two for?" the captain looked from Stephanie to Bill. "What's holding you up on this one?"

"We found out the executive producer is Gabriel Flint," Bill answered. "He's tied into prostitution, pornography—Vice has a file on him a mile long."

The captain thought for a second. "Now, why would the executive producer of a television show want to kill off his own director? Do you have a motive?"

"Not yet, but we have enough unanswered questions to keep looking," Stephanie said. "There's—"

"No, don't tell me," he said, shaking his head and interrupting. "The press thinks it's suicide; I want to be in the same boat." He turned and walked away.

"At least he's giving us some space," Bill said.

"Maybe, but I get the feeling he wants this case closed—now," Stephanie said. "I'm going to try and find a judge who might give us the papers to go after the tapes."

"You know, I think we'd better warn Cassie. If Flint's behind this in any way, she could be sticking her neck out where it doesn't belong."

Bill was right. Stephanie picked up her phone and dialed the production office.

"Josh Abrams's office. This is Cassie speaking. Can I help you?"

"Hi, Cassie. This is Detective Phillips. Can you talk?"

Cassie looked around to see if anyone was close to her desk. "All's clear for now. Josh isn't in yet; I'm pretty much alone."

"Good. I wanted to warn you, it could be too dangerous for you to be looking through office files out there."

"What changed your mind?" Cassie inquired.

"I can't go into any details yet, we just want you to be careful."

Cassie cupped her hand around the phone and leaned lower near her desk, "I couldn't find out anything on the Lasko interview anyway. It's as if someone's pulled any reference to it out of the files.

When I asked Josh about it, he said the segment was killed and not to worry about it."

"Cassie, that's why I'm calling. I want you to stop. No more questions. It's too dangerous for you. Just go about work as usual, and if anything comes up, certainly let us know. But do not, I repeat, do not go looking for anything. Do you understand?"

"Yeah, I do. But there's one more thing I need to tell you. I went over to Mrs. Bennett's house last night. She asked for help in looking into Wade's computer for any clues you might have missed."

One of the production assistants walked by Cassie's desk. "OK, Jim, that should work out fine with the schedule we've prepared for next week," Cassie continued talking without missing a beat, acting as if she was talking to Jim Schu, the executive in charge of production.

Stephanie was impressed as she listened to Cassie cover their conversation, "Good girl, I understand. Just pick up where you left off when you're alone."

When the assistant had turned the corner out of listening range, Cassie continued, "Sorry about that, she's gone now. Maybe you already know this, but we found out that the suicide note left on the computer was created at 10:35 the night before."

Stephanie was shocked. How could Ray have missed that? "Are you sure?"

"Definitely. There's a way to look at each file that gives you the date and time it was last modified. If Wade had created it the day he was killed, it would have given that information. Also, Becky swears that she and Wade were already in bed at that time. There was no way he could have been working on the computer."

"Who's got the computer now?"

"I do. It's right here at the office with me."

"Don't let anybody touch it, Cassie. I need it for evidence again. I'm going to check with my lab and see if they can confirm what you found. They copied everything onto a disk here. But remember what I told you. Things are getting too dangerous for you to play undercover detective."

Stephanie hung up and immediately called Ray.

"I don't know what to say. I'm sorry I missed it. Wednesday was very hectic. I remember I was going to check out that very thing when the earthquake hit us. Then Daryl found the skin tissue under the gun's chamber and it totally slipped my mind to go back and check the computer. I'll jump right on it. If what she says is true, I'll have the same information on my disk here. I'll get back to you."

This could be just the ticket Stephanie needed to get that search warrant.

10:45 a.m., NATIONAL STUDIOS

The arches over the gate decorated with big block letters shadowed Rick's car as he pulled up to the guard booth of National Studios. Although he had been on this lot several times over the years as a stage manager, this was the first time he was driving on as a potential director. *God, let your will be done,* he prayed to himself.

"Can I help you, sir?" the guard asked through Rick's window.

"I'm Rick Treadway. I have an appointment with Josh Abrams of 'The John Harold Show.'"

The guard looked over his clipboard for a brief moment. "Oh yes, here you are. Let's see . . . Charlie Chaplan Building, first floor. Do you need directions?"

Cassie had given Rick the directions the day before. "No, thanks, I know where it is."

"OK, sir," the guard responded with a smile as he handed Rick a security pass to stick to his interior windshield. "Just follow the yellow line into visitor parking. Have a nice day."

Rick drove through the huge gate, found a parking place, and made his way over to the production office. He was surprised he wasn't nervous. His interviews in the past had been pretty nerve-racking, especially in cases like this where he badly wanted the job.

As he neared the office building, he noticed Tina Livingston walking out, heading in the opposite direction. He had worked with her a couple of times in the past. *She must be up for the job as well,* Rick thought.

He paused by a hallway mirror to make sure his appearance was just right. He wore his dark blue sport coat over a long-sleeved white shirt, complemented with a pair of tan slacks and dress shoes, a step up from his usual casual wardrobe.

Walking through the production office, the first thing Rick noticed was the lovely young woman behind the desk in front of Josh's office. He hoped this was Cassie, the one he'd talked to on the phone, the one with the great voice. She had medium-length brown hair, a slim build, and when she looked up to greet him, Rick couldn't help but notice her beautiful hazel eyes.

"I'm glad you're doing better, Becky," she said into the phone as Rick approached. "I just wanted to check on you. I haven't had a chance to give it back to . . . them," she finally got out.

Cassie had been jumpy all day, with Wade's computer lying at her feet. She hoped Becky understood what she was talking about.

"But when I do, I'll call you right away. OK? Great. Talk to you later then. Bye-bye."

Cassie looked up as she hung up, seeing Rick for the first time. She was expecting him but had no idea how young—and she had to admit—how attractive he was. It took a moment to find her voice.

"You must be Rick Treadway."

"That's right; I'm here to see Josh Abrams."

Cassie stood up and extended her hand, "I'm Cassie Petterson, Mr. Abrams's assistant."

Rick smiled. "It's a pleasure to meet you. Your directions were perfect."

"I'm glad you didn't have any trouble finding us. Mr. Abrams is in the conference room with John Harold and our executive producer, Gabriel Flint. Let me tell them you're here."

She brushed by Rick and went to the door next to Josh's office. Rick followed her with his eyes, thinking it would be nice if his office would be nearby if he got the job. She knocked on the door once, then entered, leaving Rick alone by her desk.

He took a deep breath, trying to calm himself.

Cassie reappeared from behind the door and motioned for Rick to come in. He entered the room. Behind a large table, the three figures were rising to their feet.

"Rick, it's good to see you again." Josh met him first, shaking his hand.

"It's been a long time, Josh. You look like you did the day we left UCLA," Rick laughed.

"Flattery will get you nowhere, but thanks. Rick, this is John Harold." The two shook hands.

"I've been a big fan, Mr. Harold. Congratulations on the great success of your show."

"Thank you, but there'll be none of that. Call me John, please," Harold responded.

"And this is Gabriel Flint, our executive producer," Josh finished the introductions.

"Nice to meet you, Mr. Flint," Rick said, shaking the large hand before him. Rick hadn't heard of Flint before, but his presence was powerful within the room. For some reason, the image of Jabba the Hutt came to mind. Rick had to control his smile.

"Please, Gabriel will be fine."

"OK, Gabriel it is."

Josh continued, "Have a seat, Rick. Let's get started."

Josh briefed Rick on the show and what they wanted from their new director. When he was finished, it was Rick's chance to respond. He hoped his voice wouldn't crack as he plunged ahead with his dialogue. He began speaking, not really sure what to say, but the words started to flow, nearly without any thought on his part.

"I appreciate what you three have developed here. Your show has achieved wonderful success in such a short time, and I congratulate you all. I'm sure it's been quite a shock losing your director in midstream, and it is bound to bring a lot of anxiety to next week's production, especially for you, John," Rick looked at Harold. "You need to be able to walk out under the lights knowing your director will be right with you."

Rick turned his attention toward Josh. "Josh, I know you have a tight schedule getting the show turned around for the satellite window, and you don't want to have to worry about any editing because your director missed a shot."

Josh nodded his agreement.

"And Mr. Flint, you probably just want the production to continue to run smoothly, making you a lot of money—as long as the director is someone who'll make both of these gentleman happy."

Flint just stared back at Rick, no change of expression.

Rick paused to collect himself. "I think I'm the one who can bring all of that to you. As you can see from my résumé, I've been around the business for a long time. I've worked with some of the best directors and some of the worst, and from both, I've learned a lot. I even had the privilege to work with Wade a couple of times, so I am familiar with his style and his great attention to detail. I've had experience with talk, coming from 'Cathy and Friends.' I can handle the musical aspect of the show, having done several concert specials for cable, as well as a couple of music videos that you'll see on my reel." Rick handed over the two video cassettes he'd brought.

"Also, I'm intrigued by the social commentary your show includes, and I think my single camera experience out in the field can be of help there as well."

Rick looked from face to face to try to get a read on how he was doing. John was all ears, Josh seemed mildly entertained, but he couldn't read Flint at all.

"I don't know what else to tell you at this point. You've seen my résumé and you know what I've done. Are there any questions you'd like to ask?"

John leaned forward, "Is your schedule such that you can join us immediately?"

Now how do I make this sound like I'm not unemployed? Rick thought. "As a matter of fact, I just finished up my last project earlier this week and haven't committed to anything else in front of me yet."

"Have you done much live-to-tape, Rick?" Josh asked.

"I've directed a few live events, and *Cathy and Friends* was live-to-tape like your show is. I'm sure I can handle the pressure."

After a few more questions, the discussion turned toward what a production day on "The John Harold Show" was like. The mood shifted. They began asking if Rick saw any ways of improving their current schedule or format. Flint remained quiet in his chair throughout the whole ordeal. Rick felt like he could gain a good working relationship with John and Josh, but hoped Flint kept his distance from the production. Something about him made Rick feel uneasy.

Finally, the meeting came to a close.

"We appreciate you coming down today, Rick," Josh said as he stood up with the other men.

"It was my pleasure."

"Give us some time to go over everything. We'll have to make a decision quickly, so let Cassie know where you're going to be, and we'll get back to you."

"I certainly will, and thank you all for your time."

Rick made his way out of the room and headed back over to Cassie's desk.

"How did it go?" she asked brightly as he walked up to her.

"You never know about these things, but I feel pretty good. They want me to make sure that you have a way to reach me when I leave."

"Well, that's a good sign," she smiled. "Do you have a number you can give me?"

"I'm heading back home; you still have that number?"

"Yes I do. I'll make sure to call as soon as I know something."

"Thanks, Cassie, I appreciate it." He turned to head out of the office.

She called to him, "And Rick . . ."

He turned back to her.

"Good luck."

Rick smiled back, "Thanks." He felt like a schoolboy with his first crush as he walked out the door trying to hold in his mind the image of Cassie's smile.

Josh spoke up first after Rick left the room. "Well? Any of the three stand out to you two?"

"I like Treadway," John said right away. "I think his background is good, and I like the way he handled himself in here."

Josh was afraid of that. Rick had put on a good presentation and would probably make an excellent director for the show. But Josh wanted to hire one of the three for just a couple of weeks until he could get Carl Drake on board, someone he felt was more Wade's caliber of director. Because of their past relationship, he didn't want Rick to get the job, just to be fired a few weeks later.

"You didn't like either of the other two?" Josh inquired.

"Actually, I did," John responded, thinking carefully how he would manipulate the situation. "I liked both, and I'd place Livingston above Straton, even though she's a woman. I was impressed with her. But I still feel the show would be much better with Treadway. I didn't know he was coming in today, but the other night I caught a show he directed, and I liked his style very much."

Flint cleared his throat, and the two looked over at him. "Do you have a preference, Josh?"

"Well, of the three, I actually liked Livingston. I've known Tina for a long time and I know she'd do a fine job. I think Treadway comes in with some good shows under his belt and would probably be OK as well. But if I had my choice, I'd wait for Carl Drake. I know he won't be available to us immediately, but our choice today could be hired on a four-week contract, then we could bring in Carl."

John didn't like that plan. He knew Carl to be another director with an attitude and would probably be as hard to control as Wade had been. He looked at Flint. "What about you, Gabe? Which way do you lean?"

"Personally, I don't care that much. Treadway was right when he said I just want things to run smoothly and get someone that you two are happy with. When he made that statement, I figured we had somebody with at least the presence of mind to analyze a situation and make it work. That sounds like a good director to me. But maybe there's some merit to what Josh wants. If in a month we could have a top-notch director, maybe we should keep our options open; hire one of these now on a short-term basis then can 'em when Carl's available."

After a brief silence, Josh spoke up, "Then I guess it comes down to Treadway or Livingston for now. How do we make the final decision?"

John didn't like the way things were going. He decided he couldn't fight for Rick on the long-term basis today; he needed to just get him in the door. Then he'd have to work on making the position permanent if he liked him as much as he thought he would.

"I could go along with the short-term thing; that gives us an out if things aren't turning out the way we hope. But if we're just going for a couple of weeks here, I'm not sure I want to change the dynamics that much with a female director," he said.

He could tell Josh wasn't sure what he was getting at by the expression on his face. Flint on the other hand was right with him. John continued, selling more toward Josh, "It's just that Wade had such a dominant presence in the booth, and from what I gather, so would Carl. Do we really want to change the dynamics that much by having a woman take over for such a short time?"

Josh was beginning to understand John's argument, and really had no defense for it. Women were making great strides in

Hollywood, and Tina could definitely handle the directing of their show, but if she was only temporary, would it really be worth the change? He didn't want to put Rick in the position of being the short-term replacement, but the four weeks of shows would eventually look good on his résumé when the industry forgot that he was so quickly replaced. He decided to go along with John.

"I see your point, and perhaps you're right," Josh said. "If we keep our option opened for Carl, I think we can live with Treadway. Agreed?"

John nodded.

"That's fine with me if you two feel comfortable with it," Flint said. "You think he'll be up to speed by Monday?"

"We'll get him back here this afternoon to get familiar with everything, while the lawyers work out a deal." Flint and John both nodded. "Great. Then it's settled. We'll call his agency and make a four-week deal."

"One more thing," Flint interrupted. "I want to make sure you have a standby show ready Monday night, just in case."

"We'll have it ready to go," Josh replied.

CHAPTER 19

He sat outside a little café on Santa Monica Boulevard, finishing a cup of coffee. Nicknamed "Fast Eddie," he'd do anything for some cash, like the fifty bucks he'd just made selling a pouch of marijuana to some seventh-grade kids.

His mind floated as he glanced at the traffic on the street before him and thought about the next job he could pull off. Then he saw it drive by—the red Corvette Rudy had mentioned. It had to be the one, judging from the babe he saw driving it. He didn't remember the license plate, but he was sure that was the car. It was heading west on Santa Monica. He remembered there was a quick grand in it for him if he was the first one to let Rudy know where the girl was.

He threw himself over the little fence enclosing the outdoor tables and raced for his car. His beat-up Chrysler was no match for the sleek Corvette cruising down the street ahead of him, but Eddie hoped he could catch up to her without being noticed, then he'd call Rudy. He started the car and jerked it into gear, jumping out onto Santa Monica Boulevard while several cars blared their horns at him and slammed on their brakes. He made it into the westbound lanes and floored the accelerator, looking for the Corvette.

Vanessa continued driving until she came to the Crisis Pregnancy Center. If she remembered correctly, the woman who helped her said she worked on Fridays. Vanessa hoped so; she didn't want to speak to anyone else. She pulled the Corvette into a quick U-turn and parked along the street in front of the center. She sat for a minute in the car, making sure she was doing the right thing. Her mind had gone over all the questions during her drive down from Ventura, but she couldn't come up with any answers. She hoped Jill had some.

Fast Eddie nearly missed her, he was driving so fast. His eye caught a blur of the bright red car as he passed by. He slowed quickly, pulled over to the side of the road and found a space about a hundred feet up from Vanessa's car. He looked through his rearview toward where the Corvette was parked.

Vanessa got out of her car, put some change into the meter, and headed into the building.

Eddie saw her go through the doors, so he figured he had a little time. He got out of his car, not bothering with the meter, and ran up the street to see what kind of a place she'd gone into. He couldn't believe what he was seeing as he read the sign above the door. He kept walking to the corner, where he found a pay phone at a gas station and called the cell number he'd written down for Rudy.

"Rudy here."

"I've got the girl. I spotted the red Corvette."

"Hold on. Who is this?" Rudy blurted. He wanted that girl.

"Eddie, man, who do you think it is?"

"Where is she?"

"I'm at a gas station on the corner of Santa Monica . . . ," Eddie looked over at the street sign across from the phone booth, "and Lincoln."

"Great! Keep your eyes on her; I'm about ten minutes away," Rudy lied. He was on Sunset cruising through Hollywood looking for her. He darted in and out of traffic, looking to turn on Highland and head down to the Santa Monica Freeway. "What's she up to?"

"I saw her go into an office, some pregnancy place. I guess she needs an abortion," Eddie laughed.

"Shut up! Just keep your eyes on her, and if she leaves before I get there, follow her and call me." Rudy hung up and pushed his BMW even harder. He wanted to get there before she finished up whatever business she was up to. *A pregnancy center? She must have found out she was pregnant and found a place to take care of it. Maybe Flint would understand and let her come back,* he thought as he sped past another intersection.

Vanessa was relieved to see Jill sitting behind the counter and no one else in the waiting room. Jill looked up and smiled as she approached the desk.

"Nice to see you again. It's Rachel, isn't it?"

Vanessa smiled back, unsure of herself, "Yeah, Rachel. I almost called you last night, but I decided to come down today instead."

"How are you feeling? Everything OK?"

"I'm still not feeling great, and I'm in a lot of trouble." Vanessa couldn't hold what she'd been storing up any longer. The emotion came out in waves of tears.

Jill got up, gently leading Vanessa to one of the back rooms. She asked Grace, another volunteer at the center, to go up front and take over the phones for her.

It was hard for Vanessa to open up. Although she'd decided to come to this woman for help, it was too difficult to tell her the truth. She told Jill only what she thought was enough to solicit her help—that she had left the person she was living with and the pregnancy was unexpected. She was honest, though, about the baby being the only thing that mattered to her now.

Jill knew that she wasn't hearing all of the facts, but it didn't matter. This woman needed a friend. Jill prayed as she listened, asking for guidance.

Go. The word came to her mind. She paused for a second, praying that God's direction would be more clear. Then the word popped up in her mind again, *Go.*

Where Lord? Jill thought, not fully comprehending what she was hearing. *Go home!* she felt the Lord saying now, with a sudden urgency.

Vanessa was in midsentence as Jill interrupted her. "Rachel, excuse me. This may sound a little strange, but we need to leave."

Vanessa stopped and looked at Jill, confusion in her eyes.

Jill continued. "I'm going to take you home with me. Normally I wouldn't offer this, we're instructed not to, actually, but I really feel the Lord wants me to offer our home for awhile, until you can figure things out."

Vanessa wasn't sure what to do. "I can't impose on you . . ."

"Nonsense. I'd like my husband to hear what you're going through. Maybe together we can figure out a way to help you. But right now we need to leave. I'll explain everything when we get to my house."

Vanessa thought it over for a second. Having nowhere else to turn, she agreed.

"We don't live too far from here. Why don't you follow me in your car, OK?"

Jill let Grace know she was heading home with Vanessa, then described her car to Vanessa and told her she'd be coming around front from the side street behind the center. Vanessa was to pull in behind her and follow her.

Fast Eddie saw Vanessa exit the building. He'd been sitting on the hood of his car, waiting for Rudy to drive up. He thought about running down the street to get to the phone, but she was already stepping into the car. He'd have to follow her and hook up with Rudy later. What he would have given for a cellular phone. Eddie jumped into his car, ready to trail the Corvette.

Jill pulled out from the side street in her Grand Prix, drove past Vanessa's Corvette, and continued east on Santa Monica Boulevard. Vanessa pulled in right behind her. Two cars coming from the opposite direction forced Eddie to wait a moment before pulling out from his parking space. The moment the second car passed him, Eddie spun his old Chrysler into a U-turn, trying to catch up with Vanessa. He spotted her up ahead, going through the intersection. He was still a good two hundred feet away from it when the light turned yellow. He couldn't afford to wait. He pushed his foot to the floor and barreled toward the intersection at top speed. Two cars were already moving into it by the time his Chrysler got there.

He swerved to his right and missed a Ford pickup coming from the left, but as he did, his car was in jeopardy from a Honda approaching from the other side. He tried to turn back toward the left, but the car was moving too fast. The Chrysler spun counter-clockwise, causing the pickup to hit the rear driver's side at almost the same instant the Honda hit the front passenger's side. The impact nearly tore the Chrysler in half, sending Eddie's head into the driver's side window, shattering the glass and knocking him unconscious.

A quarter mile up Santa Monica Boulevard, Vanessa cruised along, following Jill, unaware of the wreckage left behind them.

Rudy arrived at the intersection a couple of minutes later, looking for Vanessa's car. He drove through slowly, noticing for the first time Eddie's Chrysler that was smashed in the middle. Rudy swore to himself. He must have lost Vanessa.

Rudy continued down Santa Monica a few hundred feet before pulling over. He looked up the street to see if any police cars were in view yet. Seeing none, he made his way to the intersection and walked up to Eddie's car.

"Excuse me, I'm a doctor. Let me have a look at him," Rudy said to a man attempting to help through the window.

The man stepped back, allowing Rudy access. "He's unconscious. I didn't think we should move him."

"You were absolutely right. Why don't you see if anyone else is hurt." Rudy said, trying to get rid of the man. He looked at Fast Eddie. His bloodied head was smashed against the door. He wasn't moving. Rudy could hear the sound of a siren from off in the distance. He didn't have much time.

"Eddie, it's me, Rudy. Eddie," Rudy tried to wake him. He reached in and slapped Eddie on his right cheek. He began to moan.

"What happened? Where's Vanessa?"

Eddie moved his head and winced in pain. He raised his hand to feel the left side of his head. When it came back covered in blood, Eddie's eyes widened. He was about to scream.

Rudy slapped him again, regaining his attention. "An ambulance is on the way. Now get ahold of yourself and tell me what happened before they get here."

"I waited for you . . . like you said," Eddie struggled to get the words out. "She left, I think she was following . . . someone. I tried to . . . get through the red light . . ." The sirens were nearly at the intersection. Eddie suddenly looked up at Rudy with fear in his eyes. "The trunk . . . there's drugs . . . help me get them . . . out."

"Don't worry, I'll take care of them for you," Rudy lied, "but tell me where was Vanessa going?"

"Don't know . . . followin—" Eddie's head dropped; he had passed out again.

Rudy calmly walked back toward his car, leaving Eddie at the mercy of the police. He looked over the stores along the street. He noticed a sign over one of them, "The Crisis Pregnancy Center." That must be the place Vanessa had entered. He checked his hands, making sure there was no blood on them. Confident that he looked clean, he walked up to the front of the center.

An older woman sat behind a desk in the front room. Otherwise the place was empty.

"That sounded like quite an accident. Is anyone hurt?" the woman asked as Rudy came in.

"I don't think so. It's just one of those fender benders," he said.

"That's good to hear. My name is Grace. Now how can I be of help to you?" she asked.

"I was supposed to meet my wife here; she had an appointment. Perhaps you could tell me where she's gone. She drives a red Corvette and has long blond hair, real pretty."

Grace sensed the Lord warning her to be cautious. The man didn't have a wedding ring on, and she knew the girl who had left with Jill didn't appear like she would have had her husband meet her here.

"I'm sorry, sir. I'm not aware of anyone who's been here that meets that description."

"Are you the only one here?"

"No, our director is in the back and another of our counselors just left."

"What's the name of the counselor who left? Maybe my wife's appointment was with her."

She realized that she'd already said too much. "I'm sorry, sir, I can't give you her name; it's against our policy. We guarantee confidentiality, you understand. If you'd care to leave me your name and number, I'll have her contact you when she returns . . . if she had any contact with your wife."

Rudy thought it over for a second. He could easily overpower this old woman and make her talk, probably do the same with whoever the director was. But he knew Flint didn't want any more loose ends than they already had.

Grace could see the man considering his options. She prayed for God's protection as she waited for his next move.

Rudy was frustrated. He had to get to Vanessa. His temper was about to overshadow his rational mind, lashing out at who was in front of him, forcing the information out of her.

Grace noticed him tensing up, his hand forming into a fist.

"Do you have a piece of paper and a pencil?" Rudy finally asked. Greatly relieved, Grace handed them to him. Rudy bent over and wrote down his cell number. "I'm really worried about her. If you could have that other lady give me a call as soon as she comes back, I'd really appreciate it."

"I'll be certain to give her the message."

Rudy walked outside again, contemplating his next move. He decided to enlist some help. He called one of the men on Flint's payroll to come over and stake out the center. He wanted to know when that other worker returned. She was the one he needed to talk to and force into telling him where Vanessa was.

He looked up the street and saw Eddie being lifted into an ambulance as a police officer walked around the back of his car and opened the trunk. *You're on your own now, kiddo,* Rudy said to himself as he sat in his car waiting for the guy he'd called to show up.

12:35 P.M., STUDIO CITY

Two messages were waiting on Rick's machine when he got home.

"Rick, this is Cassie at 'The John Harold Show.'" He dropped his keys and turned up the volume. "Congratulations, they want you to take over the show. I know you're probably not home yet, but when you get back, call the office. We want you to come back in and get familiar with everything before doing your first show for us on Monday." ... *BEEEP*

"Thank you, Lord," he breathed. It surprised him, but the words made him smile. The second message played: "Rick, it's Jacob

Weinberg. We did it! I just got the call. 'The John Harold Show' wants you as the new director. I'm sure you'll be excited. Give me a call as soon as you can. They want to ink out a deal fast." . . . *BEEEP*

Rick laughed. So Jacob wanted to take credit for what God had put together—that was typical. He decided to call Jacob first, then he'd call Cassie and head back over to the office. Along with the excitement of the new job, he had to admit he anticipated being able to work alongside Cassie.

"Congratulations, Rick. I think it's the perfect show for you. By the way, how come you didn't tell me about the interview?" Jacob said to Rick once he got him on the phone.

"I tried to call the office last night, but it was late when I found out about it, and you were already out."

"Well, I guess you impressed them. The call just came in from the lawyer over at National. Any specifics you want me to get into the contract?"

"Not really. You know I need the work so don't make anything a deal breaker."

"There is one thing that their lawyer mentioned off the top that wasn't standard."

"Oh? What's that?"

Jacob hesitated. He didn't know how much to tell Rick. During the conversations he'd had with Cassie, Jacob knew they wanted to keep Carl Drake in the background as a replacement if things didn't work out with their new director.

"It seems instead of the normal thirteen-week commitment, they only want to guarantee you the first four weeks."

When working for large studios, producers, writers, and directors were all under contracts that called for their commitment to be exclusive for anywhere from three to seven years. On the other hand, the studio would only guarantee their salary in thirteen-week increments. If they were fired or if the show was canceled, they would get paid only for whatever was left in that particular cycle. Lately, the trend was to make initial agreements even shorter than that. Rick had heard of other directors being offered shorter guarantees in the early stages of their contracts, so this didn't shock him greatly.

"Well, I don't have a problem with the first one being only four weeks," he said, "as long as once I've proved myself, we get to the standard thirteen-week cycles."

"I would imagine that's all this is; they want to give you a trial period before being committed to you. I'll get to work on the details with Walter over at National. By the way, there was one more thing. Because time is so short, they want you to get to work right away, even though we haven't agreed on a deal yet. Do you have any problem with that?"

"No, I think I'll be better off to get into the office this afternoon."

"Actually, I think it works to our advantage. While you're in there getting prepared, I can't imagine they'll back out on the deal over some minor point. They'll need you."

"Well, get the best deal you can, but don't play hardball. I want this job," Rick said. He knew how negotiations could be.

"I understand, Rick. Don't you worry," Jacob said, then disconnected the call.

Rick kept the phone in his hand and dialed Josh's number. It was good to hear Cassie's voice again.

"Hi, Cassie, this is Rick."

"Hi, Rick. Congratulations! Hold on, I'm sure Josh wants to talk to you."

After a moment, Josh came on and Rick agreed to head back over to the office right away. Before he left, he looked up Gary's office number and dialed. Gary answered the phone himself.

"Gary, it's Rick. I've got some great news."

"Let me guess: they want you to do the Harold Show, right?"

"How'd you know?"

Gary laughed. "What do you think I've been praying about all morning. You asked me to, remember? You must have knocked their socks off in the interview."

"I just tried to be myself. At one point, I really felt like God took over and I was saying all the right things. It must have been your prayers, Gary. Thanks."

"Don't thank me, thank the Lord. I'm sure a lot of the other people from last night were praying as well. Congratulations."

"Thanks, Gary. I just wanted to let you know. I've got to run over to the office and get things organized for Monday. I'll give you a call over the weekend."

"Sounds good. I'm still trying to be able to meet with you and Rob for breakfast tomorrow. I'll give you a call later tonight and let you know if I can."

The two hung up, then Rick gathered his stuff and headed for the car. It sure felt good to have someone like Gary praying for him, and he'd forgotten that others in the group would be praying as well. "Thank you, God, for your church," he said out loud.

12:50 P.M., WESTWOOD

It had taken Jill and Vanessa fifteen minutes to make their way to Jill's house in Westwood. Jill had taken Santa Monica Boulevard to Bundy before turning North and crossing over to Wilshire. That took them right by Vanessa's high-rise apartment. Memories flooded her, all of them bad. Memories of sexual abuse and drug parties invaded her mind. She hoped she could put that life behind her now.

"When was the last time you talked with your mother?" Jill asked her as they sat at the kitchen table.

"It's been a long time, not since I was sixteen and left the house." Vanessa decided she could open up about part of her past; she'd just protect the facts about her life now. She described how she'd been abused by her stepfather and how her alcoholic mother didn't seem to love her. It was a sad, but unfortunately too common, story. Jill felt a wave of compassion for her as they talked. The door opened, and Gary walked in. Jill had called him at his office after they'd made it home. She knew they needed to decide together what they could do for her.

"Rachel, this is my husband, Gary," Jill said.

"It's nice to meet you, Rachel." Gary extended his hand.

Vanessa felt a rush of panic. She was beginning to trust Jill, but she didn't feel ready to trust a man. Then again, she didn't have many other options right now. She finally took the hand, but kept her eyes lowered. "I hope I'm not too much of a bother to you, and . . . I'm sorry . . . I wasn't truthful. My name's actually Vanessa." She glanced over at Jill to see how she would react. "Jill's been so helpful."

Jill just smiled, conveying a message that she understood.

"I'm here to help, too, Vanessa. Why don't—" Gary was interrupted by the phone ringing. Jill walked over and picked up it up.

"Hello"

"Jill, it's Grace at the center. I wanted to make sure you were all right."

"Yeah, we're fine. Why do you ask?"

"Well, just after you left, there was a big accident on the corner. I wanted to make sure you were OK."

"No, we're fine. We didn't see anything when we left. Thank God, we must have just missed it."

"There was something else that happened after you left," Grace continued. "A strange man came in and asked about the girl you left with."

Jill's eyes grew wide and she motioned to Gary. "Hold on a minute, Grace, let me get Gary on the phone with us." Gary went into the family room to pick up another extension.

"I'm here, Grace, go ahead," he said.

"Hi, Gary. I was telling Jill that just a few minutes after she left, this large man came in, said he was looking for his wife. He was supposed to have met her here for her appointment. He described the car and the girl that you took home, Jill. I told him I hadn't seen her. He seemed real scary."

"Did you give him any information?" Gary asked.

"No ... well, I did let it slip that there was another counselor that had just left when he asked if anybody else was here. He left his name and number for Jill to call when she came back."

"Let me have the name and number, Grace," Gary said, grabbing a notepad and pen sitting by the phone.

"He said his name was Ralph, and left the number 310-555-4112."

"Anything else?"

"Well, I kept my eye on him through the window after he left the center. He made some calls in his car, and then somebody else drove over here and met with him. Now he's gone and the other man has stayed. I don't feel good about this. I think somebody is after your friend."

"I'm sure you're right. Just try and relax; continue as if nothing is going on, Grace," Gary said. "I'll call one of the men on the board of directors and get somebody down there to be with you, OK?"

"Thanks, Gary. That would make me feel better."

Gary suddenly had an idea, "Jill, put Vanessa on the phone." He waited until she was on the line. "Grace, I've got Vanessa on the phone now. Could you try and describe the man you saw?"

Gary could see Vanessa in the kitchen listening. As Grace described the man, the expression on Vanessa's face told Gary she knew who it was.

"Thanks, Grace, you've been a big help. I'll try and get someone over there right away, and don't worry. If they were going to try anything, they would have done so before the first guy left."

Gary walked back into the kitchen. "You know who the guy was Vanessa?"

"I'm pretty sure. It sounds like Rudy. He works for the man I was ...," she searched for the right words that wouldn't give away too much information, "... living with."

"They must have spotted your car somehow. Let me call someone to get over to the center; I don't want those ladies left there alone. Since I'm coming into the middle of this, Vanessa, I need you to start from the beginning, and tell me what's going on."

She took several deep breaths to collect herself while Gary made the phone call.

Gary finished the call and sat back at the table. "Bob's going to go down there for awhile and sit with Grace. He'll make sure everything's safe or he'll call the police."

Gary looked at Vanessa. "We need to know the whole story; can you tell us?"

Vanessa sat with her head down, not responding.

"Vanessa, honey," Jill spoke to her in a soothing voice, "we're not here to judge you. If you'll let us, we want to help."

Vanessa looked up and her eyes met Jill's. "I think it's best if I leave. You two have been so nice; I don't want to put you in any kind of danger."

"What do you mean by danger?" Gary asked.

"The man that lady described on the phone is dangerous. If he's looking for me and finds me with you two . . ." Vanessa couldn't finish the thought. She started to get up from the table.

"Wait, Vanessa," Jill stopped her with her hand. "When you came to me for help, that wasn't just a coincidence. I believe God brought you to us. He wants us to help you in some way. If you leave now, we won't be able to do that."

Gary wished he'd had time to talk things over with his wife. He'd love to know what kind of message she'd gotten from the Lord, but he trusted in his wife's ability to hear the Holy Spirit. "Jill's right, Vanessa. I know you're scared and facing a lot of things in your life right now. We're here; don't walk away."

Vanessa sat down, not sure which way to turn. Through tears forming in her eyes, she said, "I just want to protect this baby—it's all I've got."

"Sounds like you're doing the right thing, Vanessa," Gary responded warmly. "I appreciate your courage. In this day and age, most women would just get a quick abortion and continue on with their lives."

"I think this baby has given me a shot of hope," Vanessa said. "I want it to grow up being loved and wanted. Something I never had." She started crying again and Jill placed an arm around her.

"What do you think we should do, Gary?" Jill said, looking up at her husband.

Gary smiled at his wife, and then turned toward Vanessa, "The first thing we always do around here, Vanessa, is pray. We want to do what God would have us do." Vanessa lifted her head. This was obviously new to her.

"You see, Vanessa, we are followers of Jesus Christ. If you want us to, we'll explain what that means later. But because of that, we don't want to make any rash decisions unless we know that God is leading us. Otherwise, we'll get in a lot more trouble. If you don't mind, we'll pray right here, if you'd rather not—"

Vanessa jumped in, "Oh no, please, don't let me stop you. I've never felt more concern or love towards me, from anybody. If you want to pray, please go ahead."

Gary and Jill bowed their heads and began praying, waiting on the Lord for direction. Vanessa wasn't sure what she was supposed to do, so she just closed her eyes and listened. The last time she'd been around anything religious was when her grandmother had taken her to Sunday school. That had stopped when she died. Vanessa was ten at the time. The stories about God and Jesus then settled into her subconscious, resting among the stories about gods like Zeus and Apollo that she'd heard about from school. Now, witnessing two people who showed genuine compassion for her and who responded to Jesus as a real, living person touched Vanessa in a way she didn't know was possible.

Love one another as Jesus loves, one at a time. Gary felt the Spirit prompting his thoughts from the meeting last night. He was sure God had placed Vanessa into their lives for them to be his instrument to her.

After a few minutes, Gary looked up at Vanessa. "First of all, I want you to know that we care about you, and if you want, we're going to be with you through this."

Vanessa's eyes teared up again.

He continued, "The first thing we should do is get rid of the car. It's the only way they can trace you, besides coming back to the center. Does that sound OK, Vanessa?"

"Yeah, it does. It never occurred to me that they'd be out looking for the car. I guess I wasn't thinking straight."

Jill smiled and patted her hand. "Few people would have in your situation. Anyway, after we get rid of the car, you should spend a couple of days with us getting your head clear. But before we make any more major decisions, Vanessa, we need to hear your whole story. Is that OK, Gary?"

"That's just what I was going to say. We really need to know what's going on to be of any help. Do you feel like you can do that?"

"I think so," she said, trying to decide how much of her story she could keep to herself. "I just don't know how to thank you. I have nowhere else to turn."

"Well, you don't have to thank us. We're thankful to God that he brought you to us," Jill said.

"Now, let's get rid of that car. Then we can spend some time hearing how you got to this point," Gary said as he got up and grabbed his keys.

"Why don't we let Vanessa stay here and get some rest. I'll drive the Corvette. I've always wanted to see what one feels like—so you'll know what to get me for my birthday," Jill teased.

"Enjoy it, hon," Gary replied, "it's probably the only time you'll get to drive one. I know a good place to leave it—at the pier. Just park in the public parking. I'll follow you there and pick you up."

CHAPTER 20

Ray was huddled over a couple of computer drives in the crime lab.

"What have you got for me, Ray?" Stephanie asked as she approached his workstation.

"Well, it looks like your girl at the office was right. Look here." He pointed to the computer screen before them. "This is the copy of Mr. Bennett's hard drive. You can see all of his different files, but there are several different ways to view this information. His original computer was looking at what is called the icon view, so I didn't see this information when I made the transfer."

Stephanie was a little irritated that he'd missed this the first time. "We're all under a lot of pressure. We'll just say you owe me a dinner. Now, explain to me what you found."

"Look right here." He pointed to the file labeled 'Good-bye.' "Follow along the screen and at the end, there's a date and a time."

Stephanie saw the date on the screen: Monday, March 15, 1998, 10:35 P.M.

"Cassie was right; that's the night before his death." She felt a twinge of excitement. She turned back to Ray, "How do you explain this?"

Ray thought for a second. "There are really only two explanations. One is that Mr. Bennett would have had to create this note the night before. He then just called the note back up on the screen just before he shot himself. However, this scenario would seem most unlikely. Suicide notes are usually written right before the moment."

"Yeah. Besides, we have the widow telling us he was with her at that time of the night, not working on the computer."

"Then it leads us to the second theory. Someone came into his office and loaded this note onto his computer from a floppy disk the day he was killed. That person didn't realize he would need to resave the document on Mr. Bennett's computer to update this information to the current time of day."

Stephanie thought about this, "Let me make sure I understand the technical part of all this. If I loaded a disk on a computer, wouldn't the computer record the date and time at that moment?"

Ray reached over and grabbed a small computer disk. "Here, let me show you." He placed it into the computer.

He clicked on the disk and called up the file. "You can see here it's marked for Friday, March 19, 1998, 11:37 A.M. Now I'll copy it over onto this hard drive." Ray clicked on the file and dragged it over to the hard drive. A box appeared on the screen, indicating that the file was being copied over. After a few seconds, the screen returned to normal. Ray pointed to where the new file was stored.

"You see—the information copied with the file: Friday, March 19, 1998, 11:37 A.M."

The same date and time transferred with the file.

Ray continued, "Now, if I open up this file, as the killer would have had to do, nothing on the time information would change. You'd just have called up the file. But, if I now make some minor change, let's say type over something?" Ray typed over one of the sentences. "Then we save the new, changed document." Ray reached up with the mouse under the file menu and clicked the save button. Then he closed the document.

Stephanie looked at the date information now contained with the file: Friday, March 19, 1998, 1:17 P.M.

"So, whoever placed this note there really messed up by not updating the date information once he loaded the note onto the computer," she said.

"So it would seem," Ray agreed with her. "I'm really sorry I didn't catch this the first time, Stephanie."

"It's easy for things to slip through when we're all so swamped. At least we've got the information now. Anything new on the blood found on the gun?"

"Just that it's type A, and Wade was B negative. If you find a suspect, we'll be able to match him to the gun by blood type, even DNA if you want us to. Plus, whoever had the type A blood was also wearing surgical gloves. We confirmed the latex."

"Believe me, I'd love to have a suspect."

"Well, now that we suspect he was murdered, I'd like to have the actual computer back. Maybe there's something else I missed. I'll work with the copy in the meantime, but I want to go through the original with a fine-tooth comb."

"I've already got that in the works. Hopefully you'll get it back by the end of the day," Stephanie said as she left the lab. She hoped this information would be enough to get her a search warrant.

1:20 P.M., NATIONAL STUDIOS

It took Rick less than an hour to get his things together and get back over to the production office. This time as he drove through the gates of National Studios he felt a surge of pride. This could be the show that finally made his career as a director. It was a short-lived boost of ego, though, as he realized who had opened the doors to get him the job in the first place. God was sovereign; he wasn't. However, instead of that demeaning his fragile male ego, it was becoming a comforting thought to Rick. He realized that he had never known such peace in his life as he had over the past few days. He was learning that making Jesus Lord of his life was a thousand times better than doing everything out of his own effort.

He walked into the production office and headed over toward Cassie's desk, figuring he should talk to Josh first. Cassie greeted him warmly.

"Mr. Director, sir. So good to see you," she teased.

"Don't start with that. You can call me 'Your Highness'," Rick laughed back at her.

"Seriously, Rick, congratulations again. You must be thrilled."

"Actually, Cassie, I'm not sure it's all sunk in yet. I was just driving through the gates, and it all felt so . . . unreal."

"Well, as fast as things happen around here, by Monday you'll be too busy to have time for those introspective moments. Let me get Josh for you."

She buzzed Josh and he had Rick sent right in.

"Congratulations, Rick." Josh came around the desk and shook his hand. "When you left, I was really pulling for you. It took awhile to convince John and Gabe, but I'm thrilled they came around."

Rick felt his first sense of warning. Hadn't John told him on the phone he'd wanted Rick to have the job? One of them wasn't telling the truth. *Oh well, this is Hollywood, so what else is new?* he thought.

"I can't tell you how thrilled I am, Josh. I appreciate all you've done in making this a reality. You won't be disappointed."

Josh smiled, and crossed back over behind his desk. "I know I won't, Rick. It's amazing, our paths crossing like this. It's been a long time since those UCLA days. But we'll have time to reminisce later. I'm sure you want to get as familiar with everything as you can today. Monday will be here before we know it."

"I'm sure it will. Speaking of Monday, can we go back over the schedule?" Rick asked as he took a seat opposite the desk.

"We have a production meeting at ten, where we'll run down the show for that night. Usually each segment producer gives a quick synopsis of what they expect out of their particular guest. That's when we also look over any clips they might have and view the remote segment for that night, if we have one. That meeting usually takes about an hour. We also talk over any special needs of upcoming shows, say something that might need advanced warning for props, special effects, something like that."

"That's good; it'll give us a jump on things instead of coming in at the last minute."

"We try to avoid as much last-minute stuff as possible around here. Then, Wade would go off with the associate director and work out any logistics with the playback reel, music cues, stuff like that. By the way, do you know Chad Overton, our AD?"

Rick couldn't recall the name. "I don't think we've met."

"Hopefully you'll like him. We haven't talked about it yet, Rick, but I'm hoping you'll be comfortable with the staff we've assembled. Everyone around here works really well together."

"I don't have any plans to make any abrupt changes, but I want to reserve the right to talk about it if someone isn't working out to my satisfaction."

"That sounds agreeable. Just come to me first and we'll talk about it before you say anything to anybody else, agreed?"

"You'll be the first to know."

"OK, now back to the schedule. Once you and Chad get organized, you can grab a quick lunch before one. That's when the stage and crew are available. You have until about four for any rehearsal, musical guests, special bits, anything you think that needs to be looked at on camera. Do you think that's enough on your first day? I'm sure we can bring the crew in earlier if you think you need it."

"That'll probably be OK. Let me look at what's scheduled for that show though. I'm going to want to run through more than I'm sure would be normal. I'd rather be safe than sorry."

"Fine—just let Jim Schu know what you'll need. Then we load the audience, and start our show right at 5:15. We tape until 6:15, which gives us forty-five minutes to fix any problems. We hit the satellite at seven."

"Sounds like the perfect day."

"I'll come into the booth with you after the show, and we'll decide if anything needs to be done before we send it out. A lot of times John comes in there too. That's usually our casual post-meeting."

"Who is in the booth besides the usual staff?"

"Well, National keeps a lawyer in there to clue us into anything we need to take out for legal reasons. Often one of the executives from the studio is in there. Mr. Flint even drops by on occasion. Otherwise it's up to you who you want to allow in."

"Sounds good. When do you shoot the remote segments you spoke of?"

"There really isn't a set time. We try and schedule those for days when we don't have a musical guest. That way there's not as much rehearsal to worry about and we can take a lot of our own staff from here. If there's a conflict, we have a couple of remote directors we can tap into, to help us out if you're too busy."

"Actually, I enjoy being out in the field doing remote work, so when I can be of help, count me in."

"Great. What I'd like to do now is take you around and introduce you to what staff is in today. It's the last day of our hiatus, although a few people are in preparing for Monday. Let's take the tour and I'll introduce you around."

True to Josh's word, the majority of the staff were not in so the tour didn't take too long. Rick was shown where his new office was, a small room with two desks. He'd be sharing it with Chad, the AD. When Josh had finished the introductions, they ended up back at Cassie's desk.

"Rick, I've got some stuff I've got to get done. Would it be OK if Cassie takes you over and shows you the stage and the off-line area?"

Rick smiled; he didn't mind at all. "That'd be fine. It'll give me a chance to get to know your assistant better."

"Good, oh, and Rick, I believe John is over in his dressing room. He wanted to have you drop by while he's still here, so make that your last stop."

Cassie picked up her keys and started for the door. "Right this way, Rick. It's a little bit of a walk."

Rick followed behind Cassie, amazed at his growing attraction toward her, then remembered how messed up office romances could make the workplace. He'd have to play it cool, just establish a friendship.

"How long have you been working with Josh?" Rick asked as they stepped outside.

"Just since this show went into preproduction last summer. Josh got my name from a friend, and it's worked out pretty well."

"Have you been in the industry long?"

"Actually, no. I originally intended to go into law, but things got so expensive in law school, I couldn't stay with it. I landed a couple of production assistant jobs and ended up staying in the business. Maybe someday I'll be able to return to law school."

They crossed through what was called the "New York" side of the lot, an area made up to look like the streets of New York, used for exterior shots. Rick looked at the deli sign hung over a store across the street.

"It always feels strange to walk through here, like you've suddenly changed time zones," he said.

"I love it. This is the closest I've ever been to New York."

"Well, this version is definitely safer. I've been a few times, and I'm always glad to come home in one piece." The two laughed as they continued their walk.

Cassie pointed up ahead where the large buildings were numbered for the different stages. "That's stage seventeen, where we do the show." Rick noticed a nice awning over the entrance, with a sign above it identifying "The John Harold Show." "I'll take you in after we see our editing facility."

Cassie turned to a smaller, one-story building across from the stage marked Bungalow C. They went through the door and down the hallway to a back room. She knocked once and entered. Chad was in there working with Sid, their editor.

Chad looked up at the two coming in. "Hi Cassie. What's up?"

Cassie stepped aside to let Rick into the small room. "I'd like you two to meet our new director, Rick Treadway. Rick this is Chad Overton, our AD, and Sid Ratcliff, our editor."

Chad stood up and shook Rick's hand.

"Congratulations, Rick. I've heard some good things about you," he offered.

Sid stepped forward and gave Rick a bear hug. "It's about time you made it to the big time. How you doing?"

"It's good to see you, Sid," Rick said, smiling. "You still living like a mole in one of these bays, huh?"

The two laughed as they separated. "They let me out every month for a day or two."

Chad and Cassie felt like the odd ones out.

"I take it you two have met before?" Cassie asked the obvious.

"We go way back. I used to edit a crazy game show Rick directed. The show was the pits, but we had a good time, didn't we?"

"We tried, we tried. I didn't know you were over here. It'll be great to work with you again," Rick said.

"That it will, my man, that it will."

Rick turned back to Chad, "I hope we didn't interrupt anything."

"Oh, don't worry about that; we're almost done. It's just a standby show, in case we have a disaster sometime and have to throw something else up on the bird."

Rick's mind was quick. "This must be in case the new director doesn't cut it, huh?"

Chad's eyes gave it away—Rick had hit the nail on the head.

"Don't worry, Chad, that's pretty standard stuff. I would expect there to be a show waiting in the wings, whether it's for me or not."

"This show won't see the light of day because of something Rick's done, I guarantee you," Sid interjected.

"Thanks for the vote of confidence, Sid. Listen, Chad, I'd like to go over some things with you about Monday . . ."

While Rick had Chad's attention, Cassie caught Sid's eyes, and the two of them stepped into the hallway.

"What's up, Cassie?" he asked as they were alone.

"Listen, Sid, this is just between you and me, but I've been trying to find out some information on this Lasko interview that Wade might have been working on." At the mention of Lasko, Cassie saw a worried look cloud Sid's eyes. "I can't find anything in the files about it, who it was with or anything. Do you know anything about that project?"

"No, Cassie, I don't. Like I told you when the detectives were here, I think that's what Wade was looking at, but I'm not even sure of that."

Cassie was disappointed. "Well, if anything comes to mind, let me know, OK?"

"I sure will," Sid said, with the slightest hesitation.

The two of them stepped back into the room as Rick was finishing up with his new associate director.

As he walked across the street with Cassie, Rick felt relieved. It was comforting to have at least one old friend on the staff, and Sid was a good one.

"You and Sid seem pretty close," she said.

"Yeah, we spent a lot of late nights together. You know how an editing room can be."

As she was reaching for the stage door, it suddenly burst open and out stepped Reggie, the security guard.

"I'm sorry, Cassie, I didn't know you were on the other side of the door," he said, making sure she was all right.

"That's OK; it just startled me. Reggie, I want you to meet our new director, Rick Treadway."

"Nice to meet you, Mr. Treadway." Reggie offered his hand.

Rick felt like his hand disappeared inside Reggie's large fist. "Please, call me Rick."

"Rick it is."

"You're not Reggie Washington, are you?"

Reggie smiled; it was still fun to be recognized. "As a matter of fact, I am."

"I used to watch you all the time. You were one great line-backer. I always wondered what happened to the guys on the great Rams teams of the seventies."

"Well, one of them works as a guard right on this stage. I can't speak for the rest of them. That was a long time ago."

"Well, it's nice to meet you, Reggie. I feel safer already knowing that you're around."

"Thank you, Mr. Tread ... I mean Rick. That's mighty nice of you. Tell you what. Get together a list of anybody you'd like to have access to the control room, and I'll make sure they won't have any trouble getting back to see you."

"I'll do that, Reggie. Thanks."

Cassie led Rick down the back part of the stage until they stepped out from behind the curtain. The set opened up in front of them, the stage to their left, the audience to their right. As usual, everything looked much smaller in person than it did on television. Rick felt a sense of ownership. This was now his stage. No, he wouldn't be on it night after night, like John Harold. But he'd be in the booth, making everything happen that put John, and this set, on the air. Rick once again felt a sense of accomplishment. This time, though, it wasn't pride, but a sense of wanting to fulfill whatever purpose God had in mind in placing him here. He remembered what he'd learned from the fellowship group last night: Love one at a time, as God places those before you. *Lord, whatever purpose you have in my being here, I open my life to. You accomplish your goals. I pray I'll find those you want my life to touch while I'm here. Help me to be your light in this dark place.*

Cassie sensed a difference come over Rick, but couldn't identify it. He seemed to draw into himself. She decided it was just his way of getting used to his new environment.

"Right through this door is the control room," she motioned as the two headed through the double doors behind the audience seating. They entered a hallway with signs over all the doors. They were marked Control Room, Audio, Green Room, Video, Video Tape, and on down where Rick couldn't see.

They entered the control room. The room was dark and quiet, the row of monitors on the wall all turned off. Only the equipment showed any signs of life, the buttons on the switcher and the intercom panels casting a soft glow of light over the room. It was comforting to him, having spent so much time in other rooms similar to this one.

"I guess this will be home for awhile, huh, Cassie?" Rick asked.

"How do you like it?"

"Not bad. A pretty good layout. But like any house, you have to live in it for awhile before you know how you really feel."

Cassie laughed. She hoped his personality stayed like this. So many directors she'd encountered could be easygoing and likable before the show, but once the stress of the production started, they became something totally different. Wade had been that way, and her prayers had been for someone a lot easier to work with. So far, she liked what she saw.

Rick felt her gaze on him deepen. He wondered what was going through her mind.

"Where are you during the show?" he asked.

"Josh likes me to be out by him. He's got a position just off home base, in line of sight with John. I usually sit next to him, run a stop watch on the segments, keep his notes straight, that kind of thing."

"Have you had a chance to sit in here during a show?"

"No, I haven't. I can hear the chaos on my headset though, and I actually have been glad to be out on stage."

"You must have heard some of Wade's . . . shall we say 'intensity'?" The two laughed.

"I guess you did work with Wade before," she said.

"You bet. I've been on the wrong side of his verbal assaults before. I think Wade, and a couple of other directors, did a lot to help me find my style of directing."

"You mean that you scream and yell?"

"So loud, the cameras don't even need headsets," he teased. "No, actually, while those directors were off screaming at someone, I saw them miss more shots and cues than you can believe. I've found that in all the crews I've worked with, if somebody makes a mistake, they know it. Yelling at them isn't going to help. Usually it puts people more on edge, and they mess up again. I like to treat people like the professionals they are, and have as good a time as possible while we're putting the show together."

This guy is too good to be true, Cassie thought. Still, she decided to reserve her final judgment until after his first show on Monday. She'd noticed how handsome he was, and she'd be hard pressed to admit it, but the first time he came to her desk, she did check out his left-hand ring finger to see what was there. But Cassie was wise enough to know that there had to be more than just physical attraction for her to begin a relationship with a man. He had to exhibit a deep relationship with the Lord. After the disaster of her last relationship, this was now one of her unbreakable rules.

After going through the other rooms down the hallway, the tour ended. Rick stopped and looked directly at Cassie.

"Thanks so much, Cassie. I really appreciate your spending the time with me, showing me where everything is. You've made this little tour a real pleasure."

As Cassie looked up, she could tell by the look in Rick's eyes that this wasn't just a flippant remark. His look conveyed a sincerity that Cassie didn't often see in this business. She blushed.

"I've enjoyed it myself, Rick. I'm glad they chose you for the show. I think you'll fit in perfectly."

"I just thank God for the opportunity. Now, I'm supposed to go up to John's dressing room. I take it it's up these stairs?"

Cassie didn't catch the rest of what Rick said. *Did he really mean to thank God, or was it one of those phrases people say without conviction?* she thought. Then she realized Rick was waiting for a response from her.

"I'm sorry . . . what did you say?"

"I asked if John's dressing room was up these stairs?" He motioned to the stairway behind him.

"Yes, right up these stairs, the first door on your left." She felt silly for making him repeat the question. "I'm sorry, something you said made my mind drift."

"That's OK," Rick tried to let her off the hook without further embarrassment. "You've been an excellent tour guide. I'll have to tell the studio execs that they're wasting your talents in the production office. They should elevate you to studio page."

Cassie laughed. That was the entry-level position for most studios. "You're too kind, Rick. Well, if you can find your way up to the star's dressing room, I'll be on my way back to the office. When you get back, I'll have your office key waiting for you."

Rick watched as she walked away, then turned and took the stairs two at a time. There was definitely something special about that girl.

CHAPTER 21

Gary followed Vanessa's Corvette, driving west on the Santa Monica Freeway heading toward the Pacific Ocean. He had wanted to get the car far enough away from where they lived that anybody still looking for Vanessa would not connect her to their home in Westwood. Now he was having his doubts about driving this far. *Maybe we should have just called the police, not taken it upon ourselves to hide the car from this thug. Oh, well, it's too late now. We'll discuss getting the police involved when I get Jill back in the car,* he thought.

They'd been driving for about twelve minutes, taking the 405 Freeway south, then crossing over onto the Santa Monica

Freeway. Jill seemed to be having fun in the Corvette, cruising through the lanes of traffic. Gary tried to relax and just follow his wife, praying all the while that God's protection would be about them while they ditched the car.

Jill wasn't thinking about being seen by the people looking for Vanessa; she was just out for a joy ride. As the freeway gave warning signs of running out in the next mile, she accelerated past a silver BMW that was traveling in the middle lane, then began slowing down, preparing to exit.

At first, the driver of the BMW didn't notice the car that had just passed him. He was too deep in thought, wishing Fast Eddie had made it through that intersection and followed Vanessa to her destination. Then the image that had passed before his eyes finally made it to his brain. That was Vanessa's car.

Rudy's foot punched the accelerator, quickly catching up to the Corvette slowing down in front of him. He pulled in behind her, checking to make sure it was her license plate.

Gary had been trying to keep a close distance behind Jill, so he quickly noticed the BMW pulling in behind them. He couldn't see the driver too well because they were heading into the sun, but a sudden rush of fear enveloped him. He sensed that they'd just been found. There was no way to warn Jill.

Rudy knew that if he allowed Vanessa into the city of Santa Monica, she could easily lose him with that car. He decided to make his move now. He pulled into the next lane and accelerated along the right side of the Corvette. They were coming up to the last exit before the freeway stopped and traffic entered Colorado Boulevard.

Rudy figured that if Vanessa saw him, she'd give up and pull over. But when he looked over at the driver, he was shocked to see that it wasn't Vanessa. What was this woman doing in her car? He'd have to find a way to stop her and find out.

Jill nearly jumped out of her seat, noticing the silver car suddenly appearing next to hers. She didn't like the looks of the man staring at her, and she quickly prayed for protection. Then she saw the man hold his hand up, revealing the gun he was holding. Her prayer intensified as she stepped on the gas.

Rudy couldn't let her get away. He veered left, hitting the back of the car and nearly sending Jill into a tailspin. She screamed as her car lunged toward the cement barrier. Gary saw it all from behind and cried out for God to intervene, frustrated that he couldn't do more.

Just before the Corvette crashed into the wall, Jill regained control, keeping the car in her lane. Rudy smashed into the car a second time, with even more force. For a moment he wondered if he had misread the license plate—could he have the wrong car? But it didn't matter now, he had to finish what he started.

This time Jill couldn't regain control. She slammed on her brakes just moments before the car hit the cement barrier. The front driver's side smashed inward as the fiberglass met the concrete. The car bounced off the wall, rolling over once before settling back on its tires, sitting alone in the middle lane.

SAME TIME, NATIONAL STUDIOS

Rick approached the door to the dressing room. There was no mistaking which one belonged to John—his name was written in four-inch letters atop a large gold star on the door. Rick knocked twice.

"Come on in," he heard through the doorway.

Rick opened the door and stepped into the large room. John Harold was standing in front of a full-length mirror holding up an expensive looking dark blue suit. Standing beside him was an attractive woman, probably in her late 30s, holding a couple more outfits for John to look at.

"Rick, come on in. Congratulations," John greeted him warmly as he walked over.

"I'd like you to meet our wardrobe maven, Gena Fields. Gena, this is our new director, Rick Treadway."

Gena extended her hand toward Rick. "It's a pleasure to meet you."

Rick accepted her hand and responded, "The pleasure's mine. I'm excited to be joining the family around here."

John handed the suit back to Gena. "These will all be fine, Gena. Now, Rick and I need to spend some time together. Thanks for coming in today."

"No problem, John. You're going to look great in these," Gena said as she packed up the clothes and walked out of the room.

John walked over to the plush couch that sat in another corner of the room. "Let's have a seat and talk a bit. You did great in the meeting."

"I was just trying to give everyone what they wanted," Rick replied as he took a seat next to John. One part of his job that came easily for Rick was relating to a celebrity. He didn't have the problems of clashing egos or of feeling inferior to the exalted position they held. He just tried to treat them like any of his other friends.

"You certainly did that. I loved the part about Gabriel just wanting things to continue smoothly. You didn't see him react, but I can tell you, you hit the nail right on the head." John laughed easily, feeling comfortable with Rick already.

"Is that what got me the job? Or did you have to pull some strings?"

"Actually, between the three candidates, it was a fairly easy choice. You just felt like the right one, even without our earlier discussion. Josh was the only one that was hesitant, which kind of surprised me with your background together at UCLA."

Rick wasn't surprised that John's and Josh's stories didn't match. He had the feeling that Josh wasn't being truthful with him, and he couldn't figure out why. But then, he reminded himself, it could be that John was the one telling tales.

"Well, college was a long time ago. A friendship there doesn't mean he's going to trust me to direct the show now," Rick said.

"I don't think that's it. I believe Josh has somebody else in mind for the job who isn't available yet. He was viewing the person we hired today as just a temporary, until his choice is ready."

That made sense to Rick, recalling the offer to sign him to only a four-week contract.

John continued, "Don't count that against him. I actually think he was trying to spare you from being the one given the ax. That's why I wanted to see you; I want to make sure that doesn't happen. We've got four weeks to make you invaluable to this production company."

"I appreciate your being so candid with me, John. I'll do everything I can to make my mark around here."

"That's what I wanted to hear. Now, let's talk about next week's shows."

John spent the next half hour discussing the ins and outs of the show from his perspective. Rick used the time to gain valuable insight into the character of John Harold, and what it would take to keep him happy while, at the same time, producing the kind of product that Rick could be proud of. From Rick's perspective, John seemed like a likable, down-to-earth guy—quite a nice surprise really.

As John was talking, Rick's mind drifted back to the message from the fellowship group the night before: *Love as Jesus did, one at a time.* Rick felt the Spirit's prompting, that this was a person God had placed in Rick's path for him to show the character of God. Rick silently prayed that he would have that opportunity—to show the love of Jesus to John—in the coming weeks.

SAME TIME, SANTA MONICA FREEWAY

Gary slammed on his brakes as he watched the Corvette roll over and come to a crashing stop in the middle of the freeway. He jumped out of his car, praying his wife was still alive.

Rudy's BMW was well up the road before he could get it stopped. He looked in his rearview mirror, happy with his work, preparing to go back and find out who this lady was—until he saw a strange man run up beside the Corvette.

Gary was shocked at how smashed up the car was, but he didn't waste any time. He ran to the passenger door, forcing it open. Jill was sitting in a pool of glass, blood dripping from her face. He called to her, fearful that she wouldn't respond.

"Are you OK, honey?" he yelled.

There was no response. Gary reached out and grabbed her shoulders, "Jill! Jill!" he cried.

Then she moved, opening her eyes.

"Gary," she whispered, "what happened?"

Gary could see out of the corner of his eye that the BMW had stopped farther up ahead, and a man was getting out.

"We don't have any time, Jill." He reached in and unbuckled her seat belt. "You've got to come with me now!" he pleaded. He half pulled her from the car, quickly carrying her around to the passenger side of their Grand Prix. As he nearly threw Jill inside, he noticed the man was now running toward them, pointing a gun in their direction. Gary slid across the hood of the car, and jumped back behind the wheel, slamming the car in reverse as he did so.

Rudy couldn't believe what he was seeing. Who was this man who dared to take this girl away from him? He stopped running and tried to aim his gun toward the car.

Gary slammed the accelerator pedal down and gave the steering wheel a hard turn to the right. He crossed over the two lanes and backtracked the fifty feet it took to make it onto the Lincoln exit, sending cars squealing left and right to avoid him as he got off of the freeway.

Rudy squeezed off a couple of shots, but he was breathing too hard to get any kind of aim. The shots were way off their mark as Gary and Jill made their getaway. Rudy swore, running back to his car to try to catch up to them, but knew it was hopeless. He'd lost the lead to Vanessa again.

As he made it back to his car, he tried to remember the license plate of the blue Grand Prix he'd just seen drive off. He was pretty sure he had the right combination of letters and numbers as he sped toward the exit.

Gary got off the freeway. The last thing he wanted to do was get caught in some traffic jam so that the maniac behind them could catch up. He was fortunate to have the light at the end of the off-ramp glowing a steady green, so he took a hard left across the intersection and headed under the freeway. He decided to stay off the main streets, turning left onto a small side street, Michigan Avenue, as he made his way away from the accident.

After getting through a few of the residential intersections, Gary began to feel safer.

"How do you feel, Jill?" he asked, praying there was nothing seriously wrong with her. He just knew they had to get away from that man. He'd drive her to a hospital now if it was warranted.

"I feel OK, just shook up." She reached into the glove compartment, grabbed a napkin, and started wiping blood from the cuts on her face. "I don't think anything is broken."

"Do you want to go to an emergency room?"

"Oh, no. I'm all right. Let's get back home. I think it might be time to find out what's really going on with Vanessa, maybe bring in the police on this matter. We seem to be in way over our heads."

"You've got that right. That's what I was thinking just before that maniac ran you off the road," Gary said. "Thank God, you're all right."

"That's exactly who I thank," Jill agreed, reaching over to clasp her husband's hand.

4:10 P.M., SANTA MONICA

Rudy had driven over every street within a mile radius of where he'd run Vanessa's car into the median. Still no sign of the Grand Prix that had stolen away his only lead to Vanessa. The more he drove, the madder he got, until he almost caused an accident just crossing over a busy intersection. He pulled over next to a liquor store, deciding he needed something to calm himself down.

After coming out with a six-pack in hand, he popped open one of the beers and chugged it down as he sat in his car thinking. He looked at the slip of paper where he'd jotted down what he thought was the license of the Grand Prix. Now he needed either a police contact or someone at the Department of Motor Vehicles to look up the name and address for him.

An idea occurred to him, and he picked up his cellular phone and dialed Flint's private line in his office.

"Yeah," came the terse greeting.

"It's Rudy," he said. "I've got some news on Vanessa. You won't believe it."

"Have you got her yet?"

"I got close, but she's holed up with some couple. Don't you want to hear the news?"

"I don't have time for games! What is it?"

"I think she's pregnant, that's why she split. One of my boys saw her going into one of those prego centers."

Flint was silent for a moment. *How could she have been so careless as to let herself get pregnant,* he thought angrily.

"That doesn't excuse her running out on me. I still want her brought in, you understand?"

"Yeah, I understand. I've got a license number of the car that belongs to the couple I think she's with, but I need some help tracing it. We still got a cop on the payroll I can get to?"

"Yeah, but hold off on that. I think we've got more serious problems. There are people at the production office still asking questions about Lasko, and I hear the police are looking into my background. I want you to get over there and take care of those tapes, now!"

"I was going to go in as soon as it gets dark." Rudy looked out at the sky—there was a good hour, maybe two, of light left. "You want me to go in there in broad daylight and torch the place? What are you, nuts?"

Flint's voice rose to a rage, "Don't you ever talk to me like that! You hear me?"

Rudy kept silent.

"You make your way over to that studio and be there as soon as the sun sets, understand? Give me the license number and I'll have it checked out."

Rudy gave him the number, then hung up. He hated giving those people he saw more time with Vanessa, but he had a greater interest in getting rid of the tapes. Once they were destroyed, Mr. Flint wouldn't be the only one breathing easier.

4:50 P.M., WESTWOOD

Jill and Gary arrived back at their house with no further incident. Vanessa was sound asleep on the couch, so they quietly walked past her into their bathroom. Jill went to work cleaning up the cuts on her face. Fortunately, they were all superficial.

"Well, should we call the police?" Gary asked as she gently touched a washcloth to her face.

"Probably not until she wakes up. It has to be her decision, don't you think?"

"Yeah, I definitely think it does. If we involve the police without her consent, it could really spook her and she might run off on her own. It's probably best we let her sleep, but we'll talk about it when she wakes up. Do you want me to get you anything for those cuts?"

"No thanks, honey, I think I've got everything I need."

"You know, you were doing some pretty wild driving even before that guy ran you off the road," Gary chuckled as he recalled Jill's recreational drive. "Is there some hidden desire to try out for the Indianapolis 500?"

Jill laughed, then winced as the antiseptic sank into one of the cuts. "You know, I think I've had it with racing. Today was enough to last a lifetime. I'm just amazed at how God protected us—we could have both been killed."

"Not until God allows it. He's still got a plan for us. I just hope that goon leaves us alone now."

Jill stopped and turned to Gary, a serious look coming over her face, "What if he was able to get your license number and comes looking for us?"

Gary thought for a second. "Everything happened so quickly I don't know if he had time to see it or not. If he did though . . . any ideas?"

"Yeah, let's not take the chance. I sense the same warning I felt at the center. Let's get some things together, then wake up Vanessa. We better get out of here."

"Vanessa . . . ," Jill was gently touching Vanessa's shoulder as she lay on the couch, "Vanessa, wake up." After a moment her eyes fluttered open, looking up at Jill. A momentary panic seized her, but then she remembered where she was and relaxed.

"I'm sorry to wake you up, Vanessa, but we've run into some trouble," Jill said.

Vanessa sat up, rubbing her eyes, trying to break through her grogginess.

"We think we had a run-in with your friend Rudy," Gary said.

"Are you both OK?" she asked.

Jill assured her, "We're fine, but your car didn't fare so well."

Vanessa noticed the cuts across Jill's face. "You were hurt!"

"Just a few cuts and scratches," Jill said. "Rudy ran me off the road, but before he could come back and finish the job, Gary grabbed me and we got away."

"That's why we wanted to wake you," Gary informed her. "I think there's a chance that Rudy was able to see the license plate on our car, and he might be able to trace it back here."

The concern on Vanessa's face deepened. "I'm so sorry. I don't want you two to be in danger because of me."

"Don't worry about that. God has his hand on the situation," Gary assured her. "We said we'll be with you through this, and we mean it."

Jill took Vanessa's hand, "Gary and I feel like it's time to bring the police into this, but we didn't want to do anything without you agreeing to it."

Vanessa lowered her head, thinking before she spoke up. "I never dreamed that it would be this difficult. I just wanted to get away and start a new life." The events of the last couple of days were weighing too heavily on her. Through the tears, she finally got out, "I don't know what to do."

Jill looked over to Gary. "I think she needs a little more time. Any ideas?"

There had been an idea growing in the back of Gary's head, but it didn't really come to the front of his thoughts until Jill turned and asked the question.

"Yeah, I do have one. Let's call Rick. I know he'll be over at the Harold production offices, starting his new job. We could go over to his condo. That would give us some time to get our thoughts together before calling the police. We'll be safe there."

Gary went over to the kitchen and picked up the phone. After calling information, he got the office number and within a moment had Rick on the line.

"Gary, you're my first call here at the office. What can I do for you?" Rick said cheerfully as he came on the line.

"Rick, I can't talk long. We've got a situation here that's difficult to explain."

Rick could hear the urgency in Gary's voice. "What's up, Gary?"

"Jill and I have a friend who needs our help, and we believe someone that is after her might know where we live. I'll fill you in on all the details later, but we were wondering if it would be possible to hole up at your condo until we can figure out exactly what to do."

"Of course you can," Rick said. "I'm not sure how long I'll be here tonight, but the place is yours. I keep a spare key above the light over the garage. It's pretty easy to find if you know it's there.

Make yourself at home, and call me when you get in so I'll know you're OK."

"Thanks, Rick. You may be a lifesaver. Pray for us. You'll understand later, but this thing is pretty heavy."

"I will, Gary. Anything else I can do, let me know, OK?"

Gary hung up and went back into the family room.

"We're going over to Rick's house. Vanessa, make sure you get all of your things—I'm not sure when it'll be safe to come back here."

5:05 P.M., SHERIFF'S HEADQUARTERS

Stephanie sat at her desk fuming. She'd called two different judges in an attempt to get the search warrant she needed. Both had refused on the grounds that the evidence was too weak to assume the production company had anything to do with an apparent "suicide." She suspected the real reason was that the judges were afraid to step on the toes of the Hollywood elite. If she was wrong and they didn't turn up anything, the resulting negative press would put them all in the frying pan.

Bill came into the office and noticed her body language.

"What's wrong, Steph?"

"Just the usual problem with judges. They don't have the guts to go after someone in Hollywood."

"So you didn't get your search warrant?"

She shook her head.

"Well, we might have a break on the other front," Bill said.

"What have you got?"

"I spent a few hours at the department of records." Bill sat down with a thump. "Our Gabriel Flint owns several strip joints that fall under the city's boundaries. It was hard to research because of the various dummy corporations he's got to hide the paper trail. But with some help from Vice, I've found at least three. Let's see . . . ," Bill looked over his notes, "The Passion Palace, The Club Royale out by the airport, and The Mustang Club."

"So what's the big deal. They're all legal, right?"

"Yeah, but it seems that one of the clubs, The Club Royale, is managed by a certain man named . . . Joe Lasko."

Bill paused to let the name sink in. Stephanie looked up at him, excitement gleaming in her eyes. "Lasko . . . manages a strip joint. We've got to see those tapes, but we don't have a warrant."

Bill looked at his watch. "Look, it's getting late. Why don't we just get over to the production office before everybody leaves. I know we could come up with something to get a look at those tapes without a warrant, or at least find out if they still exist."

Stephanie smiled at her partner. "Why not? We're getting nowhere here." She grabbed her purse as she stood up. "Let's go."

CHAPTER 22

Before Rick put the phone down, he was already praying for Jill and Gary. He couldn't imagine what was going on that would put them in danger at their own house, but God knew. He prayed for their protection, and for the Holy Spirit to guide them in the decisions they'd need to make.

When he finished, Rick laughed at himself. Comparing the person he was now, who would pray for a friend at the drop of a hat, to the person who was embarrassed to pray over a meal at the deli a few days ago tickled him. It was apparent that God was working in his life. His Christian walk seemed relevant for the first time in his life. He wouldn't go back to the way things had been for anything.

He had been watching a few of the old "John Harold Shows" on a VCR in his new office, trying to get in rhythm with the flow of the show. After his tour and the time spent with John himself, he was feeling pretty comfortable that Monday would go just fine. He stopped the tape machine and ventured out of his office into the main area where desks were separated by partitions.

Nearly all of the staff members that had been around that day were now gone, but he did see Cassie sitting at her desk, working on a portable computer, the local news playing on the TV beside her desk. He looked at the clock against the back wall and was surprised to see that it was already past five o'clock.

Although the police had asked Cassie not to do anything with Wade's computer, sitting all day with it under her desk had finally gotten to her. After Josh had left for the day, she pulled the computer out of its bag and powered it up. She wasn't sure what she was looking for, or even how to find it, but she knew the computer had to hold more answers. As she looked at the screen, she prayed for God's help in finding those clues.

"Working late?" Cassie jumped as Rick spoke to her. She looked up, fear flooding her face.

"I'm sorry, I didn't mean to startle you. Are you all right?"

Cassie regained her composure, realizing it was only Rick, and sighed. This spy stuff was just too much for her. "Rick. Hi. I'm sorry. I was so engrossed in this thing, I didn't notice you walk up. Is there something . . ."

Their attention was suddenly drawn to the TV set, as the anchorman introduced Samantha Steel with the latest on the Bennett suicide.

"So far, the sheriff's office has not made any statements." Samantha was reporting with the county sheriff's headquarters behind her. "However, sources close to the investigation have told us that they have some questions as to whether he did indeed take his own life."

Cassie looked to Rick. "I wonder where she got that from. I know the detectives didn't tell her that."

Rick smiled, "I'm sure she's got her ways."

Samantha continued, "At National Studios, the job left vacant by Bennett's death, directing the popular late-night "John Harold Show," was filled today. The producers gave the show to a relatively unknown director by the name of Rick Treadway."

Rick was staring at a bad college photo of himself, surprised that this would be newsworthy. *Was it just him, or was there some animosity in her reporting?* he thought, . . . *a relatively unknown director?*

When Samantha tossed it back to the studio, Cassie turned to Rick. "Congratulations, you're a celebrity yourself now."

"I don't know about that . . . relatively unknown . . . that's quite a buildup."

"Don't take it personally. She was probably just looking for a bigger story. It's not like she has some grudge against you or anything."

Rick felt embarrassed. Cassie didn't know how close to the truth she'd just come. He decided to change the subject. "I hope I didn't interrupt anything important."

"No, not really," Cassie said, still trying to cover up what she was doing. "Can I help you with anything?"

"No, not at all. I just noticed everyone else seemed to have cleared out. I was thinking of leaving myself, then decided I'd see what you were up to."

Cassie didn't know how to respond, but something inside her prompted her to tell the truth. She wasn't sure why, but she went with the feeling, first checking to see if anyone else was around them.

"Actually, Rick, this is Wade's computer. His wife and I were checking into it last night and found something that made us believe that he didn't commit suicide. I was just getting back to it to see if there was something else in here."

"Didn't commit suicide?" Rick was astonished. He had assumed, like everyone else, that there was no question that Wade took his own life. He pulled up a chair next to Cassie. "You mean there is something the police are investigating? I thought that was just Sam trying to make something newsworthy. What did you find?"

Cassie pointed to the document on the screen and explained to Rick how it was dated the night before the suicide.

Rick looked at the screen. "You've shown the police this?"

"Well, I told them about it. They're coming out to take the computer back. They told me to leave it alone, but they didn't notice this the first time they had it. I thought maybe I could find something else before they get here. I was waiting until the office was cleared out before doing anything."

"This sounds like pretty dangerous cloak-and-dagger stuff. Who would want to kill Wade?"

"That's the mystery. I'm hoping there'll be something here to give me a clue."

"What were you going to try next?"

"Well, last night, Becky and I put this away after finding the discrepancy in the suicide note. I thought I'd look through and check the most recent documents Wade had been working on."

"That's a great idea. Can I be of any help?"

"Well, nobody else is around. Let's jump in together," Cassie responded exuberantly. She looked up at Rick. Maybe this was the answer to her prayer from a moment ago.

Cassie put her finger on the mouse pad and clicked on the apple icon at the top of the screen. The screen showed a drop down menu with all of the extras Wade kept on his computer. Then she saw what she was looking for—recent documents. She opened it and the list read: "Good-bye," "The Lasko Interview," "Lasko Pic," "Harold Remotes," "Finances."

Cassie sucked in her breath. "That's amazing." She looked up at Rick. "The day before he died, Wade had gone in to edit the Lasko interview. The next day he's dead, and I haven't been able to find one piece of information concerning Lasko anywhere in the office. When I asked Josh about it, he just clammed up and said the interview was not going to be included in the show, so drop it. Now here it shows up again on Wade's computer."

"It sounds like more than a coincidence, doesn't it?" Rick remarked.

"I would definitely say so."

Cassie highlighted "The Lasko Interview" and clicked the mouse. A moment later the computer screen showed: "The alias 'The Lasko Interview' could not be opened because the original item could not be found."

Rick always loved a good mystery. "Cassie, do a search and see if there's anything on the disk labeled 'Lasko.'"

"Good idea," she responded with a smile.

She opened up the fast-find application and did as Rick suggested. After a few seconds, the computer beeped, and a dialogue box told them there were no files with that name on the disk.

"It's certainly beginning to look fishy," Rick commented. "Whoever put the suicide note on here must have erased the files on Lasko."

Cassie looked dejected. "I'd love to try and retrieve those files. I've got Norton utilities on my computer, but I'm sure the police would nail me for tampering with evidence."

"I agree. But maybe there's another way to find out what we want to know."

"What?"

Cassie noticed the expression change on Rick's face. He looked like a kid about to embark on some wonderfully scary adventure.

"Everyone else is gone, right? Let's go over to the tape library and look for those Lasko tapes. If we find them, we'll know what Wade knew."

Cassie couldn't come up with a reason not to. "I guess it's worth a try. Let's go."

5:39 P.M., NATIONAL STUDIOS

The sunset had faded to a darker shade of purple and deep blue as the day gave way to the enveloping darkness. Rudy was oblivious to it all, waiting in his car in one of the guest parking spots on National's lot.

He stepped out of his car, cursing because of the dents and scratches of red paint along the front driver's side. He walked back to the trunk, opened it, and extracted a medium-sized box. He'd kept the contents to a minimum, knowing he'd have to walk a short distance to get to the bungalow where the tapes were stored.

He tried to look like he belonged here as he made his way toward the back of the lot. He'd worn a faded pair of Levi's, black T-shirt, and a black jacket with the emblem of the International Alliance of Theatrical Stage Employees. He whistled as he walked, acting as if he was delivering a package.

Rudy could see the Harold stage just up ahead on his right. A guard came out of the stage door and headed in his direction. Rudy kept up his casual appearance and walked right past him. He was surprised at the size of the guard—a good three or four inches taller than he was and probably forty pounds or so heavier. He hoped he wouldn't have to tangle with him tonight.

Rudy came up to the building across from the stage. In the dimming light he could see three one-story buildings in a row. He made his way to the third one, marked Bungalow C. He set the box down at his feet, then took a quick look in both directions to make sure the guard had left and that no one else was around. It appeared he was alone. He took out his knife and quickly broke the old lock on the door, making his way in. He took out his flashlight, keeping the beam low so less light would shine out the windows. He made his way down the hallway, passing the room marked Off-Line, and went to the last door. Above the knob, he saw the sign Tape Library. This door was also locked, but within 30 seconds, he'd gotten in.

Rudy scanned his light over the rows of tapes. There was no window to this back room, so he didn't care about what his flashlight hit. He quickly tried to assess how the tapes were organized in the room to verify that the ones he needed to destroy were in fact there. After a few seconds of scanning, he finally gave up on that. He didn't have a clue how to locate them.

He dug into his box and pulled out a couple of jars he'd filled with gasoline and a small timing device attached to a flint starter, like the kind used on a self-lighting gas burner. He set the timer for five minutes, giving himself enough time to get back to his car and drive away. He wanted to be off the lot when the fire started. He took his jars of gasoline and spread one of them throughout the room. The other one he emptied mostly near his timing device, with a trail leading to the first row of video tapes.

Looking around the room, he felt satisfied with his work. He wished he'd been able to locate the actual Lasko tapes, but they had to be in here. He didn't want to take any more time and risk being caught. He reached down to his timer and started the five-minute countdown, then turned off his flashlight and left the room, closing the door behind him. He made his way back down the hall and out the door heading toward the front of the lot.

He was about to walk out into the main street between the bungalows and the stage when he heard voices coming his way. He couldn't be seen now, so he ducked into some bushes next to Bungalow B and waited for the people to leave. Unfortunately, they were coming right toward him.

" . . . that's funny, Rick. So you won't be too sorry if you're working on this show and won't be able to do the next Alert One infomercial, huh?" Rudy heard a female voice say as they got closer.

"No, I won't be sorry at all. I would love for this job to last a long time. If the rest of the staff is as nice as you are, Cassie, this won't seem like a job, but a family."

The pair walked past where Rudy was hiding, not noticing the large figure watching their every move.

"I hope the Lasko tapes are still in there," Cassie said as she searched through the key ring she'd brought from the office. "If there's something on them that was worth killing Wade for, you'd think the killer would have already destroyed the evidence."

Rudy tensed at her words. How could they know Wade was murdered? He reached behind him and grabbed the gun he always carried.

Rick reached the doorway first. "We may be too late. Look, Cassie, the door's already open. Somebody broke the lock."

Cassie looked down at the door in front of her. "I wonder when this happened. Everything was fine when we were over here earlier this afternoon."

"Do you know what time Sid normally goes home?"

"Normally he's here until after we finish taping, but with the hiatus this week, he could have left anytime this afternoon."

Rick listened for any noise inside. "Well, I don't think whoever did this is in there now. Let me go inside and check it out. Wait here."

"You're not leaving me out here. Let me come in with you. I'll phone security. They can send Reggie over here."

Rick remembered the former football player and decided his presence would be welcome, so the two entered the building together.

Rick flipped on the lights, and Cassie went over to a desk in the front room, quickly dialing security.

Rudy stayed in his hiding place outside Bungalow B. He looked at his watch, trying to decide whether to let the fire take its normal course or to go in and deal with the couple directly. He couldn't hear their voices anymore, but he'd heard enough. He wondered if Reggie was the guard he had just passed. Rudy decided it would be best to get away from the area. If he was lucky, the fire might take care of these two for him. He made his way out of the bushes, but headed the opposite direction of his car so he wouldn't run into Reggie. He walked along between the buildings, heading into the night and away from the imminent fire. He kept the two names he'd heard in his mind. Flint was right about someone in the office being onto the Lasko connection, and now he knew their names, Rick and Cassie.

Cassie hung up the phone inside Bungalow C and turned around. Rick wasn't there.

"Rick," she called out, a little louder than she'd planned to.

"Down here," he answered from the hallway.

Cassie walked the length of the hallway to where Rick was standing outside of the tape library door. "Don't you think we should wait for Reggie?" she asked.

"Maybe, but look. This door was broken into as well."

Rick moved his leg out and gently pushed the door inward. His nose was immediately assaulted with the smell of gasoline. He quickly turned, keeping Cassie in front of him, attempting to get them back down the hallway. He didn't get two steps away before a loud whoosh and a wave of heat threw them off their feet and onto the hallway carpet.

Stephanie and Bill had just cleared the side gate, coming in off a street closer to where the Harold stage was. They were making a turn, headed into the parking area when they felt, more than heard, the concussion from the gasoline explosion. Bill looked to his partner to see if she'd felt what he had; her expression confirmed that she had. He slammed on the brakes and double-parked the car where they were. They jumped out, looking for any sign of what had happened. A column of smoke was rising from down the street. Without speaking, they both ran toward it.

The fumes had collected in the room long enough to let the spark from Rudy's starter create a small bomb. Rick lay directly on top of Cassie, unconscious from the impact of the concussion that threw them down. The fireball from the explosion washed over them, igniting the ceiling in the hallway. Cassie had the wind knocked out of her, but was still coherent. She struggled, trying to get Rick's weight off of her, but she couldn't get up. She could feel the searing heat, surrounded by flames. Her lungs burned as she breathed in the smoke and superheated air.

Somehow, although nearly overcome with fear, death staring her in the face, her first thought was to ask God to intervene.

Suddenly Rick's dead weight was lifted off of her. She felt a strong hand grabbing the back of her blouse and lifting her to her feet. She felt half carried, half pushed out the front door and onto the grass outside. Her body was gasping for breath, her ribs aching as she coughed out the smoke in her lungs. She looked up and saw the big grin of Reggie, which at that moment looked like the face of an angel.

"Are you all right, Cassie?"

Through the coughs, she got out a yes.

"Check on Rick. I'm going to get us some help," Reggie said as he grabbed his radio, calling for assistance. Then he ran to get a fire hose and do what he could to try and contain the fire. Cassie looked over at the body lying next to her, not moving. Somehow Reggie had carried them both out at the same time. She touched Rick's face, praying he wasn't dead, and then he too started coughing. He opened his eyes, meeting Cassie's. She smiled as she realized he was all right. Rick, with great effort, managed to sit up. He was still coughing, trying to clear his lungs from all the smoke he'd sucked in. After catching his breath, he again looked up at Cassie.

"How ...," he coughed again.

"Reggie, our friendly security guard, carried us out. Are you OK?" she asked.

"Yeah, I think I am. How about you?"

"I'm fine. I just got the breath knocked out of me. When the explosion hit, we were thrown to the floor—unfortunately, with you on top of me. I couldn't move, but I think your body protected me from the blast."

She had Rick turn around and she looked at his back. His shirt was smoldering in a couple of places. He probably had some good burns under it, but he seemed to be all right. She felt such a release of emotion to realize that they'd come out of it without great harm that she instinctively reached around and hugged Rick. "I'm so glad you're all right."

Rick felt a flash of pain as her arms touched his back, but there was such caring in her embrace that he quickly blocked out the pain and put his arms around her in return. "I'm glad you're OK too. I'm sorry; it was probably a dumb thing going inside. We should have waited for help."

The moment of serenity was interrupted as people from around the studio arrived at the burning building. Smoke poured through the front doorway, flames licked up from the back. Reggie was between Bungalows B and C spraying the end of the burning building with a garden hose. Several other security officers joined in the fight as sirens approached in the distance.

They were able to keep the fire from spreading until the fire department arrived and took over. A couple of paramedics were attending to Rick and Cassie when Reggie was able to join up with them. He was relieved to see Rick awake and alert.

"How are you two feeling?" he asked as he walked up.

"We're hanging in there, thanks to you!" Cassie got up and gave him a big hug.

Rick reached out and shook his hand. "We're sure grateful you got there so quickly. I'm sure you saved our lives."

"Well, thank God. I had almost left for the night, but when I'd locked up the stage a few minutes ago, I passed a strange-looking man on my way out. I was just about to my car when something impressed me to come back over here and make sure everything was all right."

Cassie and Rick looked at each other. They both knew what that something was, but didn't know the other knew.

Reggie continued, "I was just turning the corner down there when the call came in on the radio about you two. I wasn't that far from the front door when the fire erupted."

Cassie looked up at him. "How did you know where we were?"

"I didn't, I just knew you were inside. So after the fireball came out the front door, I ran in and was able to find you on the floor of the hallway. I grabbed the two of you and hauled you outside on the lawn."

"Well, it was fortunate for us that you were there," Rick said. "I must have been knocked out when the explosion hit. The last thing I remember is smelling the gas and trying to get Cassie out of the building."

Reggie nodded. "Well, you made it far enough to protect her and yourself from serious harm."

Relief flooded through Cassie. "My two heroes," she said as she placed an arm around each one. The three laughed, letting the tension wash away.

Rick looked over at the burning bungalow, the firemen beginning to get it under control. "I wonder if we'll ever know what was on those tapes?"

"I certainly hope so." The three turned to a voice approaching from the other side of the van. It was Detective Phillips, walking up to them with her partner. "We were hoping to get a look at those tapes ourselves."

Cassie felt relieved when she saw them. She quickly introduced everyone around the group, then filled the detectives in on what had transpired.

Stephanie frowned. "I told you to stay out of any more detective work. You could have been killed."

Cassie didn't know what to say, but Rick stepped in to defend her. "Don't blame her; it was my idea. After we discovered a missing document that Wade had on his computer titled "The Lasko Interview," I suggested we just come over here and check out the tape for ourselves. Everyone else had pretty much gone home for the weekend. I didn't think anybody would even know."

Bill looked over at Reggie. "It's a good thing everyone hadn't gone home, or you two might have checked out altogether."

Stephanie turned back toward the bungalow. "I can't believe they burned all the tapes. We were so close to finding out something." Then she faced Rick. "What did you say about Wade's computer?"

"I'm sorry, detective," Cassie explained. "I just couldn't sit there all day with his computer and not look into it further. But what we did didn't change anything on the computer, I'm sure."

"That's very interesting. I'd like you to show us how you found that out after we wrap things up here," Stephanie said.

"Do you know who's behind this?" Cassie asked.

"We have some ideas, but we really needed to see what that interview held to make sense of it all. We still don't know what would make whoever is behind this need to kill Bennett," she said as she looked over at the smoking building, "and torch a studio."

She turned to the paramedic who had been treating Rick. "Is he going to need to go to the hospital?"

"That's really up to him," the paramedic responded. "The burns on his back are minor. He's cleaned and bandaged, but it might not be a bad idea since he was unconscious for a brief moment."

Rick shrugged off the idea. "If he says the burns are minor, then I'm fine, really. I don't want to go to some emergency room and sit there half the night waiting for someone else to tell me the same thing."

"Then let's do this," Stephanie suggested. "Reggie, if you don't mind, would you escort these two back to the production office?"

"I'd be happy to."

"Great. We'll meet you back there in a few minutes. Bill, I'd like you to work with their security getting any information on anyone allowed onto the studio within the past hour. Get all you can, names, license plates, you name it. I'll work with the fire department here and see if there are any undamaged tapes. From the looks of it I doubt it, but you never know."

It was close to an hour before Stephanie and Bill finally made their way back into the office. Cassie, Rick, and Reggie had pulled out some soft drinks from the office refrigerator and passed the time trying to solve the mystery. Unfortunately, none of them were able to put what pieces they had together to make any sense of the whole thing.

"Well, I'm sorry to say, it doesn't look like any of the tapes made it through the fire, much less the Lasko ones," Stephanie informed them as she sat down next to Cassie. Bill took a seat beside Rick.

"Security's been very helpful. We've got the names of all the visitors, and the security tapes will show the license of every car that entered, so maybe we'll get lucky there."

"Mr. Treadway, Cassie," Stephanie looked from one to the other, "the press showed up after you left. The official story is that no one was in the building when the fire started. I think at this point, it is best for you two that no one knows you were looking for anything. Agreed?"

After what they had already been through, that was fine with them.

Stephanie continued, "With the loss of whatever was on that tape, we're going to have to come up with some other leads."

"Can you fill us in on anything?" Cassie asked. "I'm kind of worried about who to trust around here."

Stephanie looked at Bill, who picked up the lead. "We suspect that Gabriel Flint is behind Wade's murder."

Cassie wasn't shocked. There had always been something about that man she didn't like.

"We have a file on Flint that goes way back," Bill filled them in, "but we've never been able to convict him. He's been involved for years in pornography, prostitution, pimping, all sorts of illegal activities. As far as we know, this show is the first legitimate business venture he's been involved with."

Rick couldn't believe what he was hearing. Had he just started a job working for a pornography king?

"One of Flint's places, The Club Royale, is managed by Joe Lasko," Stephanie added. "I have to think that's the Lasko we've been looking for. There's something on that tape that would incriminate Flint in some way. But with the fire, we're back to the same dead end."

"Where do we go from here, Detectives?" Cassie asked. "Do we just go on like nothing happened?"

"For now, yes. But you have to be careful. Although we suspect Flint, there has to be someone here at the office tipping him off. Who, I can't say for sure. That's why I called you earlier to warn you."

Stephanie turned to Rick. "I guess your new job just landed you in the midst of a frying pan." She then got up, turning to Cassie, "Before I let you all go, it's time for you to show me what you found on Wade's computer."

The whole group left the conference room and gathered around Cassie's desk. It just took a few minutes for her to show the two detectives how they discovered the missing file.

"All you need to do is use a retrieval program. If the murderer left this much information on the disk, I'm sure he didn't know how to totally erase the files. It should be simple to get them back."

Stephanie sighed, "there's a lab person who's about to get a rude awakening with that news as soon as we get back to the office. Now, I think it's best if you and Rick go on home. We'll take Reggie down and see if we can get an I.D. on the mystery arsonist. If anything turns up over the weekend, we'll give you both a call. If you don't hear from us, treat Monday like any other day. Go about your business as usual."

Stephanie glanced at Cassie. "I'm letting the studio people alert the normal staff about the fire. I don't want anybody to know that we were even down here."

After locking up the office, Rick and Cassie headed toward the staff parking lot while Reggie headed with the two detectives back toward the bungalow.

The peacefulness of the moonlit night contrasted sharply with what they'd been through over the past couple of hours. As Rick and Cassie walked, there was an awkward silence, neither knowing what to say.

Rick finally broke the ice. "It's hard to believe that before today, we'd never met. After all we've been through the past couple of hours, I have the feeling I've known you for a lifetime."

Cassie liked the sound of that, but tried to keep her guard up. Tonight, though, she couldn't help responding after the events they'd shared.

"I have the same feeling, Rick," Cassie said. "When you were lying on the grass, unconscious, I was afraid of losing a friend—especially one who'd just saved my life."

"Oh, come on, you just didn't want to have to go through the process of calling all those directors and their agents back to fill my job," Rick teased. "Besides, don't forget, if it wasn't for me, you wouldn't have been in there tonight in the first place."

Cassie playfully punched him in the shoulder. "I can tell you're really the sentimental type. Although you do have a point; those agents can be a pain—especially yours!"

"Yeah, he's a pain sometimes, but he makes good deals. I wonder if he sealed up the deal for this show yet."

"If he hasn't, will that stop you from directing Monday?"

"I shouldn't tell you this—you are the assistant to the producer after all—but Jacob and I decided I'll be doing the show, even if a deal isn't solidified. This job is too important to me."

"I'm glad."

They were coming up to Cassie's car, and she slowed down, getting her keys out of her purse. Rick stopped and looked at her. "Is every night at the office going to be like this one?"

"I certainly hope not. I can't take the stress." The two laughed. Cassie touched the back of Rick's torn and burned shirt. "Is your back really all right? Do you feel any pain now?"

"It's a little tender, I have to admit. If it gets bad, I can always go see a doctor tomorrow."

"I'm just glad you're OK. Well, drive safely," Cassie said as she unlocked her car and stepped into it. "We'll see you on Monday."

Rick hated to let her go, but they'd just been through so much, he didn't want to take advantage of the emotional evening. "Until Monday then. And Cassie, thanks for being so helpful today. You made what could have been a stressful adjustment into a lot of fun."

"You're welcome," Cassie said as she started her car. Then through her open window she called, "Have a relaxing weekend. Monday will be a big day for you."

11:13 P.M., BEVERLY HILLS

Gabriel Flint turned his back to Rudy, looking at the TV set. A news reporter had just finished with the story about the fire at National Studios. Various shots of firemen working around the building filled the screen as the announcer voiced over the footage, "No one was hurt in the blaze, and firefighters are crediting the quick-thinking security staff with containing the fire. Because of the age of some of the surrounding buildings, there could have been a major disaster if it had spread. Fortunately, damage was limited to just one building, which housed the tape library of the 'The John Harold Show.' Speculation is high that this fire was intentionally set."

"You were sure they were in the building, huh?" Flint asked Rudy with disgust.

"They were in it when I left, and I heard the explosion a half minute later. They had to have still been inside. I don't see how they could have gotten out. Maybe they're keeping it out of the news for some reason," Rudy tried to explain.

"That could be true. Now you're sure you heard the two talking about Lasko?" Flint drilled again.

"Yes, and I'm positive they called each other Rick and Cassie."

"We just hired a new director named Rick. I don't see how he could be involved in this so quickly. I'll have to check the staff list to see if there are any other Ricks on the payroll. But I know who Cassie is. She's the one who's been asking so many questions."

"They even mentioned Wade being killed," Rudy went on. "They may not know what's on those tapes, but they have sure connected Wade's death to Lasko."

Flint thought for a moment. "Well, let's just hope the fire took care of this little problem. If not, we'll have to come up with something to point them, and anybody else asking questions, in another direction. Oh, by the way, I have an address on the license plate you wanted." Flint laughed. It was a hauntingly evil sound.

CHAPTER 23

Rick was exhausted by the time he made it home. It was nearly midnight. He hadn't realized how long he'd been there after the fire. He saw lights on inside his condo and was startled. Then he remembered the conversation with Gary. The last thing Rick wanted to deal with was a house full of guests.

Gary met him as he walked into the kitchen. "Rick, I was a little concerned. I saw a report on the news about a fire at the studio. They said no one was hurt, but you never—" As Gary was talking, Rick walked past him into the kitchen. Gary got a good view of the back of his shirt.

"My goodness, Rick, you were in the fire!"

Rick turned back toward him and smiled. "Yeah, I kind of was. But I wasn't alone. God's protection was really evident tonight."

"Rick, you're home." A sleepy Jill made her way into the kitchen. "Thanks so much for letting us come over—" Then she, too, saw Rick's back. "What happened to you? Are you OK?"

"Yes, I'm all right."

"Let's get that shirt off and have a look at it," Jill responded. Rick submitted to her while she gave him a proper check-over.

"Do you have some first aid stuff around here?"

"Yeah, in the guest bathroom."

Jill found some antiseptic and some bandages, then returned, checking out the paramedics' work. Rick recounted the night's events mixed in with a couple of ouches as Jill hit some tender spots.

"Wow!" Gary reacted. "I can't believe you've been through all that on the same night Jill gets run off the road and almost killed."

Rick was astonished. "Is that why you guys needed a place to stay? Tell me the whole story."

Jill had finished with Rick's back, so the three of them sat at the kitchen table. Gary began. "Well it kind of started on Wednesday, when this lady came into the Crisis Pregnancy Center and talked with Jill ..."

Between the two of them, they filled Rick in on as much as they knew. Vanessa had still been too upset to open up and tell her whole story. Rick was amazed when he heard about the car running Jill off the freeway, then Gary being shot at. He couldn't believe the turn of events in both their lives, much less happening on the same night.

"Is Vanessa resting comfortably?" Rick asked as they finished.

"Yeah, we've got her in the guest bed. When you didn't come home right away, we decided she needed some rest, and that would give her the most privacy."

"Have you guys called the police about any of this?"

"Not yet. We weren't sure what to report," Gary confided. "If Vanessa wants to make a clean break from this group, whoever they are, filing a complaint against them would just mess up her life right now. She needs to really be sure before we do anything, so we decided to just lay low here and give her a night to think about it. We hope we'll find out more in the morning."

Rick thought for a second. "But what that guy did to Jill was attempted murder. You can't let that go by."

"I'm sure it was," Gary agreed, "but how are we going to prove it? The guy can just say he lost control of the car or something."

"What about shooting at you as you two left?"

"We didn't stop and get the names of any witnesses. If somebody reported it to the police, they might believe us, but knowing LA, I doubt anyone hung around long enough for the police to show up."

"Well, you guys can't go off dealing with criminals like this by yourself."

Jill suppressed a smile. "Look who's talking."

They shared a laugh. "Maybe we should all sleep on it," Rick conceded.

"But before we turn in," Gary said, "I think we ought to give thanks to our Lord for getting us all through the night, and pray for his wisdom as we make decisions tomorrow."

"I'm all for that," Rick answered. "Since we had lunch the other day, Gary, God has really been at work. I rededicated my life to him during the fellowship meeting last night. In spite of all the church time I'd put in, I didn't understand what an intimate relationship with Jesus really meant."

Gary was nodding, and Rick could see a tear slide down Jill's cheek. He continued, "Thanks to your example, I'm a changed man."

SATURDAY, 12:10 A.m., VAN NUYS

Cassie arrived at her apartment exhausted. Her roommate, Amy, was already in her room for the evening, but Cassie felt she needed to share what had happened that night with her. She walked into her room, and whispered, "Amy? Are you asleep?"

"Not really, I heard you come in," Amy answered, sitting up in her bed and turning the light on.

Cassie walked into the room and sat on the edge of her bed. "You won't believe what happened tonight . . ." She filled Amy in on all that she'd been through.

When she finished, Amy gave her a hug as she said, "I'm so glad God had his hand on you. You could have been killed."

"It was close, all right. I'm especially thankful for Rick's quick reactions and Reggie coming back to check on that guy."

"You really like him, don't you?"

Cassie was taken aback. "Who?"

"That new director, Rick," Amy answered, grinning from ear to ear.

Cassie couldn't believe it. She hadn't even been truthful with herself about her growing feelings for Rick. How could Amy see it?

"I didn't say that."

"You didn't have to. I can see it all over your face. It kind of lights up when you talk about him."

"Oh, Amy, you're just imagining it. You know I won't let myself get involved with anybody who isn't a Christian again. You helped me through the last time I made that mistake. I don't know Rick well enough to make that judgment yet," Cassie said.

"That's easy for you to say, but sometimes our hearts don't wait for what our minds know to be right, remember?" Amy responded. "Has he said anything to make you think he might be a Christian?"

Cassie relaxed, allowing her feelings to show. "Well, this afternoon, while I was giving Rick a tour of the stage, he thanked God for the job out loud. It caught me so off guard, I completely missed what he said next. I felt like such a fool. It may not have meant anything."

"Or, maybe it did," Amy said, smiling.

12:20 a.m., SHERIFF'S HEADQUARTERS

Stephanie had given Reggie fifteen mug shots of various convicts. Several of the thugs that Vice had told them surrounded Flint were included in the pictures. Rudy Vanozzi was one of them.

Reggie flipped through the pictures. It had been dark when the man had passed him, so it was hard to remember the features. He wished he could see them in a lineup because he figured he'd remember the size of the man easier than his facial features. Stephanie and Bill watched with interest as Reggie continued through the pictures.

He flipped through them, finally pausing as he looked at one of them. "I think this might be the guy," Reggie said, as he looked intently at the picture.

Stephanie looked over his shoulder to see which picture he was looking at. It was Rudy Vanozzi. She was excited to see that it was one of the thugs who had been associated with Flint, but she couldn't lead Reggie into fingering the guy with her emotions. She spoke calmly, "Take a good look and try to be sure, Reggie."

He eyed the picture a moment longer, then looked up at Bill and Stephanie. "It was dark, and I only passed him for a brief moment. I don't know if I can be totally sure, but it looks like it could be him. I think if I saw him in person again, I'd know for sure."

Stephanie smiled at him. "That's good enough for us, Reggie. We'll put out an APB for him, and when we pick him up, we'll get you down here. I know you're probably exhausted after all you've been through tonight. Thanks for your help."

Reggie smiled. "It was my pleasure. Life can get pretty boring on a film lot. This has been the most excitement we've had in awhile. But I just thank God that nobody was hurt."

Reggie made his way out of the precinct, leaving Bill and Stephanie alone at their desks.

Bill stretched, yawning as he leaned back in his chair. "Well, I think a twenty-hour day just about wraps it up, don't you?"

"I know I'm beat. I'm just not sure what our next step is. We really needed what was on that tape."

"Well, there's not much more we can do tonight, except get the call out for Vanozzi."

"I'll do that. You head on home."

"How about tomorrow? Are we authorized to work through the weekend on this?"

Stephanie hadn't talked to the captain about it. "The way the department's been cutting back, I doubt it. I do know Ray's going to be working tomorrow after I get ahold of him." She reached for the phone, looking up Ray's home number.

"You're calling him tonight?"

"You bet. He's coming in tomorrow and going over this computer with a fine-tooth comb."

"He's going to be upset that he missed the stuff those two found on that thing."

"He should be! Look, why don't you head on home. We need to make an appearance at that memorial service tomorrow. I'll pick you up around 10:30."

Bill liked the sound of that and didn't wait around for Stephanie to change her mind. Sleeping in tomorrow morning seemed like just what he needed.

12:45 a.m., STUDIO CITY

Everyone in the house had gone to sleep for the night. Gary and Jill were in Rick's bedroom and he was on the couch. Rick flipped open his Bible. It stopped at Psalm 32. He scanned the verses, his heart quickening as he read the seventh one: *You are my hiding place; you shall protect me from trouble and surround me with songs of deliverance.*

The words were as if they were his own, pouring out from his gratefulness at how the Lord had intervened for him and Cassie. He finished the rest of the psalm, focusing on the last two verses: *Many are the woes of the wicked; but the Lord's unfailing love surrounds the man who trusts in him. Rejoice in the Lord and be glad, you righteous: sing, all you who are upright in heart!*

The words brought Rick's mind back to earlier in the week, before he had rededicated his life to the Lord. He remembered the compromising position he had found himself in with Samantha, the financial stress he'd been under with no prospect for jobs, and the lack of hope he'd found in the formalized religion he was living. He sure fit the part of woes to the wicked, although he never would have classified himself as such before. Now he wasn't so sure the life he'd lived before even included God. He definitely knew it hadn't been pleasing to him.

Now Rick could see so much of God's hand in his life. He could see the mercy that surrounded him because of the Lord, even though the circumstances were no less stressful. After being nearly killed, in the middle of a murder investigation, precariously hanging on to a job he hadn't even worked a full day on yet, Rick still felt God's peace about him.

He had read enough of the Bible and heard enough sermons to know that a committed walk with God did not guarantee all of your troubles would vanish. Quite the contrary, it brought with it a lot of sacrifice, and sometimes suffering, which would be used by the Lord in the maturing process. Rick agreed with the final verse of Psalm 32; he was glad in the Lord tonight and rejoicing in the change within his heart. He prayed that God would continue to mold him as He had been doing over the past couple of days.

Rick was still troubled about one thing: he was working for an evil man. If the police were right, and Flint was into pornography, prostitution, pimping, and now even murder, what purpose did God have in bringing this job to Rick? It didn't make sense. But then, he realized that God's wisdom is so far above his own, that he would just have to continue along the path God had ordained, and continue to trust in him.

Rick closed the Book, thinking about the one other major point of interest he had found in his life within the past couple of days—Cassie. As he settled down into the couch and closed his eyes, he saw her smiling face and caring eyes looking down at him as he lay on the grass next to the burning bungalow. Then he recalled the brilliant smile that lit up her face as she saw that he was going to be all right. There was something about that girl.

CHAPTER 24

Rick awoke to the sunlight filtering through his living room. He started to stretch, then felt the pain of the burns on his back and winced. The events of the previous night flashed through his mind.

He struggled to sit up, realizing that the combination of last night's blast and the soft cushions of the couch left him sore all over. There were no signs yet of Gary, Jill, or the mysterious Vanessa, whom Rick hadn't even met yet.

He made his way into the guest bathroom, going through his normal wake-up routine. He tried to get a look at his burns, but Jill had done an excellent job of bandaging.

When he came out of the bathroom, Gary and Jill were in the kitchen putting on a pot of coffee.

"Did you guys just wake up?" Rick asked.

"A little bit ago. We waited to come out until we heard you stirring so we wouldn't wake you," Gary answered.

"How'd you sleep? Did the burns keep you up?" Jill asked.

"I woke up a few times, but I didn't realize how sore I was until I tried to get out of bed."

"Let me get some coffee, then I'll take another look at you. The burns didn't look too bad last night, but we want to make sure you don't get an infection started," Jill said.

Coming out of her bedroom, Vanessa made a dash for the guest bathroom without speaking to anyone.

Jill smiled, looking to the men. "I'll bet you that was a morning sickness run."

"Poor girl," Gary said. "What she must be going through—all alone, pregnant, and probably dealing with some withdrawal symptoms as well. I pray God touches her through all this."

Rick looked through his cupboards, hoping to find some breakfast food he could offer to his guests. Being single, he didn't keep much stocked, especially with the financial hardship he'd been dealing with. "I hope I can find something edible, in case anyone's hungry."

"Coffee is all I really need," Jill said.

"What about your breakfast meeting with Rob this morning?" Gary asked.

"I totally forgot about that," Rick said, scratching his unruly hair. "I wonder if I should cancel until we have a plan of what to do about last night's activities."

"Actually," Gary thought out loud, "Rob might be very valuable."

"How do you mean?"

"Well, I've learned recently that whenever I come up against major decisions, it's been very helpful to get with another believer—share with them my perspective and then pray together, being willing to listen to what God might be speaking to them. I believe firmly that we all see in part, and hear in part. The more we share those parts together, submitting to the Holy Spirit, the greater chance we'll have of being in line with God's will."

Jill looked up at Rick over her cup of coffee. "Gary's right, Rick. We're all so closely involved—we, in Vanessa's dilemma; you, in this suicide-murder. Rob could be a great confirmation for direction."

Rick nodded. "I think that makes sense. I was looking forward to spending some time with him anyway. But what about you and Vanessa?"

"Well, she's going to need some time to get it all together this morning anyway," Jill looked over to the bathroom as she spoke. "This will give us more time to spend together. Maybe she'll open up some more. Then I can help her decide whether or not to involve the police. You and Gary go. We're safe here."

"All right. Then I guess we have a meeting to get to. I'm going to grab a quick shower, then we'll head off."

9:00 a.m., NORTHRIDGE

When Rick and Gary walked into the pancake house a little more than an hour later, Rob was already sitting at a booth waiting for them. He got up and greeted them with hugs. Rick winced at the pain as Rob's hands patted against his back.

"Careful, Rob," Gary cautioned, "he's got some pretty good burns back there from last night."

Rob carefully withdrew his hug. "I'm sorry, Rick. What happened?"

Rick tried to ease his concern. "I'm OK, really. Did you hear about the fire at National Studios last night?"

As the three took their seats in the booth, Rob answered, "I saw something about that on the news. I remember it piqued my interest because they mentioned your show. But I thought they said no one was inside."

"That's the official story. Actually I was inside with the producer's assistant. The blast from the fire nearly killed us. If God hadn't supplied us with a very alert security guard, I don't think I would be here today."

After they all ordered breakfast, the group spent the next few moments going over the details of how Rick got the job and ended up getting into the middle of Bennett's murder investigation. After the food arrived, they covered Gary's story with Vanessa and his heroic afternoon of gunshots and car chases.

Rob looked over the two men across from him. "I feel like I'm having breakfast with Kojak and Colombo. Or maybe more accurately with Peter and Paul. God's really had his hand on your lives."

Rick agreed. "And you know, before this week, I probably wouldn't have even recognized that. But even before the fire last night, I'd seen God's hand in my life in many ways. Gary here has had a lot to do with that. And your fellowship group the other night really opened my eyes to some things."

"I'm glad to hear that. Now, concerning your two exciting adventures, we need to put some serious prayer into these matters. Let's start with you, Gary. Do you know what God wants you to do concerning Vanessa?"

Gary shook his head. "Not for sure. When we were praying with her last night, I felt the Lord saying to be his ambassador to her. I was reminded of the sharing from the fellowship group about loving people, one at a time. I know Vanessa was brought to us to show her God's love. Unfortunately, she's still hiding some things. Jill and I feel we need to involve the police at this stage, but she's still not sure. We need to pray for God's wisdom on that decision. Being chased off the road, then shot at, involves a lot more than a boyfriend who doesn't want her to have a baby."

Rob added, "You're probably right about that. We also need to lift up her soul. She's at a real crossroads in her life. Hopefully this episode will be what God uses to open her heart to him. Let's join in prayer."

Rob reached out and grabbed the hands of the two men opposite him. Gary immediately bowed his head, while Rick hesitated. He looked around the restaurant. They were in a back corner of the room tucked away from most of the crowd, so they didn't stand out. At first the old thoughts of embarrassment began to enter Rick's thinking, then he stopped. What's wrong with praying in a restaurant with a couple of men who serve God? After all God had done for Rick lately, he decided it was time to put away any thoughts of embarrassment at looking like a follower of Christ. Rick bowed his head with the other two and began focusing his thoughts on God.

After a moment of silence, Rob began praying on behalf of Gary, Jill, and Vanessa. Moments passed. "...as we wait on you, Lord, present your direction for Gary's life, even now, dear Jesus."

The three stayed quiet as they waited. Rick continued praying for Gary in his mind until he ran out of words. Then he felt a thought enter his mind: *Take Gary to the memorial service.* Rick didn't understand it. Was it God speaking to his mind, or was he creating something during the quietness of the moment? In the past, he'd been the one to do all the talking; when the prayer was finished, he would go on to something else. He'd never been instructed to wait for the Lord to speak back. He wasn't sure if he should share what he thought or not.

Gary broke the silence. "I thank you, Lord, for the protection you gave to Jill and me. I pray that the man looking for Vanessa would be stopped by your great power. I pray for protection around Rick's house as he has allowed us to stay with him. And, Lord, I really need your direction right now. In myself, I want to let the police handle everything and keep my family out of danger. But I know that you are the source of life, and whatever you want us to do, we are willing."

There was silence for the next couple of minutes, then Rob spoke out. "Did either of you get a feeling of what the next step should be?"

Gary kept quiet and looked over at Rick. Rick's heart was beating twice its normal rate. He wanted to share what he'd thought but was afraid he'd look foolish. Finally he spoke up.

"I had one thought come to mind. I'm not sure if it's God or not. After your prayer, Rob, I felt the impression to take Gary with me to the memorial service for Wade."

Gary smiled. "That's funny," he said. "I felt the same impression, but for the life of me I couldn't figure out why I'd need to go to the service."

Relief flooded over Rick as Gary continued. "I've worked on a couple of shows with Wade, but never had any direct interaction with him."

"Well, it looks like the Lord is only going to reveal one step at a time." Rob added, "By the way, I think when you get home Jill will have some more information that'll help you decide your next step as well."

"What makes you say that?" Gary asked.

"Just a feeling. I have a hunch that Jill and Vanessa are having a heart-to-heart talk right now. I've been interceding for them as we've been sitting here."

Rick sighed, "I'm so amazed. I didn't realize the Holy Spirit brought to mind people in need of prayer until Jill and Gary prayed for me the other night."

"That's all part of walking in the Spirit. Gary's told me a little of your story," Rob said, changing the subject. "He said you have some questions that he thought I could answer for you."

Rick paused. He'd been through so much in the past twenty-four hours, he hadn't thought about the questions that had been on his mind.

"I guess the area I was questioning was about our different gifts," Rick said. "Gary challenged me with some questions the other night at dinner. It sent me on a search through the Scriptures about gifts. I guess I had some ingrown biases about ministry within the church."

Gary laughed, "Nothing we all haven't had, I'm sure."

"After seeing how your home fellowship responded, really caring for one another, it helped me to understand what the New Testament teaches about the body of Christ, and your 'one another-ing' principle," Rick continued.

Rob stopped him. "It's not my 'one anothering' principle. A lot of people across the country are catching on to the church—in other words, the people of God—serving and ministering to each other."

"I guess the main question Gary thought you could answer is where does that leave pastors? What is their job if everyone in the church is doing the ministry stuff?"

Rob smiled over at Gary; they'd been through the same discussion a few times themselves. "Rick, there's a very simple answer to your question. But, unfortunately, the church in our society hasn't responded to it."

It appeared to Rob that Rick had anticipated a more direct answer. Rob reached into his pocket and pulled out a small New Testament. " I'm not trying to be elusive, Rick. Hopefully, this will all make more sense in a minute. Let's start with what the Bible says: Ephesians, the fourth chapter."

Rob thumbed through his Bible and found the passage. Then he placed it at the center of the table and pointed to verses 11–13 so that Rick could see the words as he read: *It was he who gave some to be apostles, some to be prophets, some to be evangelists, and some to be pastors and teachers, to prepare God's people for works of service, so that the body of Christ may be built up until we all reach unity in the faith and in the knowledge of the Son of God and become mature, attaining to the whole measure of the fullness of Christ.*

Rob pulled the Bible back and continued talking, "You see, Rick, the purpose of the pastor, as it says right here, is to prepare God's people for works of service. Notice it doesn't say that he is the one to do all the serving, or in the words of your question, to do all the ministering. You're right on that score; that's the job of the whole body of Christ. Romans 12 and 1 Peter 4 are pretty clear about the body being made up of many parts, each functioning in its specific gifting."

Rick nodded. He was now familiar with those references.

"I used to pastor a church up in northern Oregon," Rob continued. "It was successful by worldly standards. We were running about 650 on Sunday mornings, had wonderful programs, a good Sunday school, and I had a great board behind me. Everything on the outside looked like a very successful church. But it wasn't."

Rick looked surprised. This sounded like every pastor's dream church.

"It took a visit to a doctor to wake me up. I'd been having trouble sleeping at night. I would wake up at odd hours, thinking about something to do with the church—a couple who was struggling with divorce, or where we'd get the money for the next building phase. Something was always on my mind. Then I started having some chest pains, and my wife convinced me to see a doctor. After an initial examination, the doctor looked at me and said, "Well, there's nothing wrong with you that a good change in occupations wouldn't cure. You're just under too much stress." Then he looked at me and asked, "By the way, what do you do?"

"I was embarrassed to admit that I was a pastor. That evening, while I once again was awake at three in the morning, I cried my heart out before the Lord. I said, *Lord I believe that you called me to this profession. But if it's going to be the death of me, I want out. Either find me something else to do, or change me so that the ministry won't affect me like this.* That was my prayer—change me, God, for I can't do it on my own. It wasn't immediate, but within the next few weeks, I started seeing things in Scripture that I hadn't seen before.

"It started here in Ephesians. The first thing that jumped out at me was that I wasn't doing very much equipping, but nearly all of the ministry myself. I was preaching three times on Sundays and once on Wednesday nights, visiting the sick, supervising the office staff and the associate pastors, presiding over the board, and scheduling counseling appointments. Then I noticed that around me there was a lack of the supporting gifts mentioned in those verses we just read. I was pretty much all alone. I've heard other pastors tell me about the burden of being a pastor, how lonely ministry can be. I was right there, buying that lie with the rest of them. But now I don't believe it's God's plan at all."

Rick was amazed, he'd never considered the enormous strain that pastors must be under.

"Don't pity me," Rob laughed. "I'd brought it on myself. You see, my identity came through being needed by the people in my church. That's what fulfilled me. Unfortunately, that's a very unhealthy relationship, both for me and for the body. In Corinthians, Paul addressed those in the body who all wanted to be the same part. He asked, if everyone were only one body part, where would the rest of the body be? I think in America today, we are doing the opposite. We expect one person, the pastor, to be and do all things. But how can a single person be a skilled leader, speaker, visionary, administrator, counselor, businessman, conflict resolver, and theologian? It just doesn't happen."

Rick spoke up, "I see what you mean. While I was thinking about some of the things Gary had asked, I realized that I would expect the pastor to handle practically everything that I thought would be categorized as ministry."

"That's a good point. Notice how we elevate the word *ministry*, like when we say a pastor is 'going into the ministry.' Actually, we are all called to be ministers. The mere fact that we distinguish between clergy and layman that way has left us with an anemic congregation, as well as either a burned-out or calloused clergy."

"That's depressing," Rick interjected.

"It's a disaster," Rob responded. "I remember when I just started working for a church as an associate pastor. One of the first things the senior pastor advised me was that I would need to get calloused in ministry. Something about that bothered me at the time, but it took years of walking through what I'm talking about to see how wrong that attitude can be."

"So what happened?" Rick asked. "Did you leave the minist—" Rick caught himself before he finished the sentence, "I mean, did you find another occupation?"

Rob chuckled, "That's OK. It's hard to stop old habits, isn't it? Actually, it took several years for the Lord to work within me what I've tried to explain here in just a couple of minutes. But I knew I was starting to change several months after that doctor's appointment when I was nursing a softball injury. I had a big scab on my knee from sliding into second base. That night, while rolling over in bed, I brushed the covers against it and immediately woke up in pain. I was suddenly wide awake at three in the morning. Then it hit me— I couldn't remember the last time I'd been awake at night worrying about something. Without sensing it, Jesus had made a change in me. I wasn't stressing out with the job. God had been working within me, and the realizations that I was seeing in Scripture about the body ministering to each other began to change the paradigm of the ministry of our church. People began catching on to the principle of the body ministering to each other. Home fellowships started springing up where people were doing the 'one anothering' thing, like what you saw exhibited in the group the other night."

"That group was a real eye opener for me," Rick said. "I'm glad I finally broke down and made it to a meeting."

"I'm glad, too," Rob said with a big smile. "Now, I think it's time we pray for your situation. We need to continue to pray for your protection and that the real people behind Wade's murder will be brought to justice."

9:45 a.m., STUDIO CITY

It took a while for Vanessa to feel like she was ready to face the world. The morning sickness had sapped her energy and the effects of withdrawal only added to her discomfort. She eventually made her way out into the kitchen after the men had left, where Jill's offer of toast and coffee helped to settle her stomach. Jill just let her sip the coffee in silence, not wanting to push her into a conversation she might not be ready for. Yet, inside, Jill was anxious to hear the whole story behind Vanessa's running away and this guy Rudy who had tried to kill her.

Finally, Vanessa took her eyes off of her coffee mug and looked up at Jill. "Jill, you and Gary are being so nice to me and you don't even know me. . . . I don't understand why anyone would do this, especially when you were nearly killed. I've never seen that kind of love before."

Jill smiled warmly at her. "It's not anything we can take credit for, Vanessa. I'm not usually the kind of person to reach out to strangers, but since I've become a Christian, God is doing a wonderful work in my life. It's because of the love he's shown me that I am able to respond to you in love."

"It's funny," Vanessa replied, "I haven't thought of anything to do with Jesus since I was a kid and my grandmother would take me to church. But all of the stories about God and Jesus have come flooding back to my mind since meeting you. I thought it was all a fairy tale. But you and Gary really believe it. I can see it in how you live your lives."

"Yes, we do believe it. Vanessa, from what little you've told me, I know you've been hurt very deeply in your past. What's worse, the hurt has come from your mother and stepfather, the two people who should have protected you and loved you the most. That's a difficult thing to get over."

Jill could see Vanessa reacting—a tear started a slow journey down her cheek. "God wants you to know that he loves you unconditionally, just the way you are. It may be hard for you to trust that, especially because of your past relationship with your parents, but it's true. He loved you so much he sent his only Son, Jesus Christ, down to earth to pay the penalty for your sins so that you might be restored to a loving relationship with him."

Vanessa was nodding her head up and down. "I remember the stories, and even the Scripture that goes along with that idea. Something like . . . 'For God so loved the world, that he gave his only begotten Son, that whosoever believeth in him should not perish, but have eternal life.' Is that right?"

Jill smiled, "That's exactly right. It's amazing how much we keep with us from our Sunday school lessons as kids. The verse is John 3:16."

"But it doesn't work for me. You don't know what I've done. The life I've lived since leaving home is not the kind that God can just turn around and forgive."

"Oh, but he can, and he does, Vanessa. You might be surprised at some of the stuff I did before I met Gary, actually even after we met. It wasn't until later that we found the Lord together. The Bible says that all of us have sinned and fallen short of the glory of God. But if we confess our sins, he is faithful and just to forgive us our sins, and to cleanse us from all unrighteousness. No matter what you've done in the past, if you believe in Jesus and confess his lordship, he'll wipe your slate clean. You can begin a new life, start all over."

Vanessa looked down at her coffee cup again, contemplating the decision that was burning on her heart. She knew what she was hearing was the truth, something she'd been running from for a long, long time. It just sounded too easy, too good to be true. She'd become so jaded and cynical over the past several years; she'd taught herself that if it sounded too good to be true, then it must be a lie. But she was at the end of her rope. There was nowhere else to turn but to a God who could love her in spite of where her life was and what she'd done.

"I think I want to do that, Jill. But before I do, I think it's only fair to tell you who I really am. If you still think God can love me and will forgive me—"

"Vanessa, I'm sure he loves you and will forgive you, and you don't have to tell me if you're not ready," Jill responded, placing her hand over Vanessa's.

Vanessa knew it was time, so she proceeded to tell Jill all that had happened since she ran away to Los Angeles to make her big break in show business. She didn't leave anything out, from the pornographic movies, to being kept as a plaything for Gabriel Flint's acquaintances. She also filled in all the details about Rudy's coming into her apartment the night before she met Jill and the beating she received.

Jill sat there stunned. She didn't realize the kind of danger they had placed themselves into. The worst Jill had feared was that there was some unstable boyfriend involved who demanded she get an abortion.

"Do you think Rudy will continue to look for you?" Jill asked.

"I'm sure of it. Gabriel doesn't leave people around who know anything about his business."

"Wow, this is serious stuff, but it doesn't change the truths of what I've told you. God does love you, Vanessa. He's got a plan for you that from here on out will be the greatest thrill of your life ... if you choose to follow him."

Vanessa thought for a moment, then lifted her head, her eyes meeting Jill's. "I want to follow him, but I just don't feel worthy. I feel so dirty inside, so guilty. How do I get rid of that?" she asked.

Jill's face broke into a big grin. "That's easy, Vanessa. . . ."

CHAPTER 25

Cassie was groggy, sitting up in her bed. After getting home so late, then talking into the early morning hours with Amy, she just couldn't get herself up for the day. She looked at the clock radio beside her—9:50 A.M. She had less than an hour to get herself together and leave for Wade's memorial service.

Becky! She needed to let her know about the events of last night. The poor woman had a right to know that it looked like her suspicions about her husband were right. She decided to try and give her a call now; it would probably be hard to talk to her about anything at the service.

Cassie slipped on her robe and walked out of the bedroom. She grabbed a staff sheet from the show that she kept by the kitchen phone and looked up Wade's phone number.

Becky's mother and her sister, Melissa, were in her bedroom, helping her get things together before leaving for the service. Becky came out of the closet holding a long black dress in front of her.

"I think that'll look perfect," her mother appraised it.

"Are you sure?" Becky answered. "It just looks so typically widowish."

Both her mother and sister looked at her, not sure of what to say. They were glad to be interrupted by the ringing phone. Melissa was closest to it so she picked it up.

"Hello."

"Hi, is Becky available? It's Cassie from the production office."

"Hi, Cassie, I'm not sure this is a good time. Becky's got a lot to do to get ready for the service—"

Becky heard and started toward the phone, "Thanks for covering for me, Melissa, but I want to talk to her."

"Oh, hold on, Cassie, she's free. Just a minute."

Becky took the phone from her. "Hi, Cassie."

"Hi, Becky. I know you're busy, but I wanted to see how you are doing and give you some information before I see you at the service."

"Thanks for calling. I'm doing as well as can be expected. We're sitting here trying to decide what will look good at the service. I'm having a real hard time dressing the part of the widow. I guess the reality of it all still hasn't hit me."

"That's understandable. Just give yourself some time. Did you see anything about the fire at the studio on the news?"

"No, I didn't even watch TV last night. What happened?"

"Well, I was able to find out a little bit more from Wade's computer. He had been working on a document called 'The Lasko Interview,' and there was a reference to a Lasko picture. From what we can tell, that's the piece Wade had come in to edit the day before the murder, but I can't find any information about it in any of our files."

Becky was listening intently as Cassie continued, "Well, the guy that helped me with the computer and I decided to go into the tape vault and look up whatever tapes we had on this Lasko thing. We figured that was the only place we'd find the answers."

"What did you find?" Becky asked.

"Unfortunately, nothing. While Rick and I were in the building, it exploded, nearly killing us and destroying all the tapes."

"Oh no! Are you all right? Was anybody hurt?"

"I'm fine, but Rick had some pretty good burns on his back." Cassie hadn't thought about that since she woke up. She wanted to call Rick and see if he was doing OK. "We were lucky, or actually the hand of God was on us. Rick protected me when the fire broke out, and then one of our guards dragged us out of the building before the flames got to us."

"That's incredible, Cassie. I'm so glad you're OK."

"Well, I thought you'd want to know. Also, the press doesn't know this yet, but the two detectives working on your case showed up right afterward. I think they're now convinced that Wade's death was murder. They're continuing their investigation."

"I'm so glad. Thanks for telling me all this, Cassie, but be careful. Somebody is determined to keep whatever Wade found out a secret. I don't want you to get hurt as well."

"I'll be careful. Now I better let you go. Is there anything I can do for you today?"

"No, I think everything is under control. Thanks for your concern."

"Becky, I know today will be hard on you. I'll keep you in my prayers. We'll see you at the memorial service."

10:03 A.M., STUDIO CITY

Gary and Rick arrived back at Rick's place a little after ten. That didn't give them much time. Rick had to change clothes quickly, then they needed to drive by Gary's house so he could get his suit before heading into Hollywood for the memorial service.

Gary noticed the difference the minute he walked in. Jill was beaming as she gave her husband a quick kiss when he entered the kitchen.

"Everything OK?" he asked.

"Couldn't be better," Jill answered. "Vanessa and I have had a great talk, haven't we, Vanessa."

Vanessa looked up at Gary and Rick and just smiled, somewhat embarrassed.

"That's great, and, Vanessa, it's nice to finally meet you," Rick broke in with a smile. "I can't wait to hear all about it, but I've got to get changed real quick so we can get to the service on time."

Rick made his way to the bedroom while Gary sat down with the two women at the table.

Jill looked up at her husband, "You're going to the service?"

"Yeah, as we prayed with Rob about the situation, it seemed like the Lord laid it on our hearts that I was to go with Rick this morning. I'm not sure why, but God's got a plan in mind. We're going to go by the house after Rick gets dressed so I can grab my suit. You two can hang around here; you'll be safe. So tell me what happened."

Jill wasn't sure she liked the idea of her husband going back to the house after what she'd just found out, but she let it slide for now. Vanessa looked at Jill, who looked back at her. Finally, Vanessa spoke up, "I've given my life to the Lord. I guess I'm a Christian now."

"That's fantastic, Vanessa," Gary said beaming. He leaned over and gave her a hug. "Welcome into the family."

In the next few minutes, Jill proceeded to catch Gary up on the events of Vanessa's life.

"We'd better get moving, Gary," Rick said, coming into the kitchen and glancing at his watch. "It sounds like I came in on the end of a pretty amazing story. You'll have to fill me in while we're driving."

"I'll do that." Gary turned toward the women. "We still haven't decided what to do about the police. But we're running late, so we'll cross that bridge when we get back. Do you both feel OK staying here?"

Jill and Vanessa both agreed. "Just go, and find out why God wanted you two to go to the memorial service," Jill said. "We'll be praying for you. And be careful back at the house. We still don't know if someone is watching the place or not. Try and check it out before you go in, OK?"

Gary looked at his wife. "We thought about that driving back here. Just to be safe, I'm going to sneak in the back from over the Winslow's fence. So if anyone's watching the house, I won't be seen."

10:35 A.M., WESTWOOD

Rick drove down Gary's street, passing slowly by his house. They looked intently for anyone who might have his eye on the place.

Rick made the turn to the next street, then looked over at Gary, "I didn't see anything suspicious, did you?"

"No, I didn't either, but that doesn't mean there isn't somebody out there. Turn left at the next street. I'll show you the house where I can jump over the back fence."

After Rick stopped the car, Gary walked up to the door first. He explained as little as was necessary to his neighbor, Mr. Winslow, who was a little puzzled, but glad to let him jump over the backyard fence. To be safe, Rick stayed at the wall and kept an eye on Gary as he made his way into the house. It took just a few minutes before Gary appeared coming out the back door, carrying a garment bag.

Rick helped him down from the wall. "Did you notice any-thing unusual?"

"No, everything looked normal. We're probably just being paranoid. The guy probably didn't have time to look at our plates."

"I hope you're right. Let's get you dressed and get out of here. This spy business is too much for me."

They didn't see the pair of eyes watching them from the second-story window of the house to the south of Gary's.

The man looking through the window picked up his cellu-lar phone and hit a speed-dial number. His partner, who'd gone downstairs and pulled their car out of the garage the minute they saw Gary go over the back wall, answered.

"Yeah."

"He's gone back over the wall and into the neighbor's house. You in position?"

"I'll be right on their tail. You call Rudy and let him know, then stay put and see if someone else shows up."

The man in the house disconnected the phone. He stood up and stretched. He hated stakeouts. The two of them had posed as FBI agents, complete with badges and identification. It had been easy to get the homeowners to let them use an upstairs bedroom to keep an eye on the house next door.

He entered Rudy's cell number and hit "send."

CHAPTER 26

Rick and Gary steered their way down Santa Monica Boulevard into the Hollywood area. As they approached the location for the memorial service, traffic jammed.

Rick surveyed the cars around him, then looked at his watch. "It's almost eleven. I hope we can find a parking place."

"Looks like Wade had quite a following. I never would have dreamed there'd be this many people," Gary said.

"Well, you know as well as I do, in Hollywood these things can become like the Academy Awards night. If you're somebody, then you have to show up."

Gary pointed to a side street on the right. "Turn down there. It looks like there might be a place to park."

Rick made the turn, noticing several TV vans parked near the front of the building. *I hope Samantha isn't covering this,* he thought. A few hundred feet down the street, he spotted an open parking place and pulled over. They didn't notice the car that had been following them continue past them. The man in the car pulled to the side, then reached for his phone and called Rudy.

"They've stopped," he said as Rudy answered. "They're at the Hollywood Mortuary on Santa Monica near Highland."

"That's interesting. They must be going to Bennett's funeral," came the terse reply. He wondered how this person was connected to Bennett. "Stay near their car so you can keep an eye on them when they come out. I should be there in about ten minutes."

"It is in this time of sorrow that we come to appreciate individual life. For we are all part of the great consciousness, and now one of us has gone on to his next stage. We honor him today." The tall distinguished man spoke from a small podium standing on the stage above the casket. "Wade Justin Bennett lived his life to the fullest. In the span of just forty-seven years on this earth, he became one of the most respected directors in television. He gave much to the world through his talent, determination, and hard work. He will live on through his many hours of creativity on videotape."

Rick found himself shaking his head in disagreement, then he heard Gary sigh next to him, probably having the same thoughts. What a bunch of worthless words. But then, what can be said at a memorial where the person didn't know Jesus Christ as Lord and Savior? Everything that the man up front was speaking about didn't amount to anything from an eternal viewpoint. What did it mean to have your name 'immortalized' on videotape, when your name was left out of the Book of Life? It was a sobering thought, and Rick realized that had it not been for the grace of God, he might have found himself in the same boat.

Rick and Gary had found two seats near the back of the room. Samantha's station did have a crew there, but Rick didn't see her as they made their way into the building. The service started just as they found their seats. The room could hold about four hundred people, and those who filtered in after them were standing around the back and sides of the room. From their position, it was hard to see the people up front, but Rick could spot Gabriel Flint and what looked like Josh Abrams next to him in the fourth row. Throughout the audience were various celebrities, Hollywood executives, and a lot of production staff and technical people that both Rick and Gary had worked with over the years. As Rick glanced around the room, he noticed the two detectives he'd met the night before walking in the back door.

Up front, in her grief, Becky was struggling with her thoughts. The empty words coming from the eulogy nearly made her wish she'd let her mom's pastor preside over the service. But it would have been harder to sit through some sermon about a gracious and wonderful God. Becky's anger and frustration were still aimed in his direction.

Next to her, Becky's sister took her hand.

Rick's eyes searched the room, studying those around him. It became a game, trying to guess what was going through each mind by the concentration, or lack thereof, on each face. There were a handful who seemed to be taking in every word like it was their sole comfort in life. Most of the others seemed as bored with the whole thing as he was, some even chatting quietly to each other as the service continued.

Then his eye caught something on the other side of the room that made his heart skip a beat. He wasn't sure, until her head turned as she flipped her beautiful hair over her shoulders. It was Cassie.

Rick was surprised at the strength of his reaction to her. Even from this distance, she looked stunning. He tried to get a read on what she might have been thinking of the service, but all he could see was the back of her head.

Then she leaned over and whispered something to the man she was sitting next to, who chuckled at her comment. The man she was sitting next to ... Rick felt like his stomach dropped to his socks. He hadn't considered there might be somebody else in her life. He began sizing up the man beside her: young, well dressed, with short-cropped hair—very handsome. Rick tried to move his head and continue scanning the room, but he couldn't keep his eyes off of her ... them. Cassie with another man. He was surprised at how much he didn't like the looks of it.

Outside the service, Rudy pulled his battered BMW up next to the man watching Rick's car.

"Good work, Ben," he said as he rolled down his window. "They still inside?"

"Yeah, with a lot of other people too."

"That's OK, we just need to keep an eye on their car and follow them out of here. I'm sure they'll lead us to where Vanessa is."

"By the way, boss, I just saw what I'm sure were two detectives walk into the place."

That made Rudy stop short. They were probably the ones investigating the suicide. He wished they would just close this case and get out of his hair. Now that the tapes were destroyed, he was sure he was in the clear, but he didn't want to take any chances.

"Tell you what, there's no need to be here together. It makes the odds greater that we'll be spotted. I'm going to drive around the side of the building. You take a position where you can see them drive off, but don't let them see you. We'll be on the cell phones when the service is over. You let me know when they pull out, then I'll be in position to follow right behind them. Got it?"

The man nodded his head.

"Good. Don't mess this up. I need that girl."

11:45 A.m., COUNTY SHERIFF'S LAB

Ray got into the lab after eleven. He wasn't thrilled about coming in on the weekend, but after missing that crucial evidence the first time, he wanted another shot at helping. He had checked the computer out of the evidence room and now it lay before him. He had also called in one of the lab assistants to give him a hand. Whenever they were going to do a procedure that could change the evidence in a case in any way, it was department policy to have at least two people present. Besides, he felt so bad about letting Stephanie down the first time he had the computer in the lab that he welcomed the extra help. He was just ready to begin when Gene walked in.

"This better be good, Ray. I was supposed to play golf today," Gene said as he saddled up next to Ray on their workbench.

"This'll be good. You know it's always exciting when we get to work together," Ray chided, knowing they'd both rather not be there.

"Seriously, what have you got?"

"This is the computer from the Bennett case," Ray explained as he powered it up. "It contained a suicide note on it when the man supposedly committed suicide. Some bright people from the production office found out the note was actually created the night before the death, and that there were a couple of documents that the man had recently been working on that no longer appear to be on the disk."

"Do they know the names of the files?"

"Yeah, I wrote them down when Stephanie woke me up last night, 'The Lasko Interview' and 'Lasko Pic.' So it's our job to try and retrieve those files. The only problem is, I haven't had a lot of experience with these Macs."

Gene filled up with a sense of purpose. "Well, it's a good thing you called in an expert then. You IBM people don't know what you're missing."

He reached up and touched the track pad, going through the same motions Cassie had used the night before. He was able to confirm to Ray that Wade indeed had recently worked on two files by those names. He did a quick file search and also confirmed that they were no longer on the disk. Ray was impressed with how easily Gene manipulated the computer. He wished he'd involved Gene the first time he had this thing in the lab.

"What's the next step?" Ray asked.

"What we need is a program called Norton Utilities. Let me just hook this computer up to my other one over here, and we'll be able to start searching for those lost files."

12:06 P.M., HOLLYWOOD

"Can you see Flint?" Stephanie quietly asked her partner as they stood in the back of the mortuary.

"Look up front. That's him in the fourth row on the left. He's sitting with Josh Abrams and John Harold," Bill responded in a whisper.

"I can't get a good look from here. I'm anxious to see what he looks like."

"Should we approach him today?"

"I don't think so. I don't want to tip our hand that we're on to him until we have enough to take him in. Keep your eyes open for his goon though. He might be stupid enough to show up."

"I have been, but haven't spotted him yet. I did notice the new director, Rick. He's in the back on the right-hand side."

"Yeah, I saw him," Stephanie replied. "I want to see how he's feeling when this is over."

The service was winding to a close. Several people in the industry and a couple of family members had stood up and recounted some memory to honor Wade's life. "So, as we conclude this time, let us remember Wade," the minister said. "For every time one of those whose lives he touched recalls a moment shared, then Wade will live on."

Rick couldn't stomach this much longer. *It's no wonder people are so messed up. Not one mention of God,* he thought. He hoped the widow had more hope in her life than was present in the ceremony. The thought prompted a quick prayer for her.

The service finally ended. Rick hadn't realized it until now, but with all the Hollywood people that had come, he felt a little funny about being the one man in the room to benefit from Wade's death. That, added to the disappointment of seeing Cassie here with somebody else, made him decide that it would be best to make a quick exit and head for home.

"Is there anybody you want to see?" Rick asked Gary, hoping for a negative answer.

"Not really. Did you want to say something to the widow?"

"To tell you the truth, no. I've never met her, and I'd feel funny since I'm the one replacing her husband on the show. Let's get out of here."

Gary agreed, but as they were heading for the door, he wondered why God had directed him here. So far, he hadn't seen any purpose to his presence.

As they stepped outside, Rick nearly walked right into Samantha and her cameraman. She held a microphone in front of his face as she asked him a question, but he was too shocked to comprehend her words. The last thing he wanted was for his presence here to be noticed, much less broadcast on the six o'clock news. Rick knew she was taping him; he saw the red light glowing on the front of the camera.

Once again, Samantha set up her question for the television audience. "I'm here with Rick Treadway, the man selected to replace Mr. Bennett on 'The John Harold Show.' Rick, how did the service affect you?"

Rick stared at Samantha, not having a clue how to respond. He knew she wouldn't want to hear his real opinion about the service. He turned toward the camera. "Wade will be missed by all of us in the industry," he finally said. "He was a very talented director, one whom I had the pleasure of working with and learned a lot from."

Samantha pressed further, a wicked smile appearing on her face from beside the camera. "Is it difficult for you being here and seeing the family, knowing that you'll be the one taking his place?"

Rick sighed, trying to stay calm. "This isn't the time to worry about how I feel. My thoughts are with the Bennett family. I pray they'll find peace during this most difficult time."

Rick held a beat, then when Samantha moved the microphone back to herself, he brought his hand up and placed it in front of the camera's lens. Looking to Sam, he asked, "Can't we talk off the record?" He still hoped he could get through to her and apologize.

Samantha held her stern gaze. "Anything you want to say to me, the rest of Los Angeles will hear as well."

This woman knows how to hold a grudge, he thought.

"In that case, no more comments," Rick replied, and walked away with Gary quickly following behind.

When they were far enough away not to be overheard, Gary whispered, "What's up with her? Do you two know each other?"

"Remember the night you and Jill were praying so hard for me?"

Gary nodded.

"Samantha was the reason I was needing the prayer."

Gary didn't need any further explanation. They walked away in silence, heading around the side of the building. Once out of visual range of the TV crews, they were quickly approached by the two detectives.

"Hi, Rick," Stephanie said as she walked up. "I didn't want the news people to see us talking. How are you feeling?"

"Actually, not bad." Rick started to go into further detail, but then he looked around at all the people still nearby and decided it would be best not to mention the fire. "Detectives, I'd like you to meet a good friend of mine, Gary Hall. Gary, these are the two officers investigating Wade's death, Detectives Phillips and Brier."

The three shook hands.

"It sounds like you two have quite a mystery on your hands," Gary said. "Any leads?"

Stephanie looked around to see who might be able to overhear them. She motioned with a nod of her head for them to follow her. They walked farther down the side of the building where there were fewer people milling around.

"I don't want anyone to overhear this." Then she turned to Rick. "I wanted to give you an update anyway, Rick. It seems that Reggie, the guard, was pretty sure that one of the pictures we showed him at the precinct was the guy he'd passed at the studio just before the fire. The man he identified is tied to your executive producer, one of his bodyguards."

"Hit men would be more accurate," Bill interjected.

Rick whistled excitedly. "So you're ready to make an arrest?"

Stephanie's face took on a sour look. "No, unfortunately there are still several problems."

Rick waited.

"Number one, we still don't know why," Bill picked up the explanation. "Nor do we have one piece of evidence, so we can't make any arrests. The only move we could make would be to arrest him for arson."

"We've still got a lot of pieces to put together before this all makes sense." Stephanie concluded, "It's got to have something to do with that Lasko interview. We really needed to see whatever was on those tapes."

"Have you found anything on the computer to help?" Rick asked.

"They're looking into it right now," she answered.

Gary glanced at Rick, trying to gauge his reaction.

"What about Josh? Is he involved?"

"Possibly. We just don't know at this point. I'd be careful Monday," Stephanie replied.

"Oh great. I get to go into work Monday and act like everything is normal because you guys can't make an arrest," Rick said, somewhat exasperated. "That sounds pretty scary."

"I don't think you have anything to worry about," Stephanie tried to reassure him. "Remember, we kept your name out of any report about the fire. As far as anyone in the office is concerned, you don't know anything about our investigation, or Lasko."

Bill agreed. "Stephanie's right. We're a little more concerned about Cassie though. She did make some inquiries. We want her to be real careful."

Rick didn't want to see anything happen to her, recalling how he felt at seeing her with someone just a few minutes ago. "I'll try and keep my eye on her."

"Well, we'll let you get on your way then," Stephanie said as she started to leave.

"Wait a minute," Rick stopped her. "Before you leave, Gary has another problem we need your advice on."

Stephanie stopped and looked at Gary. "What can we do for you, Gary?"

"Well, we're kind of mixed up in another matter that really needs police intervention. I'm not sure what to do. The other day, my wife brought home a woman who showed up at the Crisis Pregnancy Center where she volunteers. We thought it was a pretty normal case of 'woman wants to have baby; boyfriend wants to have abortion.' It turned out to be much more than that."

"What do you mean?" Stephanie asked.

"Well, we decided to abandon her car. It was registered in her boyfriend's name, and we thought he was trying to track her down. My wife was driving it toward Santa Monica, and I was following her when this guy runs her into the freeway median, crashing the car and nearly killing her. As I pulled up to get her out, this guy comes running back at us firing a gun. We hightailed it out of there before he could hit us and made our way home."

Bill was surprised. "It sounds like more than just a boy-friend who doesn't want a baby. What did the woman say?"

"Well, just this morning she opened up with the whole story to my wife. I don't have all the details, but apparently she was involved in some pornography stuff, being kept in a fancy high-rise by one of the producers. When she made a break for it, one of the men who works for this guy came after her. He was the one who ran my wife off the road. We really want to help this girl, but we're getting in over our heads, and we don't quite know where to turn."

"Listen, Gary," Bill answered. "Unfortunately, we can't be of much help unless there's a homicide. But I used to work in Vice."

Bill took a card out of his wallet and wrote something on the back of it. "Here's my card; you can use my name when you call. On the back of it I'm writing the name and phone number of the best vice cop in the city—Frank Sanger. This is his home number. He'll be able to help you. You'll like him."

Gary felt relieved. At least they had a contact. "We've been pretty paranoid. We're even staying at Rick's house in case the guy got a look at my license plate and would be crazy enough to come to our house."

"Better safe than sorry," Stephanie interjected.

"Right! Well, thanks for the name. Let's hope things don't get to the point where it's your case," Gary joked.

"Yeah, thanks, detectives. I guess I'll be seeing you later?" Rick asked.

"Oh, you will. We've got this weekend to come up with a plan to break this case. We'll think of something," Bill promised.

"I hope you do."

Suddenly something caught Stephanie's eye over Rick's shoulder and down the street. She could see a man standing by his open car door, looking at them. Although he was a good distance away, she couldn't help but think the man resembled the mug shot they'd seen of Rudy Vanozzi the night before.

"Bill," she tried to keep her voice calm, "I'm looking over Gary's shoulder at the guy down the street by the gray BMW."

Bill spotted who Stephanie was referring to as Rick and Gary started to turn their heads.

"Don't look!" Stephanie tried to stop them, but it was too late. Their heads alerted the man, who quickly got into his car, started the engine, and prepared to drive away.

"Get the car, I'll see which way he's heading," Stephanie called out. Before Rick and Gary could get some explanation, the two were off in different directions.

Stephanie got a good look at the car and the man as he made a quick U-turn, speeding away from the area. She was sure it was Rudy. She jotted down the license number, impatiently waiting for Bill to get the car around to her. She knew the man would be long gone before they could pursue him.

Rick and Gary watched the excitement until Bill picked up Stephanie and the two sped off in the direction of the other vehicle. They didn't realize that the man they were chasing was, in fact, their suspect. Gary didn't get a good look at the car, or he would have noticed the similarity to the one that ran Jill off the road.

As they walked back around the front of the building, Rick heard his name called. He turned and was surprised to see Cassie approaching him.

"Cassie, how are you?" he said, with a mixture of joy and jealousy.

"I'm doing great. What about yourself? Are your burns—"

Rick tried to hush her up with a quick finger to the lips. He reached out to hug her gently as he whispered in her ear, "Don't forget, as far as anyone knows we weren't anywhere near that fire. We don't want someone around here to overhear us talking about it. But I'm OK, really."

Cassie pulled back from the hug, changing her tone like a professional actress. "It was a nice service, wasn't it?" she said, trying to change subjects. She'd had many of the same thoughts that had gone through Rick's mind during the eulogy.

"Yes, it was," Rick decided to agree rather than risk offending Cassie with his own spiritual beliefs. He noticed the man she'd been sitting next to approaching from behind her. *This could be awkward,* he thought.

Cassie turned around and took the man by the arm, then looked back at Rick.

"Rick, I'd like you to meet my brother, Ted."

Rick could have been knocked over with a feather. He stood motionless for a second as Ted reached out his hand toward him.

"It's a pleasure meeting you. Cassie's really looking forward to your taking over the show."

Rick shook Ted's hand. "It's a pleasure to meet you as well. I'm looking forward to working with your sister. She's a wonderful woman. Oh, excuse me," Rick turned toward Gary standing next to him, "this is my good friend, Gary Hall."

Cassie turned toward Gary. "Gary, it's nice to see you again. How's Jill?"

Gary responded by reaching out and giving Cassie a warm hug. "Jill's fine. Thanks for asking."

Rick was surprised. "You two know each other?"

Gary released Cassie and turned back toward Rick, "We met a couple of months ago at the monthly C.I.F.T. meeting. I didn't make the connection that she was the Cassie you were referring to. So, Cassie, when did you start working on 'The John Harold Show'?"

So he's been talking about me? Cassie thought. A spark of hope went through her as she realized that if Rick and Gary were friends, then there was a good possibility that Rick was a Christian.

"Since the pilot last year. I'm working with Josh Abrams, the producer. It's been a blast." Cassie turned back to Rick. "So, do you have a busy weekend planned getting ready for Monday?"

"I hope not. I'm picking up my kids for the weekend and not even planning to think about the show coming up."

She smiled awkwardly. The thought of Rick being married and having kids hadn't even occurred to her. "Pick up your kids? I didn't know you had any kids." Surely he wasn't the type to be married and not wear his wedding band.

"Yeah, I've got a beautiful son and daughter. Their mother and I divorced more than three years ago. She remarried right after." Cassie tried to hide her disappointment. She was relieved to find out at least he wasn't still married, but being divorced brought up a whole different set of spiritual issues to consider.

Rick continued, "It's been hard not being with them, so I'm looking forward to this weekend. What about you? What's yours going to be like?"

"Oh, I've got nothing special planned. I may try and spend some time with Becky. She's going to need some support to get through this thing."

Rick marveled at Cassie—she was compassionate as well as beautiful. Whenever he found out something new about her, it made her that much more attractive to him. She and Ted had parked along the same street that Rick had, so when the light turned green, they all stepped across the street together.

After they had left the crowd of people behind them, Rick spoke up again, "The two detectives were at the funeral."

Cassie looked up, a bit surprised. "Really? I didn't see them."

"They were standing in the back. Before you came out of the service, they met us around the corner. We were in the middle of talking to them when they spotted somebody and took off after him. I hope it was our lovely arsonist and they can get this case wrapped up. But anyway, they told me Reggie fingered a mug shot they had of the guy that was hanging around the studio before the fire. He's one of the hired guns for our illustrious executive producer."

"Did they give you a name? Maybe I know him."

Rick shook his head. "No, they didn't mention it, just that they had an ID on the guy."

"So that should give them enough to make some arrests, right?"

"Well, that's what I thought, too, but evidently not." Cassie looked dejected. Rick tried to explain, "All it did was confirm their suspicions, but they still don't have any evidence to arrest anyone."

"I don't understand," Cassie said, frowning. The pressure around the office was getting to be too much for her, especially coming up on a taping week when things were going to be ten times crazier.

"I'm not sure I do either. All they told me was for us to go in as if everything is normal. They're more worried about you because you've asked some questions about the Lasko thing. So be careful."

"I guess I'll have to," she said. "But you'd better be as well. I'm not sure who we can trust at the office."

"Right now, I'm only planning to trust you." Rick smiled at her as he opened her car door. The gesture sent a spark through Cassie. Everything seemed so right about Rick—except the issue of the former marriage. However, finding that out now was probably great timing. It'd help hold her heart in check until she could learn more about his relationship with God.

They said their good-byes, then Rick and Gary continued on down the block heading for Rick's car. As soon as Cassie had pulled out into the street and driven past them, Rick spoke up, "So tell me everything you know about Cassie."

Gary laughed as he opened the car door. "Well she's much too good for the likes of you . . ."

Down the street, Ben was watching from his car. Remembering the plan Rudy had orchestrated, he reached for his phone and dialed Rudy's cell number. As the signal connected to Rudy's phone, Ben watched the two men get into Rick's car. Rudy answered as Rick was pulling out from the street.

"Rudy, they're just now leaving—"

"Follow them, you idiot!" Rudy screamed.

"But—"

"Don't ask questions, just drive. Keep this line open and tell me when you're behind them!" The tone in Rudy's voice sent shivers through Ben. He knew what it was like when somebody made a mistake around him.

Ben started his car, spun out of his parking place, made a U-turn in the middle of the street, and headed down the side street Rick had turned onto. His car was too big to make the tight turn, slowing him down even more as he backed up, then screeched forward again, honking at the people and cars in his way.

Rick drove back to Santa Monica Boulevard, checked the oncoming traffic, then headed east toward Hollywood. He planned to take Highland up to the Hollywood Freeway, which would take them into the valley where his condo was.

Ben pulled up to the same intersection moments later but couldn't see Rick's car. He had a fifty-fifty shot at heading the right direction, and since they'd come from the west, he quickly crossed the busy traffic on the street and headed that way, causing a black Infiniti to slam on its breaks to avoid a collision. Ben quickly accelerated, heading down the street—away from Rick as he turned left on Highland. After passing through ten blocks of traffic and not spotting the car, Ben reached over to pick up his phone. His hand shook as he brought the instrument up to his ear.

CHAPTER 27

Rick and Gary arrived back at the condo. Jill had prepared some sandwiches, and the four sat at the kitchen table to eat.

"Did you find out why God wanted you at the service?" Jill asked her husband.

"I believe we did," Gary responded, "after it was all over. But I've got to tell you, I've never heard a more discouraging funeral service before."

Rick was nodding his head in affirmation. "It sure didn't leave you with the assurance of life after death did it?"

"It was more like Wade would live on because of his wonderful work left on videotape for us." Gary said. "I wish someone would have been able to get up and share the true gospel. I can't think of any group of people who need to hear it more."

"But what about why you were there?" Jill interjected. "What did God do?"

"Well," Gary continued, "the two detectives who had been with Rick last night were there. After updating us on the situation with Wade's murder, Rick brought up our situation."

"Yeah, they were really helpful," Rick offered up.

"They gave me the number of a vice cop that they trust. They said to give him a call. He'll be able to advise us, and even protect Vanessa if need be."

All three turned toward Vanessa to see how she was reacting. She looked up, smiling.

"I'm not at all sure I want to hang around here and even deal with it. I've thought it might be much easier just to leave town and get lost. That way none of you are in danger. Hopefully, they'll just forget about me. Then I can start all over somewhere else with my baby."

Gary reached over and took her hand. "Vanessa, I appreciate what you're saying. I know you don't want to endanger us, but the truth is, we're already involved. If this Rudy character saw our license number and has traced it to our address, it won't matter if you're out of the city or not."

The room was quiet for a moment as the words sank in. Vanessa hadn't thought of it that way.

Jill broke the silence. "Look, Vanessa, what if we meet with the detective and you tell him your story. He can't do anything if you don't want him to. But maybe he'll have an idea that makes sense."

"Otherwise, we're just not sure what to do," Gary added.

Vanessa stood up and walked over to the counter. "It's just that you don't know these people. I've seen what happens to their enemies."

"Look, Vanessa," Rick said. "I know I'm kind of on the outside looking in on your problem. But let me share something with you. I've just recently found a real, living relationship with Jesus—mainly through my friendship with Gary here. I can't tell you the difference that's been in my life these past few days. If there's one thing I've learned, it's that if you've surrendered your life to God, he'll be with you in a way that you never dreamed was possible. I've seen his hand in my life miraculously this week. I know he'll do the same for you."

Vanessa listened as Rick went on.

"Listening to your story, I can already see how God led you to Jill. Then to hear how God protected these two when they were ditching your car—you've got to see that his hand is in all this. He'll complete everything in a way that's best for you. All you've got to do is hang in there. You're God's now. You have nothing to fear from those who mean you harm."

As Rick spoke the words, Vanessa sensed a deep peace.

"You are all absolutely right" she said. "I'm not sure how all this will end, but let's at least talk to this cop. Maybe he'll have an idea that will get us out of this mess."

Jill smiled at her courage. "Now you're talking."

1:11 P.M., COUNTY SHERIFF'S LAB

It took awhile for Gene and Ray to get the necessary cables to hook the two computers together. When they had finished and both computers were back up and running, Gene double-clicked on the Norton icon. "Well, here we go."

Ray's eyes were glued to the screen. A dialog box appeared with the options the program offered. Gene clicked on the unerase file box. In a matter of seconds, the program offered up a list of more than forty documents that were retrievable. They scanned the list.

Suddenly Ray pointed to the screen. "There's 'The Lasko Interview,' created March 16, 6:25 PM! But I don't see anything labeled 'Lasko Pic.'"

Gene thought for a second. "It's possible that the 'Lasko Pic' was something Bennett had used off of a floppy disk that he never copied onto his hard drive. That would account for its not appearing here. At least we've got this file."

While touching the track pad, Gene moved the cursor over to "The Lasko Interview" and double-clicked on it. In just seconds the computer retrieved the lost file.

"Let's see what the mystery is all about," Gene said as the computer booted up the file.

It took about twelve seconds, and then before them on the screen was "The Lasko Interview," created by Wade Bennett.

David Bernstein
Attorney at Law
1527 W. Olympic Blvd.
Beverly Hills, CA 90210

Dear Dave,

I'm writing this letter in case anything should happen to me. I'm planning to go to the District Attorney with what I've discovered. I've come across some information that leads me to believe I have evidence pertaining to a certain murder.

I came across this evidence while I was in the editing room yesterday. We did a remote segment outside a strip joint named The Club Royale on March 12. We were interviewing the manager of the club, Joe Lasko. Although nothing appeared out of the ordinary the day of the taping, it was in the edit room that I realized we had something on tape that amazed me. I'll put a frame from that video at the end of this letter to show you proof of what I have.

I noticed that between takes of
the interview, off in the distance, our camera recorded

"That's it?" Ray nearly screamed. "There's got to be more. How can it just stop in the middle like that?"

Gene thought for a minute. He too was disappointed. "The only thing I can think of is the automatic save feature."

"You mean when the program automatically saves the file every so often?" Ray asked.

"Exactly. The program he used, Microsoft Word, has that feature. Let me see here . . ." Gene moved to Wade's computer, moving his finger over the track pad. He opened up Microsoft Word, selected the preferences section under the tools menu. Then he selected the save feature and they saw that Wade operated his computer to save the document automatically every ten minutes.

"So that's it," Ray said.

"I believe so. Picture this. Bennett's sitting in his office, typing out this letter. After ten minutes, the computer interrupts him, prompting him to save the file, which he does. Then he continues working. Shortly after that, within the next few minutes, the killer walks in and does him in. Now we know the killer doesn't want us to find this letter, so when he closes it, even though the computer will prompt him and ask him if he wants to save it, of course he says no. So the last version saved only went this far."

"Stephanie's going to be livid. So close to some real information, yet so far. I'll page her. She'll want to know what we found as soon as possible."

2:34 P.M., STUDIO CITY

Gary got up from the couch, fingering the card the detective had given him with Sergeant Fred Sanger's name and phone number on the back. It was time. After they had prayed and Rick left,

Gary and Jill had given Vanessa a few moments to make sure she was ready to involve the police.

"It's the only way you can protect yourself," Jill said as Gary went to the phone.

"I know, I know. It's just that I've seen what that group can do to people who cross them." Vanessa folded her arms across her chest and shivered at the thought.

"Well," Gary added as he picked up the phone, "I don't care what their history is, they aren't going to be able to do anything to you without going through Jesus and his mighty host of angels first."

This whole spiritual thing was too new for Vanessa to grasp the implications of what Gary was saying. For now, the presence of Jill next to her on the couch brought more comfort than Gary's words.

Gary tapped out the numbers on the phone for Sergeant Sanger. He listened for a moment, then heard a recorded message.

"He must not be home; there's a message machine," Gary called out to the women.

After the tone, Gary tried to make it brief, "Sergeant Sanger, this is Gary Hall," he flipped the card over as he spoke. "A detective Bill Brier gave me your number. We need to speak to you about a woman we've been helping. She's in some danger, and we're kind of hiding her from some ... people who are out to get her. Anyway, we're hoping that you can help us. Please give us a call at ... 555-3265 as soon as you can."

Gary hung up and headed back toward the living room. "Well, I guess all we can do now is wait."

CHAPTER 28

Rick drove up Connie's driveway in Toluca Lake, a beautiful little community nestled between Universal Studios and Burbank. It was a lovely Tudor-style home that in this neighborhood would sell for nearly a million dollars—a home they couldn't have dreamed of owning during the time they were married. For the first time since she had remarried, Rick noticed he didn't feel jealous of her new lifestyle. His concerns focused on what kind of spiritual upbringing his kids would receive in this environment.

Jennifer and Justin came bounding through the front door as Rick got out of the car. He was engulfed in a three-way hug that brought tears to his eyes as shouts of "Daddy, Daddy" engulfed him.

How could things have gotten so bad between Connie and me that these two little lives had to take a backseat to our selfishness?

Over the kids' shoulders he saw Connie in the doorway. He wished he could turn back the clock and have a second chance with her, this time with his newfound relationship with Jesus at the center of their lives. But that wasn't to be. Connie had a new life now. He needed to concentrate on being the best dad he could be for these two that were climbing all over him now.

"Hi, Connie. The kids look great, and so do you," Rick said with a smile as he approached her with the kids in tow.

The kind greeting took her off guard. Things hadn't been that friendly between them, especially since Rick had been having trouble finding work. She'd planned to let him have it for being late with his support payment. Now she wasn't sure how to react.

"Thanks," she mumbled. "So where's your support check this month? Am I going to have to get the court involved?"

Rick's mood darkened at the terse response. He almost lashed out at her with his "not with the kids here lecture," but instead he bottled his anger and continued through a forced smile, "Look, Connie, I'm sorry. You know things have been real slow for me the past few months. But I've got some good news."

Connie's expression remained unchanged. "I don't know if you've heard, but the director of 'The John Harold Show' was ...," he wasn't sure how to say it, "... he died this week. I'm taking over the show starting Monday. So if you'll just be patient a few weeks longer, I'll get caught up as soon as I can."

Rick saw a startled look in Connie's eyes at the news before she covered it up by reaching back inside the house and grabbing the kids' bags. He was sure she was shocked because she never expected his career to go anywhere, and maybe even disappointed that she couldn't continue to harass him about his financial problems.

"Well, just because you're behind, doesn't mean the kids stop needing clothes, food, school supplies ..."

Rick tuned her out. He'd heard it all before. *Why can't she just be happy for me?* he thought. Although he didn't say anything and stayed cordial, the anger inside of him festered.

It took several minutes into the drive back to his house for Rick to cool down enough to have a meaningful conversation with Jennifer and Justin. The anger faded as he let himself become involved in their lives, hearing their stories from school and about their friends. He always experienced a mixed bag of emotions during these visits—thrilled at catching up with what was happening in their young lives, yet at the same time feeling brokenhearted at the separation the divorce caused the three of them.

On impulse, instead of jumping on the Ventura freeway—the most direct route to his condo—Rick drove through the streets of Toluca Lake, then Burbank, finally heading into Griffith Park.

"Where we going, Daddy?" Jennifer asked from the passenger seat.

"I thought we'd spend the rest of the afternoon at the zoo. Is that OK with you two?"

A loud "Yeah!" resounded through the car as Rick's smile widened and the tension of seeing Connie faded totally away. He thanked God for his children as he drove through the park, praying for God to deepen their relationships and give him the wisdom to bring them up in God's ways, even though he didn't have them twenty-four hours a day.

2:51 p.m., BEVERLY HILLS

Gabriel Flint paced back and forth in front of his pool, screaming into his cordless phone. He was agitated. The flab that hung over his swim trunks bounced up and down as he walked. A couple of feet away a beautiful young woman sunbathed in a lounge chair, but she was engrossed in her steamy romance novel, ignoring Flint.

"I'm sick of your excuses! I don't care what it takes, find that slut."

On the other end of the line Rudy was losing his cool. He'd put up with Flint's ravings long enough. You only pushed Rudy Vanozzi so far.

"Listen, Flint, if it wasn't for me, your lousy little strip joints might not even be open by now. So don't treat me like your little hired hand."

Flint stopped pacing. He was close to throwing the phone into the pool, but he still needed Rudy to wrap up the loose ends. For now he regained control. His eyes caught sight of the girl sunbathing. After his call, he'd take out some of his frustrations on her.

"I don't have enough to worry about without having Vanessa out running loose?" Flint spat back at Rudy.

"We've still got our guys watching the house of the people she's with, they'll have to come back sooner or later. Then we'll know what they've done with her. Now if you're willing to calm down and give me some help, I've got another license number for you to track down for me. My guy followed Hall after he left his house, and ended up at Wade's funeral. He got the license number of the guy he was with."

Flint took down the number, trying to keep his temper in check. "All right, but this whole thing is getting out of hand. Nobody walks out on me. Nobody!"

Rudy decided to change the subject. "What about the studio? Any word on the two who were in the fire?"

"No, nothing. The studio called and only mentioned the fire in the tape vault. Josh is over there today assessing the damage. As far as we've heard, no one was near the building when it lit up. So I don't know what you were thinking."

"That doesn't make sense," Rudy exclaimed. "I know they were inside when the timer went."

"It's just another example of your incompetence," Flint yelled, his anger rising again.

Rudy ignored the comment. "We've got to do something. Those two are getting too close."

"Then we need to give them another direction to look for their answers." Flint hesitated, a thought coming to him. "Do you still have Wade's calendar book?"

Rudy paused, trying to figure out what Flint was planning. "Yeah, I do."

"Good. I have an idea."

Flint went on to explain his plan. Rudy quickly agreed, just wanting to get off the phone and away from the man's wrath.

Flint set the phone down and turned his attention to the woman lounging by the pool. He took two steps toward her, and was interrupted by the phone ringing.

"What?" he said angrily as he picked up the receiver.

"Mr. Flint?" a female voice asked timidly.

"Maybe. Who's asking?"

"This is Samantha Steel with Channel 7, I wondered if I could speak to you about the Bennett suicide?"

An image of Samantha flashed through Flint's mind. He remembered her from the news reports. *How did she get this number?* he asked himself.

"Miss Steel, what a pleasure to hear from you," Flint's voice warmed as he sat down, a grin spreading over his face. "What can I do for you?"

"Please, call me Samantha."

"OK, Samantha. Then please call me Gabe."

"Well, I've been reporting on Bennett's supposed suicide, and I've got this feeling that there might be more to this case."

Flint laughed inwardly, quickly calculating a way this could fit into his new scheme. "You could be very perceptive, Samantha. I've been having my doubts about that very thing."

"Would it be possible to meet with you? I'd like to put our thoughts together and see where they might lead."

"I can't think of anything I'd rather do. How about coming over here this evening?" Flint looked over at the woman by the pool again. Samantha sounded like a lot more fun. "Say around 8:30?"

3:10 P.m., WOODLAND HILLS

Stephanie swore as the device attached to her handbag let out its annoying chirp. She had just spread her towel over a lounge chair by her apartment pool, wanting to get a jump on her tan early in the spring. Having come back from the memorial service without having any luck trailing Vanozzi, she decided the best thing to do would be to try and get her mind off of the case for awhile. She should have known better than to think she could spend a few minutes relaxing on a weekend while involved in the high-profile cases she and Bill were working on.

She reached for her beeper and noticed the good-looking man eyeing her from across the pool. Was it the noise that attracted him, or was she the attraction? It seemed like years since she had enjoyed a night out with a romantic interest. Most of her evenings were either spent working or hanging around a bar with a bunch of other off-duty cops.

All thoughts about the man looking at her were discarded when she took a look at the beeper and recognized the number displayed on it. It was the lab's number. It had to be Ray. She grabbed her purse and headed to the pay phone near the clubhouse.

"Ray, it's me, Stephanie. What have you got?" she asked as he answered the phone.

"I'm afraid not much, Steph, but I wanted you to know right away."

Stephanie frowned at the news. She'd hoped her day off had been interrupted by some good news.

"We were able to retrieve a lost file on Wade's computer. It spells out pretty much everything you know so far, but it isn't complete."

"What do you mean it isn't complete?"

"Well, we believe that he was probably murdered before he finished it."

"What did it say?"

Ray read to her what they had pulled off the computer.

Stephanie swore again. Every time it looked like they were going to get a break on this case, something jerked it away at the last instant. She wrote down the name and address of Mr. Bernstein as Ray repeated it. "Get me a hard copy of that letter on my desk by Monday," she instructed, "and go over the rest of that disk with a fine-tooth comb."

As she hung up the phone, the man on the other side of the pool got up and approached her.

"Must be something important to interrupt a beautiful young woman and her pool time," he said, leering.

Stephanie couldn't handle this now. A second ago she might have been interested—before she got the news and before he came up to her like Mr. Macho. She brushed past him on her way to pick up her things.

"Very important," was all she said.

4:29 P.m., LOS ANGELES ZOO

Rick laughed as the monkey jumped at his daughter, grabbing the cage just in front of her. Jennifer tried to cover up her startled look as her dad and Justin laughed. Being the older of the two, she wanted to appear in control.

"Don't laugh at me. . . . I wasn't scared," she pouted.

"No, but I'll bet the monkey is, after looking at you that close," Justin quipped.

"Come on, you two, let's get something to drink," Rick said, diffusing the moment. He walked with them over to the refreshment stand. It had been a wonderful afternoon, one of the best he'd had with the kids in the last three years. It seemed to Rick that the events leading to his journey of a deeper relationship with his Lord had some great side effects.

"What are we going to do tonight?" Justin asked as they sat down with their lemonades.

"Well, there are some people at my house I want you to meet. They'll probably be sleeping over tonight, so we'll have to pull out the sleeping bags and rough it on the family room floor. How does that sound?"

Their faces brightened up at the prospect. Somehow for kids, sleeping in anything other than a bed seemed to be more exciting, no matter how uncomfortable it might be.

"Cool!" Jennifer exclaimed.

"Great. Then tomorrow we'll get up and go to church together before I take you back to your mother."

Rick noticed the excitement leave their faces, like air going out of a balloon.

"Don't you guys go to church every Sunday?" he asked.

"Not very often," Jennifer answered. "Mom and Phil don't go at all anymore. Sometimes they send us to the church down on the corner with a neighbor, but it's soooo boooooring." She rolled her eyes.

"Well, we'll see what tomorrow holds," Rick said. He didn't want to darken the mood of the moment. "Hey, let's go look at the elephants, and then we'll make our way out of here and get some pizza, what do you say?"

Justin leaped up, heading in the wrong direction before Rick could get his attention and point the right way up the hill. The excitement was back as the kids walked on through the zoo.

Rick's mind kept churning as they walked. Out of the mouths of babes: "Church is so boring," she'd said. He never would have confessed that himself, except for the C.I.F.T. meeting he'd been to the other night. Now, if pressed, he might use the same adjective. It is amazing what adults will sit through in the name of tradition, but leave it to the kids to tell you how it really is.

4:47 p.m., WOODLAND HILLS

Stephanie hung up the phone in her apartment. After talking to Ray, she'd come in and tried to locate a phone number for

David Bernstein. Unfortunately, his home number was unlisted. She'd contacted one of the deputies on duty to find the number through the phone company. He'd just called back with the information.

She dialed the number in Beverly Hills. It was answered on the second ring.

"Is David Bernstein in, please?" she asked.

"Who's calling?" the female voice asked, sounding troubled.

"This is Detective Phillips with the LA County Sheriff's Department. I was wondering if I could speak with him for a minute."

"I'm sorry, Detective. David died in a car crash earlier this week. I'm . . . or I was, his wife. Can I be of some help?"

Stephanie sat back, dejected. Another dead end.

"I'm sorry, Mrs. Bernstein. I had no idea. I'm working on the Wade Bennett suicide."

"Oh yes, Wade and David were good friends. I couldn't believe they both died the same week, actually the same night."

That got Stephanie's attention. "The same night? Your husband's accident was on Tuesday evening?"

Mrs. Bernstein proceeded to give Stephanie the details of her husband's death.

There must be some connection, Stephanie thought. "Do you know if your husband talked with Mr. Bennett before the accident, either that night or the day before?"

"Not as far as I know. He was heavily involved in a court case. That's why he'd been working so late that night."

Stephanie asked several more questions but didn't get any helpful information. She decided it would be best to try and talk to his office staff on Monday. Maybe they knew something.

CHAPTER 29

"So, Vanessa, the most important part about your new relationship with Jesus is just growing closer to him," Jill said. Waiting for the sergeant to return Gary's call, the three of them had been discussing the new life that Vanessa had embarked on.

"And to do that," Gary continued, "doesn't stem from a system of laws of do this and don't do that. It comes from spending time with him. It's like a human relationship. You don't get to know somebody if you don't spend time with him or her. Jesus is the same way. To get to know him, you need to be in his presence."

"So you mean being in church, right?" Vanessa asked. "I remember as a kid being told that's where you get to know God."

Jill and Gary laughed, but not in a humiliating way. Vanessa smiled, "Not right, huh?"

"Not really, but we used to think that, too," Jill answered.

Gary continued, "You see, Vanessa, going to a church can be one aspect of getting to know Jesus better, and we recommend that in time you find a Bible-believing one that you feel comfortable in. But when it comes right down to it, church—in the sense that we're talking about it now—is just a building. It can be a wonderful place to go and hear good teaching, and fellowship with other Christians, but it is not the place where God is. When Jesus made the comment in Matthew 16 that he would build his church, he was talking about people. The church is all of those who profess that Jesus Christ is Lord. Do you know where the presence of God really is?"

Gary waited for Vanessa's eyes to look up and meet his before answering his own question.

"His presence is inside each one of those who profess Jesus as Lord. He's inside Jill, me, and now you, by the indwelling of the Holy Spirit. Yes, there is a special awareness of his presence when God's people get together and worship him, and it can be wonderful. As a matter of fact, we're instructed in the New Testament to gather together as believers. But that's only one dynamic of our relationship with the Lord. For most American Christians, going to church can become just a one-hour-a-week experience. The personal relationship that Jesus offers us is twenty-four hours a day, seven days a week, fifty-two weeks a year—"

"I think she gets the idea, Gary," Jill cut in with a grin. "So, the best ways to get to know Jesus better day by day are: reading his Word that he left with us; praying, or in simple terms, talking with him daily; spending time quietly before him, then listening for his response back to us; and spending time with others who know him, like what we're doing right now."

"You guys make it sound much more alive and realistic than what I've heard before. Jesus isn't an abstract being to you, but really a friend, isn't he?"

"Yeah," the two said in unison. Before Jill could continue, the phone rang.

"I'd better get that; it could be the sergeant calling back," Gary said as he walked to the phone.

"Treadway residence," he answered after the third ring.

A gruff voice could be heard on the other end. "Yeah, this is Sergeant Sanger of the Sheriff's Office. I'm looking for a Gary Hall. He left a message with me earlier today."

"Yes, sergeant, this is Gary. Thank you for returning my call."

"What's this about some woman in danger?"

Gary gave an abbreviated account of the events that led Vanessa into their lives.

"Sounds like your friend's in pretty deep," Sanger said. Gary didn't know how to respond.

"Do you feel safe where you are now?" the sergeant asked.

"Yeah, I'm sure they don't know where she is, but my wife and I would like to be able to go home. We're concerned that the guy somehow got my license plate when he tried to run my wife off the road, and they could be watching our house."

"That's possible. You're smart not to go back there until we can set something up. The only problem is, I'm not in town."

That took Gary by surprise. "Where are you?"

"Up in San Francisco running down a lead on another case. I'll be back later tonight. If you're all OK where you are now, I could come by and talk with her tomorrow afternoon. Would that be all right?"

They decided to meet at two the next afternoon. Gary gave the officer the address and directions to Gary's condo before disconnecting the call.

"Well, it looks like we're not going to get anywhere today. Sanger won't be back in town until late," Gary said as he sat down, then he looked to Vanessa. "He wants to talk with you tomorrow afternoon."

Vanessa sighed, "I was hoping we could get this over with. I don't want to lose my nerve."

"We won't let you, Vanessa," Jill said reassuringly. "It'll just give us another day to get you grounded in Jesus, then you'll know you're not facing this alone."

"That's right," Gary added. "We'll just relax and enjoy our new friendship. Besides, it'll give you a little more time to pray about all this and decide how you want to handle things."

8:15 P.M., VAN NUYS

Cassie was on the edge of her seat, immersed in the drama unfolding before her on the big screen. The man next to her reached out and took her hand in his, pulling her attention away from the film. She had met John Wellington at a singles function through the church they both attended. This was their second time out together. Cassie thought John was a nice person and enjoyed their first date somewhat. But tonight she realized that her heart just wasn't in it. The last couple of days with Rick were so preeminent in her mind that she couldn't relax and enjoy the evening with John.

Now that his touch to her hand had brought her back to reality, she was once again experiencing the turmoil of being out with him while her heart longed to be with Rick.

After a few uncomfortable moments holding John's hand, Cassie excused herself and headed toward the rest room. As she walked out of the dark theater, she silently prayed. *God, please don't let me do anything to hurt John. He seems to love you, and seems real nice. But I don't have that sense of passion with him, those feelings that I find inside me for Rick. Lord, I don't even know if Rick is your disciple, or if he even had scriptural grounds for his divorce. I pray that he does know you, Lord, but if he doesn't, and these feelings I have are wrong, please take them from me. In any case, help me to have the right words to be honest with John and not lead him on in any way. Let us have a good time tonight as two friends, Lord, and don't let me do anything that would mess up a good friendship.*

When she made her way back to her seat, she felt a little bit more at peace. She decided that after the movie she'd be honest with John, and that helped her to relax as she crossed her arms in front of her, sitting back, and once again focusing on the movie.

8:22 P.M., STUDIO CITY

It was dark by the time Rick pulled up at his condo. Jennifer and Justin had nearly fallen asleep on the drive back from the Pizza Hut. When they came through the kitchen, Gary, Jill, and Vanessa were sitting at the table munching down on some pizza as well.

Rick made the introductions, proud to see how polite his two kids were.

"Are you sure it's still OK for us to stay?" Gary asked. "We could go out and get a hotel or something."

Rick shook his head. "Don't even think about it. Jennifer and Justin are looking forward to the old slumber party with Dad in their sleeping bags, right kids?"

The two agreed with tired smiles. Rick knew it wouldn't take them long to fall asleep. "It looks like they're halfway there already. So what's the update? Did you get ahold of the police?"

"Finally, yes," Gary answered. "The sergeant is in San Francisco this weekend, but he's coming back tonight. He's planning on coming over tomorrow afternoon and talking to Vanessa. So maybe by then we'll have a plan so Jill and I can get back to our house."

"But we've had a great day here, sharing and talking about the Lord," Jill added. "We really appreciate your hospitality."

"Actually, it's been nice having people in this place. It's been kind of lonely lately," Rick said. "Well, I think the kids are tired. Let me get them bathed, and then you guys can have the bedroom again. We can talk more in the morning."

Rick let the kids have a quick bath, which revived them somewhat. He then set them out in the family room in their sleeping bags with a bag of popcorn and put *The Lion King* in the VCR for them.

Gary, Jill, and Vanessa made their way back into the bedrooms and Rick was alone with the kids. He looked at the wall clock. It was only 9:30. His thoughts went toward Cassie. He wondered if it was too late to call her. He didn't know what to say but wanted to hear her voice.

He reached for the phone, realizing he didn't even know her number. Then he remembered the staff list he had from the show. He went into the kitchen, pulled it out of his briefcase, and dialed her number.

"Hello."

"Cassie?" Rick asked, his heart racing.

"No, she's not in right now. Can I take a message?" Amy answered.

"Well, it's nothing urgent. Just tell her Rick called."

"OK, Rick. Does she have your number?"

"Yeah, . . . well, maybe she just has it at the office. Let me give it to you in case."

He recited the number and then hung up, depressed. Was she out on a date? It was Saturday night after all; an attractive young woman like Cassie should be out on a date. The thought was disturbing to Rick, bringing back the same feelings he'd dealt with seeing her at the service with her brother. Maybe she was spending some time with him. Wishful thinking, he decided. *Well, best to get your mind off it and get back to your kids,* Rick thought as he headed back toward the family room.

8:30 P.M., BEVERLY HILLS

Samantha pulled up to the massive house Flint owned in Beverly Hills. How she envied people who could live in such luxury.

Just keep pluggin', girl. You'll get there, she told herself as she stepped up to the front door.

She was suddenly dwarfed by the large figure of Gabriel Flint standing inside the foyer as he opened the door. Samantha tried to keep her shock from showing. He was nothing like what she'd pictured, or actually had hoped for. She had been flirting with the notion that she'd be meeting a handsome Hollywood producer who would sweep her off her feet, offer her a starring role, and she'd be on her way.

She'd seen this man at the funeral—you couldn't forget a person like him—but she had no idea he was the executive producer of Bennett's show. She wished now she'd done more homework concerning Gabriel Flint.

"Samantha, won't you come in?" he offered, sweeping his hand toward the interior of the house.

"Thank you, Gabe. What a beautiful house you have," she said, pulling off one of her best acting jobs.

He led her into the sitting room, showing her to a comfortable couch as he stepped behind the bar. "Can I get you something to drink?"

Samantha could see this wasn't going quite the way she wanted, but she had to play it out. "Just some wine would be nice, thank you."

Flint fixed the wine and made himself a scotch, then brought them over and sat uncomfortably close to Sam on the couch. "So, what is intriguing you about this case?"

Samantha edged a few inches away as she faced him, taking the drink in her hands. "It's just that for such an open-and-shut suicide, the police are being terribly careful with what they're saying. They seem to still be digging around. I thought it was time to talk to somebody on the inside of 'The John Harold Show', and you seemed to be the perfect choice. Thanks for seeing me."

"My pleasure," Flint said, eyeing Samantha up and down as he took a drink, a smirk forming on his lips.

Sam shivered slightly as she also took a sip. Something about her predicament reminded her of the classic casting couch situation for a young actress trying to get a break. The irony of it wasn't lost on her, as she wondered what kind of advancements this man could make for her career as well. The question in her mind was, how far was she willing to go? She definitely didn't want to stay in the rut she was in and have to do any more infomercials.

"Well, Gabe, what I was wondering," Sam continued, trying to stay on track, "is if there was any light you could shed on Wade's suicide. Do you have any reason to believe that he was murdered?"

Gabe set down his glass, reaching for her hand. "There is some information that I've just come across that I believe could give you the scoop that will make Samantha Steel a household name in this town."

Sam looked into his eyes. He had her undivided attention now.

"This could be the one event that makes your career. You'd be able to pick from whatever area of this business most intrigues you for your next project—the best scripts, television series, feature films—they could all be yours."

Samantha found herself inching closer to him as he tempted her with words. "The question is . . . ," Flint breathed, "what are you willing to do to get this information?"

11:54 p.m., VAN NUYS

It was nearly midnight when Cassie walked through the door of her apartment. She saw a light coming from Amy's room, so she walked in and flopped on Amy's bed.

"Did you have a good time?" Amy asked.

Cassie let her eyes respond.

"I guess not. There was a call for you."

"Who? It wasn't Rick was it?"

Amy waited, drawing the suspense out as Cassie sat up. "Maybe . . . let me see here." Amy reached by the nightstand for a piece of paper. "Here it is. Rick, at 9:30 tonight."

"Ahhhhhh!" Cassie looked at her watch. "And it's too late to call him back. What'd you tell him?"

"I just said you weren't in. He seemed kind of disappointed."

"What did he say?"

"Nothing, he just said to tell you he called."

"Oh, no. He'll think I was out on a date."

Amy laughed, "Well, weren't you?"

"Yes, but I don't want him to know that."

"Why not? A little jealousy couldn't hurt."

Cassie laid back on the bed. "I don't know, Amy. I couldn't stop thinking about him tonight. It wasn't fair to John."

"So, tell me about the date."

"Well, he's a nice guy and all. I was really into the movie, then John reaches over and grabs my hand. Reality set in. I felt so uncomfortable. Here I was holding John's hand, and all I could think of was Rick. It's not like me."

"Boy, you sound like you have it bad. And you don't even know if Rick's a Christian."

"Oh, I haven't seen you since this afternoon. You remember Gary? We met him and his wife at the C.I.F.T. meeting a month ago." Amy nodded. "Well, Rick and Gary were together today at the Bennett funeral. So I'm thinking, if they know each other, then maybe Rick's a believer too."

"Could be. Gary seemed like a pretty strong Christian. If he's a friend of Rick's, then I would assume that Rick has at least heard the gospel." Amy looked at her good friend. "I sure hope for your sake Rick's already saved because it looks like you're a goner even if he isn't."

Cassie laughed. "No, I'll stick to my convictions. But the way he acts, and as caring as he is, he's got to be a Christian. However, I also found out he's got a couple of kids."

Amy looked more serious as Cassie continued. "Divorced three years ago," Cassie answered the unasked question. "It sounds like there's no chance for them to get back together. His 'ex' got remarried right away. It kind of sounded like she left him for this other guy she married."

"Does the divorce bother you?"

"Well, I'll be honest. I wish he had never been married. But in this day and age, what are the chances of that?" Cassie had been dealing with her feelings alone all day. It felt good to share them with Amy. "If Rick is in God's will for me, then I'm sure I can get over that hurdle. But I don't even know if he's interested in me. He's going to have so much on his mind taking over that show, not to mention this thing about who killed Wade. I just have to go into work Monday and play it cool."

Amy let that last comment hang in the air for a minute, then said, "Yeah, right!" They both giggled like a couple of schoolgirls.

SUNDAY, 12:03 a.m., STUDIO CITY

Rick lay on his foldout couch, Jennifer under his right arm and Justin under his left. They had managed to get through only half of the movie before falling asleep. He could have stayed like this all night long, just enjoying the closeness of his children. He lay there for a moment, closing his eyes and thanking the Lord. It'd been such a good day, the best with his kids in years. It took awhile for Rick to put his finger on it, but what was different he knew was inside of him. His closeness to Jesus the past few days had resulted in quite a difference. Instead of grilling the kids on how things were at home with Connie and her husband, looking for ways to vindicate his bitterness toward her and the success of her new marriage, he'd been focused on what was happening in the children's lives, enjoying their friendship, being touched by their love. *God, whatever you're doing inside of me, please keep working,* he prayed. Then a quick thought flashed through his mind. How wonderful it would be to have Cassie as part of this picture. He quickly discarded it as silly. After all, he'd just met her Friday morning.

Rick got up and placed each child into a sleeping bag. He turned off the TV, then grabbed his Bible as he lay down again. He looked at where his kids lay. His thoughts drifted back to the discussion at the zoo concerning church, and their reaction. What should he do now? Force them to go to church in the morning, or plan something else and let it drop for now?

He opened his Bible, not really thinking about where to turn and read. After thumbing through several pages, he looked down and 1 Corinthians 4:5 caught his eye: *Therefore judge nothing before the appointed time; wait till the Lord comes. He will bring to light what is hidden in darkness and will expose the motives of men's hearts. At that time each will receive his praise from God.*

Rick wasn't one to glean a lot out of flipping to a Scripture and expecting some great revelation from it. But this one did make sense. God had placed him on a journey these past couple of days, and already he'd gained much from it. He felt like the right thing to do would be to continue on the path he was on and wait for God to reveal more to him. He guessed that would mean going ahead and taking the kids to church, then seeing what God would do. After all, Sunday was the day to be in the Lord's house.

Then verse 3:16 on the other side of the page caught Rick's eye: *Don't you know that you yourselves are God's temple and that God's Spirit lives in you?*

Rick thought that was interesting after thinking about being in God's house tomorrow. But he realized he was losing his concentration, so he closed out his prayer time and reached over and turned out the light. Then in the quiet darkness, he proceeded to give in to his thoughts about Cassie until he drifted off into a peaceful sleep.

CHAPTER 30

SUNDAY
9:30 a.m., RIVIERA COUNTRY CLUB

The titanium head smacked against the small white ball, compressing it for a millisecond before sending it soaring straight over the fairway. After about eighty yards the clockwise rotation caused it to change trajectory, slicing off to the right and into the rough, nearly out of bounds.

Flint swore again, as he often did while playing this game, or any other for that matter. He stepped back from the number eight tee at the Riviera Country Club, allowing his playing partner, city councilman Kent Samuels, to step up to the tee.

"The fairway's wide open for you, Kent." Flint offered as Kent bent over and stuck his tee into the ground, carefully placing his ball on top of it so that the label aimed toward the center of the fairway.

"Let's see if I can keep it in play this time," Kent answered. He stepped back away from the ball, planted his feet in the proper stance, and checked his grip. Just before his arms started back with the club, his head turned slightly to the right while keeping his eyes fixed on the ball. He'd picked this little move up from watching Jack Nicklaus win championship after championship through the years. What worked for "The Bear" could only help him, he thought.

His backswing was nice and smooth, pausing ever so slightly at the top, then he came back with a quick acceleration towards the ball. The ping of his metal driver meeting the ball was sweet as he powered through the impact. The shot was perfect, arching out over the fairway, landing dead center 220 yards away before rolling a good 30 yards farther.

Flint hated to be outdone in anything, but being an athlete wasn't one of his talents. He always felt that if he could get his weight into the ball, he'd be able to outdrive anybody. Unfortunately, he never mastered the golf swing enough to meet the ball square and have a chance at allowing his bulk to benefit his game.

"Great shot," he called out, hiding his jealousy.

"Thanks," Kent called back as he walked over to their cart and placed his driver back into his bag.

Flint climbed into the golf cart and accelerated as soon as Kent took his seat on the other side, speaking as they sped away.

"Kent, I wanted to talk to you about that bill that's coming up for a vote Tuesday night."

Here it comes, Kent thought. *I knew there was a catch to this free day of golf.*

"Which one is that?" Kent inquired, although he knew very well which one it was.

"That stupid one brought on by the religious right, trying to stop everyone from having fun in my clubs because they're offended."

"Oh, of course, that one. I don't think there's anything to worry about."

"Well, you never know about these kinds of things. I want to make sure that you're with me on this one. If these restrictions are accepted, it could really affect the way I'm able to do business in this city."

"Well, you know you can count on my vote," Kent tried to convince Flint. He didn't ever want to be on the bad side of this man, and he didn't really care one way or the other about the issue anyway.

"The only reason this is coming up for a vote at all is because of Perkins. Since that terrible mugging, I think it'll be quickly defeated, and then we'll just move on with the rest of the agenda." As Kent talked, the thought suddenly flashed into his mind that what had happened to Perkins could have been orchestrated by the man sitting next to him. He looked over at Flint and saw the sly grin spread across his face.

"That's what I'm hoping, Kent," Flint said as he pulled over to the area where his ball had landed, buried deep in the rough. "I know it's a terrible tragedy what happened to Perkins. I'm so disturbed by the random violence that happens in our city." As he continued, Flint stepped out of the cart and selected a club from his bag, "But I need you to make sure that this bill doesn't get any more attention, that it's just voted down and life continues on for all of us."

Flint walked up to his ball and kicked it out of the deep rough onto the carpetlike smoothness of the fairway. Kent didn't comment on the disregard for the rules of golf—he'd seen Flint disobey them consistently throughout the morning. He was more concerned with the language he was hearing. Was this a threat? It sure sounded like one.

Flint took his club back and struck at the ball, sending it flying toward the hole. It was one of his better shots of the day, landing shy of the green by only ten yards, just left of a large sand trap.

He turned back toward the cart with satisfaction in his eyes, before he bore down on Kent, "We do understand each other, don't we?"

Kent could only take a large swallow, as he nodded his head.

"Good. I'm glad we got our business out of the way. Now let's go find your ball."

11:20 A.m., STUDIO CITY

Bringing in the sheaves, bringing in the sheaves.
We shall come rejoicing bringing in the sheaves.

Rick was standing with Jennifer and Justin on either side of him, singing along with the rest of the congregation. The organ rang out the last chord, and the choir director stepped away from the podium. As Rick put the hymnal back into the pew in front of him and started to sit down, he heard Justin ask Jennifer, "What's a sheab, anyway?"

"It's the end of your shirt, stupid. Right there," She answered, tugging at his shirt.

"Shhhh, you two, be quiet." Rick tried to keep control. Inside he was laughing at Jennifer's response. He wasn't even sure what sheaves were himself. He thought back to the songs from the home fellowship and how meaningful they had been to him. His heart longed for the time of worship he'd experienced Thursday, especially for his kids. He wanted them to sense the presence of the Lord like he had.

The pastor was at the podium. "We're about halfway to our building fund goal for this coming summer, so we need a lot of help from you today," he pleaded. "Dig deep. If we're going to be able to add those classrooms we so desperately need, we've all got to sacrifice."

Rick was glad the offering was coming. He knew that soon the kids would be able to go to children's church. They had been pretty bored up to this point, and it was getting harder to keep them quiet.

"While they take the offering," he whispered, "I'll take you out and show you where your classes are."

"I want to stay with you, Daddy," Justin cried.

"Yeah, don't make us go," Jennifer pleaded.

"No, you guys will have more fun there. It'll be too boring for you during the sermon."

The kids started to argue, but Rick quieted them with a stern look. While the ushers moved through the sanctuary, Rick stepped out of his row and headed out of the sanctuary. He hadn't brought them to church in quite a while, so he wasn't sure where to take them. Eventually he found the room for Jennifer's age group and to her reluctance, dropped her off. A couple of doors down, he noticed a sign for four- and five-year-olds. He took Justin over to that room.

"I don't want to go, Daddy. Can't I go in with Jennifer?"

An older lady standing by the door heard Justin's comment, "I'm afraid not, young man," she said. "But you'll have a grand time in here."

Justin looked up to his dad, his eyes pleading.

"You'll be fine, Justin. I'll be right here to pick you up in about twenty minutes," he reassured him. The look on Justin's face nearly broke his heart. But he couldn't stay in the main service—he probably couldn't sit through the sermon, and kids weren't allowed to stay after the offering anyway.

"I'll bet you get to color or do some crafts, so have fun, OK?"

Justin finally agreed, but wasn't too happy about it. Rick made his way back to his seat in the worship hall, feeling guilty about forcing them to stay in the classrooms. He was close to just going back to get them and going home.

He settled into his seat just as the pastor was starting his sermon.

"I want to speak to you today on the importance of the church," he started. Rick perked up. He wondered how close the pastor's comments would be to what he'd been learning all week. This should be interesting.

"But before I get to that, let's talk about the family. In our culture today, the family is in trouble—it's fragmented; it's declining. When a lot of us grew up, we came from a stable family life. We lived in one home through all of our childhood. Many of us were even able to visit that home with our own children, to spend time with their grandparents. We knew our neighbors, counted them as our dearest friends. At school, it was a rare thing to know someone who came from a broken home.

"Now, look where we are. The table has turned to such an extent that it's the rare child who is still living with both of his birth parents. Did you hear what I said? Birth parents. We didn't even have terms like birth parents fifteen years ago. I was on a plane the other day and happened to be sitting next to two young ladies—one was twelve, the other was fourteen. Through a little discussion we had, I came to find out that neither one of them could name one child in their respective classes that still lived with their original moms and dads."

A collective sigh rang out from the congregation. Rick felt the burden of guilt that his children were a part of that group.

The pastor continued, "I mention these sad facts to bring to light the importance of why we're here." He paused for effect, then spoke again in a raised voice.

"The church needs to be the lifeline to our generation. Where else can you go when you're hurting? When you're needing a friend for a shoulder to cry on? When you need some food in your cupboards because the rent money won't stretch that far this month? The family isn't there anymore to do those things. But the church is. This is your family. Look around you."

Rick did as he was told, to his left, then his right. *This is my family?* he thought. He couldn't even come up with the name of anybody sitting near him.

"This is your family," the pastor repeated. Rick's thoughts went back to the discussion he'd had with Gary. *"I mean really know, as an intimate friend. Someone you'd run across town to help change a tire, or help move out of an apartment on a Sunday afternoon, spend time with in the hospital, or counsel through a difficult marriage. That kind of friend."*

"We're all part of God's family, and that makes us all family," the pastor continued, "and the Bible tells us we've got to love each other. God is love. We've got to obey his commands and love each other."

Now the pastor's words sparked another thought process in Rick. He remembered Terry speaking in the home fellowship meeting about being in the airport, when God showed him how to love like Jesus did, one at a time. That made so much more sense than what he was hearing now, loving in great generalizations. What kind of true love can you show to someone you might see rarely in the seat next to you on a Sunday morning?

"Now, getting back to what I shared earlier." Rick's attention returned to the pastor. "In order for us to fulfill our role, to facilitate making us a family, you need to help us. I mentioned the offering and how much more money we need to raise to build the new classrooms. We can't continue to supply what your family needs without the funds necessary to keep us going."

Rick looked at the people gathered around him. Of the twelve hundred or so in attendance, there was a predominance of younger couples, most accurately classified as 'yuppies' in economic terms. There had to be a vast supply of funds coming in from this group. But was that all that their Christian responsibility entailed? Was coming to church once a week and giving some money to keep the buildings going and the programs running all it meant to be a Christian in American society? Rick knew better. But he had to admit, before this week, and the questions stemming from Gary, he probably wouldn't have given today's sermon a second thought.

What was it that Rob had said. It was the job of the leadership to equip the saints for works of service. That didn't seem to be happening here. Rick's pastor seemed content to let the ministry flow from the staff, as Rick himself would have expected a week ago.

"We've got to finish God's house. After all, he deserves the best, and we're going to complete it. This church will be finished on time. How else can we carry out the programs that will meet your needs?" The pastor had raised the emotion of his sermon to a new level, and with the last words, he pounded on the pulpit. The congregation began clapping earnestly.

"*Programs,* Rick thought. *A family isn't served by programs, is it? What about the list from the home fellowship of serving, loving, caring, bearing each other's burdens?" Where did that fit in with the scheme of things around here? And what about this being God's house?* "Don't you know that you yourselves are God's temple and that God's Spirit lives in you?"

Rick thought back to the Scripture he'd read the night before. *The church isn't this building. The church is made up of persons who believe that Jesus is Lord. What was all this emphasis on the building?* Rick was amazed at how his line of thinking had changed over the last five days. He had some more questions to ask Gary when he got home. Then he remembered the other Scripture from last night that said the Lord will bring to light what is hidden. In many ways, things were looking a lot clearer to him.

Rick pulled out of the church parking lot, glancing over at Jennifer next to him, then catching a look at Justin in the backseat in the rearview mirror.

"Well, how was children's church?"

"We should have stayed with you," Jennifer said in a monotone.

"Yeah," Justin agreed.

"Why, what did you do?"

"Oh, some lady read us a story, then we colored for awhile. Pretty lame really," Jennifer informed him first.

"What was the story about?"

"It was about some boy who lost his dog. Big deal."

Rick was surprised, he thought for sure they'd have read a Bible story. Then he thought back to the sermon he'd heard. He didn't remember the pastor quoting from the Bible either. Something else to make note of.

"What about you, Justin?"

"We just colored, then had some cookies. One kid wouldn't let me use his red crayon."

"Well, kids, I want you to know something. I feel like God is showing me some things about the traditions that I've come to accept. I desire for you to understand God, and to have a real relationship with Jesus Christ. You know that when you accept Jesus, God sends his Holy Spirit to live in your heart, don't you?"

"Yeah, I guess so," Justin said.

"Well, I know you guys think church can be boring, but I want you to try and understand something. What we refer to as church is just a building. It's a place where Christians can go to celebrate Jesus together, which makes it a special place, but not where God lives. He's in here." Rick pointed to his chest. "The real church is made up of the people who have asked Jesus into their lives."

Rick knew he was probably speaking way above their heads, but there was something settling into his heart about these concepts that needed to be instilled in them. And they needed to come from him, their father, not some stranger in a Sunday school classroom.

"What I want you to realize is that our relationship with God is important, and it's exciting. I'm going to find a way to help you two understand that."

Jennifer smiled at her dad, and Justin laughed, not sure how to react.

"It's just fun to be with you, Daddy," Jennifer said.

"Well, what do you say we go home and hit the pool before I have to take you two back to your mother?"

As the kids cheered, Rick felt a reassurance that God would indeed show him the steps he'd need to take to keep his promise.

12:16 P.M., NORTH HOLLYWOOD

"Jordan drives downcourt, pulls up at the three-point line and shoots. It's good . . . the Bulls take a one-point lead with just under a minute to go." Chic Hearn's voice could be heard throughout the house from the TV as he called the final moments of the Chicago vs. Los Angeles basketball game. Sid Ratcliff lay sprawled out on his living room couch, staring at the picture in front of him, but not really seeing what was there.

"What's wrong with you, babe?" his wife, Linda, asked as she brought in some chips along with a cold can of beer for him. "You're usually crawling the ceiling, screaming your lungs out during a game like this."

Sid just stared at the screen.

"Sidney?" She repeated, finally grabbing his attention.

"What? Oh, sorry. My mind's somewhere else today." Sid sat up on the couch, taking the beer. "Thanks, honey."

Linda sat down beside him. They both munched on the chips, watching the game. It took over ten minutes for the last forty-five seconds of the game to be completed. Linda always felt that if she were told she only had a month to live, she would want to live it out within the last two minutes of a basketball game. It would seem like a lifetime.

The two sat in silence as the Bulls held on to their lead to beat the Lakers by two. Sid reached out for the remote and shut the TV off.

"I've got something to tell you, Linda."

She placed the bowl of chips on the coffee table and looked over at her husband, anxious to hear what was so disturbing to get between him and a Laker's game.

"This whole thing with Wade's death is really getting to me."

Linda held out her hand, stopping Sid. "I told you to leave it alone. You get involved in any way and you know it's gonna mean trouble."

"But I can't sit by and do nothing. It's tearing me up inside."

Linda reached out and wrapped her hand around his. "Sid," she pleaded. "We've already discussed this. It's just too dangerous. We don't know what happened to Wade, except that he's dead now. Leave it alone."

"Linda, I've tried. You and I both know he didn't kill himself." He got up and paced the room.

"So what are you going to do? You're in too deep to try anything without ending up in prison yourself."

Sid stopped pacing and sat back down on the couch. "I can't believe I got us into this mess. Just for a few extra bucks editing porno flicks at the studio after hours. Now it feels like Flint owns me." He buried his face in his hands.

"You had to call him and tell him what Wade saw on the Lasko tape," Linda said as she placed her arm around his shoulder. "Otherwise you might be where Wade is now. Just try and forget about it and this whole thing will blow over."

"Yeah, you're probably right. But I can't get rid of this guilty feeling. I told them about Wade, yet the next day he calls to warn me to be careful." As Sid confessed, the suppressed emotions finally came out as he broke into tears.

Linda just held on, not finding any words to say that could help.

CHAPTER 31

1:54 p.m., STUDIO CITY

"So, did you enjoy church?" Gary finally had a chance to ask Rick once the kids were in the back bedroom changing into their swimsuits. When Rick had arrived home, to his delight he found that Jill had made some sandwiches for lunch.

"It was depressing, Gary. Not quite as bad as the funeral service, but nearly as dead."

"That's too bad," Gary said. "I was hoping it'd be uplifting for you and the kids."

"I had my hopes too. I was kind of nervous about it because they didn't want to go in the first place. They said church was too boring. You know what? They were right. But I had a good talk with them on the way home. The sermon was all about the importance of the church, but it seemed off from what I've been reading in the Word. I really felt like God used that sermon to confirm to me that his church is not the building, but his people. I hope I can get my kids to understand that someday."

"I'm sure you will," Jill reassured him.

"I hope you're right," Rick sighed, then changed the subject. "So what time do you expect the sergeant?"

"Should be any minute," Gary answered. "He said sometime around two."

"Well, the kids and I are going to enjoy some early spring pool time. If there's anything I can do, just come out and grab me. You kids ready?" Rick called to the bedroom.

"We're ready," Jennifer called as she raced around the corner.

"Wait for me!" Justin cried, trying to catch up.

"Don't worry, we won't leave without you," Rick reassured him. "We'll see you guys in a little bit, and Vanessa," Rick turned to her as he opened the door, "I'll be praying for God's grace and courage to be with you."

Vanessa smiled. "Thanks, Rick. That means a lot."

Rick closed the door behind him, the kids already running through the courtyard toward the pool. He saw a white sedan pulling up to the visitor's parking space near his garage. *It must be the sergeant,* he thought. As he jogged to catch up with the kids, he silently prayed that God would be with Vanessa and give her strength.

"So this man who ran Jill off the road," Sergeant Sanger looked at Vanessa after he'd heard Jill's story, "you believe he's this Rudy Vanozzi. Is that right?"

Vanessa had already told him her story before Jill related the shooting incident with the car.

"It has to be, Sergeant," she answered, lowering her head. "Gabriel doesn't let people walk away from him."

Sanger nodded his head, hiding his excitement.

"Vanessa, think about this very carefully now." She looked up and met Sanger's eyes. "We've wanted to put Flint behind bars for a long time, but we never had anyone on the inside that could give us what we needed to nail him. You could be that person for us."

Gary and Jill prayed silently for her as Sanger continued. "I'm sure you're tempted to just get out of town and leave all of this behind you."

Vanessa nodded. "Yeah, I've headed that direction a couple of times, but something keeps bringing me back."

"Well, the big question is, are you willing to see this thing through and put Flint where he belongs?"

Vanessa stayed silent as she thought. Part of her wanted to just get away and protect the new life inside of her. But she didn't want to have to live looking over her shoulder, never knowing if one of Flint's boys would show up. Listening to Gary and Jill over the past couple of days, she'd decided that the God she was now willing to serve was powerful enough to take care of her. If he was in control, nothing could happen to her unless he allowed it. It was time to put her faith on the line.

She looked up at Sanger, and, with determination, answered, "Just tell me what I need to do."

She was drifting on a raft, lying on her back. Her eyes were closed as she lay still, hoping the afternoon sun would quickly warm her; the water was so cold.

He stalked her quietly. Taking one slow step at a time while on tiptoe, he made his way to the edge of the pool, fairly close to the raft. You could read the mischief in his eyes, excitedly thinking about what would come after his next step. Then he leaped, hitting the water just inches from the edge of Jennifer's raft. Justin had curled up into a cannonball, making the biggest splash his little five-year-old body could manage.

Jennifer was caught off guard, water drenching her before the wave came and rolled her off the raft. She came up screaming.

"Ahhhhhh. Justin, you little creep!"

Justin then emerged from the water giggling, struggling to get back to the steps and safety.

Rick had watched it all from a lounge chair beside the pool. The water had been a little too cold for his pleasure this early in the season, but he decided it was time to bite the bullet and get wet. He got up and ran toward the pool.

"Banzai!" he screamed and landed in the water next to Justin, who was trying to get away. Rick scooped up Justin and held him tight as he struggled and laughed. The burns on his back gave him a sharp pain as the chlorine invaded them through the bandages. But he was having too much fun to stop. He swam toward Jennifer.

"Is this the culprit who has brought harm to the lovely maiden?" he asked in his best impression of a knight from King Arthur's court.

Rick saw the anger in Jennifer quickly fade, leaving behind a broad smile as she decided to join in the game.

"Yes," she cried, "off with his head."

Justin wasn't sure what to do. This wasn't turning out the way he'd planned. "No! No! Let me go!"

"All righty then, have it your way," Rick said, and lifted him up in the air and threw him across the pool. He landed about six feet in front of the steps in a huge splash.

Justin came up laughing so hard he took in some water, but finally made it to the steps coughing and laughing some more. Then Rick turned and started wading toward Jennifer, humming the scary music from *Jaws*. She screamed again, splashing water at his face, swimming backwards in an attempt to get away.

Rick caught up with her and pushed her under the water, bringing her up quickly. She laughed as he brought her close to him in a great big hug.

"I love you, princess."

Her face lit up in a great big smile, "I love you, too, Daddy."

They made their way over to the steps where Justin was sitting. Rick decided he'd been taking life too seriously, letting the lack of work get to him. This was marvelous, just laughing and playing with the ones he loved the most.

They dried off and Rick looked at his watch. It was getting late, he'd have to get the kids back soon. He also wanted to make it to that C.I.F.T. meeting later. They grabbed their pool stuff and headed back inside. The kids went off to the back bedroom to change; Rick stepped into the kitchen and found the sergeant still talking to Vanessa, Gary, and Jill.

Rick, I'd like you to meet Sergeant Sanger," Gary said as he came to the table.

"Nice to meet you," Rick said as he shook his hand.

"Likewise."

"So, how's it been going? Do you think you can help Vanessa?"

Sanger smiled, "Actually, she's going to be a big help to us. We've been trying to get something on her boyfriend for a long time."

Vanessa's mouth rose in a half smile. Rick could tell she was still a little apprehensive about what would happen next.

"Sit down, Rick," Gary offered. "We'll fill you in on the plan."

Rick put one of the kids' towels around his shoulders and placed his on one of his kitchen chairs and took a seat.

"First thing we need to do is find a safe place for Vanessa to stay for a few days that is unrelated to Gary and Jill," Sanger briefed him. "From what I've heard, the goon that ran Jill off the road could have an idea where she lives, either from the license plates on their car or from the Crisis Pregnancy Center."

"We had an idea, but we wanted to run it by you first," Gary broke in. "We thought of Cassie."

"You mean *my* Cassie?" Rick asked. "The one from the show?"

"Yeah. Vanessa doesn't have anybody she can turn to. Anybody she knows they might be watching anyway. While we were talking about it, Cassie came to mind and it felt right to see if she'd let Vanessa stay with her for a few days."

"Well, all we've got to do is give her a call and see what she says."

"Great!" Gary responded.

"The next step," Sanger said, "is to get Gary and Jill back in their house to see if anybody's watching the place. We can also put out an APB on the guy who shot at them to try and bring him in. Gary and Jill are willing to identify him."

"What about the boyfriend? Are you going to be able to get him on anything?" Rick asked.

"Well, from what I've heard today, I'm willing to bet that after I spend a little more time with Vanessa, we're going to be able to put a lot of pieces together that will nail him," Sanger said.

"I hope so," Rick said. "Vanessa, I'd love to see you be able to get a fresh start with your new child and not have to worry about who's behind you all the time." Rick looked toward Gary. "Should I call Cassie, or do you want to?"

"I don't think it matters. I thought you'd like the opportunity to give her a call."

Rick smiled as he stood up and walked over to the phone. It surprised him that her number was already committed to memory. He dialed it, and Cassie picked it up after the second ring.

"Hello."

"Cassie, hi. It's Rick."

"Rick, hi. I'm sorry I missed your call last night. How are you feeling? The burns still doing OK?"

"Actually, not too bad. Listen, I know you've been through a lot lately, but I'm calling to ask you a favor. There's no pressure though, so feel free to say no."

He quickly explained Vanessa's situation as best as he knew it. While listening, Cassie's heart was touched by the story.

"Hold on," Cassie said, as she cupped the mouthpiece and quickly asked her roommate if it would be OK. "Rick, tell Vanessa I'd be happy to let her stay here for awhile. The only thing though, I've got plans until about nine o'clock tonight. Is that too late for you or Gary to bring her over?"

Rick thought about the timing, realizing it would work out just about right to go to the meeting and then take Vanessa over to Cassie's. "That would be great. Give me the directions to your place."

After he'd scribbled them down, he said, "This is wonderful. You're not that far from here. Thanks a lot, Cassie. We all appreciate it a lot."

"You're welcome. I'll see you tonight."

Rick liked the sound of that as he hung up. "You're all set, Vanessa," he said as he returned to the table.

"Great," Jill agreed. "Now, how do we get back to our house?"

"Well, let me ask you this," Sanger said. "Do you think Vanozzi got a good look at either of you two on the Santa Monica Freeway?"

Gary and Jill looked at each other. "It's hard to say," Gary answered. "I'd say he would have had to see Jill, but he probably only saw my car. What are you thinking?"

"I'm thinking that Jill and I would make a great-looking couple."

The comment took Jill by surprise, and she let out a giggle before she could suppress it.

"If he doesn't know what your husband looks like, it'll be a lot safer if I'm with you when you first enter the house. We'll set up a surveillance van down the street, where you can be, Gary. You'll be able to hear everything."

Gary didn't like the idea of putting his wife in any danger. But he sure didn't want them just to go back to the house on their own. He decided to go along with it.

"Is that OK with you, honey?" he asked Jill.

"I guess so. I'm sorry I laughed, Sergeant. I just wasn't expecting us to pretend to be married."

"It's quite all right. Then it's set. Let me get everything set up, and I can meet you back here . . . say around five?"

They all agreed, then the sergeant left.

"This all sounds pretty scary, doesn't it," Rick said to Jill as the four sat back down.

"Yeah, but we just need to cover everything in prayer. We have to trust God to take care of things, right?"

"Amen," Gary agreed. "Let's pray now. I want us to pray for our safety, as well as Vanessa's. Also, we need to pray that the police will be able put the pieces together to lock this group up for a long time."

They all bowed their heads together.

Jennifer and Justin came out of the back bedroom a few moments later, all changed and ready to head home. They paused in the family room as they saw the adults all holding hands around the kitchen table. Jennifer looked to Justin and raised a finger to her lips, keeping him quiet. They heard their dad praying for God to protect Jill as she went back to her house with the police officer. Justin just looked on, not realizing exactly what was happening, but for Jennifer, it was a quiet awakening. For the first time ever she felt that her dad was speaking to the Lord as if they were friends, just like Jesus was sitting at the table with them. That realization hit a tender spot in her heart.

Afterwards, as the kids gathered around Rick, he asked Gary, "I guess you won't be going to the meeting tonight then, will you?"

"No, and I was looking forward to it too. But you can still go. It starts at six and usually gets over around eight or so. That should give you enough time to get back here and pick up Vanessa and get her to Cassie's."

That's just about the way Rick had figured it earlier. "That sounds good, but what about you, Vanessa? That would leave you here alone."

"Well, you're so excited about these meetings, I was wondering if I might be able to go along with you."

Rick looked to Gary. "What do you think? Are these open meetings?"

"Sure. Especially the combined monthly gatherings. That's where all the small groups get together, at the Van Nuys High School auditorium. You'd be very welcome there, Vanessa."

"Then it's settled. Vanessa, we have a date tonight. I'll take my kids back to their mother's house, then I'll come back and get you."

Gary smiled, "And you two are going to love it."

3:45 P.m., WEST LOS ANGELES

Rudy had spent all day talking to anybody he could think of who knew Vanessa to see if they'd heard from her or would have any idea where she'd go if she was in trouble. None of them had a clue.

He'd just talked to the guys who were staking out Gary and Jill's house. Nothing happening there either. He knew it was about time to check in with Flint, but with no good news to report, he knew it wouldn't go well.

He was sitting in Vanessa's apartment, killing time. Rudy decided to head to the refrigerator for another beer when the phone rang.

"Yeah."

"Anything new?" It was Flint.

"Unfortunately, no. Everything's a dead end. Our only lead is to keep watching that house, unless you found out anything with the other car's license."

"I won't have anything on that until tomorrow. But I did find out that the investigation continues. Suicide is now being ruled out."

Rudy didn't like the sound of that but stayed quiet, not wanting to evoke any fits of rage out of Flint.

"Let's go ahead with the plan I discussed last night," Flint finally said.

"I thought you wanted to do that tomorrow when you know he won't be home."

"I changed my mind. Go on over to his house. If he's home, give me a call. I'll come up with some reason to get him out. If he's not home, then go ahead and plant it."

"OK, if you're sure."

"I'm sure," Flint spat back with a string of curses. "I want the heat off of our backs. I just had a productive day on the golf course. The vote's in the bag—as long as something doesn't come along and get in the way between now and Tuesday night. So forget the mess with Vanessa. We'll get back to her tomorrow."

4:10 p.m., WOODLAND HILLS

Stephanie was standing four-deep in a check-out line at the grocery store. She hated trying to cram in errands and shopping on Sunday afternoon, but with the caseload lately, there never seemed to be another time.

Her mind drifted as she glanced at some of the tabloid headlines displayed before her. She couldn't believe people actually bought this stuff. She rolled her cart a few inches forward as the line progressed. She needed a plan for Monday. She and Bill had talked yesterday after coming up empty trying to chase down Rudy. They didn't like the idea of Cassie and Rick heading into the dangers of the office on Monday with no plan of how to get the goods on Flint.

Then her eye caught the headline from one of the tabloids: "Prophet Declares Christ's Return Next Month."

She laughed inwardly. *Where did they get these nut cases?* Not being religious, she never really gave God much thought. But the headline struck her in an odd way. What if there was a God, and he was coming back? Her first thought was, if he came down and saw what she had to deal with every day on the job, he'd just turn around and head back up.

Then her mind thought back to earlier in the week when she and Bill had made the wager about making an arrest by next week. She knew at the time there wasn't a thing to go on. It would take a miracle for something to come up and give them a solid lead. And in just a couple of days, they'd gone from being ready to close the case as a suicide, to having a good idea who committed the murder. All they needed was the why. She knew it wasn't their great police work that had led them this far, but some lucky events centered around Cassie. Well, maybe there is a God and he's been working the Bennett case from Cassie's side of things. *More power to him,* she thought as she reached the head of the line and started putting her groceries on the moving belt.

She still needed a plan for Monday. But try as she could, she couldn't come up with one. Without that Lasko tape, they had nothing to go on. All they had was a possible I.D. on one of Flint's men hanging around the studio the night of the fire. And an arson charge wasn't going to pressure anybody to volunteer information about a murder investigation. Maybe she'd get lucky at the lawyer's office.

Stephanie sighed. They still needed that miracle. She looked up, trying to conjure up an image of what God would look like in her mind. *Send the miracle,* she thought. *I could certainly use it.*

CHAPTER 32

"With this wire on your wife, we'll be able to pick up anything she says within a half-mile radius," Sanger explained as he tucked the microphone in Jill's pocket. "You'll be in the van with my partner here, Officer Torrez." Sanger motioned to the short, solid Latino standing next to him. "You'll be parked down the street, close enough to intercede if needed, but far enough away that you'll be hidden."

"We'll be able to hear everything that is going down while keeping an eye on the front of the house the whole time," Torrez said, trying to reassure them.

Although Jill had a determined look in her eye, Gary could see underneath the exterior to the slight fear that gripped her. He gave his wife a comforting hug, then looked up to Sanger. "How long will you have to carry on with this if nothing happens?"

"If Vanozzi's watching the house, I would imagine something will present itself pretty quick. He's got a reputation for not stalling around." Vanessa nodded her head in agreement. Sanger continued, "If by morning all is quiet, I'm sure you two can go on as if everything is normal, but we'll keep a surveillance team on the house for a couple of days just to make sure." Sanger looked at the couple. "Everybody ready?"

Gary and Jill nodded their heads. "As ready as we'll ever be," Jill said.

Vanessa came up and gave them a hug. "I'll be praying. You two have done so much for me already. If anything happens to you, I don't know if I'll be able to forgive myself."

"Don't you worry," Jill said. "It's all in God's hands. He'll be there with us. You go on with Rick and have a good time. He said he'd be back here any minute. Are you OK until he returns?"

"I'm fine. I'm more worried about you two."

"Thanks, Vanessa," Jill and Gary said in unison as they made their way out the door.

Vanessa closed the door behind them and felt her pulse quicken. She hoped Rick would get back quickly.

A few moments after the group left Rick's house, a silver BMW with dents and scratches along the driver's side pulled up across the street. Rudy glanced toward number 717, looking for any signs of life inside. He needed to make sure the house was empty before he started his work.

He saw some lights on, but didn't see any movement. Maybe he was lucky and nobody was home. He picked up his cell phone and punched in Rick's phone number that he'd gotten from Flint. After two rings, the answering machine picked up. He hung up, deciding the coast was clear.

He checked his gun, then looked up and down the street to see if anybody would notice him. He just started to open his car door when a vehicle pulled around the corner, surprising him. Rudy decided to stay in his car a minute longer. He was glad he did when he saw the car pull into Rick's garage.

He cursed and looked at the digital clock on the dashboard, which displayed in bold green—5:30. He picked up his cell phone again and punched in Flint's home number.

"Yeah."

"It's me. I'm outside Treadway's place. He's inside."

"I'll have to call Josh, come up with a reason to get him out of there," Flint growled.

"Well, do it fast, I don't—" Rudy stopped in midsentence as he saw two figures come back out of the house and climb into the car. "Hold on a minute. It looks like he might be leaving."

Rudy watched as Treadway backed out of the garage, paused to hit the automatic garage door, then pulled forward. His headlights were going to cross right over Rudy's car, so Rudy ducked behind the dashboard. He glanced up as Rick's car passed by. His eyes couldn't adjust to the darkness quick enough to recognize anybody, but he did notice that there was a young woman sitting next to Rick. *Lucky stiff, he probably has a hot date tonight,* Rudy thought.

"It's clear now," Rudy said into the phone.

"Good. Just get in there and get the job done."

"You got it."

"And, Rudy?"

"Yeah?"

"Don't mess this one up."

Rudy hung up without answering. Flint was really getting on his nerves. He looked up and down the street. Not seeing anyone, he calmly opened his door and headed over to Rick's front door.

Within seconds he'd picked the lock and opened the door. He closed it behind him, surveying the room. He needed to find the right place.

He didn't find it on the bottom floor, so he headed upstairs. Bingo—Rick's office. It contained a simple desk, a computer table with a desktop Macintosh, and on another table a printer and a fax machine. *What is it with these TV people and Macintosh computers?* Rudy thought.

He walked over and turned the computer on. While he was waiting for it to boot up, he reached into his bag and pulled out a computer disk and inserted it into the Mac. It took him just a few moments to repeat what he'd done in Bennett's office. Pulling the disk back out when he was finished, he then double-clicked on the icon that was identified as "Good-bye."

He waited until the document filled the screen, then placed Wade's appointment book on the desk and made his way back downstairs and out the door. He was careful not to leave any tracks.

Once inside the safety of his BMW, Rudy started the car up and drove down the street. He dialed Flint.

"It's done."

"Any glitches?"

"None."

"Great. I'll take care of it from here."

As quickly as Rudy disconnected the call, his phone rang.

"Yeah."

"Rudy, it's Vic. That couple just got back. They're in the house."

"Don't do anything. I'm on my way," Rudy answered. He smiled as he accelerated through the streets. Things were beginning to look up after all.

5:25 P.M., MALIBU

Becky was alone. With the funeral weekend over, all of the guests and family that had come to pay their respects were all gone.

For the first time, Becky was dealing with the loss of her husband by herself.

She sat facing the sliding glass window staring out into the backyard. What was normally her favorite view didn't move her at all. She felt like crying, but no tears came. *How could this happen? What kind of God would allow this?*

Her questions were interrupted by the shrill ring of the phone. Without thinking, she reached beside her and picked up the receiver.

"Hello? Is anybody there?" the caller asked after a brief silence.

It snapped Becky out of her trance. "Hello."

"Becky, is that you? It's Paul Franklin. How's it going?"

Becky wished she hadn't touched the phone. Paul had been Wade's best friend in college. He now lived in Connecticut.

"Paul, hi. I'm sorry I didn't think to call you. You probably haven't heard."

He could sense the sadness and strain in Becky's voice, "Heard what? Has something happened to Wade?"

"Yes . . . he's dead," she finally got out.

Silence.

"Becky, I'm sorry. How did it happen?"

Becky sighed and laid her head back on the couch. "Well, we're still trying to figure that out. He was found here at the house as if he shot himself, but I can't believe that."

"I don't believe that either. He would have let me know if he was depressed. That's why I was calling actually. He hadn't returned my last several E-mails. We'd usually communicate that way every other day or so. I was beginning to worry."

"When was the last time you heard from him, Paul?"

"It was Sunday night, I think. He E-mailed about how much he was looking forward to the week off with you." Becky's eyes closed as tears formed again and slid down her cheeks.

"He was pretty excited—definitely not depressed or suicidal. Would it help if I talked with the police?"

"It could. I'll ask them tomorrow. They're looking seriously at murder, but so far they don't have much to go on. It could somehow be tied into the production office of the show."

"I'm really sorry, Becky. You must be devastated. Is there anything you need? Do you want me to fly out there. . ."

"No, Paul, but thank you. I've got my family here and everyone has been so supportive. I'm sorry I hadn't called you yet. Wade's phone book is missing. I didn't have your number."

"Let me give it to you then, so if there's anything I can do, you let me know."

Becky found a pen and jotted down his phone number before hanging up. *Poor Paul,* she thought, *he was a good friend to Wade.* She thought about other people that Wade might have been in touch with over the Internet, and it gave her an idea.

She got up and went into the office, pulled out the staff list for the show, and dialed Cassie's home phone number.

Cassie and Amy were just heading out their apartment door when the phone rang.

"Let it go or we'll be late," Cassie said.

Amy walked back inside and reached for it. "You know I can't do that," she laughed.

"Hello."

"Cassie?" Becky asked.

"Hold on, I'll get her," Amy answered. "It's for you."

Cassie looked at her watch, irritated. She hated to be late. She quickly walked back inside.

"Hello."

"Hi, Cassie, it's Becky. Can I talk to you for a minute?"

Cassie set her purse down and took a seat at the counter. "Sure, Becky, how are you doing?"

"OK, I guess. I've got a question for you. I just heard from an old friend of Wade's. They used to keep in touch on the Internet. I wasn't even able to call him about, well, you know—because I don't have Wade's address book."

Becky paused, not really sure where she was going.

"Anyway, I was wondering if there was a way to access Wade's E-mail and see if there's anybody else I might need to contact."

"Do you know what service he used?" Cassie asked.

"It was America Online."

"That's what I use, so it might be real easy. Do you know what—wait a minute. I used to E-mail Wade at your house. I know what screen name he used."

Becky was excited. Maybe she'd get to read some of the mail from friends like Paul. It might help ease the pain.

"But to get into his account, we'll need his password. Do you know it?"

"Yes, I do. He wanted me to be able to get into it if I needed to, but I was too intimidated by the computer. Could we get together and try it?"

Cassie thought for a second. "I'd be happy to, but I'm heading out right now. How about later tonight?"

"I'm ready anytime."

"OK, but the police have Wade's computer still, so you'll have to come to my place. Can you meet me here at, say, nine?"

"Oh, Cassie, that'd be great. I'm going crazy in this house anyway. I really appreciate it."

"Not a problem. Let me give you directions. . . ."

5:45 P.M., WESTWOOD

Jill's heart pounded in her chest as Sergeant Sanger pulled into their garage. She tried to act normal as she got out of the car and headed inside through the laundry room. Everything looked exactly as they'd left it a couple of days before. She saw Sanger eyeing her.

"Anything look different?"

"No, everything looks the same."

"Well, that's a good sign. If they'd known where you lived, I would have bet they'd have come in here looking for something."

"So, what do we do now?"

"Pretty much whatever you'd normally do, taking into consideration that I'm not really your husband," Sanger said with a smile.

"You don't have to worry about me forgetting that. I'm kind of hungry, do you want a sandwich or something?"

"Yeah, that sounds great."

Gary's stomach gurgled. The man beside him, Sanger's partner, Richard Torrez, laughed.

"You hungry too?"

"Yeah, I guess I didn't realize it until Jill mentioned the food. I'd love to raid the refrigerator with them."

"Look under your legs; you can raid ours."

Gary was sitting on a short stool, crammed into a small van with Richard and a bunch of electronic equipment. The outside of the van had a logo of a plumbing company on it, but inside it was all electronic gadgets. A lot of it Gary recognized, having been in the communications side of television for so long.

Gary scooted back and noticed an ice chest down by his feet. He lifted the lid and found an assortment of soft drinks and some cold sandwiches. He reached in and handed one of each to Richard, then grabbed the same for himself.

"You guys really know how to live," Gary said sarcastically.

"Nothing but the best for LA's finest."

"What kind of a microphone do you have on Jill?"

Richard's eyebrows went up. He'd never been asked that kind of question before. "It's an AT 803B omnidirectional."

"That's a pretty expensive mike. What kind of a range do you get with the transmitter?"

Richard smiled, then sat back with his eyes on the monitor showing the front of the house. *At least this stakeout will have some interesting conversation,* he thought as he began to answer Gary's question.

5:50 P.M., WOODLAND HILLS

Stephanie reached over and shut off the hot water, then lay back. She'd just settled into a bubble bath, a glass of wine on the tile beside her. The hot water tingled her skin, bringing goose bumps all along her arms and legs. It had not been a relaxing day, especially for a day off. Try as she might, she just couldn't come up with a good plan of attack to get to the bottom of the murders. She'd finally given up and decided to lay it all aside and take a hot bath. Maybe Bill would have a bright idea by tomorrow.

The quiet was interrupted by the shrill ring of her phone. She glanced at the wireless handset lying within arms reach on the counter, but decided to just let it ring. She could hear the message machine pick up in the other room after the fourth ring.

"Stephanie, it's John down at the station. Listen, I hate to bother you on your day off, but we just got a strange call concerning that Bennett case you're working on . . ."

The mention of Bennett got her attention. She grabbed the portable phone and punched "talk."

"Hold on, John, I'm here. What have you got?"

"We got an anonymous tip, and the captain wants you to get right on it. Some guy says that Bennett didn't commit suicide. It was a murder, and he knows who did it."

"Did you get it on tape?"

"Oh yeah, our machine got it. But there's more. He named the murderer as some guy named Treadway, and even said if we searched his home, we'd find proof."

"Are you sure of the name?" Stephanie asked, startled.

"You bet, Treadway, Rick Treadway. Why, you know him?"

"Yeah, something's really fishy here. Tell you what, John, get me a copy of that tape. I'll be there in half an hour."

She disconnected the call, then dialed Bill's number.

"Hello"

"Bill, it's Stephanie."

"Man, I thought I wouldn't have to deal with your ugly face until tomorrow."

"You should be so lucky. Hey, something weird just happened." Stephanie filled Bill in on what little she knew. "What do you make of that?"

"It's hard to tell. You want to follow it up tonight, I bet."

"Don't you?"

Bill looked over at his wife. They were both relaxing on the sofa, feet propped up, a bowl full of popcorn in their laps, with a movie playing in the VCR. "Not really . . ."

"Tell you what. I'll go over to the precinct and check out the phone recording. If it's worth going over to Rick's house, I'll give you a call, and you can meet me there. Deal?"

"My wife and my marriage thank you."

Stephanie set the phone down and sank back into the water. Just when she was about to relax. Her first instinct was to disregard the tip. Rick couldn't have had anything to do with the murder. He was trying to help them get the information about Lasko. But she had to remember she'd been fooled by others before Rick. She couldn't enjoy the bath any longer. She pulled the plug and reached for her towel.

6:00 p.m., VAN NUYS

As Rick and Vanessa walked into the crowded auditorium, they felt a sense of excitement around them. Most of the people were taking their seats as the first song was being sung. Rick looked around for a place for them to sit.

Cassie was just about to sit down with her roommate when she saw Rick walk through the door. First she was shocked to see him, then excited that he would be here. But the excitement gave way to fear the moment she spotted the stunningly beautiful woman at his side. If this was Rick's date, she didn't have a chance. Then she remembered the woman Rick had mentioned that needed help. Cassie hoped this was her, as she bravely made her way over to the two of them.

"Hi, Rick. What a surprise to see you here," she yelled over the music as she walked up to them.

"Cassie, wow! I didn't think about you being here. I guess it makes sense, though, because you met Gary at one of these meetings, didn't you?"

"That's right, you remembered," Cassie responded, then she glanced toward Vanessa.

"Oh, forgive me. Cassie, this is Vanessa. She's the woman I told you about on the phone."

Relief flooded Cassie as she extended her hand. "It's nice to meet you."

"And you," Vanessa answered. "I want to thank you so much for allowing me to stay with you tonight. I don't have anywhere else to turn."

"It's no problem; I'm happy to do it," Cassie said. *Anything to keep you out of Rick's house.*

"Where are you sitting?" Rick asked.

"Follow me. My roommate's over there. I think there are still a couple of seats left by us."

Rick guessed the high school auditorium was probably able to seat about six hundred people, and it seemed to be near capacity. Looking through the crowd, he saw a good mixture of people—various ages, skin tones, and economic standings. It was hard to believe that a lot of the people here had some connection with the entertainment industry. But then Rick remembered Gary's saying that the monthly meetings were growing, with people both in and out of their profession.

As he stood and listened to the singing, Rick sensed the presence of God around him, as he'd felt at the house fellowship group the other night. He smiled as he glanced over at Vanessa. She looked up at him with a grin. She must be sensing it, too, he thought. He felt Cassie's presence on his left. He was afraid to look over at her, but he listened as she sang along. Her voice was beautiful.

After the second time through, Rick was able to join in with Cassie and the others, singing the chorus. The rhythm of the guitar and drums was infectious, but more important than that, Rick began to let his love for Jesus flow out from him unto the Lord as he clapped his hands and sang.

Vanessa giggled as she leaned over to him and half yelled into his ear, "Gary was right. This isn't like any church service I've ever been to."

6:20 P.M., SHERIFF'S HEADQUARTERS

"I know who killed Bennett. You have it all wrong if you think it was a suicide. Check Rick Treadway's house. You'll find all the evidence you need. It wasn't just luck that landed him Bennett's job."

The voice was muffled, as if spoken through fabric, but the words were understandable. Stephanie rewound the tape and played it again, hearing nothing new as she listened for the fourth time. She had thought about it all the way down to the station. She was a good judge of character, and she didn't think she'd misjudged Rick. Still, she had to get to the bottom of this.

She picked up the phone and dialed her partner.

"Bill, it's Stephanie."

Bill paused the movie he was watching with his wife, his eyes apologizing to her as he responded to Stephanie.

"Hi partner, what'd you find out?"

"Well, the phone call's real specific. It names Treadway as the murderer and says we'll find some hard evidence at his place."

"Any clues on who it could be?"

"No, it's real muffled; sounds male, but you really can't be sure of that."

"Do you think Treadway could be in with Flint?"

"If so, he really had me fooled," Stephanie said. "But after all, this is Hollywood we're talking about here."

"What do you want to do?" Bill asked, knowing that he'd seen as much as he was going to see of this movie tonight.

"I don't think we have a choice."

"You going to get a warrant?"

"Definitely. It'll take me a little bit of time. Why don't you stay with your wife until I can get it. I'll let you know when it's signed, and we can meet at his house."

Bill was relieved, the evening still showed some promise. "Great, Steph. I'll owe you one."

Stephanie hung up the phone and pulled out her list of judges. Which one would be the best to bother on a nice Sunday evening?

CHAPTER 33

A silver BMW pulled past the surveillance van that Gary and Richard were crammed into. It drove slowly past Gary's house, then parked across the street, three doors down. The passenger got out and walked across the street heading toward Gary's house.

Richard noticed him first. "You have any neighbors that drive a BMW?"

"Not that I know of," Gary said as he looked out the window. It was too dark to make out any features, but the guy's build matched that of the lunatic who had shot at Jill. "That could be the guy." Gary's voice rose about an octave as he sat up with his full attention now, peeking out the window.

Richard jumped on the radio to his partner in the house as the man turned up the sidewalk to the house next to Gary's.

"Sanger, we've got a possible approaching the . . ." Richard noticed where the unidentified man was heading, "make that approaching the house next door. Stand by."

Jill jumped when the radio interrupted their conversation around the kitchen table. Sanger responded to it with a quick, "Roger," and waited.

Richard reached out and touched a joystick sitting on a console beside him. It changed the aim of the microphone from Gary's front door toward the neighbor's door.

" . . . just been inside about forty min—" was all they could hear before the man was inside the house with the door closed behind him.

"Who lives there?" Richard asked.

"Elaine and Travis McCormick. But that wasn't either of their voices." Gary was trying to get his breathing back to normal.

Richard once again grabbed the radio mike. "It looks like it's our target, using the neighbor's house as a base."

"Copy that," Sanger answered. "Get some backup over here, but keep 'em quiet."

Richard hit the transmit key to let Sanger know he'd understood, then grabbed the police-band radio to call reinforcements.

"This is X-ray. Lincoln four requesting backup at 6428 Washington near Cedar. We are on stakeout. Be advised to approach code two."

Richard listened for who would respond, and heard two patrol cars come on the air, one estimated to arrive within five minutes, the other in seven. He relayed the information to Sanger inside the house.

Inside the McCormicks' house, Rudy sat in the upstairs bedroom with his two hired guns. He swore as the police scanner next to him relayed the message of the arriving squad cars.

"The police are in the house. I'll bet Vanessa isn't even in there," he nearly screamed in frustration.

"We better blow out of here, man." Ben started to panic. One more arrest for him and he'd be doing some hard time.

"All right, we're not going to get anywhere with this tonight. I don't know how she picked this couple to help her, but they sure are going to pay for it." Rudy paused to think of the best way to cover his own hide in making their exit.

"You guys have your car in their garage?"

The two men nodded.

"OK, I'm going to go out the back door, over the back wall until I can get to my car. Load up this stuff and pack it in your car, but be driving out of here in exactly three minutes. That'll get you out of here before the first black and white arrives. I'll make some diversion," he lied. "That van will never be able to follow you. Got it?"

The two looked at each other, knowing that something was not quite right with the plan, but unable to put their fingers on it.

"Well, get going," Rudy yelled, then headed down the stairs and out the back door.

"I want you to go into your bedroom, lock the door, and lie on the floor." Sanger instructed Jill. He could see the fear in her eyes. "Don't worry, we're going to take them over at the neighbor's house. I just want to keep you safely tucked away, OK?"

"What about Gary?" she pleaded.

"Don't worry, he'll be safe in the van."

Richard studied the instruments, trying to pick up some audio from inside the other house. Suddenly Gary opened up the van door.

"Hey! What are you doing? You'll blow our cover."

"I want to make sure they're not going in the back way," Gary whispered, then jogged across the street.

"You can't—" Richard realized that he was talking to an open door. He unholstered his gun, grabbed the radio, and took off after Gary, muttering something under his breath.

Gary reached over the fence and undid the latch holding the gate. He walked through and reached the back fence that separated his yard from the neighbor's. He stopped and carefully peeked over the fence. Just as Richard ran up next to him, Gary spotted the dark outline of a man jumping the fence on the other side of his neighbor's yard.

Gary ducked his head back to his side of the yard. "Somebody just jumped into the next yard over," he whispered to Richard.

"Don't move," Richard said through clenched teeth as his eyes penetrated Gary's. He reached for the radio and whispered into it.

"It looks like our cover might be blown. We're in the backyard. Gary saw somebody climbing over the fence away from the house next door."

Sanger was mad, but he knew he'd lose precious time asking what they were doing in the backyard. Jill heard the report before she made it into the back bedroom and came back out with Sanger as he responded.

"Get Gary inside this house now!" he said, his anger erupting. "You'll stay with them, I'm going out front."

Sanger looked to Jill. "Everything's going to be OK. Just stay inside with Richard and your husband!"

Jill nodded her head, relieved that they'd be together for whatever was about to happen. Sanger made his way toward the front door but waited until he saw Richard and Gary walking through the sliding glass door in back before he stepped outside.

Sanger walked out front like he owned the house, hoping things weren't as bad as they seemed and they could still make their arrest. He walked toward the mailbox, acting like he was checking the mail after being out of town. His eyes scanned the street and the house next door, hoping for a sign of Rudy.

He saw a figure dart across the street three doors down and head for a silver BMW. Now he knew for sure that their cover was blown. He pulled out his gun and took a few steps toward the man, shouting, "Freeze! Police!"

At that moment, the garage door behind him opened causing Sanger's attention to be drawn behind him as the man he yelled at ran to his car and opened the door.

As soon as the garage door was open enough for the car to exit, the tires squealed as the driver accelerated in reverse, coming right toward Sanger. He tried to whip his gun around to get off a shot, but there was no time—the car was nearly on top of him. All he could do was dive toward the grass. While in midair, the rear bumper crashed into his left ankle. Sanger rolled on the grass, grabbing his foot as he looked up the street.

The car that almost ran him over sped off in one direction, while the other guy started his car and peeled off in the other. They were gone. Sanger slammed his gun back into it's holster, then worked his way upright to see if he could walk on the injured foot. He managed to limp back toward Gary's house.

"Get on the radio," he yelled, coming through the door. "Let the approaching black-and-whites know what to look for. I'm pretty sure one of them is Vanozzi's car. The other one's a dark sedan, probably a Ford Taurus, but I didn't get the license."

Richard ran out to the van, but Jill made her way over to where Sanger was leaning against a wall by the front door.

"Are you OK?"

Sanger tried to give her a reassuring smile. "Yeah, just got nicked by the car pulling out of the neighbor's garage."

"Well, come over here and sit down. Get your weight off of it," Jill prompted as she led him to the living room rocker.

"I'm sorry, you two. We had them. I don't know what tipped them off."

"That's OK. I'm just glad that you guys were here. What would have happened if Jill and I had come home alone?" Gary said.

Jill bent down to take a look at Sanger's left leg. "But now what do we do?"

Sanger winced as Jill touched his swelling ankle. "We'll have to have a twenty-four-hour watch put on this house and you guys until we catch them. We'll just be ready next time."

Gary smiled reassuringly at Jill. He was glad his trust was in God. The Los Angeles County Sheriff's Department would need all the help it could get.

7:10 P.M., VAN NUYS

"So, I'm watching this guy just blow his stack at the referee. He's swearing; he's throwing his racket; he's basically acting like a two-year-old who just had someone take away his little toy." Rob Stevenson was walking across the stage, acting out the emotions he was describing. The crowd was laughing with him as they listened.

Rick was thoroughly enjoying the evening. The worship had been wonderful. Some of the songs really touched him, allowing him to focus on Jesus and all his magnificence. At times he was distracted by having Cassie next to him. He found himself sneaking a peak as they sang. He was surprised at how excited he was that she was here. Something leaped in his heart as he watched her, hands lifted up, her eyes closed, singing to the Lord. Now Rick's full attention was on Rob, the man he'd learned so much from at breakfast the day before.

He was recounting a time when he had attended a tennis match years ago where John McEnroe was playing. There had been some questionable calls that didn't go John's way, and he had shown his famous temper.

"My wife and I had pretty good seats, sitting just a few rows up from where McEnroe was showing his ... displeasure," Rob continued. There were more chuckles at his choice of words. "I was embarrassed for him. But the Lord brought that back to mind in my life to show me a lesson.

"It was actually years later. God had been working on me in some areas of personal behavior. He was showing me how I can't change me. No matter what I do, no matter how hard I try, for me to become like Jesus is not something I can do. It's a marvelous work that only Jesus can perform in me."

Rick thought back to their talk at breakfast the other day about the period of time when Rob was a pastor, and the stress that had gotten to him, resulting in God's working this lesson out in his life.

"I was playing in a church league basketball game, and this guy on the other team was playing really dirty." Once again a few chuckles could be heard from those guys who could relate to Rob; Rick was one of them. "Unfortunately, I was the one he was guarding most the time. Well, as the game progressed, I found myself getting madder and madder, fighting to stay in control of my temper. I couldn't lose it and fight back with this guy. You see, I was the pastor, and the team represented my church.

"Well, there was this one moment, where I drove in for a layup. This guy was chasing after me, and knowing he couldn't stop the play, he just plowed right into me, throwing both of us into the wall under the backboard." Rob staggered across the stage, giving a visual representation of the foul.

"Well, I have to tell you, I came so close to losing it. I was beet red with anger. I wanted to shout at that guy, kick him, do whatever it would take to teach him a lesson. But you know what I did?"

There was dead silence as all waited for his response.

"Nothing. I held it all in, reached over, helped the guy up, and resumed the game." Rob paused for effect. "And I was pretty proud of myself too. I thought I'd made it. This was what being a Christian was all about. Wouldn't most of you agree?"

Rick thought back to yesterday when he picked up the kids from his wife. He'd sure been mad, and was able to control it about the same way Rob was describing. Rick also thought he'd done pretty well. What was he missing?

"You see, that's what a lot of people settle for in their Christian walk. Not for a real change within that is brought about by the work of God, but an outward covering of what's really happening inside so nobody will know what we're really like."

Rick felt like a brick had hit him. Rob was absolutely right.

"Well, later that night, God started dealing with me about all this.

"I'd like to read a passage from the third chapter of Matthew to you. It's from the paraphrase *The Message*, written by Eugene Peterson. The wording he uses really hit home to me. John the Baptist is talking about the ministry of Jesus, compared to his ministry: *I'm baptizing you here in the river, turning your old life in for a kingdom life. The real action comes next: The main character in this drama—compared to him I'm a mere stagehand—will ignite the kingdom life within you, a fire within you, the Holy Spirit within you, changing you from the inside out. He's going to clean house—make a clean sweep of your lives. He'll place everything true in its proper place before God; everything false he'll put out with the trash to be burned.'*

"You see, the truth being driven home here? You'll be changed from the inside out. It's not something we can do externally, by acting, covering up what's really there. It's not even something we can do. To walk in the Spirit doesn't mean you still get mad and just cover it up so nobody notices. Walking in the Spirit means that the problem you have with anger, or lust, or pride, or whatever it may be, is met head-on inside of you by Jesus Christ."

Rick took a second to glance over at Cassie, who was taking everything in as seriously as he was. Then he looked to the other side and realized that Vanessa was also enthralled with Rob's words. He even noticed a tear making its way down her cheek. Vanessa had never heard such down-to-earth teaching. As for Rick, he felt like he was getting a spiritual meal for a change, especially compared to the message he'd heard at his church that morning.

7:15 p.m., BEL-AIR

"Thank you, Judge," Stephanie said, standing in the doorway of Judge Jeff Reinstrom's house and taking back the signed warrant. "I'm sorry to have disturbed you on a Sunday evening."

"Well, I hope you find something useful," the judge said gruffly, then shut the door in her face.

Stephanie glanced at her watch as she headed back to her car. It wasn't that late. She picked up the radio mike once she got back into her car and asked for a patch to Bill's home phone. She hoped their movie was over because she was about to interrupt his evening again.

"Hello."

"Bill, it's Stephanie."

She heard Bill sigh. "What time and where?"

He knew her too well. "I'm in Woodland Hills. I just got the warrant signed."

"How soon until you get to Treadway's?"

"It should only take me fifteen minutes to get over to Studio City." She gave Bill the address of Rick's house.

"I can get over there in about twenty minutes," he said.

"I'll wait outside until you arrive. We'll go in together," Stephanie finished as she pulled her car out onto the street.

7:25 p.m., VAN NUYS

"That was a wonderful meeting, Cassie. I wish I'd given this group a chance a long time ago," Rick said as they headed toward the parking lot.

"They've been a great addition to my life the past few months, that's for sure," Cassie said. "What'd you think, Vanessa?"

"I'm overwhelmed. The last few days with Jill and Gary have shown me how real God can be in your life, and that meeting just capped it all off. It definitely wasn't like the services I remember as a kid."

"I'm glad you feel that way. Too often our churches get stuck in rituals and traditions. Once you see how real a relationship can be with Jesus, the celebration time of his people coming together to worship him becomes exciting. We have a saying in the group: Don't just go to church, be the church." Cassie was getting a little excited, and the pitch of her voice suddenly embarrassed her. "I'm sorry, I guess I'm getting a little preachy."

"Preach on, gal, I love the message," Rick joked. "Hey, Cassie, it's still pretty early. How about your coming by the house for a little bit while we get Vanessa's stuff together. I can stop by a store and pick up some ice cream. We can give Gary a call and see how they're doing."

Cassie looked at her watch to check the time, but inside she was thrilled to spend some more time with Rick. "That sounds great to me, but I need to be home by nine. I promised Becky I'd meet her. Is it too late for you though? If I remember correctly, you have a pretty important directing debut tomorrow, don't you?"

Rick smiled. "Actually I'd enjoy the company. Maybe I won't think about it too much with you around, and then I won't get as nervous. Besides, we need to come up with some plan of how to act at the office about the fire and everything. I don't want to say something to the wrong people tomorrow and get us both in some serious trouble."

Rick gave Cassie directions to his house while walking her to her car, then he continued on with Vanessa to where they'd parked.

Thank you, God; he is a Christian, Cassie thought as she started her car. She had never felt so strongly about a man, and now the door was wide open for a relationship. In spite of the dangers facing her tomorrow at work, Cassie couldn't remember when she'd been so happy.

CHAPTER 34

Rick pulled up to his garage to find a gathering of people by his front door. He wasn't sure what to make of it. He parked in the garage, then walked around to the front door with Vanessa. There he found the two detectives and Cassie waiting for him.

"What's going on, Detectives? Something new with the case?" he said as he approached. He looked over at Cassie, and saw a look of deep concern on her face.

"Mr. Treadway," Stephanie began. Rick didn't like the official-sounding tone to her voice, nor the use of his last name.

"We have a warrant to search your home." She handed the document over to him.

"What? You're kidding."

Cassie walked over and put her arm through Rick's. "Someone called the station, implicating you in Wade's murder. They say they have to check out the house."

Rick swayed on his feet, "That's ridiculous. You two ought to know that." He looked at Stephanie, then Bill.

"Actually, whether we think that or not, we still have to do our job," Bill said.

Rick just shook his head, "Well, you're welcome to have a look. I have nothing to hide, that's for sure."

Rick made his way to the door and opened it. The group stepped through the doorway and into the condo.

"What exactly are you looking for?" he asked.

"We never know until we find it," Bill said as he walked back to the master bedroom.

Rick looked to Stephanie. "What exactly was said by this . . . person?"

Stephanie felt awkward. Every instinct within her knew Rick wasn't guilty. But they'd played it this far; she had to finish it out.

"Just that Wade did not commit suicide; he was murdered, specifically by you. I can't comment on any more."

"Did this person happen to give you his name?"

"Like I said, I can't comment."

Rick suddenly felt uncomfortable with Bill in the back room unattended. His mind started racing on the possibility of having evidence planted in his house. He pulled Cassie aside.

"Cassie, follow Bill around the house as he searches. I'll stay with Stephanie. I don't want them left alone in here."

Cassie understood and followed Bill into the back room.

Vanessa wasn't sure what to do, so she took the ice cream they'd picked up into the kitchen.

Rick stayed with Stephanie as she looked through the family room and the kitchen areas. As time passed, he began to relax, knowing there wouldn't be anything to find.

"Red alert, red alert!" boomed out from the loft above them. Everybody jumped.

"What's upstairs?" Stephanie asked.

"My computer. I keep my office up there. That's my screen saver you heard."

Stephanie started up the circular staircase, Rick following right behind her. As he rounded the last couple of steps, it suddenly dawned on Rick that something was wrong. The computer was on, the Star Trek screen saver filling the screen with Klingon and Federation starships. He never left the computer running when he left the house, and he hadn't been on it at all that day.

"Wait a minute, Detective. Someone's been in my house. I didn't leave the computer on."

Stephanie turned to look into his face, real fear coming across his wrinkled brow. She leaned over the railing. "Bill, come up here for a second, we might have found something."

Alongside the computer was a leather-bound book, the kind used for scheduling appointments and keeping addresses. Stephanie reached over and opened it. The front page had all the vital information of its owner written in it. The person's name staring up at them was Wade Bennett.

Stephanie reached out with her pen and touched the space bar on the keyboard of Rick's computer. They could hear the internal disk working as the image of space and the starship Enterprise vanished. Rick felt his stomach drop as he realized he was looking at Wade's suicide note.

Cassie took in a quick breath and looked over at Rick. He stood there, shaking his head and saying, "This can't be happening." Bill quietly stepped up behind him, while Stephanie began talking.

"Rick Treadway, I'm placing you under arrest for the murder of Wade Bennett. You have the right to remain silent; anything you say—"

"You're arresting me? Can't you see this is a setup?"

Stephanie continued reading Rick his rights as Bill reached for his handcuffs. Downstairs, Vanessa was listening to everything going on above her. She couldn't believe that Rick could be responsible for any kind of criminal activity, much less murder. Something was bothering her beyond that, though—something about the name she'd just heard, Wade Bennett. She couldn't quite place it, but she knew she'd heard that name before.

"You can't do this." Cassie tried to think of something to stop them. "He's got a show to direct tomorrow. He's taking over for Wade."

Rick realized Cassie had just verbalized a motive for killing Bennett. He felt his anger boiling. Then he thought back to the sermon he'd just heard that night, about Jesus changing him from within. It surprised him—this was a weird time to be thinking about tonight's sermon. But rather than lashing out in anger, it stopped him long enough to offer up a quick prayer for deliverance. He glanced over at Cassie, his heart breaking at the worried look on her face. He smiled warmly at her, their eyes locking. Rick just nodded at her, trying to convince her, and himself, that everything would turn out all right. Cassie tried to smile back reassuringly, but her concern showed.

"Listen, Detective," he said as he turned back toward Stephanie. "If I was the killer, would I be stupid enough to leave the evidence on my computer, much less have the document opened for all to see? Or keep Wade's calendar book right here in the condo?"

Stephanie had already thought about that, but the professional side of her was in control now.

"We'll just have to try and settle this all at the station. You're going to have to come with us," she replied.

Bill noticed her voice didn't carry its normal tone of authority for an arrest. "How about I finish things up here and seal the place. We can look for more evidence tomorrow, can't we?"

Stephanie just nodded to him.

"You guys can't be serious." Cassie tried to come to Rick's defense. "He couldn't possibly have done this. Don't you remember they tried to kill him in the fire?"

"Believe me, Cassie, we'll take everything into account. But right now, we have a job to do, and that involves taking Rick into custody," Stephanie replied as she turned Rick around and led him down the staircase.

Bill looked at Cassie, "You'll have to leave, along with your friend down there. I'm going to tape off the house. Nobody will be allowed in until we have the lab guys go over everything tomorrow."

Cassie made her way to the staircase. She'd never been through such a radical shift of emotions before. She reached deep inside of herself and prayed for God to intervene. She thought back to teachings she'd heard about her trust in God being tested during difficult times. She knew it was being tested now, and she wanted to have the faith that he was still in control.

As Stephanie led Rick outside his condo, the blinding light of a television camera hit them in the face.

Samantha Steel rushed up to Rick and stuck a microphone in his face. "We understand you've been arrested for the murder of Wade Bennett. Any comment, Mr. Treadway?"

Rick allowed his eyes to come up and meet hers. All he could read in them was the pure evil of revenge. He tried to hold on to some kind of hope, but it was hard realizing that the press was now on to the story. He'd be the lead feature on the news tonight— Wade Bennett's killer. He looked away as Stephanie continued leading him toward her car. He figured no comment was better than giving Sam, of all people, an exclusive.

Stephanie was livid and pushed Rick into the car much firmer than she normally would have. How could the press have gotten wind of this? She felt like she was somebody's puppet, being jerked around by a string. Well, she'd play this little act out, but once she got back to the station, she'd put the pieces together—she was sure of it.

As Stephanie got into her side of the car, Samantha turned toward the camera and started her report.

"You can see behind me the car of Detective Phillips. She's just made an arrest in the Hollywood case of Wade Bennett, the former director of 'The John Harold Show.' Earlier thought to have been a suicide, it now looks like Mr. Bennett was murdered, and, ironically, he was allegedly murdered by the man the producers of the show chose to replace him, Rick Treadway. . . ."

As the car pulled out, Rick slumped back into his seat, relieved to be out of hearing range of Samantha's voice. He lowered his head in the back seat, a wave of nausea coming over him. Who could have done this to him, and why?

Jason, the camera operator, stopped the tape when Samantha had finished her story. "I can't believe you were right about this. How did you know?"

Sam just smiled. "I've got my sources. Let's get back to the van. I want to call the station and get a live-eye truck out here for the ten o'clock."

"It's done," Ben said into his cellular phone, sitting in his car about three units down from Rick's condo. He'd been sent there by Rudy to keep an eye on the place. Things were a little too hot for Rudy to show up there himself.

"Did they take him in?" Rudy asked, anxious to hear that Rick was indeed being arrested.

"Yeah, the broad just drove off with him. It was great, in cuffs, the whole works. Nice touch having the TV crew there."

Rudy didn't know there would be one, but he admired Flint's style. "Don't let them notice you. After they leave, make your way out of there quietly."

"I understand," Ben said, then disconnected. He kept his eyes on the house as the other detective led two women out the front door. It'd been a long weekend, staking out the Hall's house, and Ben was tired. He let his eyes close, thinking his work here was complete. If he'd stayed alert a moment longer, he'd have gotten a good look at the women getting into Cassie's car. There was Vanessa, standing only two cars away from his.

Rudy hung up and sighed. Finally, something about this week was working out in his favor. He quickly punched in Flint's number.

"It worked. They're taking him in right now," he said as Flint answered.

"Perfect. I'll call Josh and take care of things for tomorrow. Maybe now we can put this whole thing behind us." Flint answered, taking a big drag on his cigar.

8:35 P.m., STUDIO CITY

Cassie fought back tears as she drove down Sherman Way toward her apartment. "I can't believe they think he did it. This whole thing is insane," she said more to the air than to Vanessa.

Vanessa had remained quiet throughout the whole arresting process. The name they had mentioned upstairs kept bugging her, but she couldn't place it.

"This whole mess leads to Flint, not Rick."

Vanessa looked up at Cassie with a start. "What did you say?"

"Bennett's murder. Up to this point, everything—"

"No, the name you just used."

"Flint?"

"Gabriel Flint?"

Cassie couldn't believe it. How did Vanessa know Flint.

"Yeah, Gabriel Flint, the executive producer of 'The John Harold Show.' Everything was leading toward him, over some Lasko interview . . ."

Cassie continued on, trying to fill Vanessa in on what had transpired up to this point in the investigation. But Vanessa was off in her own world putting the pieces together. She suddenly remembered where she'd heard the name Bennett.

"Cassie!" she said, stopping her in midsentence, "I know who killed Bennett!"

Cassie freaked, her foot slamming down on the brakes. Fortunately there was no one behind her. She quickly pulled off the street and drove into a convenience store parking lot. She looked over at Vanessa. "How do you know Flint? And how can you know who killed Wade?"

"It's a long story, but Gabriel Flint was my lover, my boss ... my prison, actually," Vanessa sighed, placing her hand over her belly subconsciously trying to protect her child from her previous lifestyle. "It was one of his men, Rudy Vanozzi. He was the one who killed Bennett, but I'm sure it was on Gabriel's orders."

At the mention of Vanozzi, Cassie brightened. Vanessa must know the link between the two men that could break this case and get Rick out of trouble. "How do you know this?"

"Let me start from the beginning," Vanessa said. As they sat in the parking lot, she told Cassie everything she could remember about her past and the night Rudy had tried to rape her. Cassie took it all in like a sponge, placing the pieces into what she already knew, realizing that she needed to get Vanessa's story to the detectives as soon as she could to save Rick.

"Why didn't you say something at Rick's?" Cassie asked when she was done.

"I didn't remember who Bennett was until I heard you mention Flint. It just all came back to me now."

"Well, the police need to hear your story, and right away."

"Cassie, there's one more thing."

"What?"

"Well, they found some appointment book of Wade's up there in Rick's office, right?"

"Right."

"I saw it the night Rudy was in my apartment. He had it, along with some computer disks."

Cassie got excited. This could be the proof they'd need.

"Where are the disks?"

"I'm not sure where all of them are. I guess Rudy would still have the rest." Then Vanessa looked up with a cheerful smile as she reached into her purse, "But two of them happen to be right here."

Cassie practically screamed, "How did you get this?"

"When I was leaving my apartment, I noticed them along with the appointment book. I don't know why, but some compulsion made me grab a couple of them when I left that day."

"That's great, Vanessa! We're almost to my house. Before we head to the police station, let's give my computer a try and see if we can find what's on them."

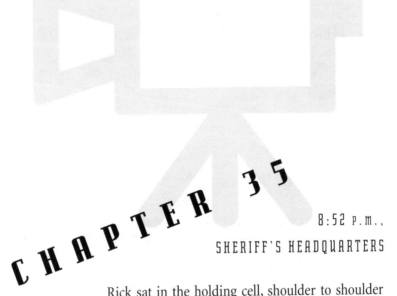

CHAPTER 35

Rick sat in the holding cell, shoulder to shoulder with some of Los Angeles' roughest characters. He couldn't remember a time when he felt lower. Even the final appearance in court for his divorce didn't come close. He'd been fingerprinted, photographed, and strip-searched; then put in this tiny cell with drunks, drug dealers, and pimps. When the flash from the police camera hit him, he had a vision of the picture being plastered over the front page of the *Los Angeles Times,* a perfect finale to the lead story by Samantha Steel on the news showing him walking out of his house handcuffed.

This week had been leading up to such a high in his life. Now, suddenly, the bottom had dropped out. Rick looked around the room, taking in the people around him. He tried to convince himself that justice would win out. He was innocent; the attempt to frame him couldn't succeed. But what little hope he still held onto was quickly being squashed by the dismal surroundings he found himself in.

He closed his eyes, and from the depths of his soul began to pour out his despair before the Lord.

As the moments passed, different passages of Scripture came to his mind. He thought of Paul and Silas being imprisoned for sharing their faith. Rather than succumb to the depression and hopelessness of their situation, they started praising and worshiping God. He remembered the admonition to count it all joy when you encounter various trials. His mind recited part of the Twenty-third Psalm, *Even though I walk through the valley of the shadow of death, I will fear no evil, for you are with me.*

He remembered earlier in the week at the deli with Gary when he had been telling him how bad things were and made the flippant comment, "I wish God would show me what he's trying to teach me quickly, so I can get some work." He'd learned so much since then. But what was it all worth if he only followed Jesus when circumstances were good? There's no test to your faith when everything in your life is going along wonderfully. Would he only serve Jesus if he had the directing job? If things were great with the kids? If he had all his bills paid? If he had Cassie?

No. Rick knew that he had no life outside of his relationship with the Lord. If everything around him was crumbling, then God must have a plan. Trust—that's what he needed to learn at this moment. Did he trust God to use whatever circumstance he was in to Rick's greatest benefit? He so wanted to. With all of these thoughts, he changed his prayer, praising God for all he'd done in his life.

Rick opened his eyes, still surrounded by the other prisoners. Nothing in front of him had changed, but he knew a lot had changed on the inside.

8:55 P.M., VAN NUYS

With her computer fired up and ready to go, Cassie inserted the first disk. After a quick moment, her screen flashed a dialogue box telling her the disk was unreadable and asking her if she'd like to format it. Disappointed, she grabbed the mouse and clicked on the cancel button.

"What does that mean?" Vanessa asked.

"The disk has never been used before, or it's an IBM one. Either way, it's no help to us tonight." Cassie took it out of the computer after it was ejected and reached for the second one.

"Let's hope there's something on this one."

She placed the other one into her disk drive. The computer sucked it in the rest of the way and they could here the drive spinning as they waited to see what would appear on the screen.

After a moment, an icon of a disk appeared in the upper right section of her monitor, with the title "Finances" beneath it.

Cassie looked to Vanessa, disappointed. "I don't think this will do us any good."

She double-clicked on the disk icon and the screen showed a folder with three files, named after the last three years. "This must be his financial records. Another dead end." She was devastated. She just knew one of the disks had to be a copy of "The Lasko Interview."

They were interrupted by the ring of their doorbell. In all the excitement, Cassie had forgotten about Becky coming over.

Amy opened the door as Cassie and Vanessa stepped into the living room. After the introductions, Cassie filled Becky in on Vanessa's story.

"Vanessa, that's incredible," Becky exclaimed. "Wade never told me a thing about Flint's history. But now that I think about it, I'm not surprised."

"Well, let's check Wade's mail real quick for you. Then I need to get Vanessa down to the police station," Cassie said, turning back to her room.

"I can wait, Cassie," Becky said. "Isn't Rick more important?"

"It'll only take a second, and you've come all this way. Come on."

The four headed into Cassie's bedroom. Cassie popped Wade's disk out and opened up her America Online application. Once the sign-on screen appeared, she selected "guest." The screen changed, showing boxes for the guest name and password. Cassie typed in: Wbennett. Then she clicked on the password box and looked back at Becky.

"He used TV9427," she prompted.

Cassie typed it in and hit "return."

They waited as the modem kicked on and the computer went through its motions to connect to AOL. Then they heard the familiar, "Welcome," followed shortly after by, "You've got mail."

Cassie clicked on the icon of the mailbox and a list of E-mails appeared on the screen. Becky didn't realize there would be so many. She had Cassie slowly scroll down through the list. She noticed several from "Paulf" dated 3/20, 3/18, 3/16. Everybody else had weird screen names that she didn't recognize. Toward the end of the list, one caught her attention: 3/16 from: MAILER-DAEMON@aol subject: Returned mail: Host unknown

Becky pointed to the screen. "What's that one? It's dated the night Wade was murdered."

"I don't know. Let's take a look."

Cassie highlighted it and clicked the read button.

The screen changed:

> The original message was received at Tuesday 16 March 09:29:08 (EDT) from root@localhost

——The following addresses had permanent fatal errors——
Dbernstein@idt.con

Becky took in a breath. "Dbernstein. That's our lawyer. He died the same night in a car accident."

Cassie leaned into the screen next to Becky and read carefully.

—— Transcript of session follows ——
Dbernstein@idt.con... Host unknown (Name server:
    idt.con: host not found)
Received: from Wbennett@aol.com
    by imo20.mx.aol.com (IMOv14.1) id 4HXUa19024
    for <Dbernstein@idt.con>; Tuesday 16 March
    09:29:08 (EDT)
From: Wbennett <Wbennett@aol.com>
Return-path: <Wbennett@aol.com>
Message-ID: <1fd837fa.355b19f5@aol.com>
Date: Tuesday, 16 March 09:29:08 EDT
To: Dbernstein@idt.con
Mime-Version: 1.0
Subject: Just in Case

—— Original message follows ——

As Cassie's eyes scanned through all the technical wording, she began reading the message out loud.

David, I'm attaching a letter—keep it in
case something happens to me. I know
this sounds dramatic, but I've run across
something that could be dangerous—this
is no joke. Get this letter to the police.
                                    Thanks, Wade

Becky grabbed her mouth and started weeping. She knew Wade hadn't killed himself. Cassie placed an arm around her.

"He must have sent this letter before he was killed," Amy spoke up behind them.

"Or maybe as he was being killed," Cassie said. "Look at the address: Dbernstein@idt.con. There's no address with "con" at the end of it, it's "com." Wade either was careless or didn't have time to put an "n" where the "m" should have been. That's why the E-mail was returned to him."

Becky looked up, "So Dave never got this letter?"

"Not if we're seeing it here," Cassie answered.

"Rudy wouldn't have known that," Vanessa spoke up behind Becky.

Becky and Cassie turned toward her. "What do you mean?" Becky asked.

"If your husband was caught sending this E-mail, Rudy would have gone after your lawyer. It seems like too much of a coincidence for him to have died in a car wreck the same day your husband was killed."

The room was quiet for a moment. Then Cassie turned back toward the screen.

"There's a file attached to this. Let me see if I can download it."

She clicked on the "download now" icon, and a dialogue box popped up asking her where she'd like to store "The Lasko Interview."

Cassie smiled to the group. "We've been looking for this file." She selected the online download file and clicked "OK." A moment later the room heard, "File's done" in that familiar computer voice. Cassie went to the folder, and there it was, "The Lasko Interview." She clicked on it, and in seconds they had the completed letter. All eyes went immediately to the picture at the bottom of the page.

They saw two men sitting in director's chairs positioned in front of what looked like a bar. It was named "Club Royale." Cassie immediately recognized the man in the left chair, her host, John

Harold. The man on the right she didn't recognize. Then she heard Vanessa give a quick intake of breath behind her.

"What?" Cassie asked. So far this picture didn't reveal anything to her.

Vanessa reached out and pointed to the screen.

"That's Rudy—right there."

In the background, she could see it now. Rudy stood profile to the camera as he walked behind another man, evidently taking him around the side of the building. One hand was resting on the man's shoulder, Rudy's left hand. Looking down, she could see that his right hand was pointing straight into the man's back, and although that part of the picture was small, there was no mistaking the gun Rudy was holding.

"Oh my God," Cassie shrieked, "I'll bet you the other man is that councilman that was murdered."

Vanessa looked puzzled. "I thought this was about Bennett's murder?"

Becky was stunned. "What councilman?"

"It's been all over the news," Cassie explained. "His body was found in some dumpster. They thought he was mugged."

She looked back up at the screen and read the letter.

> David Bernstein
> Attorney at Law
> 1527 W. Olympic Blvd.
> Beverly Hills, CA 90210
>
> Dear Dave,
>
>   I'm writing this letter in case anything should happen to me. I'm planning to go to the District Attorney with what I've discovered. I've come across some information that leads me to believe I have evidence pertaining to a certain murder.

I came across this evidence while I was in the editing room yesterday. We did a remote segment outside a strip joint named The Club Royale on March 12. We were interviewing the manager of the club, Joe Lasko. Although nothing appeared out of the ordinary the day of the taping, it was in the edit room that I realized we had something on tape that amazed me. I'll put a frame from that video at the end of this letter to show you proof of what I have.

I noticed that between takes of the interview, off in the distance, our camera recorded one of the men that work for our executive producer, I believe his name is Rudy Vanozzi, taking another man off at gunpoint. From what I've read in the news, the man being taken away is a city councilman named Perkins. His body was found the next day in a dumpster nearby. The police just identified the body a couple of days ago.

I wanted to make sure somebody had this information in case I'm discovered. Only Sid, our editor, has seen this video, and I warned him to keep it to himself.

Make sure the right people see this, and if something does happen, let Becky know how much I love her. I don't want her to know yet for her own safety.

Thanks, friend,

Wade Bennett

Becky couldn't help but break into tears again—relief at discovering the truth combined with a flow of grief over the loss of her husband. No wonder he'd been so distant that last night. If he'd only confided in her.

"Anyone game for heading to the jail?" Cassie asked as she grabbed a blank disk of her own, preparing to put the letter on a disk and print out a hard copy.

10:00 P.M., NORTH HOLLYWOOD

Sid came out of the bathroom then climbed into bed next to his wife. Their television was on, showing the 10 o'clock news. He was about to pick up a novel he had on the nightstand when the lead story caught his attention.

"Our top story tonight—local director arrested for the murder of Wade Bennett, the popular director of 'The John Harold Show' who was found dead Tuesday night at his home. Samantha Steel has been following the story all week for us. Sam?"

"Honey—" Sid's wife exclaimed.

"Shhhh," he tried to quiet her. "I need to hear this."

Samantha appeared, her name and Studio City appearing in the lower third of the screen. "That's right, Dick, we've got the exclusive story."

The scene changed to show the shot of Rick being led outside the house by Stephanie, Samantha's microphone stuck in his face while she asked for a comment. Sid was speechless.

Samantha's voice continued over the picture. "Rick Treadway was arrested tonight for the murder of Wade Bennett. The police said that through an anonymous tip, they were able to search his home and find evidence that led to the arrest. The ironic part of this story is that Treadway was the new director the studio chose to take Bennett's place. He was to direct the show tomorrow night. The police haven't told us what evidence they found, but . . ."

The sound and picture seemed to blur out as the news sank into Sid. How could this have happened to Rick, his friend. It was too much for Sid to take. He reached for the phone beside the bed.

"What are you doing?" his wife asked.

"I can't stand it any longer, honey. One man is dead, and now an innocent man, my friend, is sitting in jail. I've got to do something."

"And get yourself killed?"

"Don't worry, I've been thinking a lot about this since this morning. I've got some insurance."

"Who are you going to call?"

Sid realized he didn't know the answer to that. "I'm not sure, I guess the police department." Then a thought came to him, "No. You know what? I'll call Cassie. She was working with the detectives; she'll know what I should do."

Sid's wife started to try and stop him, but deep down inside she knew he was doing the right thing. She looked up at him and nodded. Although she was afraid, a sense of pride welled up inside her for the man she'd married.

SAME TIME, VAN NUYS

While Becky, Vanessa, and Cassie were waiting for the printer to spit out the picture, the phone rang. Cassie jumped. She didn't know how high-strung she was over all this. She laughed nervously when she realized it was just the phone.

"Let's just let it ring. I want to get over to help Rick as soon as possible."

After four rings, her answering machine picked up. Then moments later, a man's voice could be heard.

"Cassie, it's Sid, from the show. I'm not sure if I should be calling you about this or not, but your name came to mind. I just saw on the news that they arrested Rick for Wade's murder, but I know that can't be. So when you get home, call me. It's important. It doesn't matter how late—"

"This should be interesting," Cassie said to the group as she grabbed the phone beside her. "Sid, I'm here."

Sid was startled, not expecting her to answer once the machine kicked in. "Oh, hi Cassie, you surprised me. Listen, I'm not sure how to handle this, but I can't sit by any longer. I can't believe they arrested Rick."

"I know, I was there," Cassie answered coldly. Seeing Sid's name on the letter, she knew he was somehow involved. "What's so important, Sid?"

"Well, Rick had nothing to do with it. I know why Wade was killed."

"I know you do."

Sid was shocked. "How could you know?"

"That's not important now. I'll explain later. Why are you coming forward now?"

"I can't live with it anymore, Cassie. It's been eating me up. Now they're trying to make Rick the fall guy. I've got to speak up. Maybe I can strike a deal. I have a copy of the digitized video on a hard drive."

"You what?" Cassie shrieked. "Sid, do you know how much I've been through in the past couple of days because of those tapes? And you have a copy of them? How?"

"Well, that's a long story. Wade warned me to keep silent about it the day he died . . . I mean was murdered." Sid paused, realizing he couldn't deny that fact anymore. "Wade didn't erase the hard drive, I did—on Flint's orders. But not before making a copy of it, as insurance."

This was the final piece of evidence.

"Sid, that's wonderful! We can't let Rick be framed for Wade's murder. We need to get this evidence down to the detectives as soon as possible. Can you do that for us?"

Sid didn't have to think about it anymore.

"Just tell me where to go, Cassie."

10:42 P.M., SHERIFF'S HEADQUARTERS

"Are we going to make him stay in there overnight?" Bill asked Stephanie as they were finishing up the paperwork for the night. "We know he's innocent."

"Knowing that and being able to prove it are two different things. We've got to follow this one by the book. The captain somehow heard about the tip and sent us out directly."

Suddenly a crowd came rushing through the office doors, heading toward their desk, all shouting at once. Bill was tempted to draw his gun until he recognized Cassie leading the brigade—Vanessa, Becky, and Sid—coming down the aisle.

"Calm down," Stephanie yelled, trying to get their attention. "You can't all talk at once."

The group became quiet, allowing Cassie to speak.

"We've figured it all out!" she nearly screamed, she was so excited, "We've got the Lasko interview tapes and letter right here."

Stephanie looked at the group and laughed. She couldn't picture a more unlikely combination of detectives in her wildest imagination. "Bill, go down and bring Rick up here. I have a feeling he's going to want to hear this."

"I should have made the connection," Bill commented in self-recrimination after hearing the full story from Cassie.

Rick was out of his cell, giving Cassie a hug for coming to his rescue. He whispered into her ear, "Thank you, and thank God for bringing out the truth."

She squeezed back and quoted, *"He will bring to light what is hidden in darkness and will expose the motives of men's hearts. At that time each will receive his praise from God."*

Rick looked at her and laughed at the familiar passage.

"I remember the bill Perkins was pushing in the city council," Bill continued. "If it passes, it would put a lot of restrictions on club owners like separating dancers from the customers by at least six feet, closing them down by 3:00 A.M.; and, I think even requiring the dancers to get their own licenses. I just didn't make the connection with Flint."

Stephanie let out a low whistle. "I can see why any club owner would be against the new legislation. You said 'if the bill passes.' When is the vote?"

"This coming Tuesday night. If Perkins's death has anything to do with this thing, it's possible a few other councilmen are feeling the heat."

"We'll have to get ahold of the other members of the council and see if that's true. Boy, I guess we weren't on the right track with the Perkins murder at all."

"So, Detectives," Rick interrupted their discussion. "Do you think you can make any arrests now? I mean other than me."

Stephanie looked up at him. "Oh, I think we can. But be patient. I've got a plan you're going to love. Listen up."

CHAPTER 36

A murmur of chatter rippled throughout the conference room as those who had heard about Rick's arrest filled in those who hadn't. Everyone fell silent as Josh Abrams walked through the door, followed by Gabriel Flint, John Harold himself, and a woman only a few in the room recognized. Walking close behind was Rudy Vanozzi.

There was one seat left at the head of the table, reserved for Josh. Noticing the additional people, two of the writers and a segment producer wisely vacated their chairs next to Josh and stood by the window. Rudy kept his position standing behind Flint.

The quiet hung over the room like a blanket. After taking his seat, Josh cleared his throat, then looked up at the faces waiting anxiously for his announcement. He was surprised to see that Cassie wasn't there yet. It wasn't like her to be late for work—ever. He quickly dropped the thought and brought his mind to bear on the subject at hand.

"Before I begin, I'd like to introduce Tina Livingston." Tina raised a hand in recognition as Josh spoke. "Tina's a very talented director, whose presence here will become evident as I catch you up on the events of last night. I'm sure most of you, if not all of you, have heard by now about Mr. Treadway. But, just in case our rumor mill is working slowly this morning, on Friday, we hired Rick Treadway to become the new director to replace Wade. We had no idea that this was the person who turned out to be responsible for Wade's death."

Josh paused for effect. "Last night the police searched Treadway's house and found the very same suicide note that was on Wade's computer on Rick's computer. They also found Wade's appointment book on top of Treadway's desk."

"So it seems Wade did not take his own life, as Treadway would have wanted us to believe. Instead, we lost one of Hollywood's great talents because of the murderous ambition of one out-of-work director trying to get ahead in this town."

"I thought a man was presumed innocent until proven guilty."

Josh whipped his head toward the door, not believing anyone on his staff would speak out with such audacity. Rick was coming through the door, followed closely by Cassie, Sid, and the two detectives who had been snooping around the office.

Josh stared at him in shocked silence.

Rudy had been reaching for his gun as soon as he heard Rick's voice. He wasn't going down without a fight. He began bringing his arm up toward the female detective entering the room.

"Freeze!" he heard from behind her, but continued his aim.

Two shots rang out nearly simultaneously, deafening within the confines of the small room. Rudy swore as a bullet pierced his shooting arm just below the shoulder. His gun fell to the floor.

Bill stood behind Stephanie, his arms out stiff, holding his revolver. "Nobody move!" he warned. He'd come into the room with his gun already out, just in case this happened. He'd got his shot off first, sending Rudy's shot wide.

Then Cassie dropped to the floor, a small cry coming from her lips.

"*NO!*" Rick dropped immediately down beside her. Her eyes were closed, looking lifeless. He reached behind her head to support it, searching her body for any signs of bleeding. Her right hand was clasped tightly over the top of her chest. He gently reached out and pulled it away, revealing her torn blouse and blood coming from a groove across the top of her shoulder. He pulled out his handkerchief and pressed it against her wound.

"Cassie, are you all right?" he asked.

She opened her eyes and looked up—her mind flashed to the other night after the fire when their positions were reversed. It brought a smile to her lips. His face broke into a huge grin as her eyes met his.

"I think so," she managed to get out. Her shoulder burned with pain. She looked down to see the damage.

"The bullet just grazed you, Cassie," he responded gently as he helped her up and kept his arm around her to steady her.

Stephanie walked across the room, her gun now at the ready, and picked up Rudy's piece off the floor.

"What's going on?" Josh barked to Rick as the room settled down. "You're supposed to be in jail."

Rick smiled, "The reports of my demise are greatly exaggerated."

A few chuckles filtered through the room. Stephanie decided it was time for her to take over before Rick got in over his head. "Let's go into your office, Josh. There are some things we need to clear up."

She started to take Josh, Flint, and Rudy into the producer's office.

"Wait a minute. I'd like to be in on this," John Harold called after her.

She looked to Bill, who nodded. "I guess you have a right to be. Come with us."

John followed behind them as Cassie, Rick, and Sid stepped in with him.

They left two sheriff's deputies in the conference room with the rest of the staff.

"Gabriel Flint, we have a warrant for your arrest for ordering the murder of Wade Bennett and Councilman Perkins," Stephanie said with a smile as the group gathered in the room.

Flint stood there, boring a hole in her with his eyes, but saying nothing. He knew enough to wait until his lawyers were involved before starting to fight back. Then he broke into a smile, his gaze shifting over Stephanie's shoulder.

"Just hold on one minute, Detective Phillips," Stephanie heard from behind her.

She turned and saw Captain Lipton entering the room, gun in hand.

"Captain, what are you doing here?" She was stunned.

"I heard you released Treadway when I got in this morning. I figured I'd better get over here." He pointed the pistol toward Bill. "Put yours down, Bill."

Bill looked to his partner, shocked. For a brief moment he contemplated trying to get the first shot off.

"Now!" The captain ordered.

Bill set it down slowly on Josh's desk.

Lipton turned back to Stephanie. "How could you have messed things up so badly? You had everything you needed last night to close this case." Lipton gazed over at Flint. "Now how are we going to get out of this one?"

Flint smirked, "We just did."

Cassie couldn't believe what was happening. Not after all they'd been through. Rick's hand reached out and gently held onto hers.

"All right, everyone against the window," Lipton ordered. "Now I've got to figure out a way to get us—"

Josh's door suddenly burst open, a large figure crashing into Lipton, sending him sprawling to the floor. It was like a quarterback being blindsided by a blitzing linebacker as Reggie crushed him, pinning him to the carpet with all of his 280 pounds.

Both Stephanie and Bill had their guns back in an instant.

"Hold it everyone," Stephanie shouted as Rudy started moving for the door. The two officers from the conference room ran in, guns drawn.

"Keep your eyes on them for me," Stephanie said as she holstered her gun and got her cuffs out.

"OK, Reggie, let him up." She reached over and helped him off the floor. Lipton was still struggling for air; the breath had been knocked out of him. Stephanie didn't care. She rolled him over and placed his hands behind his back, cuffing them together.

"It's all starting to make a lot of sense now, Captain," she snarled. "Now I know why you wanted our cases closed so quickly, plus how they got their inside information. Flint's gotten to you."

He didn't respond, but stayed on the floor, gasping for air.

She looked up at Reggie. "How did you know?"

The big man smiled. "I was outside the window. I heard it all."

Stephanie laughed, "I'm glad you were." She got up and looked at Rudy.

"Rudy Vanozzi, you are under arrest for carrying out the murders of both Wade Bennett and Councilman Perkins, along with the arson of the studio tape vault, a hit-and-run accident involving a red Corvette owned by Mr. Flint, attempted murder of one Jill Hall, and probably for the murder of David Bernstein."

The mention of the last name got a puzzled look on Rudy's face. There's no way they could know about that.

"You can't prove anything," he managed to hiss. He knew the tapes were destroyed and Sid himself had erased the video on the computer.

Sid stepped up from the back of the room, holding out a digital disk drive. "You might be surprised to know that I have a digital copy of the Lasko interview. It wasn't destroyed in the fire; I had it at my house."

Rudy's eyes met Sid's, and even though he was surrounded by the officers, Sid felt the evil penetrate him. He hoped this man would stay behind bars for a long time.

"You'll go down with us, Sid," Rudy said with contempt.

"Don't be too sure about that. Sid's been very helpful since last night. He'll be taken care of. We also have a certain computer disk," Stephanie continued, "given to us by a woman named Vanessa. It was the property of Mr. Bennett before you took it from him the night you killed him. She can also state that she saw the address book in your possession the night of the murder."

Stephanie noticed the bandage still wrapped around Rudy's right hand as he held it up to his wounded shoulder. "How did you hurt your hand, Rudy? Perhaps the gun you forced Bennett to shoot himself with gouged it when it recoiled?" She loved watching his eyes change from confusion to fear. He knew they had him. He'd probably spill everything he knew about Flint to try and strike a deal.

"And Josh Abrams," the room once again became deathly quiet, as Stephanie turned towards Josh, "We're still not sure how you fit into all this, but until we get everything wrapped up, you have the right—"

"I don't need an attorney," Josh interrupted her. "I should have figured this out long ago. I just couldn't face the facts. I'll cooperate."

Then Josh glanced up at Rick; the pain for his old friend showed in Josh's eyes.

"I never intended for you to take the fall for all this," he pleaded. "I just didn't want to see the truth. Too much was at risk."

Rick sighed. He was glad to hear Josh wasn't a part of the murder, but he was still angry at Josh for going along with Flint's plan to frame him. Yet he heard himself responding, "You know what, Josh, I understand. I forgive you."

By now the captain had managed to sit up on the floor. "And Captain Vance Lipton, you are under arrest for all sorts of things we'll sort out later. Get them out of here." She motioned to the deputies.

John Harold sat dumbfounded as Flint and Rudy were led out with the captain.

Stephanie turned to Harold.

"We apologize, Mr. Harold, for interrupting your production like this. The facts of the case have finally come out with a lot of help from Cassie and your editor, Sid. It seems that we were getting too close to solving Bennett's murder, so Flint decided to try and frame Rick. It turns out that Flint had Councilman Perkins murdered because he was pushing for a new ordinance that would affect the operation of his strip clubs. Do you remember the day you did an interview with one of the managers, Mr. Lasko, of The Club Royale?"

Harold nodded. He remembered it all too well. It was one of Flint's clubs, and he'd been against it from the beginning.

"Well, unknowingly, the crew captured on tape Mr. Vanozzi taking Councilman Perkins behind the building at gunpoint."

It was starting to make sense to Harold now. He'd hated getting into partnership with Flint in the first place, but he needed the money to get his show on the air.

"The next day, Perkins' body was discovered, beat up and shot. We now believe that Wade saw what was captured on the tape while editing last week and was going to go to the authorities with the information. Finding out about this through Sid, Flint decided to have Bennett killed as well, instructing Rudy to make it look like suicide. Then to cover their tracks, they had to destroy the tapes that Bennett saw. Rudy was sent in to burn the tape vault, nearly killing Rick and Cassie in the process. What they didn't realize was that Wade had taken one frame of that video home, and that Sid here had made a hard disk copy of the entire video. It just took him awhile to turn it over to us."

Sid lowered his head.

"I'm shocked, Detective," Harold said. "I don't know what to say. Is there anything else we can do for you?"

"We will need to go through the production office and search for other pieces of evidence today. But we'll work around you if you want to go ahead with your show tonight."

John looked to Rick, his new director. "Still feel like directing the show for me tonight, Rick?"

"I'd be honored to, John. I think my detective days are over," Rick said with a smile.

John laughed, then looked back to Stephanie. "What about Josh?"

"We're going to need him today to help us put the rest of the pieces in place."

"You can get by without me," Josh offered. "Let the segment producers do their job. Cassie can fill in where needed if she's feeling up to it."

Cassie was still embarrassed from having fainted. "I'm fine, really."

"Would you mind jumping in and filling the void?" John asked her.

Cassie wasn't sure what he was getting at. "You mean . . ."

"I mean, would you produce the show tonight?"

"I don't know what to say," was all she could come back with.

"Say yes. We have a lot of work to do before tonight."

Rick gave Cassie a reassuring hug. "You can do it, Cassie."

"I guess yes, then."

"Great!" John then turned to Stephanie and said, "Detective, you can tear into the office all you want, but if you'll excuse us, we have a show to plan."

Stephanie smiled. "I'd be happy to get out of your way. But first," Stephanie reached out and took Reggie's hand, "thank you, sir, for coming in when you did."

Reggie smiled. "It felt good. I haven't had a chance to do that since my last days with the Rams." Cassie stepped over and hugged him, her face beaming in spite of the pain.

4:20 p.m., NATIONAL STUDIOS

Rick sat in the control room later that afternoon working through his script. They'd finished rehearsing the elements needed for the show, and it was that quiet time as the celebrities were in make-up, the audience was being brought into the studio, and the production team could take a little breather before the show.

The door to the booth opened and Cassie peeped in.

"You feel ready for tonight?" she asked Rick.

"Why, what have you got in mind?"

"The show, you idiot."

"Oh, that. Actually, yes. I think from this end everything seems ready to go. How about you? Nervous?"

"You bet I am. I knew Josh had a lot to take care of, but until the responsibility really falls on you, it doesn't sink in. I'm exhausted, and we haven't even rolled tape yet."

"You'll be fine. The hard part's already done. The guests are here; the format is set. All you have to do now is basically baby-sit John during the show, and decide how long you want each segment to run."

"Thanks, Rick. I'll remember that."

The production assistant on the other side of the room interrupted, "Hey Rick, there's a Samantha Steel on line one, wants to talk with you."

Rick's eyebrows went up. "This should be interesting."

"Hello Sam, what can I do for you?"

"Rick, I wanted to wish you the best before the show tonight," she gushed into the phone.

"I appreciate that, Sam, but I understand that from last night's broadcast, you pretty much left the city with the conclusion that I was Wade's murderer."

"Oh that! Look Rick, I was just doing my job. I only acted on the information I had at the time."

Rick mouthed to Cassie what she was saying.

"But look, here's your chance," Samantha said, all business as she tried to get her last scoop for the story. "I'm about to go on the air with my final report." *Here comes the real reason she's calling,* Rick thought. "I wonder if you'd like to make a statement for the public? Speak for yourself about this whole situation."

Rick cupped the mouthpiece. "She wants to know if I want to make a statement for her newscast."

"Give me the phone," Cassie grabbed it away from him.

"This is Cassandra Petterson, tonight's producer. Mr. Treadway is rather busy getting prepared for the telecast, but you can tell your viewers to watch our show tonight. It will speak for itself."

With that, she hung up.

Rick laughed, "Well, that should put her in her place."

"After the way she treated you, she's lucky that's all I said. Besides, maybe she'll repeat that and our ratings will soar."

"I have a feeling they are going to be through the roof tonight anyway."

6:13 P.M., NATIONAL STUDIOS

Chad counted back into the final segment of "The John Harold Show," "In five, four, three, two, one."

"Fade up on one, cue John," Rick called next to him.

On the monitor in front of the pair, John's image faded up as he spoke, "I'd like to thank my guests tonight ..."

"Ready three, three." Rick snapped his fingers as he said the camera number. "Pan right as he thanks them."

" . . . Tim Allen, Amy Grant, and Troy Aikman." The audience applauded.

"Ready back to one. One." Rick snapped again.

John looked squarely into the camera, "If you've been following the stories surrounding this show, you'll know that we've had a staff change over the past few hours. The only comment I want to make is that we plan to continue making the kind of quality, entertaining show you've grown accustomed to. Those on this staff who stepped outside the law will receive the justice they deserve. But in the meantime a couple of people have stepped up to fill the void. I'd like to personally thank Rick Treadway, our new director, who has stepped in and done a wonderful job . . ."

The people around Rick in the control room started clapping and shouting their support.

"Camera three, give me a shot of Cassie, quick. Lighting, hit the producer area with a spot," Rick ordered, not being distracted.

" . . . and I'd also like to thank Cassie Petterson . . ."

"Take three. Smile, Cassie," Rick laughed into his headset.

" . . . who stepped in at a very difficult moment and helped keep this train on the tracks. Thanks, Cassie."

"Ready one, one." Rick snapped.

"Well, that's it for tonight. Join us tomorrow when we'll have actor Tom Hanks and country music sensation Garth Brooks. Good night everybody."

"Music, ready four, four." Rick snapped again. "Roll credits . . ."

Rick continued to give camera directions while Chad counted the show off the air.

" . . . and fade to black. Nice job everybody. You're a great crew," Rick cheerfully said. The first night had gone exceptionally well. Just then, the control room door opened, and Cassie came bursting through.

"You did a great job, Rick. Everything went so smoothly." She walked over and gave him a warm hug.

"You were wonderful, too, Cassie. You really rose to the occasion," Rick countered. Then in a whisper only she could hear, "I was praying for you."

"Thanks. I knew you were," she whispered back.

John Harold popped his head into the room.

"Hey, is that my new production team hugging over there?" he joked. They quickly stopped the embrace and looked over at him.

"You two did a terrific job. Come up to my dressing room. I want to discuss our new relationship together!"

They agreed, but their minds were on another, more important relationship that was just beginning—their own.

If you would like to communicate
with Clay Jacobsen, you may E-mail him at
laskocj@aol.com